W9-ATR-597

THE BURNING MOUNTAIN

Other books by Alfred Coppel

Night of Fire and Snow

Dark December

A Certainty of Love

The Gate of Hell

Order of Battle

A Little Time for Laughter

Between the Thunder and the Sun

The Landlocked Man

Thirty-four East

The Dragon

The Hastings Conspiracy

The Apocalypse Brigade

Alfred Coppel

THE BURNING MOUNTAIN

A Novel of the Invasion of Japan

Harcourt Brace Jovanovich, Publishers

San Diego   New York   London

Copyright © 1983 by Alfred Coppel

All rights reserved. No part of this publication
may be reproduced or transmitted in any form or
by any means, electronic or mechanical, including
photocopy, recording, or any information storage
and retrieval system, without permission in
writing from the publisher.

Requests for permission to make copies of any
part of the work should be mailed to: Permissions,
Harcourt Brace Jovanovich, Publishers, 757 Third Avenue,
New York, N.Y. 10017.

The quotation from T. S. Eliot's "Burnt Norton" is
from his *Four Quartets*, copyright 1943 by T. S. Eliot;
copyright renewed 1971 by Esme Valerie Eliot, and is
used by permission of Harcourt Brace Jovanovich, Inc.
and Faber and Faber Ltd.

Library of Congress Cataloging in Publication Data
Coppel, Alfred.
The burning mountain.
Bibliography: p.
I. Title.
PS3553.064B87   1983   813'.54   82-15444
ISBN 0-15-114978-X

Printed in the United States of America

First edition

B C D E

To the survivors of C-Flight,
Class 43-A, ACFTD, Ontario, California
Summer 1942—wherever they may be

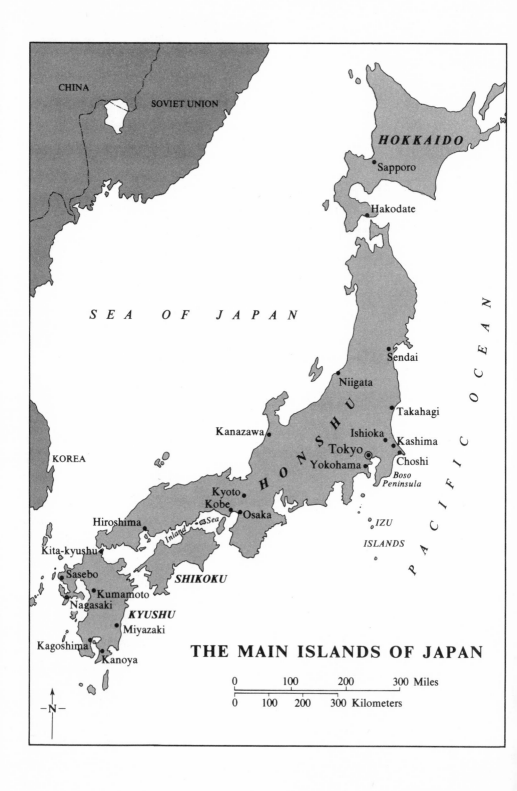

CHINA

SOVIET UNION

HOKKAIDO

Sapporo

Hakodate

SEA OF JAPAN

Sendai

Niigata

Takahagi

KOREA

Kanazawa

Ishioka

Kashima

Tokyo

Yokohama

Choshi

Boso Peninsula

Kyoto

Kobe

Osaka

Hiroshima

Inland Sea

IZU

ISLANDS

Kita-kyushu

SHIKOKU

Sasebo

Kumamoto

Nagasaki

KYUSHU

Miyazaki

Kagoshima

Kanoya

PACIFIC OCEAN

THE MAIN ISLANDS OF JAPAN

| 0 | 100 | 200 | 300 Miles |

| 0 | 100 | 200 | 300 Kilometers |

-N-

And the second angel sounded, and as it were a great mountain burning with fire was cast into the sea: and the third part of the sea became blood;

And the third part of the creatures which were in the sea, and had life, died; and the third part of the ships were destroyed.

And the third angel sounded, and there fell a great star from heaven, burning as it were a lamp, and it fell upon the third part of the rivers, and upon the fountains of waters;

And the name of the star is called Wormwood: and the third part of the waters became wormwood; and many men died of the waters, because they were made bitter.

Revelation 8:8–11

Prelude to
CORONET

Time present and time past
Are both present in time future,
And time future is contained in time past.

T. S. Eliot
"Burnt Norton," *Four Quartets*

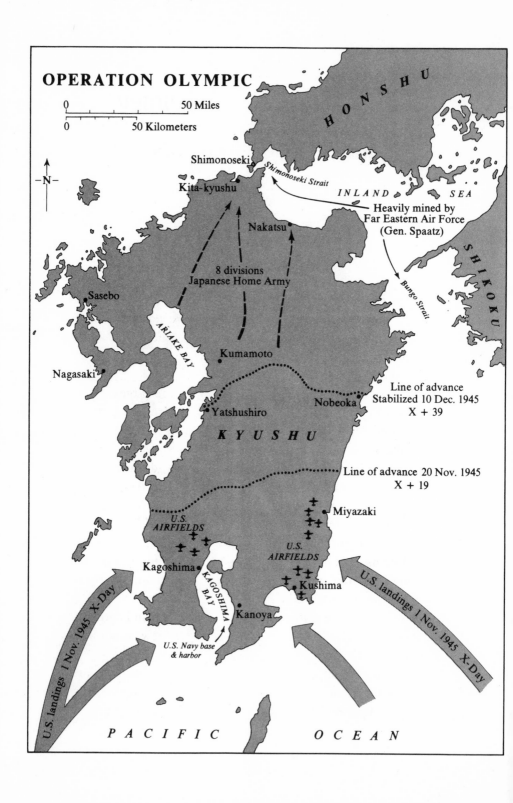

OPERATION OLYMPIC

0 ——————— 50 Miles
0 ——————— 50 Kilometers

–N–

HONSHU

Shimonoseki

Shimonoseki Strait

Kita-kyushu

INLAND SEA

Nakatsu

Heavily mined by
Far Eastern Air Force
(Gen. Spaatz)

Bungo Strait

8 divisions
Japanese Home Army

Sasebo

ARIAKE BAY

SHIKOKU

Nagasaki

Kumamoto

Yatsushiro

Nobeoka

Line of advance
Stabilized 10 Dec. 1945
X + 39

K Y U S H U

Line of advance 20 Nov. 1945
X + 19

*U.S.
AIRFIELDS*

Miyazaki

*U.S.
AIRFIELDS*

Kagoshima

*KAGOSHIMA
BAY*

Kushima

Kanoya

*U.S. Navy base
& harbor*

U.S. landings 1 Nov. 1945 X-Day

U.S. landings 1 Nov. 1945 X-Day

P A C I F I C   O C E A N

Fat Man at Dead Man's Journey

16 July 1945, 0400 Hours

The storm rides the jet stream, spinning ice veils and black cloud across the continent. At 70,000 feet, where no aircraft yet designed flies, the wind blows west to east at 200 knots, driven by the Coriolis force and by a vast high-pressure dome over the Pacific Ocean.

As the lower currents of the disturbance meet the ridges of the high Rocky Mountains, small squalls are torn from the main weather system. These lesser storms plunge down into the warm air above the great American desert. They pass over the high mesas searching for escape across the valleys and canyons of Utah, Colorado, and New Mexico. Between the San Andres and the Black mountains, a file of thunderheads drifts across a desolate plain called La Jornada del Muerto.

Early Spanish explorers gave this place its forbidding name. Men and dreams died here. It lies between the mountain ranges: flat, freezing in winter, and hot in summer. It was almost uninhabited until the scientists came.

The scientists and the soldiers built a testing place and called it Trinity Site. Here, in the center of a network of new, raw oiled roads stands a 100-foot-tall steel tower. At the tower's highest level, in a cradle of supports and a web of wiring, squats Fat Man. This is the name of a five-ton sphere with a heart composed of two machined hemispheres of plutonium, an element

3

previously unknown: heavy, strangely warm to the touch, and deadly.

Through the short night the squalls have drifted over the tower, their thunder muttering and rolling across the desert. As they move by, one by one, the men on the ground get glimpses of a clear sky brilliant with constellations. In the summer morning, the Northern Cross is sinking toward the ridge line of the Black Mountains. Andromeda is near the zenith. There is a hint of dawn in the east.

A test is scheduled at 0500 hours Mountain war time—in the awkward jargon of the time—sixty minutes from now. At 0300 hours the meteorologists reported that by time zero the weather would be clear and suitable. The forecast appears to be accurate. The squalls are passing less frequently and there are longer intervals of clear sky. The scientists begin to leave, seeking the safety of the bunkers, the nearest of which lie 10,000 yards from ground zero.

Forty minutes before the time of detonation, the general commanding the project confers with the tall, thin chief scientist. They decide that all is in order and that the final arming of Fat Man may begin.

North of Trinity Site the last thunderhead in the squall line drifts toward the tower. As such storms go in this part of the Southwest, the squall is not large. But like all cumulonimbus clouds it contains a massive positive electrical charge. From time to time this energy is released in lightning flashes within the funnel of the cloud. Twenty-five minutes before time zero, the squall drifts over a slight rise in the ground north of Fat Man's tower. The electrical equilibrium is disturbed, and a lightning bolt strikes the ground with an explosive blue-white flash that dims the pale dawn light now illuminating the valley of the Dead Man's Journey.

The general and the chief scientist, ten miles away at the command post, see the strike and immediately order a hold in the test countdown. It is a futile decision.

Fat Man rests atop the tallest structure on the plain. The steel legs are anchored in concrete caissons buried in earth dampened by the earlier squalls. The tower is now a perfect lightning rod, and as the squall moves directly overhead a vast shift of electromotive forces takes place. A second, far larger, bolt of lightning flashes from the cloud, seeking earth.

Thunderclap and bolt strike the tower almost simultaneously. A sonic wave booms across the desert plain. The strike meets the northeast corner of Fat Man's sheet-metal shelter and explodes it into ragged ribbons of glowing steel. The charge flows in milliseconds into the heavy supporting members of the tower. Rootlets of fiery light rampage over the skein of wires covering Fat Man. Instruments in the control shelters go dead. The lightning covers the five-ton sphere in a cascade. Heat melts inner circuits, switches, capacitors. The plutonium hemispheres inside Fat Man distort. This is fortunate, because the high-explosive charges surrounding the hemispheres, meant to drive them together to achieve critical mass, detonate. There is a sudden flurry of neutrons and alpha particles around the bomb, but the damaged hemispheres jam and do not begin their chain reaction.

Nonetheless, Fat Man is dead, a dangerous shambles of fused and melted electrical components and two scarred and damaged plutonium half-spheres.

The lightning bolt pours down a tower leg and through the cables bracing the structure. The bracings melt. The tower leg collapses. The tower begins to buckle.

The time between the first impact of the lightning on Fat Man's housing and the buckling of the tower leg is less than one second.

Things move more slowly now.

The leg folds. Insulation fires hiss in the sudden rain shower. The platform supporting the bomb tilts. Yards of cables spill like entrails from the falling tower. For another second or two, Fat Man hangs on its supports before its great weight tears the fastenings free. The sphere falls heavily to the wet ground, imbedding itself to a depth of a third of its radius. Then, with a creak of raped metal, the tower completes its collapse and crashes down on the ruined bomb.

The line squall, elemental and innocent, drifts on. Overhead the desert stars are fading in the dawn.

Excerpts from *A History of the Pacific War 1941-1946*

By E. A. Schorr and K. K. Tsuboi. New York:
Harcourt Brace Jovanovich, 1989

From Chapter VI: "Trinity and Its Aftermath"

With the failure of the initial test of the atomic bomb at Trinity Site came a period of uncertainty for the policy makers in Washington.

Major General Leslie R. Groves, director of the Manhattan District project, promptly reported the circumstances of the test disaster to President Truman, and in a top-secret memorandum on July 25, 1945, the general took upon himself the responsibility for the decision to test on July 16 despite the inclement weather.

He offered a new testing schedule, explaining to the President and the Joint Chiefs of Staff that although a uranium bomb was, in fact, immediately available (the U-238-fueled device known as Little Boy), it was his opinion that the uranium bomb should be held in reserve until such time as another full test of the plutonium-fueled bomb could be completed.

Appended to General Groves's memorandum was a personal appeal from Dr. J. Robert Oppenheimer, the Manhattan District project's chief scientist. Oppenheimer, in characteristically dramatic language, assured the President that the misfortune at Trinity Site had been "an act of almighty Providence, perhaps intended as a lesson in humility to those of us who would harness the incalculable powers of Nature." For Oppenheimer, an avowed agnostic, to write in such terms to Harry Truman, a man with a strong middle-American religious sense, but one with whom Oppenheimer felt no emotional or intellectual kinship, is remarkable. It is a measure of Oppenheimer's determination to continue with his work on the frontier of physics.

The Manhattan District scientists, Oppenheimer wrote, could reprocess the plutonium fuel [1] from the damaged Fat Man bomb and be ready for another test in February 1946.

He also informed the President that some of his fellow scientists were having second thoughts about the morality of using an atomic bomb on the Japanese.[2] Perhaps, he suggested, the enforced delay could be used to contrive a demonstration on some uninhabited Pacific atoll to show the enemy the weapon's power.

This course of action was never seriously considered by either the Joint Chiefs of Staff or the administration. The President and his advisers were aware of a substantial "peace party" in Japan, but they doubted its ability to affect the suicidal resolve of the members of the War Cabinet. And, given the failure of the Trinity test, a request by Oppenheimer to test the next plutonium bomb in the presence of enemy observers was, in the words of Admiral Ernest J. King, the chief of Naval Operations, "utopian—to say the least."

Almost as an afterthought, Oppenheimer asked the President not to accept the resignation of General Groves, which had been offered immediately after the New Mexico fiasco. "To begin again with a new director," Oppenheimer wrote, "would cause enormous problems and further delays." Between Oppenheimer and Groves there existed a genuine mutual respect and regard and there is no reason to suspect Oppenheimer's motives. He

1. At this time the plutonium core of the Fat Man bomb contained 99% of the total supply of this element in existence.

2. Most historians agree that there would have been no such doubts about using the weapon on the Nazis. Many Manhattan District scientists were refugees from National Socialist oppression. It is an interesting point in view of the many revisionist historians, most writing thirty or more years after the event, who accused Truman and his advisers of racism in making the final decision.

had worked well with Groves for three years and he did not relish the prospect of having to "break in" a new, and possibly less understanding, major general.

In Washington, however, the basic decision to continue the Manhattan District project—and under its current leadership—had already been taken.

President Truman had learned of the effort to build an atomic bomb only after the death of President Roosevelt at Warm Springs in April. He did not immediately become an advocate of the project. His experience as a senator and chairman of the Truman Committee investigating arms contracts had made him suspicious of any program based on large secret expenditures. The Manhattan District project was one of the most expensive and most secret ever undertaken by the United States. Furthermore, the President's background of close association with the Pendergast political machine in Missouri caused him to be extremely sensitive about any program that might, after the war, come under hostile scrutiny by his political enemies in the Congress. Although he did, in the event, decide to continue the Manhattan District project, it was not a decision he made with enthusiasm.[3]

With the decision made and General Groves retained as project director, the scientists in New Mexico began the long and demanding task of assembling another plutonium bomb. The

3. Edward R. Stettinius, in his memoirs, suggests that the President was tempted, on moral grounds, to discontinue work on the atomic bomb, and that the decision to go forward was based on the foreseen need to contain a truculent Soviet Union after the war. A number of Truman's biographers accept this view. The authors, however, find it a questionable one. The Cold War was not, in 1945, yet an accepted fact of life in Washington. It is far more likely that the President was seeking a method of shortening the Pacific conflict at a time when American public opinion was growing impatient with battles won that did not seem to bring the end perceptibly nearer, and the administration's Republican opponents had begun to question the conduct of the war. Stettinius, in any case, would not have been privy to the decision to continue the Manhattan project, having been replaced as secretary of State by James F. Byrnes on July 3, 1945.

question of staging a demonstration was never seriously considered. Meanwhile, it was still necessary to press the war against Japan to a military conclusion and force the Japanese to accept the unconditional surrender demanded by the framers of the Potsdam Declaration.[4]

From Chapter X: "The Decision to Strike"

As early as the end of 1944 discussions were taking place on the most effective way to conclude the war in the Pacific. Most naval strategists favored isolating the Japanese homeland from its conquests in the rest of Asia by means of landings in Formosa, Korea, and on the east coast of China. The exponents of strategic air power advocated encircling the Japanese archipelago with an air and naval blockade while battering the Japanese into capitulation with massive, round-the-clock incendiary bombing by the fleets of B-29 Superfortresses that were beginning to stream in great numbers from plants in the United States. The Army and Marine Corps, in rare agreement, believed that the methods advanced by the other services were likely to be too slow or ineffective. The soldiers and Marines, supported by General of the Army Douglas MacArthur, argued that the Japanese could be defeated only by direct invasion of the home islands. It would be costly, but it would be certain. And it would be relatively swift.

4. At Potsdam, President Truman and his advisers had been seeking a commitment from Marshal Stalin that the Soviet Union would enter the war against Japan by year's end. But by October 1945, it had become obvious that the Soviets did not intend to withdraw their troops from any territory liberated by the Red Army. The installation of Communist puppet governments in Poland, Czechoslovakia, and the Balkan states had finally alarmed the Anglo-Americans. Soon the need to keep the Soviets out of China (where a Soviet-supported insurgency was defeating the U.S.-supported Kuomintang), Korea (where Communist guerrillas were active against the occupying Japanese), and, above all, Japan proper had become a major preoccupation in London and Washington.

This last consideration was growing in importance. The European war had ended in May. The methods offered by the sailors and airmen to end the Pacific war might work, but they could take months—possibly even years.

In Washington, President Roosevelt's wartime bipartisan coalition was beginning to disintegrate. On the home front, the public was growing impatient with wartime privations and inconveniences. President Truman, who lacked the charismatic touch of his predecessor, but was a consummate politician, sensed difficulties ahead for the Democratic administration if the war continued indefinitely.

MacArthur, upon whom command of the invasion would devolve, was well aware that an assault on the Japanese islands would take an enormous toll of American lives. Despite his lack of personal regard for the new President, MacArthur considered it his duty to warn that staff estimates of American casualties were running as high as three-quarters of a million Americans killed, wounded, or missing. Japanese casualties, MacArthur's planners believed, could be three times the American figure. "But nothing less than a massive assault on the Japanese homeland," he wrote, "can accomplish our national war aim of unconditional surrender. The political and strategic constraints on a campaign of pure attrition against Japan, one lasting a year or even more, are compelling."

Therefore, on May 25, 1945, while American forces were deeply committed on the island of Okinawa in the Ryukyus, the Joint Chiefs of Staff issued "J.C.S. 1331/3, Joint Chiefs of Staff Directive for Operation Olympic."

The operative paragraph of this directive, sent to MacArthur, Admiral Chester W. Nimitz (commander in chief, Pacific Fleet), and General Curtis E. LeMay (commanding general, Twentieth Air Force [1]), was: "The Joint Chiefs of Staff direct the invasion of Kyushu (Operation Olympic), target date 1 November 1945."

1. The new Superfortresses had already begun attacking Japanese cities from bases in the Marianas, displaying some sensitivity in choosing targets. The

Although Operation Olympic was to require the commitment of 500,000 men (necessitating large-scale redeployments of troops from Europe), it was only a stepping stone to a much larger operation, now known as Coronet.[2]

Olympic's purpose was to seize the southern third of the island of Kyushu, the most accessible of the four main islands of the Japanese archipelago. Two large bays, Ariake and Kagoshima, dominate the coastal plain of Kyushu. These bays were to be taken and equipped as major bases for the naval forces needed for Operation Coronet. Airfields were to be built near Kagoshima and at Miyazaki on the eastern coast to accommodate bombers, fighters, and fighter-bombers. With these strips in operation, no part of the main island of Honshu would be out of range of American air power. And Honshu, of course, was the target of the next, and final, invasion.

X-day for Operation Olympic was set for November 1, 1945. March 1, 1946 was designated as Y-day for the assault on Honshu, Operation Coronet.

From Chapter XXI: "Bakas and Bushido"

In March 1945, General Masakazu Amano, one of the officers entrusted with the task of evaluating enemy intentions, wrote the following:

"Because it is the economic and political center of the empire, as well as the best tactical terrain in the homeland, it is on the

---

Imperial Palace in Tokyo and the ancient cultural capital of Kyoto were protected by strict orders from Washington. Asian specialists within the State Department had convinced the military planners that bombing these would be counterproductive. But all else in the home islands was considered to be in a free-fire zone.

2. Although "J.C.S. 1331/3" was issued on May 25, not one of the logistic or strategic redeployments had actually been made at the time of the Trinity test on July 16. On July 18, two days after Trinity, theater commanders were instructed to begin the planned movements at once.

Kanto Plain that the Americans will seek the final, decisive battle with the Japanese Army.

"First they will attempt to secure bases in southeastern Japan by means of large-scale amphibious lodgements. Upon completion of their objectives there, they will invade the Kanto." [1]

Amano's vision of the future was a chillingly accurate one. On April 8, 1945, Japanese Imperial General Staff Headquarters began to prepare a defense of the home islands by issuing Ketsu-go Number 6, an operational outline for resisting enemy landings on the island of Kyushu, and Ketsu-go Number 3, an outline of plans for the defense of central Honshu and the Kanto Plain. The commitment of the General Staff to a last-man, last-bullet defense was absolute.

It has often been said that the Japanese did not know how to surrender. This is not strictly true. In the feudal civil wars preceding the Tokugawa Shogunate, side-changing and honorable surrenders were common.

But Japan had never lost a war to an external enemy. The destruction—by divine intervention, the Japanese believed—of two invasion fleets sent against Japan by the Mongol Emperor Kublai Khan, the successes against China, and the defeat of a Russian fleet in the Russo-Japanese War all tended to establish a myth of invincibility.

By 1945 the war against the United States was clearly lost, but the Japanese ability to accommodate national policy to strategic reality was also lost. The Bushido of the modern samurai, the Way of the Warrior, was quite different from that of his forebears.

It is written in the *Hagakure* [2] that one should never hesitate to correct oneself when one finds that one has made a mistake.

1. Major General Masakazu Amano, Chief of Operations, *A Situation Estimate for the Latter Half of 1945 and the Spring of 1946.* Tokyo: Army Section, Imperial General Staff Headquarters, 1945.

2. Written, it is believed, in Nabeshima fief, Kyushu, about 1716. An edition available in English today is *Hagakure: The Book of the Samurai*, Tokyo: Kodansha International, 1979.

After four years of war against the world's greatest industrial power, it was obvious that Japan had, indeed, made a very serious mistake. Her conquests had been stripped away, her Navy lay at the bottom of the sea, her air units were reduced to suicide cadres, and her cities were under continuous devastating attack.

There was a faction in Japan, consisting mainly of aristocrats, former diplomats, and intellectuals, who wished desperately for peace at almost any price. But the government remained firmly in the hands of the *gumbatsu*, the military clique that had planned the war against the United States, and set it in motion.

As early as July 1944, dissatisfaction with the conduct of the war had resulted in the resignation of Premier General Hideki Tojo and his replacement by retired General Kuniake Kioso. Though there were other changes to follow, none of them opened any avenues to an acceptance that the war was being lost and that only surrender could save the Japanese homeland from a blood bath and eventual occupation by foreign troops.

By the winter of 1945, with American forces firmly in control of southern and eastern Kyushu, a political convulsion within the Japanese officer corps produced the Crimson Dawn Coup, ending all pretense of parliamentary government and returning General Tojo to power as virtual shogun.

It is also written in the *Hagakure* that "the way of the samurai is found in death."

From Chapter XXIII: "The Commanders"

On December 20, 1945, General of the Army George C. Marshall and Fleet Admiral Ernest J. King received a secret report from General of the Army Douglas MacArthur. This report was written personally by the general, in collaboration with Fleet Admiral Chester W. Nimitz, on December 18.[1]

"On the island of Kyushu a line has been established between

1. In 1961, when the documents relating to the conduct of the war in the Pacific were reviewed and declassified, this report was not among them. It is a personal communication from MacArthur and Nimitz to Marshall and King,

Nobeoka in the east and Yatsushiro in the west. Japanese resistance is diminishing, and it appears that they are now stripping this front and redeploying the troops to Honshu. According to plan we shall make no further attempt to advance into the northern half of Kyushu. Halsey's carrier pilots have been given the task of interdicting Japanese movements between Kita-kyushu and Shimonoseki. Spaatz's long-range bombers have mined the strait heavily and are now doing the same to Suo Sound and the Bungo Strait, between Kyushu and Shikoku Island.

"The Japanese are engaged in a 'Dunkirk' operation, moving troops in small boats under cover of darkness, and it is to be expected that many of the soldiers we fought on Kyushu will be on the beaches of Honshu to meet us again.

"Our airfields at Kagoshima and Miyazaki and the satellite strips at Kanoya, Nango, and Kushima are complete. The performance of the construction battalions, often working under fire, has been magnificent. The first long-range fighter units, P-47Ns and P-51s, have arrived and are taking over defensive patrolling duties from the squadrons of the fast carrier task groups. There has been no Japanese air activity here since X + 10. G-2 believes they have withdrawn all their remaining aircraft to Honshu.

"We understand that the President has certain political problems at home brought on by the intransigence of our so-called ally the Soviet Union combined with a certain sensitivity about casualties in this theater. We remind you that he was told that Olympic and Coronet would be costly.

"We have taken 37,000 casualties in the forty-eight days since we landed on Kyushu. The Marines have been hardest hit, with a loss of 9,000 effectives. We cannot overemphasize the need for

---

and as such was intended to supplement the normal report submitted by the Pacific commanders to the President and the Joint Chiefs of Staff. The authors attempted in 1982, 1983, and 1984 to obtain this document under provisions of the Freedom of Information Act. Not under 1985 were they able to do so.

---

replacements *at once*, so that they may be trained and conditioned for Operation Coronet.

"From X − 2 through X + 10 the Kamikazes hit us hard. The loss of three fleet carriers and eleven transport vessels is not surprising in view of the fact that the assault force was under continuous suicide attack for twelve days. It is a bitter thing to contemplate, but we will have to absorb even larger losses as we close in to land on Honshu. Captured documents say that the Japanese still have 10,000 aircraft hidden on the main island. Many of these are trainers, and they will be flown by inexperienced pilots. But we do not underestimate the damage they may do.

"On Kyushu, and most particularly in the area around Kagoshima, our troops were repeatedly attacked by civilian irregulars and volunteer defense forces, some of them armed with bamboo spears. As on Okinawa, the Japanese military has totally convinced the population that our soldiers will rape and kill like Russians (like, in fact, the Japanese did at Nanking and other places in this war). The result has been hysterical flight in some cases, and, in others, fanatical resistance by old men, women, and even schoolchildren. We have not been able yet to estimate Japanese casualties, but be assured that they are astronomical in number.

"The resistance of the soldiers of the 16th Home Army and the treacherous guerrilla actions of many civilians have, regrettably, resulted in some unsoldierly excesses by a few of our troops. A Marine gunnery sergeant with twenty-two years' service is awaiting court-martial in Kagoshima for mutilating enemy dead; there was some looting and there were a few cases of sexual assault. There has been nothing to justify what the press seems so delighted to call 'atrocities' and even 'war crimes.'

"In any case I have made it known that indiscipline of any sort will not be tolerated in my command.[2] It has not been in the past

2. Even without the personal pronouns here, it would be apparent to historical scholars that this section of the report was composed by General MacArthur.

and it will not be now merely because we have penetrated the enemy homeland.

"Training is being carried on under an accelerated schedule, conscious as we are of the imminence of Coronet and the largely unblooded quality of the troops we must use. Weather has been a problem, but once again the construction battalions performed yeoman service in repairing necessary facilities.[3]

"May I suggest that the President consider with care how much information he will release concerning our losses during Olympic. They have been high, and when Coronet begins they will be much higher. What the war effort cannot afford at this time is a weakening of resolve on the home front. No one, believe me, feels the loss of each soldier, sailor, or airman more keenly than I. But even the President, with that minimal military experience of which he is so inordinately proud, knows that in war there is no substitute for victory—at whatever terrible price it must be purchased. . . ."

Though written in the terms MacArthur customarily used to address posterity, the modern reader can easily discern in this report the great commander's need to explain the high cost in lives of Operation Olympic, and to reiterate his previous warnings of the even higher cost to come of Operation Coronet.

3. The typhoon of November 1945 struck on X + 2 and did great harm to the orderly advance of the American forces as it swept across the island of Kyushu. But in the event it did far greater damage to Japanese defensive installations, flooding many and drowning civilians and soldiers alike as rivers rose and bridges and roads were destroyed. By December, the American Seabees had repaired all damage. The Japanese were unable to and so suffered additional terrible privations.

CORONET

And how can man die better
 Than facing fearful odds
For the ashes of his fathers,
 And the temples of his gods?

Thomas Babington Macaulay
"Horatius"

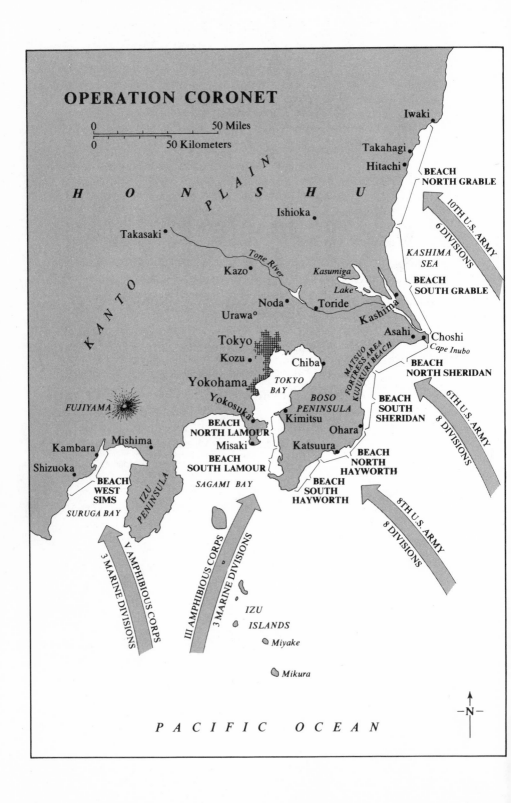

OPERATION CORONET

0   50 Miles
0   50 Kilometers

H O N   *PLAIN*   *S H U*

Iwaki

Takahagi

Hitachi

**BEACH
NORTH GRABLE**

10TH U.S. ARMY

6 DIVISIONS

Ishioka

Takasaki

*KASHIMA
SEA*

Tone River

Kazo

Kasumiga

Lake

**BEACH
SOUTH GRABLE**

Noda

Toride

K A N T O

Urawa

Kashima

Asahi

Choshi
Cape Inubo

Tokyo

Kozu

Chiba

*MATSUO
FORTRESS AREA*

KUJUKURI BEACH

**BEACH
NORTH SHERIDAN**

6TH U.S. ARMY

8 DIVISIONS

Yokohama

*TOKYO
BAY*

Yokosuka

*BOSO
PENINSULA*

**BEACH
SOUTH
SHERIDAN**

FUJIYAMA

**BEACH
NORTH LAMOUR**

Kimitsu

Ohara

Kambara   Mishima

Misaki

Katsuura

**BEACH
NORTH
HAYWORTH**

Shizuoka

**BEACH
SOUTH LAMOUR**

SAGAMI BAY

**BEACH
SOUTH
HAYWORTH**

**BEACH
WEST
SIMS**

*IZU
PENINSULA*

SURUGA BAY

8TH U.S. ARMY

8 DIVISIONS

3 MARINE DIVISIONS

V AMPHIBIOUS CORPS

III AMPHIBIOUS CORPS

3 MARINE DIVISIONS

*IZU
ISLANDS*

Miyake

Mikura

N

P A C I F I C   O C E A N

Y-day minus 1
28 February 1946

On the date specified by the Joint Chiefs of Staff, the invasion force will assemble and proceed to the designated points off the coast of the island of Honshu, Japan, where it will disembark the forces required to penetrate and occupy the Kanto Plain.

> Staff Study Operations: "Coronet"
> General Headquarters
> U.S. Army Forces in the Pacific

1700 Hours

Between longitudes 139° and 140° West, the surface of the Pacific was alive with ships. Steaming at the optimum cruising speed of the slowest ship in the fleet, the 3,000 vessels of the Coronet Amphibious Main Force closed on the east coast of Honshu.

The sun, low on the horizon, made a broad amber path on the sea. A bank of clouds marked the division between sky and ocean to the west. Lookouts and radar scanned sea and air, and the low-flying scout planes and fast ships of the screen prowled the enormous periphery of the fleet, alert for submarine contacts. For twelve hours there had been none. The sea belonged to the advancing armada.

The columns of ships stretched from horizon to horizon. Even the pilots of the high-level Combat Air Patrol above the landward flank of the fleet could not see its full extent. They shared the air only with the sea birds that wheeled and soared over the ship-troubled ocean.

Thirty nautical miles to the east of the Main Force's seaward flank steamed the five Fast Carrier Task Groups. Each of the fifteen carriers took its proper turn launching and recovering aircraft in a rota that kept no fewer than fifty fighters above the fleet at all times. These operations would continue through the night; suspending standing "darken ship" orders, the carriers floodlit their flight decks for flying operations whenever necessary and without regard for the possibility of submarine or Kamikaze attack.

On the escorts, destroyers and cruisers of the screen, the ships were now at Condition Two, a state of readiness with half of all guns manned constantly by their regular battle-station crews. They would remain so, barring emergencies, until the fleet went to General Quarters and the beachheads were secured. All ships steamed extremely close to maximum watertight integrity.

Only on the attack transports was there a semblance of momentary ease. They were fifteen hours from their anchorages off the beaches. The ships moved in clear weather across a calm sea with a long, gentle swell. And the half-million soldiers and Marines about to be committed were allowed to relax and be alone with their thoughts.

Standing at the rail of the attack transport USS *Portola*, First Lieutenant Harry Seaver looked to the west across column after column of gray ships. As the sun reddened with the onset of dusk, the sea grew darker. He could see the silver flash of dolphins sporting in the avenues between frothy wakes.

Portola steamed third in a column of fifty ships carrying the assault teams of the 11th Airborne Division of the U.S. Sixth Army. A new ship, she was packed with men and equipment. Along her sides were festooned furled landing nets. The fast assault boats of Seaver's Ranger team were stacked amidships under the cargo cranes. The amphibious tanks of the armored landing teams were lashed to the deck, and the LCIs, the Landing Craft Infantry, hung in davits ready to be swung outboard from the boat deck. *Portola* could put 5,000 men ashore with enough matériel to maintain themselves for twenty-four hours of combat. There were 170 ships of her class in the fleet.

Far to the rear, somewhere in the line that stretched back thirty miles or more, the supply ship carrying the division's food, ammunition, and thin-skinned vehicles kept her station. On Y + 1, when the 11th Airborne's section of Beach South Sheridan was secure enough to send the supplies ashore, she would do so.

At that time she would take aboard the dead—those who could be recovered.

As it happened, Harry Seaver knew the 30,000 yards of South Sheridan assigned to the 11th Airborne Division well. When he was a boy, he had swum and sunned himself on these twenty kilometers of gray sand that the villagers of Choshi, Asahi, and Kochiba called Kujukuri-hama, Ninety-nine-Mile Beach.

He wondered who had decided to name the invasion beaches after movie stars and a big-band vocalist: Grable, Sheridan, Sims, Hayworth, and Lamour. It was such a typically American thing to do. The Japanese would think it insulting, an example of the Yankees' lack of *makoto*—a word that translated roughly as "sincerity," though it meant much more. But then, Seaver thought, the Japanese had never quite believed in the Americans as serious-minded people. For that error in judgment they were paying a terrible price.

Down in the troop compartment Jim Tanaka was deep in his obsessive study of the map of the Ranger team's operational area. A Nisei from California, he had fought in Italy with the 442nd Regimental Combat Team. All that he knew of Japan, he had learned from his parents, who were still living in the Tule Lake Relocation Camp. Now *that*, Seaver told himself, was *makoto* with a vengeance.

At the sound of airplane engines, Seaver looked up, suppressing an impulse to take cover. A flight of four Grumman Bearcats swung low over *Portola*. Their deep-blue paint looked black in the light of the low sun. So far there had been no sign of Kamikaze activity. During the Olympic landings on Kyushu, and before that, during the assaults on Okinawa and the Philippines, the suicide attackers had taken a substantial toll of ships and men. But the attacks had cost the Japanese casualties of 100%. Now, Divisional Intelligence reported that the Japanese had reconstituted their Kamikaze forces for use against the fleet when the assault on Honshu began.

Seaver's father had been a banker in Tokyo, manager of McKinley-Manhattan Trust's office there, and Seaver had been born and educated in Japan. He wondered what he would find in the homeland. Reports of the havoc caused by the Twentieth Air Force and the Navy's carrier raiders suggested that nothing remained standing on Honshu. But flyboys and zoomies tended to make wild claims, he well knew. Documents captured at Kagoshima—which he had translated for the division's commander —suggested that the Japanese still had airplanes for suicide attacks and a million soldiers with which to resist Operation Coronet.

Seaver had lived through two bloody campaigns by now. He found himself wondering if he could live through a third. He was three weeks past his twenty-fourth birthday.

Corporal Saigo Noguchi lay in his narrow bunk under two meters of earth and tried hard to ignore the shaking of the ground. The bombardment had been continuous for more than six days. This meant, according to the honorable company commander, that the Americans would be coming soon.

Noguchi tried to calculate the number of shells the prowling cruisers and destroyers had fired into the support area behind Kujukuri-hama. It was an almost impossible exercise. Hundreds of shells had fallen each hour of the day and night. The numbers were astronomical; the weight of explosives even greater. It was difficult to conceive of a Navy that could squander artillery in this fashion.

The Americans' prodigality was even more astonishing considering that the so-called Matsuo Fortress was only a line of log-and-earth bunkers hastily dug into the sandy, damp earth of the bamboo forests behind the beach. Some of the bunkers held artillery, it was true, but most of the shelters housed only light machine guns or, like his own, 50mm mortars.

The cavelike compartment in which Noguchi and his two mortarmen waited out the bombardment was a space three meters by two. A vertical slit in the seaward-facing wall of the bunker gave the mortar a field of fire down an open avenue to the beach, and a small gap between the logs supporting the roof allowed the men to raise a bamboo periscope to search the area immediately surrounding their position.

But the earth erupting from near misses had clogged the periscope port and nearly closed the firing slot. If and when the bombardment eased, they would have to set to work to clear them. Until then nothing could be done.

There was no proper egress from the cave. Each time a mortar section was relieved, an opening had to be dug to permit the exchange. The departing section would then shovel earth back into the opening, both protecting and isolating the men inside.

Until the most recent bombardment had begun, these reliefs were made every three days, each new mortar team bringing its own supplies of rice and water to the position. But Noguchi and his men had now been isolated for twice the customary time. When the shelling had begun, Noguchi had instituted a rigid rationing system, allowing each man only one cup of water and one bowl of rice each day. But they had stretched their supplies to the limit and beyond. They had eaten nothing for twenty-four hours, and even the water was now gone.

The stench inside the bunker was intolerable. The twenty-centimeter pit in the rear of the cave that served as a latrine was overflowing. Drainage was bad in this wet lowland soil.

The corporal was aware that soon they would have to send someone to the *taii-san*, the company comander, to ask for supplies. This meant that they would have to dig themselves out from inside and that the man chosen would have to run at least two kilometers through the rain of shells from the American warships cruising so impudently a few thousand meters off the beach. The commander, a middle-aged former schoolmaster from Shikoku who fancied himself a samurai, was a harsh disciplinarian and might become very angry with anyone who left his post during an alert.

Noguchi, upon whom the mantle of leadership rested heavily, resolved that if anyone went, it would have to be himself. He did not relish the idea of leaving his precious mortar in the care of

Superior Private Koriyama and Second Class Private Iwaka, but the responsibility for feeding his men was his.

Koriyama was a hulking man from Hokkaido. He claimed to have been in training to become a sumo wrestler when he was drafted, and it might well be so. He weighed more than 100 kilograms even after weeks of short rations. The big man also fancied himself a strategist. The Americans, he said, would not land here at Kujukuri, but farther north, beyond Choshi, so that they could advance on Tokyo on the other side of the Tonegawa. The terrain was better on that side of the river for their tanks, so that was obviously what they would do. The constant shelling and the reported appearances of frogmen off Kujukuri-hama were tricks, nothing more.

It was plain to Noguchi that Koriyama wanted to believe the things he said. Yet he had fought the Americans, as Noguchi had, on Kyushu, and he should know that the Yankees mounted enormous operations. They would probably attack the Kashima beaches north of Choshi, as Koriyama said. But they would attack Kujukuri-hama as well, and almost certainly the beaches of Sagami and Tokyo bays for good measure. They had the ships and men to do it.

The company commander, Captain Kitaname, had impressed upon all the noncommissioned officers of the Matsuo company that once the Americans came ashore, a Japanese soldier's duty was to fight and die. Noguchi accepted this as right and proper, but he was not certain that Koriyama did. He hoped that he had sufficiently impressed on both Koriyama and Iwaka that the *taii-san* meant exactly what he said.

The corporal twisted in his earthen niche so that he could survey the interior of the bunker. Iwaka, a sixteen-year-old conscript from Aomori Prefecture in the north, was terrified by the bombardment and had been since it began. His eyes seemed to bulge from his flat, hungry-gaunt, sallow face each time a shell struck nearby. His trousers were constantly wet and smelling of urine, though his stink could add little to the already rank stench of the overflowing latrine.

Each half-hour for days, it seemed, Iwaka asked: "How soon will the Americans come, *Gocho-san*? What will they do when they find us?"

For the first thirty or so times the questions were asked, the corporal, conscious of his duty as leader, had replied that the Americans would appear only after the ships' guns were silent. Then, he explained, the men of Matsuo, together with many, many others nearby, would drive them back into the sea, because even American Marines could not withstand the Yamato spirit, the spirit of the Land of the Eight Islands.

Instead of reassuring the boy, the mention of Marines added to his fright. He had heard from men who had fought on Kyushu that Marines wore necklaces of human ears, taken from murdered prisoners.

Noguchi had no doubt that Americans did such things. But though it was horrible and totally uncivilized, what did it really matter to the dead what happened to their ears? Particularly if they had so far forgotten duty as to allow themselves to be captured? Such persons would not be among the honored spirits at Yasukuni Shrine.

Noguchi had tried hard to be understanding and, insofar as duty permitted, sympathetic with the boy. He was a long way from home and parents, and the chances were that he would never again see Aomori. But in the confined bunker's foul air, without food or enough water, and under the incessant shelling, never knowing when a direct hit might bury them all, Noguchi's patience had begun to run out. Now when Iwaka whimpered or asked stupid questions, Noguchi silenced him by hitting him in the face with his fists. This brought tears, but it did tend to inhibit Iwaka's whining.

Noguchi, who was not a brutal person, disliked having to enforce discipline with blows, although it was common practice in the Army, and it did achieve its purpose. From time to time the corporal even found it necessary to strike Koriyama, who could easily have beaten the slender Noguchi senseless.

Koriyama, for all his wishful thinking, was not really a bad soldier. A *yobeiki*, a conscript of the First Reserve, he at least understood military discipline. He was thirty-five years old, twelve years Noguchi's senior, and his strength and size were useful when it was necessary to carry the heavy mortar from place to place. Of course, here, Noguchi thought, a sumo wrestler's bulk and girth were an imposition on his comrades. Koriyama took up far more than his proper share of space in the cave.

The steady pounding of exploding cannon rounds made the corporal's head ache. The gnawing emptiness in his belly didn't help either. And his mouth felt dry and unpleasantly furry.

He closed his eyes against a fall of dirt from the roof of the bunker. A new, deeper, rumbling series of shocks made the entire shelter tremble. These explosions were stronger than any they had felt before, and Noguchi recalled that his platoon leader, Lieutenant Fuchida, had warned him that there were American battleships off the coast of central Honshu, ships armed with sixteen-inch guns.

The jolting explosions of the huge shells caused some of the dirt jammed in the firing slot to come free and fly across the bunker's interior. Noguchi felt the overpressure in his ears and against his eyeballs. He brushed dirt from his face and got to his knees. The arrival of the bigger shells presented him with an opportunity. Frivolous use of the field telephone was cause for punishment, but it was clearly his duty to inform the company command post that Matsuo was now being bombarded by large warships. That done, he could also remind the *taii-san* that his men needed food and water. It would be less hazardous to say this to Captain Kitaname on the field telephone than face to face. The *taii-san* had been known to use his scabbarded sword on insubordinate noncoms.

Iwaka was huddled in a corner, chin buried in his chest, his rifle in the dirt. Though it was difficult to tell in the darkness, it looked as though he were crying again. Koriyama leaned against the mortar tube, his cheeky face expressionless under the grime. Noguchi suspected that he was thinking about food. He was the only man in the Matsuo company who ate Army victuals with enjoyment, even when the rice was contaminated with sand and insects.

"Give me the telephone," Noguchi said.

Koriyama handed Noguchi the instrument in its moldy leather case. Noguchi hoped the wires were still intact. He cranked the handle and put the handset to his ear under his helmet.

A small distant voice said, "Command post."

"This is Mortar Section Number Six, Corporal Noguchi speaking. The enemy is shelling our area. They are using large guns now."

"Yes," the disembodied voice said without interest. "The observation post says there are battleships offshore. Your report is noted."

Before the command post could break the connection, Noguchi said, "May I please speak with the honorable company commander."

"He is busy."

"Then, if you please, may I speak with Lieutenant Fuchida?"

"Fuchida's dead. Sergeant Okamura is in command of 2nd Platoon now."

Though Noguchi had become familiar with death, the news about Fuchida stunned him. He had been a good officer, always considerate of his men, and he was fond of Noguchi. He had even lent him his own binoculars to watch the beach. They were stored carefully, wrapped in cloth, in Noguchi's personal kit. It was a shock to learn that Fuchida had been killed.

Weeks ago, while the company was training at Sendai, Fuchida had done 2nd Platoon the honor of attending the sake party given on the Emperor's birthday. Noguchi remembered that there had been a good-natured argument, amid much shouting and drunken laughter, about whether Fuchida's rank gave him precedence over the spirits of lower ranks when they died and went to report to Yasukuni Shrine. Fuchida, grinning, had said that of course rank had its privileges, even among the dead at Yasukuni. Everyone there would be a soldier and would understand. But Okamura and Noguchi had held out for a precedence based on first come, first served.

Now, Noguchi thought, feeling tears in his eyes, Lieutenant Fuchida knows the proper answer—whatever it might be. This war was very tragic.

"Ask them to send a runner with something to eat, *Gocho-san*," Koriyama said, shouting to make himself heard over the noise of the bombardment. "My belly is empty as a drum."

Noguchi emerged from his melancholy with a start. The constant strain and the hunger made it difficult for him to keep his mind on what he should be doing. He said, "Command post, are you still there?"

"Yes," the voice said irritably. "What do you want?"

"We need rations—"

An explosion nearby brought a torrent of dirt down from the inadequately shored roof. Noguchi hunched over the telephone, protecting it. Iwaka sobbed and Koriyama cursed.

"Command post?"

The line had gone dead. Noguchi cranked the handle again and said, "Can you hear me, command post?"

There was no reply. The last salvo had torn out the wires. Noguchi threw the instrument against the earthen wall in a burst of frustrated anger. He kicked at Iwaka furiously and said, "Get your entrenching tool out and start digging." It would begin to get dark soon, and with luck a man could make it to the command post and back in an hour.

"Me, *Gocho-san*?" Iwaka said stupidly. "You want me to dig? What shall I dig, please?"

Noguchi clenched his fist and threatened to hit the teary face. "Dig *there*, idiot! I'm going out. You, too, Koriyama. Dig, you stupid bastards!"

He knelt in the damp earth, feeling his empty stomach tremble with unreasonable rage. He wondered suddenly if he was going mad. He hoped not. The spirits of madmen would probably be unwelcome among the shades of honorably dead warriors at Yasukuni Shrine.

1730 Hours

In the Combat Intelligence Center of the Coronet Main Force command ship, the massive cruiser *Alaska*, Radarman Second Class Bertram Temko guarded the cathode-ray tube of his long-range search radar as he had been taught to do. Behind him, the CIC specialists went about their tasks with a murmuring of voices. The plots for enemy activity, plexiglass partitions upon which positions were marked in grease pencil, were empty. But the tension in the compartment was growing. Temko could feel it in the prickling of the short hairs on the back of his neck.

Temko's LRSR was the newest piece of equipment on the ship and he was proud of it. The secondary radars, the CRTs banked along one of the compartment's bulkheads, kept watch on the shifting patterns of ships keeping station on *Alaska*. But the antenna of Temko's radar was powered and angled to ignore the clutter of electronic returns from the nearby vessels and focus on the horizons. At the moment, the rotating antenna high above the cruiser had begun to pick up the image of the Izu archipelago, which lay seventy miles southeast of Sagami Bay.

Bert Temko was a modest young man but he was aware of the importance of his position. *Alaska*, as command ship for Operation Coronet, was in effect the headquarters for the biggest amphibious operation of the entire war. Overlord had had only the English Channel to contend with. Coronet was aimed straight at the heart of the Japanese empire from the open ocean. And Temko and his long-range search radar had the job of guarding her against surprise attack by the defenders.

The sounds of the CIC were familiar: the humming of the ventilating blowers, the all-pervasive, deeper hum of the great geared turbines driving the cruiser through the water. There was a group of Army officers in the CIC, all of them colonels and lieutenant colonels. Commander Muller, *Alaska*'s gunnery officer, was briefing them on the capabilities of the ship's secondary battery of five-inch thirty-eights.

Members of the crew often made black jokes about the CIC, which was off limits to anyone not stationed there and thus mysterious. The hands said that CIC was an abbreviation of Christ I'm Confused and, by God, *they* wouldn't like being stuck in a steel box below the water line, not in *these* waters. Temko, who was only nineteen years old, considered that sort of talk the product of uneducated and immature minds.

He heard other talk, too, from the crews of cans and aircraft carriers. They didn't have a good word to say for cruisers. Too small to do real damage, they said, and too damned big a target. But they didn't know what they were talking about. The three new cruisers, *Alaska* and her sisters, *Guam* and *Hawaii*, classed as "large" in contrast to the smaller "heavy" and "light" cruisers, were the pride of the fleet.

Though it was no part of his assigned duties, Temko made it his business to know a great deal about his ship. On his own time he had talked the engineering sections into giving him a comprehensive tour of *Alaska*. He had stood beside her 150,000-horsepower turbines and on the gratings that surrounded her eight Babcock and Wilcox boilers. The sense of power surrounding all this machinery filled him with an almost religious awe. It seemed impossible to him that anything could resist, let alone damage, this throbbing cathedral of force.

As much as Temko loved the gleaming machinery that drove *Alaska*, he loved his radar even more. To him, the ability to reach out to the horizon with an invisible beam of electrical energy and collect on the CRT a glowing picture of what hid out there was nothing short of a miracle. The specialist school he had attended had supplied him with all the technical information he needed to understand how his set worked, but the fact that it actually *did* filled him with wonder. The LRSR was *Alaska*'s eyes, the indispensable faculty she needed to seek and find the enemies who would destroy her.

On the bulkhead over his narrow bunk he had taped a page from a ship-recognition manual on which had been printed *Alaska*'s silhouette. He had carefully modified the line drawing into a fair rendering of *Alaska*'s black-and-gray dazzle and he had added, in careful lettering, all the ship's dimensions: Displacement/Standard 27,500 tons; Full Load 32,000 tons; Length 808 feet 6 inches; Beam 89 feet 6 inches, Draft 27 feet 6 inches. He had drawn an arrow pointing to the LRSR antenna, and, despite the fact that he was but one of the ratings qualified to operate the set, had labeled it: Mine!

Though his back was to the center of the compartment, he could hear Muller and the Army officers discussing fire missions. *Alaska*'s primary assignment was that of command ship, and did not include the bombardment of preassigned positions ashore. But her main battery of nine twelve-inch rifles would be available, Muller was explaining, to take on what the ground troops called "targets of opportunity": pillboxes, tank traps, and strong points behind the beaches. Muller was a broad-shouldered mustang, a regular risen through the ranks, who loved his guns as much as Temko loved his radar set. Temko had never spoken to the commander, but he regarded the grizzled regular as a kindred spirit.

The outlines of the Izu island chain were growing more distinct as the fleet moved closer to the coast. Temko could see that the destroyers of the inshore screen had altered course toward the southernmost island, Mikura. All of the islands had been subjected to almost constant air attack and sea bombardment for the last month to suppress the *shinyo*s, the suicide attack boats, based there. During the Kyushu landings, the Japs had used

35

dozens of hastily built *shinyo*s, armed with torpedoes, bombs, depth charges—anything capable of blowing a hole in the hull of a ship.

The Jap technique for attacking an assault force was to approach under cover of darkness at slow speed and, when discovered, to crank on thirty knots to ram, so that whatever they carried exploded close aboard. Against unarmored ships the tactic had been devastating. Twenty ships of the Olympic force had been sunk by *shinyo*s in Kagoshima Bay. Even against armored vessels, attacks could be deadly if the charge used was a large torpedo or depth charge. What sort of people, Temko wondered, could devise such a style of warfare? Failure meant death under the guns of the defenders and success meant death in the explosion that mauled the target vessel.

Because his duty station was deep inside *Alaska* and well below the water line, Temko feared the *shinyo*s more than he did the airborne Kamikazes. He had heard that *shinyo* sailors were all men his own age or younger. And Chief Vucinich, the CPO in charge of his section, said that the Japs were chained to their boats by their officers so they wouldn't chicken out at the last minute and go over the side trying to save themselves. Temko wondered how it was possible for the chief to be sure of this, since, as far as he knew, no one had yet captured a *shinyo* intact. But Vucinich was a thirty-year Navy man and usually had the absolute, genuine word on practically everything.

Lieutenant (jg) Potkonsky, the radar watch officer, paced the deck behind the operators, looking over their shoulders at the sweep of each green-glowing radar tube as he passed. He was a sallow young man from Boston, who had bad skin and lank sandy hair. His pale eyes were set close together, so that he seemed always to be peering at the end of his long, thin nose. Temko could see that Mr. Potkonsky was nervous. He always grew nervous as the hours of darkness closed in on *Alaska*. The radar crews were convinced that their officer hated and feared the CIC, but Temko suspected that Potkonsky was simply a jittery, intense sort of person. His family was Polish, and Temko's father always said Poles were like that. "Nervous in the service," Vucinich would say.

A regular procession of Army and Marine officers paraded through the CIC, some of them guided by the ship's own brass: Commander Michael Armitage, the exec, and once even the skipper himself. When Captain Weed came, it was with two major generals, Pedro del Valle and Lemuel Shepherd of the 1st and 6th Marine divisions.

Temko was increasingly aware of the rank topside. With his shipmates he had lined the weather decks at Buckner Bay to watch most of it come aboard, including General Walter Krueger, the officer in tactical command of the assault force, General Robert Eichelberger of the Eighth Army, and General O. W. Griswold of XIV Corps. Someone had pointed out to Temko a weazened stick of a man in wrinkled combat fatigues and an old cavalryman's hat. It was "Vinegar Joe" Stilwell, brought from the China-Burma-India Theater to command the Tenth Army, the outfit that was going ashore on North and South Grable and charging, so the rumor was, straight for Tokyo to capture old Hirohito himself.

Temko would like to have seen General MacArthur and Admiral Nimitz, but they were far out to the east, on Main Force's right flank, in the carrier *Midway*, the new 45,000-tonner everyone in *Alaska* had been talking about. The brass on *Alaska* were the tactical commanders; the two five-star flags, representing ultimate authority and responsibility, flew from the main yardarms of *Midway*.

Midway was one of the fifteen carriers steaming roughly parallel to Main Force. With each seaward sweep of the search radar, Temko's screen would show a faint return from the carrier groups. He had heard that there was even a Limey task unit somewhere in the area. The combined fleet reminded him of the hunting dogs of his native Kentucky hills, closing in for the kill.

As *Alaska* sortied from Buckner Bay at Okinawa to rendezvous with the assault force, Vucinich had told his men proudly that there were more than 3,000 ships involved in this

landing. The chief had been at Pearl on December 7, 1941—
"Sneak Day," he called it—and he hated Japs with a passion.

Potkonsky had completed another walk along the bank of radar sets and returned to stand behind Temko. The radarman could feel him fidgeting and shifting his weight from one foot to another as the ship rolled slightly in the long, calm swell.

At the edge of Temko's screen a faint spot of light appeared. Potkonsky noticed it instantly. "Turn the gain up full, Temko," he said.

"I already have, sir," Temko said reproachfully. "It's a genuine contact."

"Then report it, man," the officer said testily.

Temko pressed the speaking button on the sound-powered piece of his battle phone. "Unidentified radar contact. Aircraft. Bearing 310 relative. Range 42,000 yards. Altitude unknown."

Temko heard the talker behind him repeating the sighting to the bridge and to the flag bridge, where Admiral Joshua Kinsey, the officer in tactical command, and his staff were situated.

The sweeping raster painted the contact again on the tube face, and Temko felt the adrenaline begin to flow. All Allied aircraft had been equipped with a black box known as the IFF—Identification, Friend or Foe—which sent back a distinctive radar recognition signal. There was no such signal coming from the lone aircraft flying at the edge of Temko's radar.

"Contact bearing is 311 relative. Range 41,000 yards decreasing. No IFF." He studied the lingering fluorescent echo on the cathode-ray tube, measuring its movement across the etched grid. "Target speed is 200 knots. Two zero zero. Bearing unchanged. Target course is 90 degrees true."

"It's a Jap," Potkonsky said positively.

Temko agreed, but said nothing. He watched intently as the raster swept around the circle once more. The target's course was changing, bearing away to the north to parallel the fleet's track. "Target changing course. New course is 019 degrees true. Target speed 200 knots. Target bearing 310 relative. Range 40,000 yards."

On the plexiglass panel behind him, the target's course was beginning to take shape as he reported subsequent bearings. The sound of voices in the CIC had diminished. The talkers' repetitions could be clearly heard over the hum of the ventilating system. It has begun, Temko thought tightly. The Japs know where we are now.

On the flag bridge, Lieutenant Arnold Deighton, Admiral Kinsey's flag lieutenant, took the sighting report from the signalman wearing the headset. He stepped across the compartment to where Kinsey stood with members of his staff at the chart table. "Contact is holding his distance, Admiral. He's changed course to track us."

"All right, Arnold. Pass the word, if you please."

The flag lieutenant stepped to the TBS operator and handed him the signal pad. "All ships."

"All ships, aye, sir," the signalman said. He opened the switch on the talk between ships and said, "All Santa's Helpers. This is Sleighbells. We have a bogy. Bearing 310 relative, range 40,000 yards. Bogy's course is 019 degrees, speed 200 knots. Acknowledge dog charlie schedule."

On the ship's navigating bridge deck above, the officer of the deck, Lieutenant Commander John Steinhart, said to his quartermaster, "Call the captain to the bridge." To his signalman he said, "Flag hoist, Trasker. Make easy sail." The signalman hurried aft to the signal wing to comply. Easy sail—the alphabet flags for E and S—was one of the most ancient and traditional signal hoists in the Navy: Enemy in sight. John Paul Jones in *Bonhomme Richard* had made that signal when he sighted *Serapis.*

Captain Weed, commanding officer of *Alaska*, appeared on the bridge. "What do we have, Commander?"

"Contact bearing 310, sir," the OOD said.

The captain stepped out onto the port bridge wing and raised his binoculars to scan the sky. He could see nothing against the glare of the setting sun. "Range?"

"About twenty miles, sir," Steinhart said. "Single contact. From the speed, I'd say a Lorna or a Betty."

"Course?" Weed continued to search the sky between the breaks in the low-lying clouds to the northwest.

"Zero one nine, sir."

Weed lowered the binoculars and said, "Tracking us and probably squawking his little Jap heart out." He removed his cap and ran a hand through his thinning gray hair. The bullion on the bill of the cap was tinged with green. "All right, John. Let's come to General Quarters just to be safe."

"Now hear this. The ship will go to General Quarters in one minute."

A few moments later the general alarm sounded throughout the ship, and *Alaska* came alive to the sound of running feet. On the bridge could be heard the radio acknowledgments of the sighting from the divisional command ships: Reindeer, Pine Tree, Juniper, Redwood, Holly. All the divisional command ships had code names related in some, often far-fetched, way to Christmas.

Overhead, a flight of Bearcats headed west, throttles to the fire walls. The zoomies were practically racing to see who would intercept the Jap plane first, Steinhart thought. The aviators were always eager for a kill.

The OOD's quartermaster appeared with gray-painted steel helmets for the OOD and the captain.

"You still have the conn, Commander," Weed said. "I'll be in flag plot with the admiral." A thin smile touched his sunburned lips. "Reassuring the doughboys." The captain had served as an ensign on a destroyer in World War I and he had never lost the habit of referring to soldiers in that archaic way.

Steinhart watched the captain go down the ladder toward the flag bridge. Then he turned to scan the northwestern horizon with his own binoculars, waiting for the smear of flame and smoke that would mark the end of the Japanese spotter plane.

Lieutenant Harry Seaver had completed an inspection of the

Ranger unit's fast inflatables and had walked to the stern to smoke a cigarette when the general alarm sounded in the ship.

The sun's edge, flattened by atmospheric distortion to the curve of a scimitar's blade, was cutting into the bank of low clouds that had formed on the western horizon. The sea—only moments before a vibrant deep-water blue—had turned green except where the sun path glittered on the water like a trail of dull copper coins. Sea birds wheeled and quarreled over *Portola*'s fantail, occasionally indulging in plummeting dives into the thrashing water of the ship's wake. Seaver had been wondering what they found there that made such an apparently hazardous maneuver worthwhile.

The abrupt clangor of the alarm disturbed them, and they scattered into the darkening sky. The public-address system bellowed orders, and sailors were running. In the gun tubs dotting *Portola*'s superstructure, helmeted crews appeared. The quad forties of the antiaircraft battery began to quest the sky.

"Air action port! Air action port!"

Seaver scanned the sky to the west to see if he could discover what it was that had changed *Portola* into an overturned beehive of running sailors and searching gunners. Except for a flight of four Navy fighters that were unmistakably Grumman Bearcats, there was nothing in sight. Across the intervening water he could hear the general alarms being sounded in ships near *Portola*: bells and whooping sirens.

"Now hear this, now hear this. All personnel not involved clear the weather decks!"

Reluctantly, Seaver jogged toward the hatchway leading down into the Rangers' troop compartment. Before he reached it he caught sight of one of the escorts veering away toward the setting sun, her bow wave suggesting a hound with a white bone in her teeth.

The members of his team were on their feet to meet him as he stepped over the coaming into the steel box that had been their home since leaving Buckner Bay. Corporal Angelo Tangelli, the heavy-weapons man, looked both angry and frightened. A thick-set Sicilian with sloping shoulders and a thatch of coarse black hair that grew low over his black eyes, he had won a Silver Star on Okinawa and was probably the most savage member of the Ranger Battalion. But he disliked being confined, whether in a military stockade (where he had spent considerable time) or in the hold of an attack transport. He said, "What the fuck's happening, Lieutenant?"

"I'm not sure, Tangelli," Seaver said. "Maybe a spotter plane."

Joe Buie, Seaver's commo man—the corporal who carried the team's radio—was bulky in his life jacket. "Oh, shit. Here come the fuckin' Kamikazes."

The other members of the team gathered around Seaver and shouted questions. All of them shared Tangelli's dislike of being belowdecks in a ship under attack. During the Okinawa landings they had been on the USS *Napa*, which had taken three near misses from suicide attackers.

"Will they hit us tonight, Lieutenant?"

"Can they do it after dark?"

"How many of the fuckers are there?"

"At ease," Seaver said, "at ease for Chrissake. All I saw was four Bearcats. Hardin, where's Tanaka?"

Staff Sergeant Hardin—more familiarly known to the Rangers as Sergeant Hard-on—was the senior NCO. He was a stick-thin, leathery man whom Seaver had once seen hump an 81mm mortar up a thirty-degree slope and reach the top without losing his breath. He was a rarity in the Rangers, a regular with twenty years' service. Regulars were not often drawn to Ranger battalions. They found it difficult to adjust to the seemingly lax discipline.

"He said he was going up to the wardroom to talk to the straight-legs, Lieutenant," Hardin said. Troops who were not jump-qualified and therefore wore their trousers unbloused at the ankles were called a number of things by the Rangers; "straight-legs" was the least insulting. At Bragg, where the Rangers and other airborne units were trained, it was an invitation to serious injury for a soldier to be seen in town with his trousers bloused and no parachute wings on his chest.

"Get him, Sergeant," Seaver said. "I don't think we'll run into too much tonight, but if that was a spotter causing all the fuss with the swabbies, we might get a surface attack. I want the team to stay together." It was only the silver bars of a first lieutenant that gave Seaver command of the battalion landing team's Rangers. Tanaka was a second lieutenant. Seaver was also white, and Tanaka was not. This was ironic, because in many ways Harry Seaver was more Japanese than Jim Tanaka.

Hardin left the compartment, and the other men dispersed to their bunks. It was Navy practice not to billet the officers of the landing forces with their men. Seaver's sleeping quarters were on the deck above, in a cubicle he shared with Tanaka and two straight-leg lieutenants from the battalion artillery. But the place for officers, Seaver believed, was with their men as soon as there was gunfire.

He wondered if he was afraid. He knew, of course, that any man who would almost certainly be shot at within the next twenty-four hours could be expected to feel normal anxiety. But where, exactly, did anxiety end and outright fear begin? He had fought in the Philippines. No landing under fire there—he had arrived after the action had moved inland. But he and his Rangers had been given an assortment of really nasty jobs: using flamethrowers on log pillboxes, grenades on hillside caves, and sometimes knives on Japanese patrols. They had taken casualties, too, and by the time Okinawa was assaulted, the team members had considered themselves blooded troops, impossible to shock.

Toward the end of Operation Iceberg, when the population of the island retreated into the mountainous north with the Japanese Army, the battle became a horror. For the first time, American forces were encountering large numbers of Japanese civilians, and even Seaver, who knew the Japanese intimately, had been unprepared for what the Okinawans did.

The Jap Army fought with a ferocity unknown in previous

Pacific campaigns. In the Ryukyu archipelago they were defending a part of the home empire: islands that had been Japanese for generations. The civilians, women and children as well as men, had resisted the advancing Americans fanatically. Seaver had expected that. They had refused to surrender when trapped or surrounded. He had expected that, too. He had been prepared for the sight of old men and farm women eviscerated by grenades issued to them for that purpose by the retreating troops. But what he had not expected was the sight of hysterical women throwing their children off rocky cliffs and then following them, arms and legs waving absurdly, to death on the rocks at the edge of the sea.

Seaver thought of the boys with whom he had attended school—sons of the samurai class, most of them, though in theory the warrior-servant class had been eliminated by the Meiji Restoration. It had not been, of course. The class system was so deeply ingrained in Japanese society that a mere eighty years of aping Western ways was unlikely to have made any basic changes in the way Japanese lived.

Seaver had a recurring nightmare in which he always met one or another of his schoolmates on a ruined jungle island. In the dream his opponent was always armed with a magnificent 300-year-old Saotome sword, while he himself carried only the bamboo stick used for his lessons with the *kendo-sensei*, the fencing master. The dream was never resolved, and he always awoke from it drenched with sweat.

He was thinking of his dream when he heard the far-off, muffled coughing of gunfire. He realized that though the fleet was still far from the landing beaches, the battle for Honshu had actually begun.

Chief Naval Aviation Pilot Masao Nakano had served more than eleven years as an instructor at the Imperial Naval Advanced Aviation School at Yokosuka when he was chosen to join the scouting force of the 3rd Air Fleet and assigned to the Hamamatsu Squadron.

At thirty-three, Nakano was considered elderly for combat flying, and his record of achievement and discipline at the aviation school easily qualified him for a staff assignment. But the times were not normal, and most of the young men he had helped to train had long ago been commissioned, sent on operations, and, sadly, died. Pilots of any sort, even half-trained cadets, were now being pressed into immediate service. The nation's need had at last provided Nakano with the opportunity to serve the Emperor in a direct way in action against the American enemy.

As a boy, in his native village of Murakami, Nakano had attended a Paulist mission school. In Murakami, a small settlement forty kilometers up the coast of the Japan Sea from Niigata, the school had been regarded with some suspicion by the villagers. It had been an article of faith that the American missionaries had come to Japan to spread subversive thoughts and to disturb the population by preaching Christianity and teaching English. Nakano's father, a fisherman with few resources, had argued against the notion of enrolling a member of his family in such a school, but his wife had insisted. It had always been the hope of the Nakano family, who had five daughters, that their only son would eventually enter the Imperial Navy and serve the Emperor as his grandfather had at Tsushima in the war against the Russians. The mission school had offered them the only opportunity to obtain an education for this son, an education that would permit him to seek an honorable naval career.

The Paulist brothers had done an excellent job with young Nakano, and they had even entertained the hope of placing the fisherman's son on the list of students eligible to compete for scholarships to Tokyo University.

Masao's mother had been bitterly disappointed when they were unable to make good this promise. For a time she had allowed her ambition to cloud her judgment with thoughts of her son as a professional man, a doctor or lawyer, or, failing that, a commissioned officer of the Navy. But when the scholarship list was published without Masao's name on it, she went to the local shrine to proclaim her *haji*, her shame, and to ask the local deity to intercede for her son with Amaterasu Omikami, the mythical founder of the Japanese nation. The sin of ambition, she told the goddess, was hers alone. She had lost sight of her proper place and had allowed herself to indulge in unhealthy imaginings. Her son, she declared, had never wanted more than to serve the Emperor as a warrior in the Imperial Navy, emulating his honorable grandfather, who had been a sailor on Admiral Togo's flagship. She offered the earnings of a full month's catch of fish to the shrine, in return for which she hoped that the goddess would not hold her lack of good manners against her son.

The following week, Nakano, then fifteen years old, had traveled by train alone to Yokosuka to enlist in the Navy. He was large for his age, with a round, sallow face and a thatch of black hair that grew over his ears. His clothes smelled of fish, but he had a good grasp of geography, mathematics, and English of a sort.

Ordinarily, such a country yokel's appearance at the office of the naval recruiter would have been the occasion for equal portions of levity, vulgarity, and brutality. But the result of the Paulists' educational efforts, while failing to qualify young Nakano for the university, did impress the noncommissioned officer on duty that day. The Navy had only just published an appeal for young men of good physique and education to come forward and apply for the expanding Naval Aviation Service. Each petty officer had been given a quota of candidates to fill, and Nakano's appearance had been fortuitous.

The recruiter had taken him outside and down to the piers, where a pair of floatplanes were docked. Nakano looked wide-eyed at the great gray warships out in the roadstead. They had interested him far more than the mothlike Nakajima seaplanes.

"Look there," the petty officer said. "Have you ever seen anything finer? You don't see things like that in Murakami."

Nakano, fascinated by the enormous steel ships, agreed that this was so.

"Good," said the petty officer. "It is an honorable thing to volunteer."

Young Nakano was enlisted that very day for naval training, with a special notation on his papers specifying that he had expressed enthusiasm and determination to seek flying training as a naval aviator as soon as his first enlistment was completed.

After six years as a seaman and signalman in a series of destroyers and light cruisers, and having attained the rank of petty officer second class, Nakano found himself at Kasumigaura, the Imperial Navy's primary aviation school.

The course, which he had not sought but which he was determined to complete, had been a nightmare. The training routine was harsh, unremittingly demanding, and conducted with the utmost brutality. Physical beatings were common, discipline was severe. Of his class of 100 pilot candidates, forty had been washed out for ineptitude, twelve had been killed in accidents, and six had committed suicide. One, the son of a serving admiral, had gone berserk after a particularly degrading beating by the *hancho*s, the military instructors, and had attempted to murder the commanding officer of the training squadron. He had been hustled off the base in the dead of night, never to return. There were hair-raising tales of imagination about what might have happened to him.

Nakano's pilot training lasted two full years, after which, having borne the discipline with a native stoicism and the training with the skill of a natural flier, he was graduated as a full-fledged naval aviator.

He looked forward to service in China or with the fleet, but it was not to be. His aptitude was his undoing. He was posted to the advanced school of naval aviation at Yokosuka as an instructor, and there he remained for the next eleven years, as class after class of young cadets struggled through the course and departed for careers as honorable warriors of the Emperor.

In all those years in the Navy, Nakano had never once seen an enemy of his country. Students who had learned their craft in the rear cockpit of his Nakajimas and Mitsubishis, and who had felt the correcting sting of his *hancho*'s bamboo cane, participated in the attack on Pearl Harbor, in the battles of Guadalcanal, Midway, and the Coral Sea. His cadets had bombed American warships and shot Grummans out of the sky. Some—recently—had tied *hachimaki* around their heads and plunged into the hulls of enemy ships as Kamikazes. All this while Nakano chafed as an instructor far from battle zones.

But at last the war had come to Japan, and Nakano was free.

In the pilot's seat of his Kyushu Q1W, a patrol airplane known as an Eastern Sea, Nakano searched the ocean.

The Hamamatsu Squadron had been driven from its normal base by repeated Grumman attacks that had pocked the runways with bomb craters and burned the buildings. The day Nakano reported to the squadron commander, he had been ordered to fly one of the remaining Eastern Seas to a camouflaged airstrip inland on the banks of the Haruno River. It was from this primitive base that he had taken off in the late afternoon of this last day of February to fly his scouting patrol on the suspected line of advance of the American invasion fleet.

To avoid the marauding American carrier planes and the long-range AAF fighters from Kyushu, he had flown southeast over the Izu islands, staying a mere 100 meters above the surface of the sea. At the limit of the southeasterly leg of his search pattern, he had climbed to 2,000 meters and swung in a wide circle to the south.

The sun was sinking into a low bank of clouds in the west when he ordered his radioman, Aviation Gunner Masuda, to inform home base that he was returning. It was at that moment he first saw the ships of the American fleet's forward screen.

He swiftly ordered Masuda to cancel his previous message and send a sighting report. Then he pushed the throttles fully forward and nosed the Eastern Sea into a maximum climb.

The poor-quality fuel made the two 600-horsepower Hitachi engines clatter and vibrate with detonation. Nakano knew that he was damaging a valuable piece of equipment by demanding so much of his airplane, but it could not be helped. He must see what lay behind that forward screen of destroyers before the

Grummans appeared—as they surely must, and undoubtedly soon.

At an altitude of 3,000 meters, the reddish light of the setting sun seemed to turn the sea to fire, which made accurate observation difficult.

"Masuda. Send this: 'Amplification of sighting message. Enemy vessels advancing at approximately ten knots. Have identified twenty destroyers or light cruisers in forward force. Large force of assault transports and warships proceeding estimated three kilometers behind screening vessels—' "

He broke off and let his breath escape in an explosive sigh. Behind the destroyers came rank after rank and column after column of ships. There were thousands of them. He had never seen so many ships. They covered the sea from horizon to horizon. The fading light made accurate identification difficult, but he could recognize at least eight cruisers, fifty or more transports, hundreds of infantry landing ships, hundreds more attack ships. The sight chilled the blood.

Darkness was pooling on the surface of the sea, a common sight when flying at this time of day. The brassy light of the sun turned to magenta, while the sky remained white, as though the darkness had bled color from the air.

Nakano spoke again to Masuda. "Send this: 'Many ships, many. Warships, transports, and auxiliaries. Fleet course is 019 degrees true—' "

Below the Eastern Sea's flight level a spray of antiaircraft bursts opened like flowers against the magenta sea. Nakano thought of the Paulist brothers who had educated him. They had been austere men, with little appreciation of beauty. Yet their gardens flamed with blossoms each spring, and in winter they had wrapped the cherry trees in fanciful garments of straw, just as the Japanese did. They had come to the Land of the Eight Islands to spread their Christian creed and troubling thoughts. Instead, they had become Japanese. Now, here were their countrymen. Thousands of them, perhaps millions. What would the end of all this be?

Quite suddenly he heard Masuda's single, rear-facing 7.7 machine gun firing. The unpleasant acrid smell of cordite filled the cockpit.

At last, Nakano thought, I have come to battle. He twisted in his seat to look back through the greenhouse. As he did so, he was dazzled by the fiery half-ball of the setting sun, a swollen, shimmering disk with watery, indistinct edges. I must see my enemies, he thought. It is my right, earned by so many years of patience. But he saw only the glare of the sun and felt the heat of it on his cheeks.

The concentrated fire of sixteen fifty-caliber machine guns in the wings of the first element of Bearcats shattered the plexiglass canopy and sent a million shards of it spinning away into the Eastern Sea's invisible wake. Nakano heard the explosive impacts and felt a hot wind in his face. The controls went flaccid, and the airplane fell into a rolling plunge that he was quite helpless to control. The sun's fire expanded into a searing curtain, and he felt himself being consumed by fire. His last thought was that it was a tragic thing that he had worked so long to face the Emperor's enemies and that they had killed him without ever once being seen.

The Eastern Sea, mortally hit, fell toward the darkness in a long, twisting smear of oily flame and smoke. Chief Naval Aviation Pilot Masao Nakano was the first man to die directly as a result of Operation Coronet.

Aviation Gunner Masuda, who had been blown from the aircraft by the explosion of the unarmored fuel cell in the starboard wing, but whose parachute was damaged and failed to open, was the second.

The USS *Sarasota* steamed at the head of her squadron in the westernmost file of transports. *Sarasota* and her sister ships carried the men and equipment of the three Marine divisions that made up V Amphibious Corps, the force destined for Beach West Sims on the rocky shore of Suruga Bay.

Because the Marines of V Amphib were experienced veterans of Admiral Nimitz's campaign through the islands of the Central

Pacific, they had been given one of the most threatening and least bombarded beaches on Honshu.

The southwestern shore of Suruga Bay consisted of a narrow strip of beach immediately backed by steep rock embankments rising to a shallow coastal plain no more than a half-mile in depth backed in turn by the mountains of Shizuoka Prefecture. Though G-2 believed that the nature of the terrain had encouraged the Japanese to rely mainly on fortified defensive positions rather than massed manpower, it was clearly understood by every man in the three divisions of the landing force that they were expected to land on an unprotected strand and then advance up steep mountainsides under heavy fire from positions the Japs had been preparing for more than a year. By Y + 1, V Corps was expected to have anchored the flank of the entire invasion force and to have cut the Tokaido highway and rail line connecting Tokyo and Yokohama with the coast of southern Honshu.

On V Corps' northern flank they would have their fellow Marines of III Amphibious Corps, whose task it was to effect a landing on the beaches code named North and South Lamour, isolating—and no later than Y + 3 liquidating—all Japanese troops trapped on the Izu Peninsula.

By Y + 4, according to the op orders for Coronet, Suruga Bay would be secure and available as an anchorage for the supply ships now steaming far to the rear of the attack transports.

The battalion commander, Lieutenant Colonel Cleghorn, had briefed his officers in the *Sarasota*'s wardroom that afternoon, and they, in turn, had brought the word to the platoon sergeants and squad leaders in the troop compartments.

Sergeant Edward MacCauley, leader of Fox Company's reconnaissance squad, had listened to the details with a griping pain in his belly. He had heard it all before, and he was remembering Peleliu.

MacCauley had been a nineteen-year-old rifleman that terrible, hot September day in 1944. For the first time, the Army and Marines were attacking an island on which there had been no coast watchers. All intelligence had come from the frogmen of the underwater demolition teams assigned the task of clearing the beach of obstacles and from small parties put ashore from raiding submarines. Maps had had to be constructed from high-altitude aerial photographs. The result had been a dreadful mis-calculation about the topography of Peleliu. The Marines and GIs had gone ashore expecting to fight on a flat coral atoll. What they had found were jagged limestone cliffs overlooking the beaches and the island's airstrip, bastions of fractured boulders, deep gorges, and splintered spurs of rock—all laced with Jap pill-boxes of thick concrete reinforced with steel. And there had been 11,000 Japanese waiting.

The assault had been a horror. The preliminary bombard-ment, carried out primarily by cruisers armed with five-inch guns, had been too short; in any case, too light to crack the fortifications.

It was at Peleliu that the Japs had changed their tactics for resisting amphibious assault. Prior to Operation Stalemate II—as the attack was so appropriately code named—they had concen-trated on meeting the invading force on the beaches, and when resistance was broken there, all that remained to them was a series of hopeless banzai charges in which they were steadily decimated by superior Marine fire power. But on Peleliu the beaches had been swept by all that they could muster in the way of cannon fire, mines, and small-unit enfilades, while the main forces kept to their fortifications. It had become necessary to dig them out with grenades and flamethrowers. Nor could the strongpoints be by-passed. The Japs had given themselves fields of fire in all directions, so that troops failing to clear them out of their bunkers found themselves attacked from the rear.

By this time, Tokyo knew the war was lost. Word had come down the chain of command that the garrisons of islands in the way of the American advance toward Japan were to be consid-ered expendable. Their purpose was attrition: butcher Marines and GIs, make each mile toward the homeland so costly in lives that the Americans would have to grant honorable terms.

MacCauley had landed in the second wave of Lieutenant Colonel "Chesty" Puller's lst Marines. Since the island's terrain was so rugged—what was not guarded by cliffs and ridges was made impassable by mangrove swamps—the lst, 5th, and 7th Marine Regiments had all come ashore on Peleliu's southwestern coast, on open beaches protected by the usual coral reef some distance offshore.

The moment the Amphtracs had begun to lumber over the coral, the entire reef had exploded into a curtain of fire. Mines that had been missed by the UDT men had crippled many of the amphibious tractors, marooning them on the reef and forcing the succeeding waves of Marines to form files to avoid the blazing wrecks. The storm of fire from behind the beaches had been so savage that the Marines had been forced to abandon the exposed vehicles and wade ashore through water up to their shoulders. Those who had reached the beaches unwounded had found that they were being taken under fire from pillboxes built on a spit of land called The Point. The carnage had been incredible. Mac-Cauley's company had reached shore with an effective force of eighteen men. On the beach, the Marines had been forced to pile corpses to protect the living from the enfilading fire of the Nambu machine guns.

MacCauley had attached himself to another company. By evening of that first day, he and other Marines had actually reached the airfield, a mile from the beaches. It was there that he had been wounded. At 1700 hours the Japanese had counterattacked across the airstrip with thirteen light tanks and several hundred infantry. Screaming, the Japs had charged at the exhausted Marines, who had met them with bazookas, antitank guns, pack howitzers, M-1s, bayonets, and even pieces of sharp coral. The fighting had been hand to hand. MacCauley, attempting fruitlessly to dig into the rock-hard ground near the runway, had looked up to see Japs coming fast out of the mangrove swamp. There had appeared to be thousands of them following their clumsy-looking tanks. As he watched, great gaps had appeared in their ranks as Marine gunners in the few Shermans that had managed to get ashore opened up on them at point-blank range. It had seemed as though violent pistons of invisible force were punching holes in the Japanese mass. Bodies had exploded into bloody smears; arms and legs had flown through the air in a shower of blood and entrails. He had thrown himself flat on the sharp coral, firing his M-1 until the barrel was too hot to touch. As the human wave had drawn nearer, he had been able to make out individual faces and figures—strange, flat-featured faces and small bodies in dirty uniforms that seemed sausage-tight. A Marine SBD dive bomber had appeared from nowhere and made a low pass over the charging Japs, its machine guns making a strange tack-tack-tacking sound.

The Jap charge had been within a dozen yards of him when he rose, dry-mouthed, with his M-1 held at the hip. He had felt something thud against his thigh. He had staggered but did not fall. A Jap officer, quail-fat, wearing polished boots and holding high a samurai sword from which yellow silk tassels dangled, had come at him screaming *"Tenno! Banzai!"* MacCauley had shot him in the groin, and he had jolted to a stop, a look of stupid incomprehension on his face. His tight trousers had bloomed red. MacCauley's bullet had exploded the femoral artery, and blood had gushed from the torn cloth, pumped by the Jap's laboring heart. The sword had fallen to the coral, and the fat officer had lowered himself carefully to a kneeling position. He had begun to weep. MacCauley had caught the stench of flushing bowels. That was when he learned that dying men were incontinent. He had felt his knees shaking and he, too, had knelt. For a moment the two men had faced each other in an attitude of prayer. Then the Jap's eyes had glazed and he had rocked forward onto his face, his fat buttocks pointing at the sky. MacCauley had vomited. When he had tried to stand, he found that his leg could not bear his weight. His green camouflaged dungarees were bloodied. He had taken an Arisaka rifle bullet in the thigh. It had missed his femoral artery by an inch. He had realized with a shudder of cold horror that that was the margin by which he had escaped dying a death exactly similar to the Jap lieutenant's.

The corpsman who had found him on the airstrip among the Japanese and Marine corpses after the attack had kept the sword. Somehow, MacCauley had not regretted that. He did not enjoy remembering his single afternoon on Peleliu.

MacCauley had been evacuated to a Navy hospital ship and thence, not to the States, with his "million-dollar wound," but to Ulithi, where he was treated and allowed two months to recover. From Ulithi, along with several hundreds of Army and Marine casualties who were, in the words of the medical staffers, "capable of rehabilitation," he had been shipped down to Fremantle, in Australia, for re-equipping and rearming. By mid-1945 he had found himself reassigned to the 2nd Marine Division of the V Amphibious Corps on Okinawa—a unit marked for a prominent part in both Operation Olympic and Operation Coronet.

When the Marines stormed ashore at Kagoshima Bay on the island of Kyushu, Sergeant MacCauley had been fortunate enough to miss the first assault. His unit had gone ashore on X + 12, in company with an infantry brigade assigned the task of providing security for the new fighter strip at Miyazaki. The battle for Kyushu had moved north to the Kumamoto-Nobeoka Line. There it had stabilized. Both Japanese and American troops had begun to withdraw, leaving the mountainous front to be held by entrenched forces. The battle for Kyushu was over, despite the fact that one-half of the island remained in Japanese hands.

Now MacCauley lay in his bunk, which was one of a stack of six between deck and overhead in the hold of *Sarasota*. This time, once again, MacCauley and his recon squad were destined for the first wave. He had seen the maps and photographs of Beach West Sims. It would be Peleliu all over again.

The compartment was crowded with Marine infantry. In the dim illumination from a dozen feeble lights protected by wire cages, the men had spent the day writing letters, sharpening bayonets and trench knives, blackening the sights of their weapons, checking carefully the belts of ammunition for their machine guns. Bunks were piled with personal gear: canteens, knives, first-aid kits, webbing, spare skivvies, shaving kits, mess kits, helmets, helmet liners, camouflaged helmet covers, shelter halves, ponchos, hand grenades, extra bandoliers of M-1 ammunition, entrenching tools, and knapsacks.

The men either lay amid the chaos of military impedimenta or stood in the narrow spaces between the tiers of bunks smoking, talking, some whistling tunelessly, some just staring at the deck, overhead, or bulkheads. The air was hot and thick with the smell of soldiers—a mixture of sweat, new canvas, cosmoline, soap, and cigarette smoke.

MacCauley had reacted to the sound of General Quarters with an aching sickness, but he had remained in his bunk, wedged into place by the clutter of his personal gear. He looked at his watch. It was just after 1730 hours, local time. About sunset, he estimated. He heard the starboard antiaircraft guns firing, felt the vibration through the steel fabric of the ship. His mouth was dry, but he did not feel up to shoving his way through the crowd in the compartment to reach the scuttlebutt in the companionway.

There was a stir among the men when Second Lieutenant Scowcroft appeared at the hatch. Scowcroft was a plump Ivy Leaguer fresh from OCS at Quantico. MacCauley distrusted all new officers and he had little faith in Scowcroft, whose beardless face and fatuous manner seemed to promise that he would not live long in combat.

The Marines at the forward end of the compartment gathered around Scowcroft demanding news.

"It was only a Jap spotter," the baby-faced officer said. "The Bearcats splashed him." He delivered his news as though he had personally dispatched the Japanese patrol plane.

MacCauley suppressed with some effort the surge of irritation that Scowcroft's manner aroused in him. It was an unreasonable, and unreasoning, response, he knew. But the new officer was one more burden to be borne by the Marines of Fox Company, and his ignorance, trumpeted by his pronouncement that he expected a walkover tomorrow when the landing force hit the beaches of Suruga Bay, made MacCauley want to shout at him to get the fuck out of the troop compartment and leave the men alone.

How much of his anger, MacCauley wondered, was really caused by the annoying lieutenant and how much by dread of going into action yet another time? The appearance, however brief, of a Jap spotter plane meant an attack on the fleet, by submarine, *shinyo*, or suicide bomber. And it seemed to Mac-Cauley that every enemy action was aimed directly and personally at Edward MacCauley.

I'm near the end of my rope, he thought. He had always believed *other* guys suffered combat fatigue. But recently he had started snapping and snarling at his men and verging on insubordination when anyone gave him an order. Classic symptoms. He closed his eyes and pressed his face against the field pack that served as a pillow. God, he thought, just let me get through it one more time.

1800 Hours

Superior Private Koriyama, on his knees, dug at the wall of the bunker like a dog about to bury a bone. His smell was pungent: sweaty cotton, feces. He was not a fastidious man. And fish. Corporal Noguchi was certain he could smell fish on Koriyama. That was plainly impossible. It had been weeks since the men of the mortar section had seen even a strip of fish. It was his hunger, Noguchi thought, that was tricking his senses.

The corporal knew that his own odors were contributing to the foul air inside the bunker. How he longed for a bath! To wash with soap, to feel the clean water running down his back, to soak in the heat of the *ofuro*, to smell the delicious scent of wet cedar—

"*Gocho-san?* One of the logs has shifted. I cannot lift it alone." Koriyama's great back muscles were straining the filthy cloth of his shirt.

Noguchi scuttled forward on his knees and cuffed Second Class Private Iwaka, who was digging ineffectually at the sandy soil with his bayonet. "Help him, idiot. Lift the log," Noguchi ordered.

Together the three men strained at the great cedar log. It was one of those taken from the torii of the small shrine in Matsuo. There had been superstitious grumblings when the gate had been dismantled for use in the fortifications behind the beach, but Captain Kitaname had chided the men, telling them that the local deities, like all true Japanese, would be grateful to sacrifice their torii to the defense of the sacred homeland.

The noise of the shelling had subsided slightly as the gunners in the ships offshore shifted their aim to concentrations farther inland.

With a great effort, the men of the mortar section shifted the log, freeing a slide of damp sandy earth. Noguchi could now see through the widened gap. The light was fading. It would soon be dark. Returning to the company's CP, he would have to pick his way carefully through the minefields. The ground behind Kujukuri-hama had been sown with explosives to a depth of three kilometers. Those parts of the bamboo forest not covered by the fields of fire of the pillboxes and bunkers formed open lanes to tempt the men of the assault forces. In these places, mines had been buried, one to every two square meters.

Koriyama, throwing dirt like a madman, cleared an opening and thrust his head out into the open. Noguchi caught him by the shirt collar and dragged him back. He slung his Arisaka over his back and crawled past the large man through the hole.

He sucked in his breath at what he saw.

The sky was covered by low clouds except for a few streaks through which a red sky could be seen, a bloody monochrome left by the setting sun. A stench of charred wood and cooked vegetation assailed Noguchi's nostrils.

The beautiful stretch of bamboo and red pine forest in which the emplacements of Matsuo Fortress had been dug was gone. In its place was a splintered wilderness of shattered, blasted trees. Blackened limbs extended in a kind of supplication from the mass of churned debris that had once been a graceful and carefully tended grove.

For a moment Noguchi was perplexed, wondering how such a change could have come about in so short a time. But the time had not been short, he reminded himself. It had been more than six days. Long days of the Americans throwing tons of steel and explosives into the soil of the homeland. The men inside the bunker had not smelled the burning because it had been masked by their own stink. Now, in the open, Noguchi gagged on the cordite fumes that seeped from the churned, raped earth. They worked their way deep into his nostrils and brought tears flooding from his eyes.

The flat, crumping noise of shells bursting still filled the air, but the focus of the bombardment had moved to the west. The terrain behind Kujukuri-hama was flat country. Beyond the groves lay rice paddies and a single line of hills so low as to be almost imperceptible. There the Home Army had built a vast interlocking system of pillboxes and strongpoints. These were now the targets of the warships offshore, enormous vessels that could, it was said, fire a sixteen-inch shell across the entire width of the Boso Peninsula into the waters of Tokyo Bay.

Noguchi felt an overpowering hatred for the people who had done this terrible thing to the once serene forest. Even the Yokoshiba road was gone, vanished. What remained was a strip of wildly plowed earth littered with the remains of trees smashed into matchwood.

Iwaka, staring open-mouthed through the hole from which Noguchi had emerged, uttered a ridiculous, frightened giggle. "*Gocho-san*," he said foolishly, "look at what they have done."

Noguchi exploded with rage and kicked at Iwaka's moonish face. "Shut your mouth. Get back inside," he yelled at him. The farm boy was speechless with fear, unable to move. But it was not fear of Noguchi. It was panic at the sound of the huge shells whirring overhead. In the open they had the sound of a train bruising the air. The warships' guns had registered their targets and were now firing for effect.

Lieutenant Fuchida had always said that a soldier must maintain a sense of inner calm, no matter what his situation. Noguchi felt sudden shame at his outburst. He said, in a more controlled voice, "Stay under cover, Iwaka. I will return with rations soon."

"It is getting dark, *Gocho-san*," the boy whined.

"Koriyama," Noguchi said.

"Hai, Gocho-san." The large man's face appeared over Iwaka's shoulder.

"Keep watch. I will try to get us something to eat and drink."

"Hai," Koriyama said.

"I am afraid," Iwaka said hoarsely.

"Be a soldier," Noguchi said. He unslung his rifle and began to walk in the direction he believed the command post to be. It was difficult to be certain because the landmarks were gone and the light was going. To the west, the flash of exploding shells lit the underside of the lowering clouds.

In the far distance he could now hear another sound, one all too familiar. It was the deep humming sound made by hundreds upon hundreds of *Bi-ni-ju-ku*, the Superfortresses with which the Americans had burned Tokyo to the ground. They were on their way to the north. Not to Tokyo this time. The rolling, thundering sound of thousands of bombs exploding in waves made the air tremble. They were attacking the rear areas behind the Kashima beaches—the northern leg of the V formed by the coastline, with the town of Choshi at the apex. Not that anyone would now suspect that there had ever been a town on Cape Inubo. Weeks ago, Choshi and the adjacent hamlet of Hasaki at the mouth of the Tonegawa, had ceased to exist under the rain of shells and bombs. Hundreds of civilians of the Volunteer Defense Force had perished in a futile attempt to control the fires there. To-night's attack was as savage as it was senseless. There was nothing on Inubo left to destroy. But still the bombs fell in a torrent. Even at a distance of thirty kilometers, Noguchi could feel the concussions.

Stumbling across the blasted ground, he felt curiously disembodied. His feet felt light, as though he had to exert a special effort to make them stay on the earth. With each step he had the odd sensation of floating. His head ached abominably, and there was a foul taste in his mouth. The continuous jolting of the air by falling shells pressed against his eardrums, making him yawn and grimace to keep them clear. He had covered perhaps 200 meters when he realized that he had walked in a great semicircle and that the bunker, which he had left behind him, had reappeared ahead and to his right. He stopped in confusion, looking up at the dark and threatening sky as though he might find some signpost. There was nothing but the yellow reflection of the explosions, which appeared to have encircled him.

He clambered over a tangle of shattered, charred logs and fell, losing his rifle. He got to his knees and looked about for it frantically. It was wedged between some blackened bamboo shafts, huge ones with great prominent ribs. He reached out to retrieve it, and then recoiled in horror. One of the bamboo sections was not bamboo at all, but an unexploded five-inch shell. He sucked in his breath and scuttled backward, on his knees, until a fallen log cut off his retreat.

He remained there, staring at the scarred steel cone of the American shell, his breath coming in short, shallow gasps. Something had happened to him during the six long days of shelling. His brain refused to function properly. He knew that he should retrieve his Arisaka. To appear at the company CP without his weapon would be cause for the most severe disciplinary action. Yet he could not force himself to reach for it. His hand refused to move. He quoted to himself the lines from the *Hagakure*: "When it comes to either/or, there is only the quick choice of death. It is not particularly difficult." In his mind he could actually see the hiragana symbols on the page of his book, which, carefully wrapped in paper, was at this moment lying in his pack next to the binoculars Fuchida had lent him. He was absolutely certain that what was written in the book by the swordmaster Tsunetomo Yamamoto 300 years ago was no less than the clear and simple truth. Yet he could not force himself to touch the rifle that lay beside the unexploded shell. A sense of humiliation, of deep shame, filled him.

He tottered to his feet and looked dazedly around him. A flat, cracking explosion flung shards of wood and clods of earth into the air not a hundred meters from where he stood. Two more bursts followed the first. He looked toward the sea, down the slight slope to the beach, where tangles of wire and the laboriously constructed log tank traps had been ripped apart and scattered by the bombardment. In the deepening dusk, the sea looked black. The breaking surf was small, a pattern of ghostly white against the dark water.

Far out to sea there was a flicker of lightning that was not lightning. It was the muzzle flash of great cannon. Within seconds he heard the whirring beat of shells passing overhead. A rolling thunder came in with the onshore breeze, the voice of a battleship's main battery. The Americans were using their largest warships. From far inland came more thunder, deeper and more threatening, as the barrage rolled from one target to another.

The shattered forest, meanwhile, was lighted here and there by smaller shell bursts as lesser warships raked the area behind the beaches again and yet again. The explosions were sharp and quarrelsome, filling the air with steel splinters that whined and chattered across the ruined, leveled pine-and-bamboo forest. Each burst shocked the air and hurt Noguchi's battered eardrums. He staggered and almost fell. He surveyed his surroundings. Why was he here? Yes, now he remembered. He had started for the company post and he had allowed himself to become confused. He could only just make out the mound of the bunker he had left. How long ago? It seemed hours. And he had lost his rifle. In the fading light he could no longer see the unexploded shell.

On the sea he could make out the silhouettes of ships steaming south, parallel to Kujukuri-hama. Destroyers, he thought. From time to time they stood out in the bright, electric flashes of their own gunfire. A salvo of five-inch shells struck the rubble of the Yokoshiba road with a sound like a string of giant firecrackers.

Once again he tried to orient himself to strike out toward the company CP. His hunger had gone completely, but in its place he felt a searing thirst; his throat was raw with the stench of explosives and burning.

The ruddy glow of the sunset had vanished, leaving a stark

topography limned in black and shades of gray. He climbed over the trunk of a fallen pine and twisted his ankle badly as he slid to the ground. He was still in sight of the bunker. He recognized it because the painted cedar logs from the dismantled torii were the only patches of color in the terrible landscape.

The destroyers offshore fired again, and he heard the shells coming this time. They made a whispering noise, like the colored paper windmills one folded for Boys' Festival. The first shell of the salvo struck a mere fifty meters away with a yellow-white flash and a crack of sound. The second shell was short and landed somewhere between where he crouched and the beach. The third shell hit thirty meters from him, and he tried to fall flat, though not in time, because the concussion threw him against a tree stump headfirst, dazing him. He did not actually hear the last shell of the salvo strike, because his head was ringing and his eyes were unable to focus clearly. But he felt the explosion in the earth, which seemed to shift under him. He rolled onto his side in time to see a painted cedar log spinning in the air, like a matchstick flung aloft by some giant's thumb and forefinger. Beside the torii pillar, seemingly attempting to fly through the debris in the air, the body of Superior Private Koriyama pinwheeled, spewing blood.

Open-mouthed, Noguchi watched as what remained of the would-be sumitory fell into a jumble of broken pine and bamboo, impaling itself on one of the few slender shoots still standing. The weight of the corpse bent the bamboo double, but did not break it.

There was a moment of near silence, broken by the patter of falling dirt and debris. Noguchi rubbed at his eyes and at his stubbled head. The bones of his skull felt strange. There were ridges and lumps where there should be none. Another salvo of shells landed, but south of where he crouched, reeling dizzily.

He hauled himself to his feet and looked for the bunker. It was gone. In its place there was a fresh shallow crater still smoking. He walked toward it unsteadily. It was difficult to keep his balance. The ground felt as though it were pitching and rolling beneath his feet. Inside the crater there were pieces of paper scattered everywhere. He recognized the red paper cover of his copy of the *Hagakure*. He went to his knees in the churned earth, feeling the heat left by the exploding shell. He caught a pungent trace of the latrine, which had been at the rear of the bunker. He looked about in confusion, not knowing what he searched for or why.

He saw a foot protruding from the ground. A foot with a tabi on it. It was the farm boy Iwaka's foot, he thought. Iwaka was always whining that the military-issue boots and the puttees hurt his feet.

Noguchi seized the foot and pulled. "Come out of there, you stupid person," he said. The foot came away quite easily. It was not attached to anything. It trailed bits of skin and muscle and bloodstained shinbone. Noguchi fought hard to avoid giggling at the absurd sight of Iwaka's lonely foot.

His head ached and throbbed terribly. He had struck the tree trunk hard and he wondered if he had injured himself. The blow had, indeed, fractured the occipital bones, but Noguchi was mainly aware of the pounding ache of the bridge of his nose. It was plainly broken, and blood drooled from his nostrils. He wiped at it with his fingers and tried to remove the sticky stuff by rubbing it onto his thin khaki uniform. He looked at the state of his clothing and told himself that he would certainly have to clean up before presenting Lieutenant Fuchida with his request for water and rations for his mortar team.

The destroyers had moved south, firing all the while. Noguchi sensed the salvo falling at a great distance now. He stood. He should not have wanted to laugh at Second Class Private Iwaka's severed foot. To have done so would have shown a serious lack of good manners. Useless as Iwaka might be, he was a soldier of the Imperial Army and was therefore entitled to consideration, if not respect. He apologized to Iwaka and stumbled away from the wreckage of the bunker.

He tripped on a hard object. He looked down, and there by his boot were the binoculars Fuchida had entrusted to him.

It hurt his head terribly to stoop, but he retrieved the field glasses and wiped them carefully with a shirttail. One lens was shattered. They were valuable—officer's equipment. Fuchida would be angry. But hadn't someone told him that the *chui-san* was dead? Could that be right? It didn't matter. In war many people died, but the war went on. It always went on. He looped the strap of the binoculars over his shoulder and began to walk. It was difficult going through the splintered forest in the fading light. The thought of having to account for the damage to an officer's property troubled him more and more as he lurched and stumbled toward the beach. He wondered why he was going in this direction when any other would do as well. Then he knew that he had decided what to do. Koriyama and Iwaka no longer needed rations, and he was not hungry himself. To return to the command post would only mean trouble with Captain Kitaname, who had never liked him. So the corporal had decided that he would walk down to Kujukuri-hama and hide himself there until the Americans finally decided to come. Then he would kill some of them. It was the correct thing to do. The Americans had killed his men, destroyed the lovely pine-and-bamboo forest, and damaged Fuchida-san's field glasses. They were without honor and they deserved to die.

Second Lieutenant Lloyd Hansen crouched knee-deep in the mud of the rice paddy and struggled to free himself from the tangled straps of his parachute. The nylon canopy was sinking in the muddy water, and he felt as though the weight of it would soon drag him under.

In the darkness he could hear shouting: high, hysterical-sounding alien voices. Far to the east he could see the glow of the burning B-17. He wondered if anyone else had made it out safely. As bombardier, he had had access to the ventral nose hatch first and he had jumped even before Kowalski, the aircraft commander, gave the order to bail out.

The water was cold, and at his first attempt to move, the thick mud had sucked the flying boots from his feet. He had been told that the Japs used night soil to fertilize their paddies and he could well believe it. The water had the stink of a latrine, though that was the least of his worries.

He reached the shore of the paddy with his breath rasping in his throat. The landscape was flat, featureless, lost in shadows. The sky was overcast, with the last faint light of twilight imprinted on the low clouds like the suggestion of a silver patina. To the west he could make out the indistinct bulk of a house. It was not what he had expected. He had been told that the rural Japanese lived in wood-and-paper houses, but the structure seemed far more solid than the low, flimsy buildings with which his imagination had populated the rice-growing farm area of the Kanto Plain.

From the north, the soft breeze carried a steady rumbling sound, like that of distant thunder. It was the first time Hansen had ever heard the sound of shells and bombs falling. He stood, undecided, trying to form some sensible plan of action. Within a day or two—possibly within a few hours—Allied forces would be landing on the beaches of Honshu. If he could avoid capture for even a short time, he could be reasonably certain of survival. But he had no idea what the local Japs might be doing, what attempts they might be making to capture American airmen shot down in the Kanto. Colonel Rivera, the group Intelligence officer, who had conducted the briefing at Miyazaki, had warned that the Japanese were not signatories of the Geneva Convention, and that anyone shot down in central Honshu should make every effort to stay out of the hands of the local police and, above all, out of the clutches of the Kempetai, the quasi-military secret police. "These people are animals," the colonel had said grimly. "They torture and kill for pleasure. They have no standards of decency." The briefing had upset the newer crewmen and those who had been redeployed to the Pacific from Europe, as Hansen had been.

His eyes having become more accustomed to the darkness, Hansen found himself standing on a low dike between two paddies. To the east the paddies stretched as far as he could see. To the west lay the boundary of the rice field and a slightly higher dike, on which there was what appeared to be a graded road. Automatically he started in that direction, but the going was hard because his feet were bare and his clothes were heavy and sodden; the quilting of his flight jacket and trousers had soaked up the foul-smelling water eagerly.

When he reached the road, he paused again, trying to orient himself. His instinct led him to follow the road away from the silent, blocky farmhouse and toward the sea, which was a long hike off.

He had walked for five minutes when he heard the sound of voices behind him again, still quite distant but nearer than before. The road curved away from the paddy field and into a grove of bamboo trees. When he paused, he could hear the tall fronds clicking softly against one another as the breeze made the trees undulate. His feet were already sore and he knew that he could not travel far without doing something about them. He limped ahead as swiftly as he was able and pushed his way into the bamboo grove. It was difficult because the fronds grew close together, but he told himself that this would be an advantage if it became necessary for him to hole up in the grove. It almost certainly would be. He needed to stop, to rest, to organize himself, and, most important, to hide.

He was well into the grove when he heard the noise of a truck on the road he had just abandoned. He crouched, not moving, and tried to see the source of the sound. The vehicle, headlights reduced to slits by blackout masks, cast a feeble illumination on the road. Ahead of the truck, which was moving at walking pace, went two soldiers in mustard-colored khaki, rifles at the ready.

The sight of the Japs brought a constriction to Hansen's throat. This was the first time he had seen a real Jap soldier. Even the corpses had been disposed of by the time his B-17 group had moved into Miyazaki, and in the course of his three missions over Honshu he had seen only one Jap airplane—and that at a great distance, its pilot fleeing from some hunting Mustangs. Now here was the actual enemy: two Jap infantrymen, small, compact figures—what his uncle, who raised horses in Wyoming, called "cobby." They had short backs and legs, heavily muscled shoulders and buttocks. In the uncertain light and at this distance, Hansen could make out nothing more. There were voices coming from the back of the covered truck—conversations, probably, though the sounds were gibberish to him. There was probably at least a full infantry squad in the truck, perhaps more. And they were looking for him, for Lloyd Hansen specifically. He was certain of that. Someone must have seen his parachute against the dark sky.

As the truck rolled slowly by, Hansen suddenly heard a voice that was unmistakably American. It said, "Watch it, you Jap bastard!" It sounded like Sergeant Stansky, the flight engineer. There was a sound of scuffling, and then a Jap screamed with fury. The sound chilled Hansen. It was like a noise a rabid animal might make. There were more shouts in Japanese, followed by a flat, muffled crack that could have been a shot from a light-caliber pistol or one of the Arisakas Jap infantrymen carried. The Yankee voice turned shrill and was laced with agony. "Oh, God! *God!*" Hansen shivered and huddled against the roots of a knot of bamboos. He did not move until the truck had gone completely out of sight and sound down the track toward the rice paddies.

As he crouched against the segmented stalks, he closed his eyes. He had never imagined, when the group received orders in England to fly across half the world to Miyazaki, that it would end like this.

Everyone had expected, of course, to be redeployed to the Pacific. The entire Eighth Air Force was making the move. But the aircrews had thought that at least they would be shipped back to the States first to be re-equipped and retrained to fly B-29s. Instead of that, they had made a mass flight with three other B-17 groups from England to Italy to Egypt to India to the Philippines and finally to Kyushu. Within three weeks of arrival at the newly captured airstrips surrounding Miyazaki, they had begun flying missions over Honshu.

69

The opposition had been light, almost nonexistent. From time to time a Zeke or a Hamp would appear to challenge the massed bomber formations, but they were almost instantly blasted from the sky by one of the hundreds of USAAF or Navy fighters that roamed freely over the Jap homeland.

Sometimes the B-17s were used against Tokyo and Yokohama at night, supplementing the raids being flown by the Superforts of the Twentieth and Twenty-first air forces. Hansen had seen the strike photographs after such raids, and the square miles of ruins had him and his squadron mates convinced that the war was all but over and that they would be home by midsummer at the latest.

And now this, he thought bitterly. He had a wild impulse to break into hysterical laughter. Little Lloyd Hansen, barefoot in Japan. It was crazy. If the war was almost over, what was he doing here, soaked to the skin and hiding from Jap infantrymen?

He removed his flight jacket and padded trousers, trying fruitlessly to squeeze the foul-smelling water out of them. He laid them aside and removed his shoulder holster and .45 automatic. He had never fired the heavy pistol and he doubted he could hit anything with it even if he tried. The weight and feel of it made him uncomfortable, as though he were being forced to play at the game of soldier. He had been in the hospital at Roswell Army Air Base when his class had received its two hours of instruction on the Colt pistol and he had never made up the course. It hadn't been a thing the cadets' instructors took very seriously, not like the Norden bombsight.

Shivering with the cold, Hansen removed his shirt and used his jungle knife to cut it into strips. When he had done that, he took the pieces and wrapped his feet and ankles with them. It wasn't much protection for his feet, but it would be better than nothing. He would have to walk—somewhere—eventually. He couldn't just cower in this bamboo forest and wait for the bloody invasion, after all. Who knew when that would be? Not second lieutenant bombardiers, that was for certain.

But where would he go? For a moment he had to concentrate

completely on holding off the waves of panic. He thought about the scream of pain he had heard coming from the Jap truck—Stansky's voice. Christ, what had they done to him? Would they really shoot a helpless prisoner of war? Even the Germans didn't do that. But these were not Germans, and this wasn't Germany. A terrible sense of alienage came over him. It was as though he were suddenly marooned on another planet, a billion miles from home.

He finished wrapping his feet and replaced his flying trousers and jacket. They were still wet but they were familiar and soon his own body heat would dry them. He returned the jungle knife to its scabbard and considered what to do about the pistol and shoulder holster. It frightened him to think of walking anywhere in this strange landscape without a weapon. But it frightened him more to think of having to use it. Perhaps the best thing to do would be to find someone and simply surrender. He had heard hideous stories about Jap treatment of POWs, and Stansky's scream seemed to confirm them. But what else could he do? He compromised by putting the heavy Colt in his pocket and using the straps of the holster to reinforce his makeshift boots.

He took an oiled silk map from the sleeve pocket of his flight jacket. Kowalski always insisted that each member of the crew carry an escape map of the target area. It was a rule that most of the crew ignored, but not Hansen, who was not the sort of young man to defy even such authority as Kowalski exercised. God, he wondered, where was Kowa now? Killed by that freakishly lucky flak hit, probably, along with Stegeman, the copilot, and Jerry Pavoni, the navigator. Their B-17—known as "The Cornhuskers," after the Nebraska football team on which Les Kowalski had been second-string tackle—had taken its deathblow from a 75mm antiaircraft shell fired blindly up into the dark by a battery hidden somewhere in Narita, about halfway between Tokyo and the coast. It was a miracle, Hansen thought, that the exploding shell had not killed him as well.

He spread the limp map carefully and fumbled in his pocket

for the sealed capsule of matches he always carried. He struck a flame, shielding it with his body and open jacket, and tried to read the map in the flickering light.

As far as he could tell, he was down somewhere between Narita and a Jap landing strip—long made unusable by the raids—at a place called Yachimata. To the north the map showed both a road and a rail line. The road skirting the bamboo grove did not even show. He estimated he was at least fifteen miles from the coast, possibly more.

The matchlight died. He folded the map and replaced it carefully in the sleeve pocket of his flight jacket. The area between this grove and the coast would be, he knew, stiff with Japs. It was the defensive zone behind the invasion beach called Kujukuri. It would certainly be a tangle of pillboxes, wire, minefields, and troop concentrations. There was absolutely no way a single enemy was going to be able to penetrate such a deadly maze.

He thought again about surrender. What else could he do? he asked himself. It seemed a cowardly act, but there was no genuine alternative.

He thought again about Stansky and shuddered. As he crossed his arms for warmth, and in an unconscious gesture of despair, he touched the leather gilt bars on his flight jacket. God damn it, he was an officer. Japs were really chickenshit about rank. Everybody said so. If he could only find a Jap officer and surrender to him, perhaps he would not be treated too badly. And how bad would a Jap POW camp be? He could take it for a month or so—until the Marines or someone came to liberate him. Jesus, Hansen, he told himself, the fucking war is *over*. . . .

Thinking this, he lurched to his feet and out of the bamboo grove. When he reached the graveled road he began to walk—westward, away from the invasion coast.

1900 Hours

It was not Radarman Bertram Temko, sitting at the CRT of USS *Alaska*'s powerful long-range radar, but twenty-year-old Leading Seaman Albert Cummins, shivering in the foremast lookout's bucket high above the deck of HMS *Ramsey*, who first detected the approach of the *shinyo*s, the suicide boats, from Mikura.

Ramsey, an angular four-pipe destroyer, had a long and checkered history that would have fascinated young Cummins—a former education student at a red-brick university in the English Midlands—had he been aware of it.

Built in 1914 and commissioned into the United States Navy as the USS *Meade*, she had seen Atlantic convoy duty in World War I and had actually sunk a German U-boat off the coast of Ireland. After the armistice, *Meade* had fallen, like many veterans, on bad times. Shunted from one hardship station to another, she had even suffered the ignominy of serving as part of the U.S. Coast Guard during the years of Prohibition, frustrated by swift rumrunners and gambling-ship tenders in a most unnaval and undignified series of mismatches along the eastern seaboard of the United States.

By 1934, *Meade* had been considered worn out and unsuitable for further service to a Navy shrunken by congressional constraints to a token force. She was decommissioned and scheduled for scrapping. But a bureaucratic foul-up (or the surreptitious sentimentality of some officer who might once have served in her) saved *Meade* from the wrecker's yard and assigned her to the mothball fleet, where she remained, stationary and rusting, until September 1940.

The old destroyer's resurrection was brought about by the destroyer deal of 1940, under terms of which she and forty-nine of her sisters were eventually transferred to British ownership in exchange for basing rights for American naval forces in Bermuda and other British islands.

By January of 1941, *Meade* (rechristened *Ramsey* and wearing the White Ensign) was once again rolling and pitching in the familiar seas of the North Atlantic, helping to guard the convoys that were keeping Great Britain alive and fighting through the bleak months of German Continental victories.

Ramsey, in her best days an idiosyncratic ship, had been loved and loathed by a series of Royal Navy crews. Lightly built (the members of her class were known as "Thousand Tonners"), narrow of beam, and flush decked, *Ramsey* was a hellship in a seaway. She would bury her knife-sharp prow so deeply into advancing waves that the uninitiated aboard would despair of her ever rising again. Tons of green water would turn her decks into a series of rapids more violent than any mountain stream's, washing away and smashing any gear her crew had neglected to secure to stanchions with chain or wire rope. On one occasion she had performed her submarine act to such effect that her forward deck gun was uprooted and sent plunging over the side along with a deck cargo of a ton of American beef intended for the messes of the Home Fleet's destroyer squadrons based in the Clyde.

At speed in heavy seas, her thin plating would flex like the skin of a nervous thoroughbred, convincing the fainthearted aboard that she was destined to collapse like an empty bully-beef tin with the very next onslaught of the sea. Her ancient power plant was still capable of driving her at thirty-two knots for short periods, and to be aboard her at that speed in any but the calmest sea was a thing, once experienced, never forgotten.

But in smooth waters such as the long Pacific swell in which *Ramsey* now found herself, she could display an impeccable set of manners, which her commander, Robert Stacey-Munro, Lieutenant, RNVR (a former America's Cup trials helmsman and a devoted yachtsman), described often as "yare," meaning sweet, quick to the helm, swift and graceful.

In the normal course of naval affairs, *Ramsey* would certainly have been retired at the end of the war in Europe. In a Royal Navy that was dwarfed, to be sure, by the immense American fleet, but which had almost fully recovered from the disasters of the early years of the war, a ship such as *Ramsey* would never have been sailed all the way to the Pacific to take part in this enormous, and largely American, Operation Coronet.

But politicians dispose, while officers can only propose. Through the summer and fall of 1944 and even into the spring of 1945, as it became apparent that Japan would have to be invaded to bring the Pacific war to a satisfactory conclusion, Winston Churchill had waged an unremitting campaign to assure British participation in the operation.

In Washington, the notion of a British presence in the waters of what Admiral King regarded as an American lake-to-be was bitterly opposed. The dour chief of Naval Operations wanted no dilution of a Pacific command structure with troublesome allies. Nor, as it happened, did General MacArthur. Both men professed the greatest admiration for British courage and endurance, but as American strength built to enormous proportions in the Southwest and Central Pacific theaters, they saw any British participation as a desire solely to win a seat at the table when the Japanese, as they surely must, sued for peace.

But they reckoned without the persuasive powers of Winston Churchill. Focusing these powers first on Franklin Roosevelt and then on Harry Truman, the "Former Naval Person" succeeded in drawing from them a promise that the British (who, after all, had suffered great losses of prestige and power in Asia) would be allowed to have a share of Operation Coronet.

The result was that a British carrier task force of a dozen ships now sailed toward Honshu thirty nautical miles behind the fast carriers commanded by Admiral Halsey. And a grab bag of smaller British ships—frigates, corvettes, and destroyers—had been added to the offshore screening force that now lay between the vast invasion fleet and the Japanese coastline.

Even political decisions would ordinarily have been insufficiently all-inclusive to assign a thirty-two-year-old destroyer to the Operation Coronet force. But *Ramsey* had found herself in the Indian Ocean, actually destined for still another change of flag—this time to the Indian Navy—when the ships began to gather for the invasion of Japan. The change of nationality was postponed when the Admiralty, searching for candidates to show the White Ensign in this last, greatest naval fight of the war, signaled *Ramsey* to join the warships assembling in Buckner Bay, Okinawa. And had anyone with any naval knowledge presumed to tell the new Prime Minister, Clement Attlee, that, due to the insistence of his rival and predecessor, one of the fifty antique destroyers leased by the Americans to Britain was to help represent England in the battle for Japan, he would probably have ordered *Ramsey* withdrawn instantly. But no one did inform the Prime Minister. Among his close associates it was common knowledge that Mr. Attlee was still shocked—pleased, as well, but shocked—by the ease with which the British people had discarded their crusty war leader, Churchill, to make a socialist their new commander.

Attlee, a less sanguine man than Churchill, would have been quite willing to allow the Americans to fight this last engagement of what had become in the Pacific a primarily American war, after all, without further expenditure of British lives and British treasure. He would surely have preferred to spend Britain's resources elsewhere.

But for the British contingent in the Coronet fleet, the die had been cast months earlier, before the British elections, and no one had removed the die from the table.

HMS *Ramsey*, her White Ensign streaming gallantly, was about to fight her last battle.

· · ·

Seaman Cummins was a frail young man given to unexpected bouts of seasickness and an endless succession of head colds. The surgeon-lieutenant in *Ramsey*, a recent graduate of Edinburgh University's medical school, after having prescribed all the customary nostrums for Cummins's complaints to no avail, had been driven to attempt to persuade the captain, on humanitarian grounds, that Cummins should be put ashore and assigned to one of His Majesty's shore installations that did not pitch and roll as *Ramsey* did.

Lieutenant Stacey-Munro, a natural sailor, equated motion sickness aboard a destroyer with malingering and he had promptly refused the doctor's request. He had his own way of treating malingerers. "Fresh air and isolation are sovereign remedies for the pukes, doctor," he said, "and for the sniffles as well." He assigned Cummins to a four-on-and-four-off spell of duty at the masthead.

Thus it was that as night fell on the invasion fleet, Seaman Albert Cummins was performing his second tour as lookout in a sheet-metal perch three-fourths of the way between *Ramsey*'s foredeck and the rotating half-dish of her temperamental masthead radar.

Ramsey was zigzagging at twenty knots on the port flank of the fleet in company with a motley assemblage of similar ships: frigates and destroyers, most of them American, but some of them ships of the Royal Australian and the Royal New Zealand navies.

From his position on the needle-thin foremast, Cummins could see the frothing, phosphorescent wake of the destroyer next ahead of *Ramsey*, an American with the odd name *Jacob W. Onstott*—a Yankee admiral in the War of 1812 who had won fame ("notoriety," according to the dour Stacey-Munro) by sinking a British man-of-war before receiving word that the war had been over for eighteen days.

The *Onstott*, a ship twenty years younger than *Ramsey*, signaled a change of course, which Cummins noted and duly reported, and then heeled sharply as she began the landward leg of her next zigzag. Cummins braced himself against the icy sides of his steel bucket, his stomach heaving in anticipation of *Ramsey*'s twenty-five-degree heel as she changed course to follow in *Onstott*'s wake.

Ramsey started her turn, rolling sickeningly, her masthead swinging in a violent arc of forty degrees. At the same moment the following wind wafted a haze of stack gas over Cummins, and his gut muscles gave a great churning spasm. He had had only tea and dry sandwiches since leaving the anchorage at Buckner Bay, and not even that since morning. But the mere fact that his stomach was empty didn't prevent the bile from rising into his throat. He hung helplessly onto the rim of the crow's-nest, his head wobbling weakly on his neck, and vomited over the side.

Fortunately, no members of the crew except the gunners at the foredeck four-incher were on the weather decks. He wiped his mouth and his watering eyes on the sleeve of his duffel coat and gasped for air. The ship was now on a northwesterly course and the wind was abeam, carrying the stack gas clear of the foremast. He sucked in cold air and squinted at the dark sea to the west.

It was then that he saw the white wakes in the darkness, a dozen or more of them, approaching from the direction of Mikura.

Ensign Koji Takahashi, assault commander of the naval contingent of the Mikura-jima Special Surface Attack Force, crouched behind the narrow spray screen shielding the helm of his *shinyo* and tried to pierce the darkness ahead with his salt-burned eyes.

The boats, ten Navy *shinyo*s and eight Army *renraku-tei*s, motorboats, had been towed into position by two I-class fleet submarines in the late afternoon, and had been abandoned swiftly by the submariners as the last daylight faded. For two hours the fleet of plywood craft had bobbed in the gentle Pacific swell, lashed together with light lines to prevent dispersal. Many of the Army boats' pilots had suffered badly from seasickness; Takahashi had heard them retching miserably in the darkness. The two hours of waiting had been the worst time the twenty-three-year-old ensign had spent in the Navy. The beatings and discipline of his cadet-school weeks were as nothing compared to the fearful hours spent on the dark sea waiting for the appearance of the American ships.

Now all that was forgotten. Just as his tactical officer had predicted, he had heard first the sound of the American airplanes of the Combat Air Patrols and then the beat of ships' engines rolling over the silent sea.

It had been a calculated risk for the submarines to tow the boats the twenty kilometers from Mikura. At any time the plywood armada and the valuable I-boats could have been detected by enemy aircraft. But when the last light of day had gone, both the submarines and the Special Attack Force were reasonably safe: the submarines because they could return toward the coast submerged and the boats because their thin wooden shells would not register on the enemy radar sets.

As the fleet was being cast adrift, Takahashi had been hailed from the conning tower of the I-boat nearest him. It was a boat called *Anemone*, and it was commanded by Lieutenant Commander Kunamoto, the officer who had presided at the sake party given the previous night by the submariners to honor the crews of the Special Attack Force.

Kunamoto, the *hachimaki* he wore around his head still visible in the swiftly fading light, had called out that the American fleet had been spotted by an Eastern Sea patrol plane. "You will have good hunting tonight!" Kunamoto had added, and behind him some member of the submarine's crew had waved a Rising Sun banner to raise a ragged cheer from the men in the bobbing crash boats.

Takahashi had felt a surge of pride and emotion, but when the submarines had gone, slipped beneath the surface with a hiss of compressed air and swirling water, his courage faltered. The onset of darkness on the empty sea had filled him with a terrible foreboding. He told himself that his dread was of failure, of some sudden onslaught of cowardice, but he knew better. He had known better ever since leaving the naval school at Yokosuka with the orders assigning him to the suicide fleet on Mikura-jima in his pocket.

It was all very well to think of oneself as a samurai ready to die at any time for the Emperor, but it was another thing entirely to ride on the breast of the black sea knowing that this dark night, with even the stars hidden from view by the low clouds, was to be one's last night on earth.

Takahashi had been an art student at Kyoto University when the war began. He had rushed, with most of his classmates, to the naval recruiters on the morning of December 9, 1941. But so strong had the Navy been at the time, so flushed with the pride of great victory over the Americans, that art students of seventeen were not, the recruiting officer said disdainfully, needed.

Crestfallen, Takahashi had returned to his studies. He had written an abject letter of apology to his father for his having failed to convince the Navy recruiter that he was a suitable candidate for the officer school at Yokosuka. The elder Takahashi had served as a naval officer in the Great War of 1918. His ship had participated in the world-wide search for the German commerce-raider *Emden*. Now the Germans were Japan's allies, but the head of the Takahashi clan still spoke of his service days with great pride.

He had written kindly to his son, assuring young Koji that the time would come for him to offer his life and duty to the Son of Heaven. "Patience, as well as courage, is the mark of the samurai," he wrote. And he had added a quotation from Musashi's *A Book of Five Rings*: "There is timing in the whole life of the warrior, in his thriving and declining, in his harmony and discord."

The Takahashis were not a truly ancient clan: Koji's great-grandfather, a descendant of farmers, had attained samurai rank only in the last decade of the nineteenth century. Barely in time, actually, to lose it to the reforms of the Meiji Restoration, when all such class distinctions were, theoretically at least, abolished. But their parvenu status tended to make the Takahashis prouder and more self-demanding than other, older, families. And Koji had been certain that he had disappointed his father by allowing himself to be rejected by the naval recruiter that December morning in 1941.

For that reason he had devoted himself to the military arts, abandoning the art faculty at Kyoto as unworthy of attention in wartime. In 1943, when the Navy was no longer so flushed with victories, it had been glad to accept Koji Takahashi as an officer cadet.

Now he had written his death poem and selected the prayers he wished his family to say for the comfort of his soul at Yasukuni Shrine. He had toasted his comrades in sake and dedicated his death to the Emperor. All the proper forms were fulfilled. All that remained for him to do was to lose this terrible cold fear and perform his duty as a Japanese and a member of the Takahashi clan. Silently, he prayed to Amaterasu Omikami to guide him bravely against the American ships.

The *shinyo*s and the *renraku-tei*s were essentially similar craft. Both were built of plywood and had flat-bottomed hulls five and a half meters long. They were powered by automobile engines, most of them products of the now-destroyed Mitsubishi factories around Nagoya, which could drive the boats at twenty-six knots in a reasonably calm sea.

The *shinyo* carried a single 250-kilogram charge of explosives in the bow. This warhead was triggered by a contact fuse, and the proper technique was to approach the target ship slowly, making as small a wake as possible until the moment of discovery. Then one was expected to open the throttle wide and crash the *shinyo* into the side of the enemy vessel. Warships, the operations officer at the Special Attack Force base warned, were to be avoided. Troop transports were to be the targets of choice, since they were unarmored and sinking them would cause the greatest number of casualties.

The war, Takahashi had been given to understand, had reached the point of simple choices. Tactics and strategy had been reduced to one simple directive for all Japanese forces:

"Inflict casualties." Only by bathing the Americans in blood could Japan hope to obtain tolerable terms for the ending of hostilities.

The Imperial Japanese Army, always ready to compete with the Imperial Navy—even at this late date in the war—had established its own special attack squadrons, with crash boats, oddly named *renraku-tei*s, liaison boats. The specially trained soldiers who piloted them had been told to crash into enemy targets only as a last resort. The *renraku-tei* was armed with two 160-kilogram depth charges, mounted on either side of the cockpit. These were to be carried at top speed toward the enemy ships and dropped beside them as the boat was hauled into a tight U-turn. The charges had fuses with a six-second delay. This made attacking in a *renraku-tei* or a *shinyo* equally hazardous. In either case, the chance for escape after a properly executed attack was exactly nil.

During the American reconquest of the Philippines, the operations officer had told his pilots, seventy *renraku-tei*s had attacked the assault transports of the Americans in Lingayen Gulf and a similar force of *shinyo*s had sortied against the ships of the American Navy anchored in Mariveles Bay. The destruction of enemy vessels, the operations officer had declared, was enormous. Takahashi, as well as the other boat pilots, had been rendered silent by the disclosure that Japanese casualties in those attacks had been 100%. This was to be expected in a *tokkotai*—special attack—action. But not even the operations officer of the combined Army and Navy squadrons could claim that the American landings had been in any way delayed by the self-immolation of almost 150 soldiers and sailors.

The boats of both the Army and the Navy were supposed to be under Ensign Takahashi's tactical command after leaving the submarines. But clearly nothing of the sort was possible, he realized. The boats began to separate as soon as the lines connecting them had been cast off at the sound of the Yankee airplanes. The night was too dark to see more than sixty or seventy meters, and none of the craft carried a radio.

As the plywood fleet floated in the darkness, Takahashi strained to interpret the sounds that came over the black sea from the south. He had heard the grumbling of ships' engines many times before, but this was different. It was a deep susurration—gentle and distant at first, but growing swiftly in intensity. The sound seemed to rise from the sea itself, through the thin planking of his *shinyo*'s fragile bottom, and as the throbbing increased, it seemed to Takahashi that the sea was vibrating, as though some enormous stringed instrument were being bowed somewhere deep beneath his feet.

Next came the smell. At first there was only a whiff of acrid stack gas, a taste of the oily mist made by fuel burning in the steel bellies of the oncoming ships. But the odor grew steadily stronger, thicker, more pungent, until it burned the throat and eyes.

The stringed instrument was joined now by the uneven beat of gigantic drums, a heartbeat that was felt rather than heard. It was as though Takahashi's own bloodstream had joined with the deep sea, becoming cold and terrible and yet infinitely alive to the steel prows that knifed through it somewhere just out of his range of vision.

He heard a soughing now, the sound of great shapes rushing through the water. The beat of engines became much louder, a rumbling, booming noise of huge machines working their steel arms and legs inside vast hollow caverns of iron.

Takahashi's hand rested on the starter-pull of his engine. It was trembling, but he could not make it stop. Images of sea dragons and monsters from the ancient fables filled his mind. The stink of their gaseous breath brought the bile into his throat.

A shrill voice in the darkness called out: "I see them! I see them!"

The noise of the engines was deafening; it rolled across the water like a tsunami. How many ships would it take to make such a sound? Takahashi wondered. A thousand? Ten thousand?

Again the shrill voice from one of the drifting boats to the south: *"Banzai! Tenno banzai!"*

Takahashi heard an engine start, then another. Engines were coming to life all around him. He pulled the starting lanyard, and the Mitsubishi power plant of his own *shinyo* burst into life.

Directly over his bow a dark shape was materializing. It towered into the night like the wall of a sheer cliff. White foam boiled along the water line as an American destroyer pounded past at twenty knots. Terrified, Takahashi twisted the helm. The jagged silhouette, as big as a block of houses, stinking of fuel oil and stack gases emitted a booming throb that was like the pulse of a giant beast. The sloping fantail appeared, a tumbling chaos of boiling water under the stern where the screws tormented the sea to phosphorescence.

Quite suddenly, the low clouds parted slightly, allowing a thin starlight to shine on the water. Takahashi stared. It seemed to him that the sea was alive with enormous indistinct shapes. Ahead of him he could see what was surely another destroyer: long, low to the water, with four high stacks, the spaces between which narrowed as the ship completed a turn and began to steam toward him.

He heard the sound of a klaxon aboard the heeling ship. It made a hysterical sound, a sound filled with fear and anger. Then he became aware that his hands had ceased trembling. He felt as cold as before, but it was no longer terrifying. Instead, the iciness centered in his belly seemed to steady him. He shoved the throttle forward against the stop and felt his boat surge forward.

A searching tongue of fire appeared on the foredeck of the oncoming destroyer, and for a joyous moment Takahashi imagined that one of his boats had already scored a hit on her. But as the water around him erupted into geysers of spray, he realized that the gunners on the ship were firing at him.

Other ships were firing, too, and he could see the arching flight of tracers lacing the air over the sea and balls of yellow fire wobbling through the night until they were extinguished in the darkness. A huge explosion lighted the scene as one of the attack boats, struck by enemy fire that set off its bow charge, volcanoed into the sky.

A star shell fired by one of the vessels of the screening force ignited high in the air and hung in its parachute, bathing the combatants in cold white light.

Takahashi looked to the south and west. There were ships as far as he could see. All seemed to be shooting wildly, creating a monsoon rain of fire.

He put the helm down hard to swerve his boat into an intersecting course with the onrushing destroyer. He felt his bladder flush with the mingled terror and elation he was feeling. He raised his face to the fiery sky and shouted hoarsely. He knew with an unswerving certainty that in the next sixty seconds he would experience the apotheosis of the samurai and that all of his twenty-three years had been only preparation for this moment.

From his position high above the deck of *Ramsey*, Seaman Albert Cummins could see the reaches of the surrounding sea bathed in the cold light of the star shells and the hanging parachute flares. The surface of the water reflected the light like a black mirror, an undulating plain that was marred by frothing wakes and sudden geysers from exploding shells. The air was painted with fiery streaks and the wobbling trails of tumbling tracer bullets.

At eleven o'clock, some ten points to port off *Ramsey*'s sharp bow, a shabby slab-sided boat, lying low in the water, was circling to come onto an intersecting course. *Ramsey*'s gunners, working the four-incher on the foredeck, were firing at some target on the starboard side. Cummins could not see what they were trying to hit because shell bursts from other ships of the screen were raising a curtain of spray laced with the yellow flashes of explosives.

The *shinyo* on the port side straightened into a collision course.

Cummins picked up the bridge telephone and screamed a warning. *Ramsey* heeled again in a turn from the threat, but her motion seemed slow, far too slow.

The beam of a searchlight from the *Onstott* swept across *Ramsey* and onward until it caught the green *shinyo* in its glare. Immediately the water around the boat began to boil with heavy 40mm fire from the American destroyer's fantail. There was a momentary interval of fiery darkness when the parachute flares quenched themselves in the sea. When another constellation of flares reilluminated the scene, Cummins could see that the *shinyo* was still coming on. It struck him as amazing that a plywood motorboat could drive through such a storm of steel and fire apparently unscathed. He could make out clearly the bulbous explosive charge in its prow. A tiny dark figure crouched behind a low splinter shield amidships.

The gunners on the foredeck seemed of a sudden to become aware of the onrushing boat, and the four-incher swung left, firing at full depression. Cummins could not distinguish the bursts from the sheets of water raised by the barrage of fire from the swiftly departing *Onstott*.

In the light of another star shell's burst, Cummins saw that the attacking boats were scattering, three of them were capsized and sinking, two more had dissolved into a scum of wooden wreckage on the water. Far astern something burned brilliantly, spreading blazing gasoline in a trail behind it, and even as he watched, the boat exploded into a ball of oily flame. He heard himself yelling incoherently, his voice hoarse with mingled rage, excitement, and fear.

Behind the nearest boat he could see the frothing wake of another, of slightly different shape. It angled away from its leader as though racing to be the first to reach *Ramsey*.

A shell from the four-incher struck the first *shinyo*, but failed to explode. It sent pieces of wood spinning into the air and yanked the boat around as though on a tether. The quarter wave overtook the boat as it went dead in the water, washing over it and filling the cockpit. When Cummins could see clearly again, the green boat was down by the stern, swamped. *Ramsey* drove past, leaving it astern.

For a moment Cummins felt an urge to cheer, but then he saw the second boat charging in, only 100 yards from *Ramsey*'s port quarter. The foredeck gun's muzzle flash illuminated the deck gear, but the cannon could be depressed no more. Cummins realized with a sick certainty that his ship was about to be hit. He could do nothing more than grip the steel rim of his perch and watch in horror.

When the dud four-incher grazed Ensign Takahashi's *shinyo*, it demolished the port side of the hull, dismounted the engine, and smashed the steering linkages. The boat stopped as though it had run into a solid wall, and the quarter wave overtook it, filling the cockpit with water and unignited gasoline. Takahashi felt himself lifted by the inrushing sea and flushed from the shattered boat like a bit of flotsam. His first reaction was terror; his second, furious frustration. In the bleak light from the flares he saw his boat break into three pieces, the bow—with its precious explosive charge—and the stern section—with the engine— sank like stones into the black water. What remained was a section of the foredeck and cockpit, a jumble of plywood frames and planking. He began to swim desperately as the cold struck him.

Seemingly out of nowhere, a *renraku-tei* thrashed by, almost running him down. He could see the pilot hunched over the helm and the portside depth bomb glistening as the spray sluiced over it. Streaks of tracers made a lattice overhead. The noise of shells bursting was deafening. He could scarcely hear the rumble of the *renraku-tei*'s engine as it swept past, racing toward the heeling destroyer, now only 100 meters away.

The Army pilot was going to score a hit, Takahashi thought. Unless the enemy gunners could explode the boat's charges, there was no way the destroyer could escape. Impressions were jumbled in his mind. He shouted encouragement to the *renraku-*

tei pilot. Simultaneously he knew that if he was in the water at the moment the charges exploded, at this range he would be crushed and disemboweled by the pressure. He thrashed frantically through the water to reach the floating remnant of his own *shinyo*.

The destroyer swept by, water hissing and tumbling along her side. In the battle glare Takahashi was startled by the flag flying from her fantail. It was not the striped banner of the Americans. It took him a moment to realize that the flag was the White Ensign of the English Navy. For some reason this useless bit of information filled him with despairing rage. It was not enough that the Americans could cover the sea with thousands of ships, they were even drawing others into the battle with them, like scavengers gathering to tear the body of the sacred homeland.

Takahashi reached the remains of his boat and pulled himself up just as the *renraku-tei* crashed into the hull of the destroyer. The shock wave of the explosion almost swept him back into the sea.

Albert Cummins failed to die with his shipmates by a happenstance so improbable that it approached the miraculous. As the 320 kilograms of high explosive carried by the *renraku-tei* ripped HMS *Ramsey* apart, the foremast was snapped cleanly off at deck level and sent into a high, lazy arc fifty feet above the sea. Wedged into the narrow steel container of the crow's-nest, Cummins went with it.

The air over the dying *Ramsey* was filled with spinning debris—shards of white-hot steel ripped from the ship, exploding ammunition, flaming oil.

The *renraku-tei* pilot had immolated himself and the men packed into *Ramsey*'s thin, narrow hull by detonating his charges directly abaft the central ammunition storage. *Ramsey*'s plating collapsed inward with the force of the explosion. For the first few microseconds, raw fire blew like a red hurricane through the ship, blasting away watertight doors and turning bulkheads into sheets of glowing-hot metal. As the flame front seared the midships ammunition storage, it detonated a dozen torpedoes and nearly 100 rounds of four-inch high-explosive ammunition. The old four-stacker twisted in agony, her decks bulging in a futile attempt to contain the force of the blasts tearing her apart. A column of flame gushed up the ammunition hoist to erupt like a geyser at the four-inch gun mount. The cannon was ripped from its mountings and blown high into the air, surrounded by the pinwheeling, broken shapes of the gun crew.

The bridge crew felt the first shock and almost before they could react spears of flame erupted from the voice pipes connecting the bridge with the compartments below. The helmsman, an RN veteran who would never see Liverpool again, felt the flames searing his face, but before he could properly feel the pain of the burns, he was crushed between the overhead and the suddenly bulging, superheated deck. On the bridge wing, Lieutenant Robert Stacey-Munro was literally torn in half by a piece of deck plating that had been driven upward through the ship from the floor of the number-one ammunition hoist.

Belowdecks men died before they could even give voice to their terror as the flame front gutted the crew compartments, scouring decks, bulkheads, and overheads with thousand-degree heat.

Ramsey herself screamed in agony as her back broke in two places, sending bow and stern spinning off through the water as though they weighed ounces instead of tons. The midships section simply disintegrated into steel splinters and debris and a vertical column of flame.

The destroyer's death was witnessed by one Japanese only, the shaken and drenched survivor clinging to the remnants of his shattered suicide boat. The others who had left Mikura-jima that afternoon were all dead, some already fathoms deep in the cold Pacific waters, others floating burned or dismembered by the withering fire of the fleet's defenders.

Seaman Cummins saw nothing. Aware only that he was alive and that he was somehow high above the burning sea, he shut his eyes and made sounds of animal terror as the mast fell, spinning like a jackstraw in a whirlpool.

The steel shaft struck the surface like a spear, and Cummins, protected from the impact by the steel crow's-nest, found himself in darkness, water pressure compressing his lungs. The mast had plunged to thirty feet before he freed himself and struck desperately for the surface. After what seemed an eternity, he reached it, gasping for air. The night was strangely silent, unbroken now by any sounds of battle. The fight had been, for all its fury, only a tiny skirmish on the landward flank of an enormous fleet, a fleet that covered hundreds of square miles of sea.

In the distance some oil or gasoline burned on the water, but that was all that he could see. The fleet, reacting to the threat of the suicide boats like some vast animal reacting to the pinprick of an insect's bite, had flinched away from the point of attack and rolled on. He could hear the sound of engines, but from his low position could see nothing.

Ramsey was plainly gone, sunk with all hands. The suicide boats were gone, too. Cummins floated, exhausted, in his life preserver. The dark overcast had parted into scattered clouds, and he could see tiny, brilliant points of light that were the stars.

He felt reasonably certain that he would be rescued by morning. The fleet carrying Coronet's forces was so enormous that six hours from now, as the sun rose, ships would still be passing.

Then he heard a human sound, and had a flashing hope that it was one of his shipmates, spared by some miracle like his own, who had made it.

He listened carefully to establish a direction, and heard water lapping against something: a raft, perhaps, or a bit of floating debris.

Soon he saw the fragment of the wrecked *shinyo*. The ragged ruin looked as big as an island to him. He began to swim toward it, confident for the first time since the attack had begun that he was going to survive this night.

In flag plot aboard *Alaska,* Lieutenant Arnold Deighton reported to Admiral Kinsey: "Signal from *Onstott,* Admiral. The inshore screen has beaten off an attack by eighteen *shinyos.*" With some difficulty, in the red battle-lighted compartment, he read the typed flimsy. "All Jap boats destroyed. We lost *Ramsey. Onstott* asks permission to drop out of column to search for survivors."

Kinsey did not hesitate. "Permission denied. Notify the rear pickets to make a sweep when they reach *Ramsey*'s last position." He paused, his deeply lined face bleak. "*Ramsey* is one of the Limey cans, isn't it?"

"Yes, sir," the flag secretary said.

Kinsey stood for a moment, a spare, hunched figure in rumpled khakis. It was beginning, he thought. How many more men would die before Operation Coronet forced the Japs' backs to the wall? "Carry on, Arnold," he said quietly, and returned to his scrutiny of the charts of the anchorages, now only hours away from the advancing invasion force.

Cummins reached the floating wreck of the *shinyo* and looked up. Outlined against the starlight a man knelt on the remnants of the boat's deck planking. For a moment, Cummins thought that the man was extending a hand to help him aboard. But in the next instant he saw the flash of a blade and felt the burning touch of its edge as the Japanese thrust at him.

Ensign Koji Takahashi, terrified by the sudden appearance from the sea of a white enemy face, thrust again with the *wakizashi,* the short sword he had worn against the possible need to commit seppuku if in danger of capture.

Cummins felt the blade tear deeply into his cheek. In silent desperation he released his hold on the wreckage and seized the arm that guided the blade. He arched his back and thrust himself away from the wreck, pulling Takahashi with him.

Takahashi felt the footing under him sink away; he found himself in the water. He tried to wrench himself free of the grip on his arm, but all he succeeded in doing was to lose the *wakizashi* into the depths. He sobbed with mingled rage and terror and in the process ingested a pint of sea water. Instantly, his throat constricted and his lungs convulsed as the salty fluid seared tender membranes. He clutched Cummins with the strength of panic.

Cummins thrust his clenched fist between Takahashi's arms and broke the Japanese's grip. In a fury, he battered the close-cropped head with all the strength he could muster. The cold of the sea was striking deep, and he felt himself weakening. Finding a grip on Takahashi's throat, he shoved down as hard as he could. The Japanese struggled spasmodically, but Cummins did not release him. For a full two minutes or more he held the smaller man down. When at last he opened his hands, the Japanese slipped away into the abyss below.

Cummins, chattering and sobbing, looked about for the wreckage of the *shinyo*, but it, too, had vanished.

He raised his fingers to his face and felt something hard, sharp. Then he realized that he was touching his own teeth through his gashed cheek. "Oh, God," he whimpered. "Oh, *God.*"

He hung in his life jacket, shivering with shock and cold, as the dark ships, thrumming like dragons, passed all around him on their course to the north.

2100 Hours

The light of the oil lamp fell gently on Katsuko Maeda's smoothly contoured face, her gleaming black hair, and the gold and silver embroidery of her formal kimono. Deftly she completed the brushing of the tea in the porcelain cup and passed it, with properly averted eyes, to her brother.

Kantaro Maeda rotated the cup the prescribed one-half turn and sipped the tea, murmuring a suitable compliment.

Outside the *chashitsu*, the teahouse, the same sea wind that stirred the dark pine boughs brought the muttering of gunfire, like the sound of a distant thunderstorm, but different, without the resonance of thunder. Katsuko closed her eyes and wished for serenity, but she felt none. Even the grace of the tea ceremony had failed to ease the dark fear she felt in her heart.

Kantaro had arrived at the Maeda villa without warning, bringing the long-expected news that the *ketsu-go*, the decisive battle that the Army had planned for so long, was about to begin. It was both his *oya-on*, his familial duty, and his *giri*, his obligation to his name, to visit his sister and their ancestral villa this one last time before meeting his death in the service of the Emperor.

He was handsome, Katsuko thought, looking sidelong at her brother. Tall for a Japanese, and graceful in his movements, he knelt on the delicately bordered tatami of the teahouse wearing a heavy black silk kimono decorated with the double hyacinth-leaf *mon* of their cadet branch of the ancient Maeda clan.

Katsuko knew that she should be composing her spirit for what fate must come, preparing to meet the ancestors as Kantaro was doing, with an air of inner calm. But she found it beyond her capability to do more than mask the tumult of emotion within her.

That morning she had gotten up before the sun and climbed the path to the family shrine on the cliff overlooking the Pacific. As the sun rose, the long sweep of the light had turned the dark ocean to a wonderful pattern of blues: ultramarine where the water was deep, cobalt and turquoise in the shallows. She had found it nearly impossible to accept the reality of what the horizon concealed. Japan's enemies were out there on the living sea, out there in their hundreds of thousands, in ships beyond counting. She still could scarcely believe it. Had it actually come to this? Would the Westerners really be storming ashore on the beaches of Honshu—some of which were visible from the mountain shrine—to kill, burn, rape, and dishonor?

Filled with sadness, she watched Kantaro complete the rituals of the *chanoyo,* and she found herself remembering Harry-san. Was it possible, she wondered, that he was out there on one of the enemy ships, or in one of the marauding bombers that flew each night over the villa on the way to burn Tokyo? It didn't seem reasonable. Harry-san had been born in the Land of the Eight Islands. When he was seven, the Seavers had given him his first *hakama*, the samurai skirt, even as Kantaro received his. Harry-san was *Japanese*, Katsuko thought, no matter what the color of his skin or the shape of his eyes.

As children they had played together, Harry, Kantaro, and Katsuko. They had acted out the deliciously tragic legends: the *Hogen Monogatari,* the tales of Yamato Takeru and the Forty-seven Ronin. How could Harry-san return to Japan as an enemy?

Kantaro placed the fragile cup on the tile hearth and folded his hands. He bowed formally to his sister. "It is done," he said.

Katsuko touched her forehead to the tatami, and, still on her knees, scuttled to the doorway, which was very low, to instill humility. She waited for her brother to crawl through the opening into the dark garden, then followed him out of the teahouse.

There was still that muttering in the wind that brushed the pines. Katsuko had become accustomed to the sound of distant gunfire; she recognized it for what it was. Through the trees, when the vista opened to the sea, she could discern a faint flickering of light on the underside of the clouds. She could not actually see the ships, but it was plain that they were there—and in battle.

Kantaro said, "Yes. They are really coming this time. Are you afraid, Katsu-chan?"

"I am afraid for you," the girl said. "Is that too Western?" She wanted to be correct. This night of all nights, she wanted everything to be in perfect order.

Kantaro half smiled in the darkness. "We are what we are," he said, and started up the path toward the villa.

Katsuko followed him, a submissive one pace behind. Since his unwilling return from Saipan (he had begged his commander to allow him to stay and die with his soldiers), Kantaro had abandoned all the Occidental ways he had acquired from the family's prewar friends and associates. He had become totally Japanese, fanatically so.

At the villa his soldiers waited—the squad he had brought with him to leave on the mountain road, where they would build strongpoints and set ambushes to greet the Americans when they came.

It seemed unreal to Katsuko that there would actually be fighting here, and yet Kantaro assured her that it was a certainty. The Maeda family had owned this land high in the rugged terrain of the Boso Peninsula for a hundred years. It was land unsuited to agriculture—unsuited, really, for anything but a mountain park, which is what the Maedas had made of it. The villa had been first built in 1859, before the overthrow of the Tokugawa Shogunate. It had been enlarged and rebuilt many times, and eventually it had become the principal lodging of the

---

95

clan. In the early years of the war, it had been, to Katsuko, an island of tranquillity in an increasingly turbulent time.

The gardens, the villa, much of it closed off and unused now because the number of servants needed to run it properly was too great, and the shrine on the ridge—all the physical properties remained, but as an establishment it had gradually been bled, by necessity, so that it was now more memorial than home. General Sanjiro Maeda, the head of the clan, was dead somewhere in China. Tokichiro, who would have been the heir, was dead in the battleship *Yamato*, somewhere on the bottom of the East China Sea. Minoru, the second son, had died piloting a Kamikaze against the American fleet in the Philippines. It was reported that he had sunk an American *Essex*-class carrier, but who could really be certain of that? Katsuko knew that it was improper of her to have such doubts, but she could not completely control them. Perhaps it was the Western taint in her upbringing. She had been educated at the American School in Kyoto until the government closed it in 1940. Her elder sister, Nuiko, and their mother had been killed in Tokyo. When the air raids had begun, Katsuko and Kantaro had tried to convince their mother that the Maeda house was unsafe, but Lady Maeda refused to leave the city. "As long as the Emperor remains in Tokyo," she declared, "here I stay." On the night of the first low-level fire raid by B-29s, when sixteen square kilometers of the city burned, Nuiko and Lady Keiko Maeda died fighting the fires.

Now all that remained of the Double Hyacinth Clan were the youngest of the children, Kantaro and Katsuko, and Kantaro, a newly promoted Imperial Guards colonel, was preparing to die on the beaches tomorrow. What had become of the graceful, spacious world they had all known before this terrible war?

Katsuko followed her brother up the path, past the villa, to the shrine on the ridge. Kantaro's back was as straight as a bowman's finest arrow. He was not wearing the family sword; to have done so in the *chashitsu* would have been inappropriate. But he might just as well have the ancient blade at his side,

Katsuko thought. He could not have been more samurai than he was at this moment. The flash of mingled anger and pride she felt unsettled her. What have we become? she wondered. Before the war the younger Maedas had been sophisticated cosmopolitans, aristocrats who had traveled in Europe and America, members of a set of outward-looking young Japanese supposedly unbound by the old ways. Those were the Maedas who had been friends of Harry Seaver and a dozen or more sons and daughters of Tokyo's foreign community.

She remembered the long and coolly reasonable discussions with Harry-san about the war in China, about Japan's need for space and raw materials. She remembered Harry once saying to her that she was persuasive because she was *neko-kawaigari*—familiarly using the idiom that meant she was like a loving cat. At nineteen, she had been woman enough to treasure that not-so-subtle statement of Harry's fondness for her.

But those times were gone, she told herself severely. The war had changed everything, and what it had changed most of all was the way in which Japanese of her age and social standing regarded themselves. Cosmopolitanism had begun to die on December 8, 1941. After five years of fighting, it was ashes.

They reached the shrine, which had been built on the crest of the hill on which the villa stood. The *kami*, the divine spirit, was an ancient stone, none knew how ancient, but family legend had it that it had stood on the mountaintop for a thousand years. When the Maedas took the land, first as a fief and later as outright owners, a torii had been built of cedarwood, under which one passed as one approached the *kami*. The hemp rope hung at the shrine's last purification, after the death of Tokichiro, swung gently in the sea wind.

From the shrine the ground dropped away to the east in steep terraces to the Mobara-Katsuura road, which followed the smoothly curving coastline of the Boso Peninsula. The brother and sister could see no light below: the villages were dark; those still standing had been heavily fortified. Some dozen kilometers to the northeast, Kantaro had told Katsuko, the Home Army had constructed the enormously powerful Matsuo Fortress Area to anchor the first line of defense behind Kujukuri-hama, where a strong attack by American amphibious forces was expected.

Kantaro's unit, a crack Guards regiment of the 52nd Army, was deployed on the flank of Kujukuri, to guard a concentration of tanks and armored vehicles painstakingly gathered for the counterattack that was intended to decimate the Americans once the invaders had reached the killing ground.

The northern reaches of Kujukuri, which were hidden from the shrine by a shoulder of rocky land, had been under bombardment for days. Katsuko and the three old servants who remained at the villa had been able to watch the American warships cruising a scant 2,000 meters off the beaches. They had not actually seen the guns firing, because as the ships came abreast of the ruins of Katsuura they began the turn to reverse course and continue the bombardment.

For weeks Katsuko had stood at the shrine, fascinated by the lean gray ships that sailed so confidently up and down the coast, unchallenged, arrogant, and powerful.

The radio broadcasts from Tokyo (at least they claimed to originate in Tokyo) spoke glowingly of the heroism of the Kamikaze pilots who daily gave their lives for the Emperor and the homeland. The announcers, who spoke between long intervals of patriotic music, said that the Yankee fleet was in ruins, burning and sinking, its sailors terrified by the ferocity of the attacks by Japanese warriors. But the ships that cruised off the Boso Peninsula seemed undamaged, and the sound of their guns was a constant muttering thunder.

In her heart Katsuko knew that the war was lost: worse than lost. The enemy was coming, closing in on the home islands. For months now, not a word had been spoken on the air about the battle for Kyushu. It was useless to pretend that anything at all remained of Japan's vast prewar empire—or of the immense territories conquered in the first year of the war. Now one of the sacred home islands was gone and the enemy was at hand. Yet so long as Kantaro, now head of the clan, declined to speak of

Japan's terrible losses, Katsuko was required to pretend that they had not taken place.

In the villages between the mountains and the seacoast, the women, children, and old men were being drilled by soldiers of the Imperial Army. For three hours a day—a killing schedule for people existing on the edge of starvation—they were instructed in how to fight with bamboo spears. The spirit of Bushido, it appeared, was more important than arms, training, food, sleep, or warmth. Katsuko, as a member of the ruling class, had tried to set an example for the Boso peasants by presenting herself for spear drill dressed in the drab, mud-colored cotton of the national uniform. But the Army NCOs in command of the parades had been scandalized that a lady of the Maeda clan should be seen in such circumstances. Whatever else we lack, Katsuko thought ironically, the Japanese people have a powerful sense of the fitness of things. We are expected to fight ferociously, like samurai, and then to die—but in proper form.

Like her brother, Katsuko had become, in adversity, more and more purely Japanese. But her Westernized education sometimes betrayed her into agonies of silent protest.

Kantaro stood before the *kami*, inclined his head, closed his eyes, and clapped once to awaken the spirit of the shrine.

He should have felt the presence instantly. The souls of his Maeda ancestors should be all about him, guiding him toward the inner serenity he craved.

But he felt nothing—only emptiness, despair.

He opened his eyes and searched the dark sea far below. Small flashes of light, like heat lightning, flickered against the clouds. The American fleet was under attack—probably by the few pitiful boats the Navy and the Army had managed to gather in the Izu Islands. Brave men were dying, he thought—few on the American ships, many on the Japanese Special Attack Force boats. He had met some of the sailors and airmen of the *tokko* units. Almost without exception they were very young men, children, actually. Among the aircrews were pilots with fewer than fifty hours in the air. It was bad enough to find Japan reduced to fighting a war by suicide attacks; in addition, most of the attackers were so inexperienced that only a pitiful few could make it through the swarms of Grummans and Mustangs to reach the ships. Imperial General Staff Headquarters told the nation that the attacks were 80% effective. They admitted to field-grade officers that the percentage of successful attacks was much lower; forty of each 100 reached their targets, Intelligence claimed. Kantaro placed the degree of success still lower than that. If one in twenty actually struck a ship, he would be surprised. It was a tragedy, he thought. It was national seppuku perhaps—but it was not war.

He had not planned to visit the villa before going into action. In fact, it was a court-martial offense for him to have done so. He was risking extreme dishonor to have separated himself from his men at this critical moment. And he would never have done such a thing, no matter how much he had longed to see Katsu-chan once more before the end, except for what he had encountered in Misaki that day.

Misaki was a village a dozen kilometers from the sea, hidden in a fold of hills that had protected it from the worst of the naval bombardment and air attacks. It was a place he had known all his life, living as he had for part of every year on the Maeda lands on the Boso Peninsula. Maeda servants had come from the local villages, Misaki among them. It was a place that time, it seemed, had forgotten. Even in the late 1930s, when he and Harry Seaver had been schoolmates in Kyoto and had spent their holidays at the villa, they had spoken of Misaki as something out of the ancient legends, untouched by the modern world's changes. But Misaki was undergoing a change now. Under the guidance of the Kempetai, soldiers were working in Misaki.

Kantaro had seen the spear drills in other villages. The sight of old men and women posturing fiercely with sharpened stakes of bamboo no longer disturbed him. In war, the entire adult population was expected to fight. That was the Way of the Warrior.

But as he had marched his men through the single narrow street of Misaki, he had seen sappers outfitting boys and girls, some of them as young as five and six years old, with explosive back-packs. The children were being instructed in the proper method of approaching an American tank from the front, hands held high to gull the tank crew, and then dashing forward to squirm under the machines and detonate the packs.

Many of the children of Misaki were too small to carry the regulation twenty-five-kilogram satchel charges. So the soldiers were reducing the amount of high explosive to ten and even five kilograms: not enough to put a Sherman out of action, but more than enough to blow the tiny attacker to bloody jelly.

To do them credit, many of the sappers looked unhappy with their task and, despite the presence of the Kempetai, worked unwillingly. Others were smiling and laughing and making a game of it, as though they were preparing their pupils for *Tango-no-sekku*, Boys' Festival.

Kantaro had left Misaki sickened and resolved to visit the family shrine—and his sister—one last time, to seek some sort of inner peace before the final battle. But he had not truly found it, and he stood now more troubled than before he had made his way up the mountain road to the villa.

For almost five years he had acted strictly as a true samurai should, despite the fact that it had required him to put aside much of the intellectual facility with which he had been born, and which his excellent education had honed to a sharp cutting edge.

At the war's beginning he had been little more than a boy, filled with romantic notions of what was required of him as a man and a Japanese. He had suppressed the doubts he had felt about the wisdom of the war: it had been planned and begun, in heroic style, by men older and wiser. He had suppressed, too, the sadness he had felt at the loss of good friends among the *gaijin*, the foreigners—Harry Seaver most of all, an almost-Japanese white man who had been, he suspected, close to being in love with Katsu-chan.

101

He had made his sacrifices willingly enough, believing that any deprivation he felt was compensated by the joy of fulfilling a particularly Maeda destiny. Despite his partially Western education, Kantaro had the Japanese sense of family and honor.

His experiences in the Army had toughened him, built considerable scar tissue over the sensitivity he had carried into military service. Life in the Imperial Army was brutal: but properly so, he came to believe, because war itself was brutal. Without dedication and discipline, a soldier could become simply a bandit, a criminal, in uniform.

As a captain, he had fought on Saipan, fought well. The Americans he faced there had not been Harry Seavers. They had been sweating, red-faced young men whose fear of the Japanese had made them behave savagely. His own troops had behaved in the same bloody way. And it had begun to occur to him that war—any war—was *not* the stuff of the sagas and tragic legends.

The defeat on Saipan had been complete and absolute. Kantaro was still alive only because his commander had ordered him out on one of the last aircraft, to carry his final obeisance to the Emperor.

Kantaro had heard that when the Americans took Okinawa—the first time they had encountered large numbers of Japanese civilians—they had been shocked by the sight of women throwing their babies into the sea and then following them off the cliffs. It was a measure of how deadened his own sensibilities had become that he found nothing whatever unsettling about such an act. It was, after all, an affirmation of the Yamato spirit: the inner strength that had sustained Japan since feudal times without a defeat in war.

Then Kyushu was lost, and the certainty of defeat was inescapable. The entire nation was now resolved to offer itself as a sacrifice. The directive that came from Imperial General Staff Headquarters was couched in the simplest possible terms: "Make the enemy pay." Kill him by the hundreds, by the thousands, by the millions if need be.

It struck Kantaro as wildly improbable that the Americans would, at this late stage of the war, be driven by high casualties to grant "honorable terms." And even if some secret party existed within the American government ready to seek peace, plainly they would never deal with Hideki Tojo. The Crimson Dawn Coup of last November, which had returned General Tojo to power and dissolved the Diet, had surely sealed the fate of any peace movement in America. Yet the *gumbatsu* imagined that honorable terms were available—if only they spilled enough American, and Japanese, blood.

The *ketsu-go*, so beloved by Japanese *bushi*, would now be fought on the Kanto, the plain where Tokyo stood, the ancient Eastern Capital, a city that had never been taken in war.

How contradictory it all was, Kantaro thought. How could Japan demand, as part of the price of peace, that she be left free of invaders? The enemy was in Japan; in Okinawa and Kyushu—and tomorrow or the next day here where I stand. It was tragic and mad. For surely it was madness to arm farmers and fishermen with bamboo spears and put satchel charges on the backs of children.

A wave of utter desolation swept over him. That he, Kantaro Maeda, was certain to die disturbed him little. Life and death, after all, were but aspects of the same eternity. And when one is weary and filled with sorrow, life is not a great thing to surrender. But something should remain. It was not right that the old men in Tokyo should totally sacrifice all of Japan's future.

He turned to face his sister. Her shape was indistinct in the dark, limned against the pines by the few pallid stars shining through the trees. "Katsu-chan," he said, "we've had no chance to talk these last few months. I apologize for that." He noted her polite gesture of denial and wondered bleakly what had become of the energetic, lively girl with the clever, questing mind he remembered from before the war. He hoped that she still existed somewhere inside that pretty kimono-clad, doll-like figure. "I want you to listen to me carefully, Katsu-chan," he said, again using the warm, familiar diminutive of her name. He longed for her to know that she was very dear to him and that all he wished for was that she should survive whatever was to come.

He faced the sea again, feeling the near presence of a hundred thousand enemies who must be outwitted. "The Americans will begin to land tomorrow," he said. "We will not be able to stop them. They have too many soldiers, too many tanks and ships and airplanes. Too much of everything."

For a moment he was afraid she was going to say something about having confidence in the fighting spirit of the Army. It was the sort of remark Japanese had learned to use as a talisman against any sort of terrible news. But, thank the gods, she did not. Instead, she stood attentive and submissive, the very model of a woman of samurai family, ready to endure the unendurable. Nothing he could now do would absolve him of the responsibility for his part in making her what she had become. Before the war she might have escaped the dark karma that was overtaking her, and all Japanese. Though perhaps that was fantasy. He and his sister were the last of an ancient and noble line. Whatever fate decreed was to be Japan's destiny, he and Katsuko must share it. There was no escape.

The Japanese concept of *on* was one that few Westerners could ever understand. One received an *on* at birth from one's family: an obligation that must be repaid and yet, peculiarly, could never be completely repaid. *On* was lifelong, but it was a source of virtue. One derived virtue from repayment, which was, like *on*, never-ending. From the Emperor one received *ko on*; from one's parents one received *oya on*; from one's lord or superior, *nushi no on*. The repayment of these debts was *gimu*, mandatory, essential to honor. Yet repayment was always partial because the debt was eternal. Even death left the debt undischarged.

Yet death, thought Kantaro, is all that I have left to offer. The despair he was feeling was un-Japanese, he knew, and a product of his early contamination with Western ideas.

He faced his sister and bowed deeply and formally. "Katsuko-sama," he said, "I apologize to you for all that you have endured and all that you must endure in the future."

As custom dictated, Katsuko received the apology in respectful silence. It was understood between them that Kantaro, as the last remaining male of their line, must make such an apology. It was *gimu*.

He said, more practically, "This place will probably be overrun tomorrow or the next day. The Americans will move directly across the peninsula to secure the eastern shore of Tokyo Bay. I can give you a letter to a friend stationed at Chiba. He may be able to obtain transport for you out of the battle zone."

"I prefer to remain here," Katsuko said. The idea of running away, of leaving this place untended, repelled her. She, too, had her obligation, her *oya on*.

"If that is your decision," Kantaro said.

"The battle is lost, then?"

"We can't stop them, Katsu-chan. We can only make them pay." The more fanatical officers spoke of "making the barbarians swim through a river of their own blood." Would that make them grant honorable terms? Kantaro wondered. Or would it goad them to the killing rage he saw unleashed on Saipan? The horrid memories of that island were fresh in his mind: men broiled alive by flamethrowers and napalm bombs, soldiers mashed into bloody piles of offal by the Marines' incomparably superior fire power. Would men who did such things give terms to men who put explosive charges on children and sent them into battle against tanks?

He looked at his beloved sister in the darkness and savagely suppressed his terrible sense of loss. "I must go now, Katsu-chan," he said.

She returned with him to the villa, waiting while he changed clothes. On the rack in the central room he had placed his sword, the long-bladed *katana* made by Saotome in the sixteenth century, together with its short companion *wakizashi*, reuniting the *daisho*, the matched pair, for the first time since he had departed for overseas service. The swords were plain, severe, and very beautiful.

Kantaro appeared dressed in uniform, and Katsuko handed him the long sword, holding it with reverence. The Maedas had owned many fine weapons, but this *daisho* had been given to Kantaro by his father, the general, personally.

He accepted the sword from Katsuko and secured it at his side. Then, departing from tradition, he took the companion blade from the lacquered stand and put it silently into Katsuko's hands. "You may be the last of the Maedas," he said sternly. "Bear this with honor."

Katsuko, kneeling on the tatami, bowed until her forehead touched the floor. She remained in that position until her brother strode from the room and out into the courtyard, where his troop of soldiers waited.

Presently, Katsuko heard the two trucks in which they had come start down the mountain road toward the sea. Only then did she straighten her back to kneel in the silent room, the short sword in its black lacquered scabbard across her knees.

Y-day
1 March 1946

It is most probable that the main [enemy] attack will be directed against the Kujukuri Beach sector, with secondary attacks being carried out in the Sagami Bay and Kashima Sea areas.

> Homeland Operations Record, Vol. II
> Imperial General Staff Headquarters, Tokyo

During approach and landing, our assault waves will be opposed by the fire of such coastal guns and beach groups as have escaped destruction during our preliminary bombardment, and by long-range fire from artillery and mortars emplaced behind the beach defense zone. The effectiveness of this fire will depend on the extent to which the enemy's fire plans have been disrupted; however, it is probable that some groups, particularly those in the rear part of the beach defense zone, will survive our bombardment and will continue to offer isolated resistance as our troops advance inland. These groups will be well dug in and will act principally by fire. In general, counterattacks during the early phases will probably be limited to occasional small-scale "banzai" charges, principally at night.

> Staff Study Operations: "Coronet"
> General Headquarters
> U.S. Army Forces in the Pacific

0200 Hours

The men of the Ranger platoon commanded by Harry Seaver had experienced the skirmish with the suicide boats from Mikura only as a series of alarms and harshly delivered naval orders to *Portola*'s crew on the public-address system. At the beginning of the engagement, the distant sound of gunfire had penetrated the troop compartment indistinctly, and they imagined they felt some changes of course as the ship maneuvered—though they were unsure of this.

Jim Tanaka had hurried down to the compartment when the Japanese spotter plane had first sent a tremor of alarm through *Portola*'s squadron, and shortly thereafter he had heard the announcement that suicide boats were trying to engage some of the destroyers of the inshore screen. Since that time there had been no information, and now he lay in a bunk at the far end of the hold housing the platoon's men and equipment.

He was there, rather than in the quarters assigned him by the Navy, because Seaver was insistent that the men never be separated from their officers while guns were firing.

Second Lieutenant James Monroe Tanaka was a stockily built, athletic young man. At five ten he was taller than most Japanese—an anatomical anomaly that gave him great satisfaction. Born in Mountain View, California, and educated there, he had been a star performer on the high-school track team and a blocking halfback on the Santa Clara Valley Athletic League championship football team of 1940. In an area where racial prejudice was far from unknown, he had been a popular student—until December 1941.

The land around Mountain View was largely agricultural: the acres between the Bayshore Highway and the foothills of the Coast Range mostly devoted to orchards of apricot and plum, those between the highway and the shore of San Francisco Bay planted in produce and flowers. The bayside farms, over time, had almost all come into the hands of Japanese immigrants.

Tanaka's father, Isoroku, had gone to the United States from northern Honshu shortly after the end of the Great War, as it was then called. Prohibited from ownership of land by California's Alien Exclusion Act, and denied, by his race, even the privilege of seeking United States citizenship, Isoroku Tanaka nevertheless intended to make a success of his life in America. This he proceeded to do.

In Japan, he often told his son, a man was what he was born and he remained in his place. In America, there was a miraculous possibility of change.

He was a small man, scarcely more than five feet tall, with bowed legs and myopic eyes that, in later life, were hidden behind thick, never-quite-clean spectacles. He was almost a caricature of the "Jap" that had, after Pearl Harbor, become a staple of American cartoon journalism.

Yet Isoroku was a fiery patriot, an apologist for America at all times and under any circumstances. And it was he who had formed Jim's character.

Isoroku had arrived in the United States from Tohoku with his belongings in a paper bag, speaking no English and friendless. He had seen few Occidentals in northern Honshu, but if the oversized, pale-skinned Californians intimidated him, he did not let it show. He was healthy, able-bodied, accustomed to both grinding poverty and long hours of backbreaking labor. He considered himself equipped to succeed in the new land.

Within a week of his arrival he was working as a laborer on a truck farm in the northern Santa Clara Valley. The farm was owned by an absentee landlord of Slavic extraction, no stranger to hard work himself. Within four years, Isoroku had learned as much English as he would ever learn and he was farming the fertile land as a tenant, making it pay more than it had ever done before. He had become fast friends with Stepan Grgich, the farm's owner, and was contriving with him a plan that would allow him to purchase the farm he had grown to love with the same ferocity of affection he bestowed upon the United States.

What was needed first was a wife. Next, there must be children—Nisei, born in the United States and therefore citizens. The land could then be purchased in the names of these children and so belong to the Tanaka family forever.

Accordingly, Isoroku wrote to his aged parents. In due course the letter was delivered in the village where they still lived with Isoroku's younger siblings. It was taken to a scribe who could read the strange Romaji characters in which Isoroku's scribe had written it. The message was concise: Send me a wife.

Eight months after the arrival of Isoroku's letter in Japan, Miyako Akagi arrived in San Francisco. She was plain, smaller even than Isoroku, but strong and eager to please. The wedding, at which fewer Japanese than Caucasians appeared, was held at the home of Grgich. Nine months, almost to the day, after the wedding, James Monroe Tanaka was born. He was followed by three sisters and a brother.

By the autumn of 1941 Jim and his siblings owned a section— 160 acres—of the richest farmland in the Santa Clara Valley, and Jim was ready to enroll at the agricultural college of the University of California at Davis.

Pearl Harbor shattered the Tanaka family's plans. By planting time in the spring of 1942, the Tanaka farm was in the hands of others, a family of white dirt farmers from the Midwest. The land had been sold at far below its value, together with the house and the greenhouses where Miyako and her daughters raised flowers for sale in the florist shops of San Francisco.

The Tanakas were taken, with thousands of their fellow Japanese, first to a temporary camp at Tanforan racetrack near South San Francisco, and then to a bleak new thousand-acre relocation camp at Tule Lake, California.

Many of the interned Japanese were citizens, but more were Issei—immigrants from Japan disqualified from the hope of citizenship and eventual redress. In the camp many became bitter. Some demanded repatriation to Japan, but not many. Mostly, the internees waited, stunned and fearful, for whatever might come.

Isoroku, by then in his sixties, remained an unregenerate American patriot. It did not matter, he said, that what was being done to American Japanese was wrong. What did matter was that Japan had dishonored herself by attacking America in a sneak strike against Hawaii. This was *haji*, an act both shameful and unworthy, and it was the duty of all American Japanese to disassociate themselves from the homeland and prove their loyalty to America "ten thousand times over."

His statements attracted the attention of the Kokuryu-kai, the pro-Japanese secret society in the camp, a violent group of young men who, for the most part, had been sent back to the homeland to be educated. On a night in late 1942, Isoroku was attacked and severely beaten by these young toughs. The thrashing cost him nearly two months in the hospital, but he remained undaunted.

When the U.S. Army came to the camp seeking volunteers for military service, Isoroku, as head of the family, offered the recruiters the services of his eldest son, James Monroe Tanaka. Jim, conditioned by a lifetime of his father's love for America, did not hesitate.

In Italy, with the 442nd Regimental Combat Team, he won a Silver Star and a battlefield commission. In 1945, he was returned to the States and assigned to a course at the Military and Naval Language School at Monterey, California. There he worked hard, but fruitlessly, to lose the accent of northern Honshu that permeated his Japanese. He was also taught Japanese history, and, at neighboring Fort Ord, he was qualified as a Ranger.

From Ord, he was sent to Fort Benning, where the 11th Airborne's Ranger battalion was forming, and it was there he met Harry Seaver, whose Japanese was perfect. Tanaka, in his rare moments of envy—rare because he was not an ungenerous person—called him the "White Samurai."

Now, within a matter of hours, he would be wading ashore to the land of his ancestors in the company of a million (give or take a few thousand) apprehensive and angry men, none of whom was more willing to do violence to everything Japanese than Lieutenant James Monroe Tanaka.

Seaver made his way through the clutter in the troop compartment to Tanaka. As far as the Nisei was concerned, the jury was still out on the White Samurai. Seaver was unlike anyone he had ever known. In the 442nd, all had been Japanese-Americans. Few had visited Japan or wished to. But Seaver had been born there, and it had not taken long for Tanaka to learn that Seaver had a deep affection for Japan and the Japanese. True enough, he had fought for two bitter years in the islands of the Southwest Pacific, and he had killed often. But, Tanaka felt, he did not have the hard core of anger and hatred needed now.

Seaver didn't talk a great deal about his years in Japan—at least not to Tanaka. Tactical information, terrain, and the Japanese Army's fighting abilities were the sum total of Seaver's conversations. He was a good commander, Tanaka admitted, solicitous of his men and yet capable of driving them hard when he needed strict obedience. There was no question of his courage, either. He wore the same decorations Tanaka did, and he had won them the same way. But Tanaka sensed a softness in Seaver, a concern for the Japanese and what was going to become of them when the Americans and their allies began to overrun the home islands. Because there was no question at all in Tanaka's mind that that was the only possible outcome of this enormous, overpowering invasion of which he was a part.

While the fleet had been assembling in Buckner Bay, he had said to Seaver: "We are going to steamroller them, Harry. We are going to roll over them and bury them." And Seaver had only shrugged and turned away with an almost sad "I suppose we will." As though, Tanaka thought sourly, Coronet was aimed at the coast of California instead of the Kanto.

Seaver stopped at Tanaka's bunk and said, "Officers' call, Jim. In the battalion commander's quarters."

The two of them crossed the compartment to where Joe Buie, who looked like an olive-drab bear in his flotation gear, carried on a desultory game of poker with Angelo Tangelli. Gambling had reached a peak two days out of Okinawa; it had fallen off rapidly as the fleet closed on the invasion beaches. Most of the men were either writing V-mail letters or simply lying in their racks, smoking and staring at the overhead.

"Where's Hard-on, Joe?" Seaver asked his radioman.

"In the latrine, Lieutenant. Or the head—whatever they call the crapper on this bucket."

"Tell him we've gone up to Colonel Bolton's quarters for a briefing. And have him check everyone's personal gear. Then all of you try to get some sleep."

"Yeah, sure, Lieutenant," Buie said sourly.

"I know. But try," Seaver said. "Knock off the card game."

"Okay, Lieutenant," the radioman said. "I'm tapped out anyway."

Seaver and Tanaka left the compartment and climbed a ladder to the weather deck. The night air had turned cold, and the few stars shining through the breaks in the lowering overcast looked like diamonds on black velvet.

"I didn't expect it to be so goddamned cold," Tanaka, the Californian, said. "My old man always claimed it was warm in the Kanto."

"Your dad is from Tohoku," Seaver said. "There's five feet of snow up there right now. A Tohokujin wouldn't even wear a coat this far south."

They made their way along the cluttered deck between lashed-down boats and fieldpieces and amphibious tanks, to the ladder to the ship's island, where the senior officers were quartered. All around *Portola* there was darkness, but they could feel the presence of the other ships in the squadron. They could hear the soughing of the sea along the transport's steel flank, and from time to time there was a dull flash of deep light as the black water phosphoresced.

"I hate the ocean," Tanaka said with feeling.

"I thought all Californians were beachboys," Seaver said wryly.

"The beach is one thing. This—" Tanaka looked at the darkness that hid the fleet—"this is something else. It gives me the creeps."

"You won't have to put up with it much longer," Seaver said, leading the way into a red-lighted companionway.

Tanaka said, "What's it like, trying to land on a beach under fire?"

"No worse than fighting in those Italian mountains," Seaver said.

"Listen."

Over the grumbling sounds of the ship they heard another, more threatening, noise. It was faint, distant.

"Gunfire," Tanaka said. "Big stuff."

"The wind must have shifted. It's probably battleships working over the landing areas. Sound carries a long way at sea."

"I hope they know what they're doing."

"Yes," Seaver said noncommittally. He was thinking of the bamboo forests that in many places came down to the sea: the way the wind made patterns in the pale-green leaves and the sound of the stems clicking softly against one another. There was such a forest inland from Kujukuri Beach. He remembered walking through it with Kantaro and Katsuko.

In the companionway outside Bolton's quarters stood a crowd of officers from other companies of the Ranger Battalion. Captain Milton Grosser, their company commander, said, "How's your platoon, Seaver?"

"Sweating, Captain," Seaver said.

"Aren't we all," Grosser said heavily.

The Rangers filed into Lieutenant Colonel Bolton's quarters, filling the tiny compartment. Bolton had a map of the battalion's landing area taped to a bulkhead. He stood by it impatiently as the officers found space on the bunks, the chairs, and the deck.

The colonel was a leathery man of forty whose face looked like a bronzed skull, with sunken cheeks and large, feral-looking teeth. He wore his webbing harness over his jungle fatigues, a vicious British Commando knife suspended hilt down on one strap. Sam Bolton was famous for that knife; on at least two occasions Seaver knew about, he had put it to use.

Captain Rufus Kizer of Dog Company lit a cigarette. Bolton fixed him with a cold stare. Kizer snuffed the cigarette and slipped it into the breast pocket of his fatigues.

"All right," Bolton said. "Here it is." He turned to the map of Beach Sheridan and began swiftly to give the assembled Rangers an update on the latest Intelligence reports about Japanese dispositions.

"We've received word that the ground immediately behind the beach has been heavily fortified in the last two weeks. Log bunkers here, here, and here." He rapped the map to indicate the positions of the suspected major works of Matsuo Fortress. "Field guns have been brought up from Kyushu; eighteen of them have ended up in our area. Down here, near Mobara, the Japs have built some concrete blockhouses and redoubts to house three eight-inch naval guns they managed to fish out of the Inland Sea. They think we don't know they're there, but an F-5 got some low-angle pictures of them yesterday. They are your babies, Kizer."

"In addition to my other duties, Colonel?" Kizer asked wryly. It was a standing joke in the Ranger Battalion that Kizer drew all the unwanted tasks, from PX officer to morale officer. Such assignments were always made in orders reading, in traditional Army language, "in addition to his other duties."

A ripple of tense laughter swept the compartment. It was short and no one had his heart in it. The Japanese positions marked on the map taped to the bulkhead tended to wring the humor out of the battalion's situation.

For another fifteen minutes Bolton briefed his men on the most recent information. From time to time he would let Major Vanzetti, the battalion Intelligence officer, elaborate on what the Japs had done to strengthen the defenses.

Finally Bolton said, "You will be facing troops of the 52nd Army. You may have heard that the Japs are down to their skivvies and reduced to fighting with sticks. Don't you believe it. The 52nd Army includes the 3rd Imperial Guards Division. They've had years to get ready for today and they are going to try to beat our brains out. We aren't going to let them do that. We are going to kick the living shit out of them." He favored his officers with a death's-head smile. "After today, the fucking Marines are going to stop bragging about Tarawa and Iwo. They'll be busy on the left flank taking Lamour and Sims. But the real invasion of Japan takes place right here!" He rapped again on the crescent of Kujukuri Beach. "From here, the U.S. Army goes straight to Tokyo—with Rangers from this battalion leading the way."

Actually, as all the officers present knew, the Rangers would be in the lead only until the beaches were secure and the armored forces landed. It would be the tanks of the 1st Cavalry Division that would roll first into Tokyo. Despite his bombast, Bolton meant what he said, however, and if he could possibly arrange it, his Rangers (those still alive) would be riding the 1st Cav's tanks through the rubble of the Ginza when the spearheads crossed the Edo River into the Japanese capital.

"All right, then," Bolton said. "I'll see you on the beach. Captain Grosser?"

"Yo, Colonel."

"You and your recon platoon commander stay for a moment. The rest of you get back to the troops."

When the others had cleared out, Bolton said, "How well do you know the Boso Peninsula, Lieutenant?"

"Quite well, Colonel," Seaver said.

"I don't like leaving you a platoon short, Captain," Bolton said to Grosser, "but I'm afraid I'm going to have to do it. Your bad luck for having a resident Jap as a platoon leader."

Grosser was about to protest when Vanzetti cut him short. "This came down from General Krueger's staff, Captain."

Bolton said, "I'll give you Lescher's platoon from the reserve, Captain. Not the greatest solution, but it's the best I can do. G-2 has a chore for Lieutenant Seaver's outfit."

"Yes, sir," Grosser said reluctantly.

"That's all, Captain. You can rejoin your company now," Bolton said. "Lieutenant, come over here and take a look at the map."

Grosser left the compartment and closed the door behind him. It was unusual—and usually unwise—to make changes in a unit's order of battle this near to H-hour, and it left him feeling unhappy. But if he was going to lose a platoon to some special chore for the Army commander's staff, he was just as pleased to have it be Seaver's recons. The platoon was understrength, and had been ever since the last fire fights in southern Kyushu. It was lightly armed, for mobility—a mobility that Grosser suspected would serve no immediate purpose on Beach Sheridan. And it was commanded by two Japs—one white, one yellow. Grosser tried hard to suppress his racial prejudice (he had been on the receiving end of enough bigotry as a student at Rutgers to know it was irrational), but he could not. His elder brother had been killed at Pearl Harbor.

Of the two recon platoon officers, Seaver was the more mysterious to Grosser. For a white man to have been born and raised in Japan was exotic enough to cause deep uneasiness in the company commander. Seaver's record in battle was sound enough,

118

but in a really tight spot, on a Jap home island, how could you ever be sure what Seaver would do?

Then there was Tanaka. Grosser watched his bandy-legged, muscular figure as the Nisei went down the steel ladders to the troop compartment ahead of him. There was a man whose parents and friends were still sitting behind barbed wire in a relocation camp. What the hell is he doing here? More to the point, Grosser thought sourly, what is he doing in my company of Rangers? Who needed this kind of problem? No, the Old Man was doing the company a favor by replacing the recons with Lescher's reserve platoon.

Bolton unrolled a larger-scale map of the Boso Peninsula and taped it over the first. Seaver studied it carefully. It was a mosaic, made of aerial photographs pieced together. The landing beaches, North and South Sheridan, covering the entire sweep of Kujukuri, were marked in red. To the south of Kujukuri, west of Katsuura Point, lay the less open beaches designated North and South Hayworth, where General Eichelberger's Eighth Army would, in the course of two days, put ashore eight infantry divisions, led by the 93rd and the 96th. The tip of the peninsula was too mountainous for an amphibious assault and would have to be taken by soldiers of the 93rd from the landward side, supported by units of III Amphibious Corps, whose three Marine divisions were assigned the task of assaulting the western shores of the Boso Peninsula to secure the entrance to Tokyo Bay.

"The Marines will take and hold this sector across from the Yokosuka Naval Base, Lieutenant," Bolton said. "If they can break out to the northeast across the Koito River, they'll be in a position to turn the flank of the Jap 52nd Army—*our* Japs. MacArthur has told Krueger to leave the west side of the peninsula to the Marines, but the staff thinks the Marines don't have the punch they'll need to make it across the Koito. That's where we come in. Are you following me?"

"Not yet, Colonel," Seaver said.

"By Y + 1, we'll have five squadrons of Shermans ashore on South Sheridan. Krueger proposes to detach one of those squadrons and send it across the peninsula to support Shepherd's 6th Marines. They'll have the Japs pinned down here, at Kimitsu." He indicated a village on the Koito River a half-dozen miles from the strait separating Sagami and Tokyo bays. "That'll get the Marines across the Koito and give them a free run at the 52nd's flank. With luck, we can roll the bastards up in twenty-four hours. They'll never get a chance to get out of the peninsula and onto the Kanto Plain. See it now, Lieutenant?"

"Yes, sir," Seaver said. "What you want is a road across the peninsula from South Sheridan to Kimitsu."

"That's it, Lieutenant. Only, aerial recon says there aren't any roads suitable for Shermans. What do you say?"

"There's one, Colonel. Or there used to be. It depends on what the bombardment has done to it."

Vanzetti said, "Show me, Lieutenant."

Seaver studied the aerial mosaic carefully. It exposed very little of what lay on the ground in the folded terrain of the middle of the Boso Peninsula. The mountains were heavily forested, and the trees covered the topography too well.

"There was a road—nothing fancy, Major—that we used to use to get from Koito village across the mountains and down to Katsuura Point."

"We?"

"Family friends, Major. The Maedas. They owned a villa in the mountains just south of Katsuura."

"Does that villa show on the aerials?" Bolton asked.

"No, sir. But there is a shrine on this point. It is only about a sixteenth of a mile from the compound."

Bolton looked at Vanzetti and said, "We've got the right man."

"So it would appear, Colonel," the Intelligence officer said.

Bolton said, "This sector south and west of South Sheridan is supposed to be defended by the 52nd Army—some regulars and *yobeiki* conscripts, but mostly Volunteer Defense Forces. If your road has survived at all, it will probably be defended by that sort of troops."

"The road is very steep on the Pacific side, Colonel. It wouldn't take much to hold it against tanks. There's no room for maneuver and the tanks couldn't leave the road."

"I want that road, Lieutenant. I want your platoon to scout it. You'll establish OPs to keep it under observation until we can detach the tanks and enough infantry to make sure they get across to the west side of the peninsula."

"I see, Colonel," Seaver said slowly.

Vanzetti essayed a thin, cold smile. "It isn't exactly a coincidence, your outfit getting this job, Lieutenant Seaver."

"I didn't imagine it was, Major," Seaver said dryly.

"Any problems with it?"

"Plenty of problems, Major. But none that can't be handled."

"I don't mean tactical problems, Lieutenant."

Seaver reined his sudden flare of resentment and said in a flat voice, "I've been killing Japanese for two years, Major. Do you think I'm going to have trouble killing more?"

"You did say the owners of that villa were friends, Lieutenant. That could make a difference. I'm sorry, but the question has to be asked."

"And answered," Bolton said.

"I doubt there are any Maedas left at the villa, Colonel. Or anywhere else. The man I knew would have been in the thick of things from the beginning. If he has survived this long, it will be a surprise."

"And a pleasure?" the Intelligence officer pursued.

"There hasn't been much pleasure in this war for people like me, Major," Seaver said icily. "I doubt there will be any tomorrow or the next day."

"All right, that's good enough for me," Colonel Bolton said. "Your platoon will stay aboard *Portola* until H − 5. You'll be put on the beach just as soon as it looks as though we can begin to move inland. Get back to your men and tell them what you are going to do."

"Yes, sir," Seaver said.

"And Lieutenant—"

"Sir?"

Bolton's lupine face was grim. "We've all lost friends in this war. No one takes pleasure in that."

0330 Hours

In the troop compartment of USS *Sarasota*, the Marines of V Amphibious Corps lay sleepless in the dim light. They had heard the skirmish with the suicide boats quite clearly, and for several hours they had been wondering just how close to destruction their ship had been. No one had taken the time or the trouble to tell them. The fight had been over in ten minutes, or even less, and their ship had continued on its way. That was all they knew and, according to Gunnery Sergeant Peltzer, all they fucking well needed to know.

Sergeant Edward MacCauley lay sweating in his bunk, conscious of the pressing nearness of bodies as sweaty as his own. It wasn't all that warm in the troop compartment. In fact, a cold wind blew in from the ventilators. Under other conditions the men would be complaining bitterly about the lack of heat. But tonight—this morning, MacCauley amended his thought—the sweat was simply the physical prelude to what was coming. The human body had its own way of protesting the outrages forced upon it by the human mind. *Sarasota* was filled with brave men; yet MacCauley was certain that not a single man aboard was free of fear.

MacCauley looked up to see Lieutenant Scowcroft standing in the narrow aisle between the racks. His new green fatigues—the Corps had stopped issuing jungle camouflage now that operations had moved this far north—clean and neatly pressed, had obviously been tailored to his rather dumpy figure. On his webbing hung an enormous amount of lethal gear: trench knife, spare clips for his M-1, a canvas-holstered .45 automatic, and at least a half-dozen grenades. The Gunny never let anyone in Fox Company walk around on shipboard with grenades hanging from the rings. It was asking for trouble. And Peltzer ate second loots for breakfast. But MacCauley made no comment. New officers needed at least one dressing down from the bull-necked Peltzer before going into action. It taught them humility—and saved lives in the long run.

No one in Fox Company much liked Scowcroft. It wasn't difficult to understand why. He had a fat ass, a pink face, and a condescending manner. He had come into the Corps late, from an Ivy League college—Brown or Dartmouth; MacCauley didn't know which—and he moved with an air of mingled superiority and unknowing incompetence. He assumed that enlisted Marines were, without exception, working-class and ignorant. In fact, there were at least two dozen college degrees in Fox Company's enlisted ranks.

Scowcroft tried, MacCauley thought. One had to give him that. But his idea of fitting in was patronizing and a source of annoyance to everyone in the company. He had asked all the officers to call him C. J., which was what his friends, he said, had called him in college. Instead, Captain Freeman and all the other company officers called him Chauncey.

He had concluded, somewhere along the line, that as a member of a *corps d'élite*, it was his privilege, even his duty, to despise all other branches of the service. In casual conversation, this was a common-enough practice among Marines. But it was a privilege to be won in battle, and Chauncey Scowcroft had yet to hear that proverbial shot fired in anger. The Marines of Fox Company were irritated by his comments about the Navy, the Army, pilots in general, and civilians—whom he referred to as feather merchants. The raggedy-ass Marines of Fox Company considered their newest replacement officer hardly more than a feather merchant himself.

MacCauley, in his more tolerant moments, realized that basically there was little wrong with Lieutenant Chauncey J. Scowcroft that a week in combat would not cure—if he lived. Experience in war had taught him that men lived by different values in an environment where bad luck and mistakes were irretrievable. The laws of combat were Draconian, and no one, not even the most battlewise veteran, could ever be certain he knew all the rules.

Since enlisting in the Marine Corps, MacCauley had seen much death and pain. His education told him that it was a military truism, repeated down the ages, that casualties of 30% were all that any fighting unit could sustain before losing its willingness to fight. Military *élan*, so the students of war claimed, could not survive a more savage winnowing. Yet at Tarawa, the Marine Corps suffered 40% casualties and won. On Peleliu, an island MacCauley would never hear mentioned without shuddering, the 1st Marines lost 56% of the landing force and still took the island. And on Iwo-jima the 26th Marines lost 76% and hung on to win their battle, while on Okinawa the 29th lost 81%. Perhaps, MacCauley thought, there was something the students of war did not know about the United States Marine Corps. And it was that mystic something that had sustained Marines quite literally "from the shores of Tripoli" to this very moment, hours from the beaches of Honshu. If that was jingoistic, MacCauley thought, then thank God for jingoism—because neither he nor any of his fellow Marines would be able to face what was coming without it.

All Marines had a claim on history, but before one claimed bragging rights, one should have paid one's dues. Lieutenant Scowcroft was still very much a probationer, and it was a pity he was too insensitive to realize it.

MacCauley noted a thin sheen of dampness on the lieutenant's pink upper lip. In a spirit of sudden charity, he said, "I wouldn't carry grenades around that way on shipboard, Mr. Scowcroft."

"Oh, really, Sergeant? Care to tell me why?" Scowcroft's tone was clearly intended to suggest that MacCauley had committed an impropriety by addressing gratuitous advice to a superior.

MacCauley was already sorry he had spoken. He should have let the baby-faced bastard run headfirst into Peltzer's roaring contempt.

He was tempted to give Scowcroft a graphic description of what he had seen happen aboard the transport on the way to Ulithi after Peleliu. A battle-happy corporal had refused to be parted from his grenades, and one had caught on a projecting bit of gear in a troop compartment. It had pulled free of the ring and safety pin and rolled under a bunk. A four-second fuse didn't give men in a crowded troop bay much chance to get clear. No one had been killed, which was a miracle, because the bunk had been stuffed top to bottom with sea bags. But five men had been seriously wounded.

MacCauley's nerves were stretched too tight for patience. He reached up and, with a swift, smooth motion, pulled one of Scowcroft's grenades free, leaving the safety pin dangling from the ring on the officer's webbing.

The grenade was now live, the fuse prevented from igniting only by the lever held in MacCauley's closed fist. He displayed the lethal handful to Scowcroft.

"*That's* why, Mr. Scowcroft," he said.

The lieutenant's foolish face went white.

With his left hand, MacCauley disengaged the ring and safety pin from Scowcroft's webbing. He replaced the pin through the lever with care and opened his fist so that the grenade lay on his palm, inches from Scowcroft's nose.

"That one came out hard," MacCauley said quietly. "Some come out much more easily than that." He favored the plump officer with a mirthless smile. "Didn't they teach you that at Quantico? Sir?"

For a long while Scowcroft's watery blue eyes remained fixed on the grenade. Then he looked at MacCauley and said hoarsely, "You are on report, Sergeant."

"Yes," MacCauley said. "Sir."

Scowcroft turned and retreated through the narrow space between the racks.

"Mr. Scowcroft," MacCauley said.

The lieutenant stopped, turned. His face was still livid with residual anger and fright.

"Don't forget this," MacCauley said, and tossed the grenade.

Scowcroft caught it with both hands, gave MacCauley one more furious look, and hurried from the compartment.

MacCauley looked at the men staring at him from their bunks. "What's the matter?" he said. "Haven't you gyrenes ever seen a stupid lieutenant before?"

The men did not reply. MacCauley climbed back into his bunk and lay there, hands clasped behind his head, his face rigid from tension and disgust with himself. There had been no need at all for that display of petulance. It was inexcusable for a combat veteran to bait and belittle the man who would be leading him into combat within hours.

He closed his eyes to shut out the oppressive sight of the bunk above, ten inches from his taut, pale face.

0350 Hours

Sometime after midnight, the shelling from the sea had begun again in earnest, and Corporal Saigo Noguchi had taken shelter between the stripped trunks of two fallen pines. For the first hour he had simply huddled in the narrow space between the trees, cradling his throbbing head in his arms, screaming from time to time as his pain or his terror dictated. The entire stretch of ground that had been designated as Matsuo Fortress was now a churned waste of burning bamboo and pines in constant shuddering motion as the heavy naval artillery missiles struck again and again, changing the topography with each mammoth salvo.

The American ships had been reinforced with rocket-firing barges, and for hours there had been a fiery spider web of rocket trails across the lowering sky. The air was pungent with the acrid smell of explosives, and the ground heaved and rolled under Noguchi as though an earthquake were continuously shaking and shifting the earth.

His brain seemed to have been shocked and shaken into some lower level of activity. It functioned automatically, all semblance of reasonable human thought pounded out of it by his injury and the constant concussion of exploding shells.

The patch of demolished terrain in which he cowered was no more than 200 meters from the gray-white sand of Kujukuri-hama, where other soldiers huddled in sea-wet pits reinforced by logs, their weapons overturned and buried by the bombardment from the great ships prowling offshore.

As each of the shells passed overhead, it seemed to tear the very fabric of the air, and Noguchi could feel the changing pressure in his ears, from which a thin trickle of blood had begun to flow. He was only partially conscious of how long he had alternately wandered and crouched in this ruined wilderness lighted by flickering hellfire. He had begun his aimless movement as a soldier with some specific purpose in mind, though he no longer remembered what that purpose might be. He wondered why a pair of binoculars with one shattered lens hung around his neck, what had become of his rifle, why his head ached and throbbed so. Enough coherence remained to him to remember that it was the damned Americans out there in their huge battleships who were shelling this piece of ground, and he knew, with his gut rather than with his mind, that soon enemy soldiers would be wading ashore. He clung desperately to the idea that he must kill these invaders, though in his wandering he had apparently lost the implements the task required.

The continuous thunder of explosions moved inland, and the wounded heaving of the ground under Noguchi lessened. This tiny respite was enough to bring him staggering to his feet again to continue his wandering.

He looked at the sky, trying to guess what time it might be, but there was no hint of dawn, nothing but the occasional stream of fireballs wobbling in from the sea.

He started to run, the binoculars thumping against his chest. Fuchida! That was it. *Chui-san* Fuchida had entrusted the glasses to him and he had allowed them to be damaged. For a moment he surrendered to a sharp thrill of shame. Then he recalled that Lieutenant Fuchida was dead, undoubtedly killed at the company command post by a shell from one of the American battleships.

His own men, who had been entrusted to him by the Imperial Army—and so, by the Emperor himself—were also dead. He had allowed them to be killed. The sense of his own failure as a soldier was so strong that tears leaked from his eyes and streaked his grimy face.

He stumbled down almost to the high-tide mark, where the bamboo forest once had given way to sea grasses, but where now there was nothing but a stinking, smoking jumble of earth and sand. In the flickering illumination from fires inland, where the bombardment had set alight the splintered trees and bamboo fronds, he could see the beach, glowing palely. It stretched away to seeming infinity in both directions, and it was littered with the wreckage of laboriously built tank traps and obstacles. Chevaux-de-frise fashioned from desperately needed steel rails had been twisted into metal curlicues. And yet the sea laved the strand as it had always done, small waves breaking and washing in out of the vast darkness of the sea, froth tinged with gold from the fires breaking against the shattered remnants of the beach obstacles, washing around them uncaring.

He walked stiffly down to where the sand was wet and firmer. There were great shell craters at the water's edge, but the waves filled them, rolled over them, smoothing the torn edges, making them glisten in the dim light.

Noguchi realized that the beaches must have been heavily mined, and yet he continued to walk along the water's edge, as though the sea that washed around his feet and ankles would somehow protect him. From time to time he encountered an unexploded mine, uprooted by the bombardment but miraculously intact. These he stepped over, convinced of his invulnerability. But his lack of fear did not lessen the wrenching sorrow he felt as he thought about Fuchida and Koriyama and Iwaka. The knowledge that they were dead made him feel as though he were walking, totally alone, on the surface of some terrible unknown planet.

On the edge of the high-tide mark a half-kilometer from Noguchi, the survivors of a heavy-machine-gun crew were pulling themselves out of the sand. Two of the men had been buried beyond rescue, but the surviving pair, miraculously unwounded despite the bombardment that had repeatedly rolled over their position, labored in silence to pull their Model 92 free of the sand that had almost filled their foxhole.

The senior soldier, a private, raised his head long enough to risk a quick glance to the northeast, where Kujukuri-hama stretched away into the darkness. By the light of an exploding shell, he saw what plainly was a single man walking toward their position. "Hurry, *hurry!*" he breathed hoarsely. "The Americans—they are here!"

Lieutenant Lloyd Hansen shuffled through the darkness, stumbling on unseen obstacles in the roadside ditch he had chosen as a path. He did not have a clue as to where he was or where he might be going. It was even possible, he realized, that he was traveling in a circle. He could not have imagined that finding his way inland would be such a problem.

All around him the horizon was lighted by the reflected brilliance of explosions and fires, but he seemed to be moving in an island of darkness, a flat plain of rice paddies and burned-out houses, gravel-surfaced roads and stinking, sewage-filled irrigation ditches.

He was staggering with fatigue: he had been walking for hours. And while it was true that he had decided he would surrender himself to the first Japanese officer he encountered, each time an opportunity seemed about to present itself, he panicked and threw himself down, hiding until the danger of discovery passed.

He had seen a number of detachments of troops moving on the roads, some in blacked-out trucks, others on bicycles or on foot. On one occasion, as he lay hidden in a collapsed culvert, a battery of field guns drawn by horses had clattered over his head. He found it hard to believe that the Japanese still used horse-drawn artillery, but there they had been, cannons and limbers and six-horse teams, looking like phantoms from World War I.

Sometime around midnight he had crossed the ruins of a railroad line that his map indicated ran between Yachimata and a village called Sakura. The only indication of what had once been on the raised roadbed was a tangle of rails that had been uprooted and twisted into a cat's cradle of curled steel by the bombs of the fighter-bombers. The incredible destruction made it difficult to use the rail line as a landmark, but it had served to show Hansen how far he had come since parachuting into the darkness the previous evening. The discovery had not been good. He had managed to put only a few miles between the paddy where his boots and parachute lay in the mud and where he now found himself.

He was getting hungry, too. He seldom managed to eat well before a mission, and last night's flight had been no exception. Now he felt a grinding emptiness in his belly, and there was a sour bile-flavored taste in his mouth. He wondered if the Japs would feed him when he surrendered. *If* he could bring himself to surrender, he amended. Yet what else could he do? This wasn't Europe, where downed airmen could at least hope to find help from the underground resistance. Suddenly, the war in Europe—which he had hated with a terrified passion—seemed the most desirable of wars. He was sorry it was over. He was even sorrier that he had been dragooned into the Pacific war, which was a very different thing from what he had experienced flying over Nazi-occupied Europe. The enemy here was blank-faced, alien, dreadful.

He stopped walking and rested his hands on his knees, trying to catch his breath and ease the throbbing ache in his legs and back. Now it seemed that he had hurt himself dropping into that shit sink of a paddy. And his feet had worn through the strips of shirt he had wrapped around them. They were cold, scraped, probably raw under the coating of slime on them. He wondered what terrible assortment of germs and diseases was being driven into his flesh with each step on this wretched foreign ground.

He was, he estimated, now about twenty miles from the coast. That meant that he was out of the military zone of greatest Jap activity, but he was probably still surrounded by soldiers.

The flickering lights behind him indicated that the naval bombardment was intensifying, while the same threatening flashes reflecting on the overcast ahead of him meant that the Tokyo-Yokohama area was being bombed yet again by the B-29s.

The thought of the Superfortresses and their crews made Hansen shiver with frustrated envy. Hell, Eighth Air Force brass had as much as promised the B-17 crews that they would be retrained and re-equipped with B-29s before being sent against the Japs. Of course none of it had happened. Wasn't that just like the fucking Army, he thought. The crews from Europe had been shafted, just the way any dogface infantry would have been. Before the redeployment orders had come down from Eighth Air Force, there had been wild rumors of some sort of superbomb that was going to be used against the Japs, something that would blow them out of the war in weeks. And the rumor had it that it was the European veterans who were going to carry it in those brand-new Superfortresses waiting for them in the States. Yeah, sure, Hansen thought. What we got was a long flight around the anus of the world, cold Quonsets in Miyazaki, and the privilege of nursing the same old war-weary B-17s over Japan. And now, here he was, hunched over in a ditch on the Kanto Plain, smelling like a Jap turd and scared—yes, god damn it, he thought, scared shitless.

The sound of the distant shelling and bombing was a steady, echoless rumbling. The underside of the heavy clouds was like a screen illuminated by the flashes. For a time Hansen crouched, just watching them and thinking about the airplanes flying above the overcast, bombing by radar and turning to fly back to Kyushu or Iwo or Okinawa. He was almost moved to tears by his wish to be up there, away from this place, on the way back to safety and American voices, hot food and clean clothes.

The road he had been following ran straight between the rice paddies, and all but the most solid structures had apparently been strafed and burned into black ruins. Now, as he went on, the character of the ground was changing slightly. The road rose to run between a series of wooded mounds; Hansen supposed some might call them hills, but to his Wyoming-bred mind, these wrinkles in the ground hardly deserved the name.

Cover was more plentiful here, and as he walked he resolved again to surrender at the first suitable opportunity, though he was as uncertain as before about what sort of meeting with the Japs would be suitable. He was, after all, an invader in their country, and there were those terrible tales of prisoner mistreatment.

The night seemed endless. He looked at his watch, and the glowing hands told him that dawn could not be far away. He felt a deep ambivalence about the coming of daylight. He hated and feared the alien darkness, but he felt an equal dread of the coming of morning. Not only would it strip him of cover—and therefore of choice—but it would herald the beginning of Y-day, the first day of the assault on the Honshu beachheads. The Japs would go wild when that happened. He had it on the authority of people who had been involved in the Olympic landings on Kyushu. The Japs, the veterans said, had gone absolutely berserk when the American soldiers and Marines had poured into the landing areas around Kagoshima Bay. The issue had seriously been in doubt, despite an American numerical advantage of three to one and an edge in fire power that was almost impossible to calculate. The damned Japs had actually held the landing forces pinned down on the beaches for almost two full days, and an airborne company dropped at Yatsushiro, on the west coast of Kyushu, had been wiped out to a man by a screaming horde of civilians, for God's sake—old men and women, thousands of them, armed with farm implements and bamboo spears. At least that was what the Olympic participants had claimed. Maybe it was just a war story, Hansen thought, but how the hell could one be sure?

He came up out of the drainage ditch and studied the wooded hillock ahead and to the right. It looked surprisingly intact, a sparse grove of squat red pine with stands of the ubiquitous bamboo intermingled.

He was bone-weary and footsore and he had been frightened for so long, it seemed to him, that even the tightness of his chest and belly had come to feel like the natural state of things. How much longer, he wondered, could he just continue to wander about in the fire-shot darkness before he ran into a pack of civilians with their knives and sharpened sticks?

The noise of the bombs was muffled by distance, but it never stopped. It sounded as though giants were dropping great stones to earth from fifty miles up. But stones did not burn like that, he thought, his face reddened by the glow of the far-off dying city.

He began to climb the hill into the grove of pines. The air smelled fresher here. It was tainted by the smell of fire, of course, and by the stink of the paddy he carried with him, but there *was* just the faintest scent of pines, and it flooded him with memories of home, of the tall trees and high mountains of Wyoming. He was almost staggered by the surge of longing that struck him. Oh, God, how he wished he were there instead of here.

The ground in the grove was littered with sharp rocks, and they pierced his inept foot wrappings, making him wince with each weary step. It took him almost ten minutes to reach the thickest part of the grove, but there the soil and rocks were covered with a carpet of fallen pine needles. He sank down against the trunk of a largish tree and began to unwrap the tattered remnants of the shirt with which he had attempted to protect his feet. He didn't dare risk striking a light—not here on high ground. It could too easily be seen from below.

Massaging his aching feet blindly, he was conscious of the odd fact that even the pain this caused was mildly pleasurable. He stopped presently and rested his head against the rough bark of the tree and closed his eyes. He was so tired that his muscles twitched and jumped as he stretched out his legs and tried to find a comfortable position.

Ten minutes, he thought. Maybe fifteen. And then he would move again. He could not force himself to plan beyond that. He had been awake since six in the morning of the day before. He shivered with the cold and hugged himself to stop the chills.

Fifteen minutes, he thought. No more.

He opened his eyes to a gray-lighted dawn. There was movement around him, and his heart seemed to leap about in his chest. A circle of dark figures, silhouetted against the uncertain light, surrounded him.

He scrambled to his knees, reaching for the pistol in the pocket of his jacket in a panic. The encircling figures rushed forward; he felt the prodding of the sharpened bamboo spears they carried. He could not see their faces because the light was behind them. But he interpreted their menace accurately, and the feel of the sharpened spears pushing against his flight jacket was real enough. There was no hope that this was simply a nightmare.

He raised his hands slowly and clasped them on top of his head. He had seen dozens of newsreels in England of German soldiers doing that. Now it was his turn. The realization that his fate was now totally in the hands of others seemed to drain all emotion from him. He was experiencing what he had never expected to experience, what no soldier since the beginning of war is ever truly prepared to experience. Still on his knees, Lieutenant Lloyd Hansen surrendered and waited for he knew not what.

0400 Hours

The dugouts in which the pilots of the Takasaki Special Attack Squadron slept were damp, dark, and cold. The floor, of stamped earth, was three meters below the surface of the surrounding ground, and it was impossible for most of the dugouts' occupants to stand erect without striking their heads on the log-and-tamped-earth ceiling.

The pilots slept on the ground, those who slept at all. Some were fortunate enough to have been issued moldy *futon*s, but most made do with a single thin blanket, one of the thousands that had been captured from the Americans in the fall of the Philippines.

Naval Aviation Cadet Kendo Matsumoto lay shivering in the farthest reaches of Bunker Number One. He had not been able to sleep more than an hour since lights out. The cold and his growing anxiety had kept him staring sightlessly at the darkness and listening to the mutterings and night noises of his companions.

Today would be the day, Matsumoto knew. There was no doubt of it now. The American fleet had been sighted and reported by an Eastern Sea pilot at dusk yesterday. Ensign Yoshi Kashiwahara, the flight commander, had told the *tokko* pilots that there had been a great sea battle—a night engagement—and that many American ships had been destroyed by *shinyo*s from

Mikura-jima. "But," he had added, "the American invasion force is very large, and it is our turn next to attack and destroy them."

In the late hours of the night, all the chosen pilots had presented themselves at the squadron shrine to ask the help of the ancestors and the gods and to prepare for meeting old comrades at Yasukuni once duty was done.

Matsumoto had found the simple ceremonies moving, but unfortunately he had no close comrades waiting at Yasukuni, where the war dead assembled. Until four months ago, he had been a student at the prefectural secondary school in Oga, a tiny village on the coast of Akita Prefecture.

In ordinary times, a village boy like Kendo Matsumoto would never have been given the opportunity to become a naval aviator. But these were not ordinary times. In November, a chief petty officer of the Imperial Navy had appeared at the Oga school to tell of the marvelous life of a Navy flier. The people of Oga had welcomed him enthusiastically as an emissary from the wide world few of them had ever seen. Oga lay on the south coast of a peninsula that thrust itself out into the gray Sea of Japan near the northern tip of Honshu. From time to time the people of the village had seen American airplanes flying very high, and once a fishing boat from the village had actually seen warships cruising along the coast. There had been much discussion about the nationality of the warships: some claimed they were Russian; others, American. But the villagers had concluded that they were Japanese, ships of the Imperial Navy. What others would dare cruise so openly near the coast of the Eight Islands?

News of the destruction in the south and of the reverses that had preceded the attacks on Japan proper had filtered into Oga from time to time. But the people of the village did not travel; nor did strangers come often to Oga. The result was that the progress of the war was not a subject about which the Ogajin were well informed.

When the recruiter appeared, he was presented to the students as a representative of the Emperor—which, of course, he was. Kendo Matsumoto was one of the young men chosen to accompany him south to the training base, where he would become a naval aviator in the service of the Emperor. Kendo's parents and his other relatives were deeply honored. His three younger brothers and his schoolmates were envious. Only his sister, Ochacha—an unprepossessing girl with an unfortunate tendency to be outspoken—had expressed any doubts about the wisdom of the decision. Her only favorable comment had been: "Well, perhaps now there will be more for the rest of us here to eat."

Often, during his training, Kendo had thought about Ochacha. Though she had not actually said so, it had been plain from the outset that she believed he was making a mistake. She, of all the family, had traveled. For a short time in 1943, she had worked in a munitions factory at Sendai. But she had disliked the life and had returned to Oga at the first opportunity. It was Ochacha's quietly held opinion that Japan was not winning its war against the Americans, though even she was not so outspoken as to put such doubts into words. The people of Oga had never seen a Kempetai, but they knew that such officials existed and had great powers to punish the disrespectful.

From Oga, the petty officer had taken his charges—a number of youths from the northern villages—to Yokosuka and deposited them there for basic training.

It had been immediately apparent to all of them that training of any sort was by now impossible at the once great naval base. Matsumoto and the others had been shocked by the destruction around them. The naval facilities were a tangle of twisted steel and burned housing; the anchorage a graveyard of ruined and beached ships. And the *Bi-ni-ju-ku* raids were coming more often, and with increasing strength.

The Navy had quickly moved the trainees by boat across the Tsushima Strait to Pusan, in Korea. Neither Matsumoto nor any of his class of trainees would ever forget the short voyage. Their ship, sailing in convoy with two small gunboats, had been repeatedly attacked by American Navy fighters. The gunboats had been sunk, and their own ship had survived by a miracle, arriving in Pusan with twenty dead and forty wounded aboard.

From Pusan, the now diminished cadre had been taken by truck to an airfield at Andong, where a half-dozen battle-worn pilots had begun instructing them in Akatombo Red Dragonfly trainers. One of the cadre, a boy from Kanazawa who claimed to have been preparing for a university career, pointed out that the Red Dragonflies were actually Army trainers, and not naval aircraft at all. For his presumption he had been severely beaten by the petty officer in charge of their group.

The airplanes, which were as worn and tired as the flight instructors, killed an even half-dozen of the group before the first two weeks of training were complete.

But Matsumoto found that he could manage flying reasonably well. Though from time to time the airplane's behavior frightened him, he was among the first to solo.

On an evening in January, by which time he had accumulated almost eighteen hours of flying time, the training group commander assembled his young men and informed them that it had become necessary for all pilots to return at once to Japan. "Since no transport is available," he said, "we will return to the homeland in our own aircraft."

A murmur of mingled excitement and apprehension rippled through the assembled cadets.

"The distance between Andong and Hamada, where a landing ground has been prepared for us, is just under 400 kilometers. This is within the range of the Akatombo, but barely. The flight will require precise navigation."

The apprehension grew among the trainees. None had progressed beyond the bare rudiments of flight. Navigation had not been touched upon by any of the ground instructors.

The flight commander, a naval lieutenant and a survivor of the air battles over Okinawa, quieted the group with a stern gesture. "There is no need for concern. The air navigation will be done by the crew of a Mitsubishi G4M1, which will lead us safely to Hamada."

The flight was an experience that haunted Matsumoto's dreams. The move had been ordered for January 30, a heavily overcast and rainy day. The flight instructors, some of whom were to fly Type Zero fighters patched together from the wreckage of the frequently bombed Korean airfields, encouraged the trainees by saying that the bad weather would protect the flight from the Grummans of the American carriers, which were now roaming almost at will around the home islands.

The trainees, eighteen of them, in Akatombos, took off one by one from Andong because they were insufficiently trained to attempt formation takeoffs. The result was that four of the trainers entered the clouds and rain and were never seen again.

After too long a time spent trying to assemble something like a coherent formation, the four Zeros and the remaining Akatombos attempted to rendezvous with the Mitsubishi bomber assigned to lead them across the Tsushima Strait. The bomber never reached the assembly area over the Korean coast. It had been shot down by a Bearcat fighter from the American carrier *Lexington*, whose task group was doing picket duty north of Ceju-do Island.

The weather grew steadily worse as the trainers followed their instructors east. Heavy rain and a lowering overcast forced them down to wave-top level, and three Red Dragonflies went into the sea.

When, at last, the survivors picked up the coast of Japan, they discovered that they were too far south, over the Shimonoseki Strait between Honshu and Kyushu, one of the most strategic and heavily defended places in the home islands. Two more trainers and one of the flight instructors were shot down by Japanese antiaircraft fire.

The ragged formation scattered, and another trainee was lost, seen to go down in the murky waters of Suo Sound, east of Shimonoseki.

As darkness fell, the three remaining Zeros led a shaken and weary group of trainees down onto the hastily leveled field at Hamada. Of the original group of eighteen trainees and four flight instructors, eight cadets and three officers completed the flight from Korea.

The following morning, four American Mustangs appeared out of the still-heavy overcast, attacked the field, and destroyed a Zero and four Akatombos. In the strafing, twelve naval ratings of the ground contingent were killed.

Once again the group was ordered to move, this time to Takasaki, where camouflaged revetments had been prepared for the aircraft. On arrival there, the cadets were informed that they were now designated the Takasaki Special Attack Squadron and that their Akatombos would be modified to carry a single 250-kilogram armor-piercing bomb. It would be their honor and privilege to deliver their bombs onto the decks of the ships of the American invasion fleet when it attempted to land troops on the beaches of the Kanto.

That had been a month ago. Since that time, no member of the Takasaki Squadron had flown an hour. The airplanes had been modified, armed, and hidden. The pilots had spent their time in bunkers or under camouflage netting studying American ship models. Every day, sometimes several times each day, American fighters—Mustangs from Kyushu and Iwo-jima, Grummans from the prowling carriers—had swept low over the squadron. The men, pilots and service troops, had remained underground or under cover and had miraculously escaped notice.

But now was the time, Matsumoto told himself. Today he would fly, fight, and die.

Counting the nightmare crossing from Korea, he had twenty-three hours of flying time. Some of his classmates had more, most had less. He considered himself fortunate.

He heard Superior Seaman Yatabe, a burly sailor from Shikoku, beginning to make the rounds of the dugouts, waking the pilots. He forced himself to put aside the thin blanket and squat in the darkness. Today, he thought again, it will be today.

In a strange way, the happenstance that he must die on this particular day was almost mystically significant. He touched the belt of one thousand stitches around his narrow waist. His mother had roamed the village of Oga, politely asking the village women to contribute a stitch or two to the garment that would keep her eldest son safe. For a moment he simply closed his eyes and remembered his home: his mother, whom he loved deeply; his ancient, weathered father, to whom respect and honor were due; his younger brothers, who would in their turn serve the Emperor; and his plain, too-outspoken sister, Ochacha. Why was it, he wondered, that he felt certain it was she whom he would miss most when he entered the holy precinct of Yasukuni Shrine as a spirit? He fumbled under his belt and found the *hachimaki* Ochacha had given him to wear around his head.

Today, he thought yet again as Yatabe shone his pocket flash-light into the crowded bunker. Today.

It was surely an omen that this had turned out to be the chosen moment. Because this was the morning of his sixteenth birthday, a time to deny the fear in his belly and do his duty proudly. On this day of all days, the Emperor had chosen to honor Kendo Matsumoto.

Because excessively long concentration on the rotating raster of a radar tube produced fatigue, evidenced by a soporific glaze in the eye of the watcher, CIC had a "utility" radarman for the periodic relief of the regular operators. The Coronet Main Force had gone to General Quarters some five hours ago. Radarman Bertram Temko's relief had just approached him when the first images of the Honshu beaches began to appear on the row of cathode-ray tubes banked along one side of the compartment. Despite his long watch at the LRSR and the aching of his back, he was unwilling to leave the set now that the anchorages were in sight.

Actually, it was not strictly accurate to speak of "anchorages," since the bulk of the fleet would not immobilize itself off the beaches. The plan for Coronet specified that the bombardment now being carried on by the heavy warships farther offshore would continue until the last moment, and the ships of the in-shore screen would add their fire power as they made their first approach to the landing areas. Then *Alaska* and the other warships in her supporting group would take up a position in the center of the fleet, where she could control the landing operations. The other warships would steam north and south to guard the flanks of the assault against submarines, *shinyos*, and Kamikazes. Her task as command ship did not free *Alaska* from the duty, shared by all the warships in the fleet, of delivering fire on targets as requested by the troops ashore.

Temko and the other radar operators had a peculiarly clear picture of what was actually happening across the miles of open sea as the electronic images blazed and faded with each sweep of the radar antennas far above the *Alaska's* deck.

Temko had seen the attack by the suicide boats enacted in brilliant miniature on his screen, had watched in horror as *Ramsey* had vanished from the CRT. None of the *shinyos* had approached *Alaska*, so the short, sharp battle had no reality to the men in the CIC. But Temko's imagination had been stimulated enough so that he could envision the terrible, swift death of *Ramsey's* crew. He wondered if there had been any survivors, and whether they were still clinging to wreckage or floating in their life jackets far back along the track of the fleet. By now, he supposed, ships of the rear screen should be approaching the spot where *Ramsey* had disappeared. Lookouts would be searching the sea in the first light of dawn. It was not likely they would find anything, he thought with a shudder.

"All right, Temko. I'm relieving you." Radarman Third Class Peter Hergesheimer, a young New Yorker with an acne-riddled face, stood at Temko's shoulder, ready to slip into the operator's chair. Hergesheimer was known as Lucky Pierre, because he claimed to have screwed the daughter of one of the French officials at Nouméa. Not one of the radarmen and seamen in his watch believed the claim for a moment. They were convinced that no one below the rank of commander could even approach the Frenchwomen of Nouméa. In this they were almost correct. The women of Nouméa were available only to captains and above.

"Okay, okay," Temko said, fascinated by the smooth contours of the enemy coast, now less than fifteen miles away.

"What's the problem, sailor?" Lieutenant Potkonsky appeared out of the red battle-lighted dimness.

"I'm relieving Temko, Mr. Potkonsky," Hergesheimer said.

"Well, get on with it," the officer said.

Hergesheimer sucked his teeth in a gesture of secret insubordination as Potkonsky turned away.

Temko slid from the chair and stood by until Hergesheimer took over the controls of the LRSR.

"You shouldn't hang personal crap all over the fuckin' set," Hergesheimer said in a complaining voice.

Temko patted the sign he had pasted on the console weeks before and said, "It's my baby, Lucky. You just get to use it sometimes. My Eye-in-the-Sky. Are your hands clean? Did you shave the hair off your palms?" Before Hergesheimer could make a retort, Temko moved through the crowded compartment to the dogged hatch and waited for the Marine guard to open it. He stepped over the coaming and out into the companionway.

He was supposed to head immediately for his quarters in the crew area, but he had found a secret space on the weather deck, available from the series of ladders ahead, and it was his normal practice to sneak up there and get a breath of fresh air after his watch on the radar set.

He had never done this so near to action, but the thought of being in the open for a moment rather than in his rack below-decks was immensely appealing.

He hurried along the narrow steel passageway to the ladders and climbed up and away from the throb of the turbines and the constant whine of the ventilator fans.

Presently he stood below a small hatch that opened onto the foredeck forward of the number-one turret. He undogged the hatch and cracked it. A stream of chilly, salty air washed over his face. He opened the hatch a trifle more and stood on the ladder so that his head and shoulders were out in the open air.

The dawn was trying to break through the clouds. Here and

there he could see stars against a sky the color of slate. The sea around *Alaska* was gray as lead, oddly smooth in the uncertain light. The ship was moving swiftly but gently through long, low swells. Each time the bow dropped into a trough, there was a soft susurration of water rushing along *Alaska*'s steel flanks. Temko estimated the cruiser was closing the coast at some eighteen knots, well under her top speed.

He positioned himself higher, looking around for other ships. He could see none, though he knew from the radar images he had been watching that there were at least 1,000 vessels of all sizes within visual range of the cruiser.

Of the column *Alaska* was leading, there was no sign. The ships supporting her were all astern or still invisible in the dawn.

He looked again at the sky. The overcast was breaking up. He was sorry to see that. An overcast would make attacks by Kamikazes more difficult. But no, March 1, 1946, was going to be a clear day along the southeastern coast of Honshu.

Quite suddenly, the darkness to the right of the ship turned to an orange daylight. Great funnels of yellow fire materialized out of nowhere, and immediately Temko heard the booming crash of a salvo of naval guns. Somewhere out there in the dark a cruiser had opened fire.

He strained to pierce the gray-blue twilight in the direction of the coast. But the fleet was still too far away from the landing beaches for him to see anything but a suggestion of lights flickering against the underside of the clouds.

Another warship, farther still to starboard, opened fire, and Temko caught a glimpse of the first ship, silhouetted against the muzzle flash of the more distant one. The first ship to have fired was a *Brooklyn*-class light cruiser—most probably the *Nashville* or the *Savannah*, both of which had been steaming in the center of the van. The fact that the cruisers were firing told Temko that the fleet course had changed and that Coronet was now aimed directly at the Kanto beaches.

He realized that he should not be standing in an open hatchway with the ship still at General Quarters. If Potkonsky ever got wind of it, it would mean a captain's mast at the very least.

Temko's concern over possible disciplinary problems was all at once blotted out by the most unholy noise he had ever heard. The air around him was set ablaze with a terrible yellow light. A stink of cordite washed over him with a wave of heat and a spinning shower of tiny burning bits of silk. *Alaska* had just joined her sisters in troubling the enemy coast. Her six forward-mounted guns had fired a salvo directly over his head.

Slapping wildly at the shreds of burning powder bag that had showered him, Temko slammed shut the hatch and sat trying to recover his hearing. His face felt as though he had been in the sun too long. His ears rang. There were burned spots on his dungarees.

If it was this bad just under the muzzles of the guns, he thought shakily, my God, what was it like out there where the shells were landing?

The fifteen kilometers between Katsuura and Ohara on the east coast of Honshu consisted of a number of rocky spurs that spilled down out of the mountains that spanned the southernmost bulge of the Boso Peninsula and were the highest topographical features of the Kanto.

There had been an enormous amount of propaganda disseminated about the extensive fortification of the Kanto, but in actual fact it was only here, where the mountains met the sea and divided the vast sweep of Kujukuri Beach from the smaller and steeper strand southwest of Katsuura, that any genuine attempt at fortress building had been made.

It was not for lack of desire and concern that the high command had failed to do more. It was Japan's exhaustion that had made it impossible. Log bunkers and spider holes reinforced with tank obstacles and concertina wire were all that could be built in the inland sectors behind Kujukuri and the equally vulnerable beaches north of Choshi in the Kashima Sea area.

But between Katsuura and Ohara there had been an extensive building program: concrete emplacements, strongpoints, and bunkers connected by deep trenches or tunnels honeycombed the seaward-facing hillsides, and both field artillery and reclaimed naval ordnance had been sited to flank any attack from the sea on Kujukuri Beach. Caves had been blasted from the rocks to accommodate the guns, and the underground chambers had been garrisoned with the best troops available. These units of the 52nd Army had been stiffened with units of the 3rd Imperial Guards Division and with the few remaining companies of the Imperial Naval Landing Force. It was expected that these troops would launch a counterattack on the southern flank of the United States Sixth Army after that force established itself on Kujukuri, and before the Americans could begin to move inland.

Japanese Intelligence was by now almost nonexistent, and even elementary reconnaissance was near to impossible owing to the total command of the air by the invaders. It was assumed by the planners in Tokyo that other American units would attack around Sagami Bay, to the west of the Boso Peninsula, and this supposition was correct. But no Japanese military planner had yet quite grasped the size of Operation Coronet. Between Katsuura and the southernmost tip of the Boso Peninsula lay a series of small beaches. On these, the U.S. Eighth Army intended to land eight divisions of infantry. Within hours now, the fortifications built at such great cost in materials and effort between Katsuura and Ohara would lie between two American armies consisting of sixteen veteran divisions.

Colonel Kantaro Maeda was aware that he had lied to his sister. A less honorable man would temporize and tell himself that he had not actually lied—he had simply interpreted certain facts in the most congenial way.

To reassure her, he had said that the areas behind Kujukurihama were massively defended and fortified. It was true that two years earlier, when the works were planned, the defenses of Kujukuri would have been considered formidable. The earthworks and log bunkers, of which there were thousands, were the same kind of fortifications that had taken such a toll of American lives on Tarawa and Saipan. But time and war had taught the Americans that such defenses could not be reduced with a day's—or even two or three days'—bombardment from the sea. The so-called Matsuo Fortress Area had been saturated with shells and bombs for fourteen days. The earth-and-sand defenses were by now churned and pulverized into uselessness. Even the unnamed fortifications in which he and his men were now assembled—defenses that were the best Japan could construct—had been heavily damaged by the constant gunfire from the large warships cruising so insolently offshore.

The galleries were dark: the electrical generators had been smashed. Many of the tunnels had collapsed, and the batteries were filled with rubble from concrete roofs held in place only by the reinforcing rods imbedded in the cement slabs. The troops had been housed in the lowest levels, ten to fifteen meters below the surface strongpoints, and thus far casualties had been light. But many of the large guns salvaged from beached warships and transported from the south with such great effort lay thrown off their mountings and were damaged and useless.

Maeda walked carefully through the dark gallery, picking his way among fallen rocks and chunks of broken concrete. The seaward-facing wall was pierced at intervals with gunports, and a mixed bag of artillery pieces had been sited behind them, surrounded by sandbags. The crews slept by their guns, and a few of the men nibbled at scanty rations of rice mixed with millet that had originally been intended as fodder for the artillery horses. The animals themselves had been devoured long ago.

Maeda noticed that none of the men stood or saluted or in any way took notice of his passing. Unlike most of the young men of his social class and military rank, he felt no personal affront. The men were tired and hungry, and the continuous bombardment made rest difficult to come by. But it troubled him that an army so long noted for its ferocious discipline had become so lax that no effort at all was made to display the military courtesy his rank demanded.

The relatively short trip down from the villa had been interrupted several times by shelling from the sea. The gunners on the ships undoubtedly had reasonably accurate maps and photographs of the road across the mountains and, though it could be nothing but a secondary target of little military value, they had sent in a number of salvos during the early-morning hours.

He had been able to site a number of heavy machine guns and mortars on the steep hillsides overlooking the road. He hoped that the random, probing gunnery had not found any of his men. Though he would not admit it to himself, he had placed the guns and men on the mountain mainly to defend the approach to the family villa and Katsuko-chan. He had heard, and by now half believed, the stories of rape and murder of civilians reaching the homeland from Okinawa.

He moved on through the gallery to a ladder descending to the lowest level of the fort. He had been summoned to a meeting with General Shibata, who had arrived from Tokyo with his staff to make an inspection of the Katsuura-Ohara defenses.

From his own officers Maeda had heard that Shibata had arrived with a large party, including several Kyoto geishas. He found this hard to believe, though he was acquainted with the general and found him a difficult officer to respect.

On the lowest level of the fort, the rumbling of the American bombardment was muffled. The warships had been concentrating for the last three hours on the ridge line above the fortifications. The concussions from the fall and explosion of the heavy naval shells could be heard, and felt, like a distant earthquake.

Maeda looked at the luminous face of his wristwatch. In two hours it would begin to grow light outside. Through a half-collapsed gunport he could not yet see the dark surface of the ocean to the east. Below the lowest gallery and a half-kilometer to the north lay a series of road tunnels. He wondered if the American shelling had destroyed them. If it had, there would be no chance whatever for resupplying the defenders once the assault on the beaches began. Not, he told himself, that there was much chance of that in any case.

A number of troop concentrations had been ordered in the

beach areas, but it was questionable that the orders had been carried out. Assembling troops and armor under the sort of bombardment the Americans had been conducting for two weeks was almost impossible. The general war plan, known as Ketsugo Number 3, called for swift movement of the 36th and 52nd armies to the beachheads once the enemy began to land. Then all available units of the 12th Home Army, which had been sheltering in the eastern Kanto, were to be rushed into action. But how, precisely, he wondered, was this to be accomplished? For months nothing had been able to move by rail or by road without attracting a swarm of fighter-bombers from the south or from the roving carriers.

This thought triggered, as it always did, a typical foot soldier's resentment. Where were the Japanese air forces? How did it happen that the Americans could roam at will through the skies of the homeland? He had been told last week, at a meeting of senior officers, that there were 25,000 Army and Navy airplanes ready for *tokko* attacks on the Americans. Even if one cut the number in half, there should still have been enough air power left to make it possible to keep the defenders of the coastal works supplied at least. But neither Maeda nor any member of his battalion had seen a Japanese airplane for more than a month.

He suppressed a surging, angry feeling of despair. How had this happened? How had the thrilling victories of 1941 become the catastrophes of today? What must the Emperor be thinking of the soldiers, sailors, and airmen sworn to enthrone him at the apex of the Greater East Asia Co-Prosperity Sphere? And with a tiny echo of his unfortunately Westernized education, he wondered: What fool invented that cumbersome, pompous phrase?

He entered the narrow tunnel leading to the command bunker and was promptly stopped by a sentry with a bayonet fixed to his Arisaka rifle. Maeda was shocked to see that the man wore the uniform of the Kempetai and not the Guards. The implication that senior officers needed to be guarded against their own men by the loathed secret police stunned him. Surely that was General Shibata's doing and not an indication of the way Imperial

General Staff Headquarters regarded its defenders on the firing line.

"I am Colonel Maeda," he said harshly.

The Kempetai man studied him suspiciously, using a flashlight to check his face and badges. Maeda reined in his irritation. If the stupid policeman expected treachery, surely he should know that badges of rank could be easily obtained by any potential assassin. But he said nothing. He had learned that it did not pay to argue with the Kempetai.

The man straightened to a semblance of attention and said, "Please go on, *Taisa-dono*. The *chujo-dono* is expecting you."

Maeda noted that Shibata, whom he had last known as a major general, had been promoted to lieutenant general. Promotions were flowing out of Imperial General Staff Headquarters now. His own, from major to colonel, had been one of the first. What it implied was sobering. On Okinawa and Kyushu, casualties among officers had been high. Many senior men had been killed in last-man, last-bullet defenses, and others had committed seppuku. As the American thrusts began to touch the homeland, the Japanese armed forces had begun to react convulsively, like a sensitive organism responding to a violation of its innards.

He moved on down the gloomy damp corridor, his boots making a hard sound on the wet concrete. From ahead came noises he had not heard for many months: the minor notes of a samisen, the sound of women giggling and laughing. Then it was true, he thought. That *baka-mono* Shibata, that foolish man, had actually brought geishas into the fighting zone. Maeda understood that a man needed women, and that Shibata, who was known throughout the Army as a satyr, needed them more than most. But to bring geishas to this place from Kyoto—the one place in all Japan that was never, would never be, bombed—was the act of a madman.

He was met at the entrance to the command bunker by Captain Azumi, Shibata's aide-de-camp. He knew Azumi from their days at the Military Academy. Back then, he had thought Aiko Azumi a serious young man. He was not serious now. He was

152

giggling drunk. A sake party was under way inside the bunker. The place was lighted by candles. One of three kimono-clad geishas was playing the samisen while the other two circulated with sake bottles among the half-dozen officers seated on tatamis and cushions that had been spread about the rock-walled room. Maeda became aware again of the slight shuddering of the earth beneath his feet as a salvo walked heavily across the ridge line two kilometers from the fort.

As he entered the room, the geishas quite properly placed the sake bottles on the floor and bowed until their foreheads nearly touched the tatami. Maeda was racked by a sense of total unreality. The candlelight in a room cut deep into the rock, the situation maps on the walls that spelled out a hopeless military strategy, the silent radios and field telephones pushed into a corner, the Kyoto girls with their lacquered hair and white-powdered faces, and the giggling, drunken officers gathered around the fat figure of General Shibata, who had put aside his uniform tunic and wore a heavy black silk kimono embroidered with the bamboo-frond *mon* of his clan—all combined to compose a scene as unreal as any in a *bunraku* play. Maeda had the mad impression that there were black-clad puppeteers crouched, unseen, in the smoke-filled chamber.

His own regimental commander, Colonel Ogaki, a fierce gray man as lean as a lance with a fearsome war record in Manchuria, sat cross-legged on the mats, reeling drunk. When Maeda entered, he raised his cup and said thickly, "*Kampai*, a toast, Maeda-san! Come in and drink. The sake is warm and the company is good!" The other officers, all of them senior to Maeda, shouted greetings. For the first time, Maeda's doubts coalesced into a dull fear. The drinking party was an ancient tradition in the Japanese military, but these were the men to whom the Emperor had entrusted command of the best troops of the best remaining army in the homeland, and the battle was only hours away.

The fatigue of a night without sleep made his thoughts sluggish. He found that there was a terrible temptation to do as his seniors were doing. How easy it would be to settle down on the tatami and drink himself into insensibility. Once, on Saipan, he had done just that: on the night before battle he had gotten mindlessly drunk and he had still been drunk when he had drawn his sword and led a screaming charge against an entrenched unit of American Marines. For one wild moment that bright morning, his actions had seemed the apotheosis of the samurai code, an act of Bushido beyond compare. But when he had counted the dead after overrunning the mere twenty Marines, he had been sickened. One hundred and forty of his men lay dead or dying, another dozen screaming in pain from the burns inflicted by the enemy's flamethrower. He had vowed to himself then that he would never again give his men that kind of insane leadership. They deserved better than that. It was a soldier's duty to die, but it was an officer's duty to make his death count for something. For months after that fight on Saipan, he had dreamed that he was dead and that his comrades at Yasukuni Shrine refused to accept him because he had wasted his men in a fit of drunken bravado.

Shibata, his black eyes glittering in the candlelight, shouted, "Well, Maeda, will you drink with us?"

Maeda looked into the general's face and wanted to strike him. How had he dared come to this place and seduce men of lesser rank to this shameful neglect of their duty? How bad were things at Imperial General Staff Headquarters to permit a high commander to do a thing like this?

He said, "*Chujo-dono*, please forgive me, but I must see to my men."

Major Higashi, the headquarters company commander, protested. "One drink, Maeda. And then perhaps another. For the honor of the regiment." He looked at one of the geishas and roared with laughter.

Ogaki lurched to his feet and came to the door. He looked closely at Maeda, and the younger man realized that the regimental commander was not so drunk as he seemed.

In a low voice Ogaki said, "That fool Shibata appeared here

last night. He is talking about leading a charge against the Americans. He won't be able to walk in another half hour. I'll get you out of this. Go back to the troops."

Maeda came to attention, saluted, and bowed. Then he hurried from the command bunker, blocking his ears to the calls of protest and invitation that followed him along the cold, damp corridor.

0410 Hours

Major Richard Stanley Connel, commanding officer of the 337th Fighter Squadron of the 332nd Fighter Group, Fifth Air Force, sat in the cockpit of his Mustang and watched the control tower for the green flare that would send him and his squadron into the air.

Miyazaki Number Six airfield was ablaze with lights. No effort whatever was being made to keep a blackout. It would, Connel realized, have been absurd to try. The whole of eastern Kyushu had been converted into an enormous complex of airfields, so many of them that the pilots flying in and out of the area had been warned repeatedly to fly with their landing lights on, even in daylight, to lessen the possibility of collision.

The Army's field at Miyazaki, raw from the attentions of the construction battalion's bulldozers, was larger than many of the military fields on which Connel had trained in the States. It was now the operational base for no fewer than three full groups of B-17s redeployed from Europe. In addition to the bombers, four groups of C-46 and C-47 aircraft of the Troop Carrier Command had recently arrived from the CBI theater, and C-54s of the Air Transport Command arrived from and departed for Hawaii, Guam, Saipan, and the States on an hourly schedule. Around Miyazaki, the engineers had built a complete ring of auxiliary fields on which to base the fifteen fighter and fighter-bomber groups of the Fifth and Eighth air forces now present on Kyushu.

The 332nd FG did not have Miyazaki Number Six to itself. Far from it. The Mustang group shared the field with a Marine fighter group of Corsairs that had been bumped off its carrier by the arrival in the theater of a new group of Navy Bearcats fresh from the West Coast of the United States.

The pilots of the Army and the Marine Corps managed to share the base facilities with a minimum of physical conflict, but a lively rivalry had arisen between the two units over the number of kills made. At the moment, the Marines were ahead, owing to what Connel considered their extraordinary good fortune to have been based on Okinawa during the flurry of Kamikaze attacks on the ships carrying the Operation Olympic invasion force. The Army Mustangs had been stationed on Iwo at that time and had been limited to flying escort for the B-29s of the 20th and 21st bomber commands.

Connel himself had contributed heavily to his unit's record. There were seventeen Rising Sun flags painted on his P-51 and two more awaiting confirmation before being stenciled under the busty blonde girl painted on the aircraft's long nose.

Connel, a West Pointer and a natural flier, was on his second tour in the Pacific. It had taken some heavy wire-pulling to manage another eighteen months of combat. (The AAF was already beginning to husband its regulars, looking forward to the needs of a peacetime independent Air Force.) But Connel's father was a major general in the Pentagon who happened to have served with one Captain Harry Truman in World War I.

Major General Stanley Connel, who despite being a dedicated soldier was a rather gentle man, had been shocked by the changes in his son when the younger Connel, heavy with decorations, had returned from his first tour in the Pacific. Young Dick had always been what Army people called eager. But the Dick Connel who had returned from the war zone was considerably more than that. General Connel was a realist and he had always understood that the business of a soldier was killing. However, men killed in different ways: regretfully or hungrily. That was the basic difference between a soldier and a killer. Few soldiers, even professionals, were true killers.

Dick, the general discovered, was both. It had taken only one long late-night conversation between father and son in the dingy study of the general's quarters at Fort Myer to convince him of that. The next morning General Connel had approached General H. H. Arnold's chief of staff with a request for another overseas tour for Captain Richard Stanley Connel, USMA Class of 1941. No gift he had ever given his son had been so enthusiastically received as the AAF HQ Special Orders assigning him to Miyazaki.

Since assuming command of his new squadron, Major Connel seldom thought of his father. But he was remembering him now as he waited for the green flare that would send him hunting again.

The old man's way had always been oddly gentle with his only son. Connel remembered quite happily the succession of Army posts where he had spent his childhood and adolescence—cavalry posts, most of them, because that was the old man's branch of service. Even then there had been indications that young Dick was made of steelier stuff than most of his fellow Army brats. When he fought in schoolyard scuffles, he had always fought not only to win, but also to inflict injury on his opponents. He faced these childish encounters coldly, with a calculation of tactics far beyond his years.

At the Point he had excelled at the individual, rather than the team, sports, He had been an intercollegiate champion fencer. Short of stature, lean and almost fragile in body, he had avoided the contact sports, not for lack of desire, but because his physical limitations made it impossible for him to punish his opponents.

After being commissioned, he had been selected for pilot training and had been graduated from Randolph Field in the sixth class of 1942. By January of 1943 he had been in combat, flying P-38 Lightnings from Henderson Field in the Solomons. He had lost wingmen, but he had never lost an engagement with a Japanese pilot.

On the night he spent with his father at Fort Myer, he had told the old man of one single battle that had become an epiphany.

A flight leader at the time, he had surprised a full squadron of Mitsubishi bombers of the type code named Betty. It was apparent, he told his father, that the Jap pilots were inexperienced. The quality of the opposition had been declining steadily through the summer and fall of 1943, and he could tell by the sloppy formation of the Japanese squadron that the pilots were green.

On the first pass, the four Lightnings of Connel's flight had shot down three of the bombers. The remaining ten had scattered, four of them clinging desperately together and diving for the treetops of the jungle that covered most of that part of Bougainville.

Connel had ordered the second element of his flight to pursue the Mitsubishis that had attempted to fly out to sea, while he and his wingman followed the four Japs who were maintaining a semblance of formation discipline.

On his initial attack, Connel blew the wing off one Betty, and it spun wildly into the trees, exploding on contact. No parachutes appeared. It had been a three-second burst from the four fifty-calibers and the single 20mm cannon in the nose of the Lightning that had disintegrated the Mitsubishi's wing. The kill had left Connel excited, but unsatisfied. It had been too simple, he told his father, too quick.

Flying just over the trees, he had closed in on a second bomber. The Jap pilot had gone into wild evasive maneuvers, but they proved useless. The Betty was no match for the Lightning. One quick, short burst into the fuselage had set it on fire, and it, too, plunged into the trees, to be marked by a column of oily smoke.

The two surviving Japs, frantic now, had attempted to climb away from the pursuing fighters. The fuselage gunner on the trailing bomber had actually managed to get his weapon into action and score a lucky hit on the coolant radiator of his wingman's left engine. Connel watched him feather the propeller and swing away from the enemy airplanes. "I told him to bug out and head back to Henderson," he told his father that night in Virginia. "I don't know why I did that. He could have hung around on one engine and at least confirmed my kills; the rest of the flight was twenty miles out to sea by then. But I suddenly just wanted those two Japs all to myself. I can't explain it. I just did."

His father had sat quietly in the semidarkness of the rainy evening, with the shadows of his empty house around him, and Connel had wondered if he really dare tell him what he had discovered about himself that day in the sky over the Solomons. They had finished a fifth of bourbon between them. Drink had always been one of the old man's antidotes for the loneliness that had descended on him when Dick's gentle Southern mother died one bleak winter amid the barrens of Fort Hood.

"I followed them," he said. "They didn't separate, but they didn't support one another, either. It was as though no one aboard knew quite what should be done." He had shot down first one, he said, and then the other, calmly, at close range. And when the last Jap crew managed to jump from the disintegrating Betty, he had circled and used the last of his ammunition to kill them as they hung in their parachutes. He remembered with delicious clarity the way the last of them had struggled, his arms and legs working wildly, like the limbs of a spider impaled on a pin. The Jap, bulky in his quilted-cotton flying suit, had shredded away as the heavy fifty-caliber bullets struck him. For Connel, it had been an act of love. He had felt it in his loins. He had balked at telling the old man that, but somehow he had known. His eyes had grown teary and he had stumbled off to his cold bed in that cold, empty house. Had he realized then, Connel wondered, that some men found no release in the company of women, or even in the love of other men, but only in those rare moments war could bestow? And that his only son was such a man? Perhaps, Connel thought. At any rate, the very next day Major General Connel had set in motion the process of presenting his son with the only genuine treasure still within his gift: an extension of his license to kill and another eighteen months of war.

"Skipper? Green flare, sir."

The voice of Lieutenant Donaldson, his newest wingman, came through the earphones in his helmet.

Connel came out of his reverie with a start. The flare fired from the tower was falling, an ember, to the earth. He advanced the throttle and let his airplane roll onto the steel-mesh runway. It troubled him that he had been woolgathering at so critical a time. That was unlike him.

He glanced over his shoulder at Donaldson. The lights that blazed everywhere on the field reflected from the shiny duralumin skin of the lieutenant's Mustang in streaked and shimmery patterns.

"Broadsword Squadron rolling," he said into his throat mike, and advanced the throttle until the glowing needle of the manifold pressure gauge showed fifty inches of boost, steadying there just under the red box labeled "War Emergency."

With a massive, whining roar of their Rolls-Royce engines, the sixteen airplanes of the 337th Fighter Squadron took to the air above the brilliantly lighted coastal plain of eastern Kyushu, turned to the northeast, and climbed into the predawn darkness over the Pacific. At precisely sunrise, they would rendezvous with the great air armada converging now in the sky over the beaches of Honshu.

Leading Seaman Albert Cummins, half-delirious with cold and shock, weak and numb from loss of blood, was a young man who should have been dead. He had floated in his life jacket for nine hours. The frigid sea should have killed him long ago. But he had a powerful grip on life that neither the dark ocean nor his wounds could loosen. He had drifted in and out of consciousness many times. He had no notion of the passage of time; his ordeal was without boundaries, and after the first four hours without reality.

With his mouth grotesquely enlarged by the wound inflicted by the Japanese *shinyo* sailor's blade, he would have drowned almost immediately in a breaking sea. But the surface had remained smooth ever since *Ramsey* had disappeared. He had been alternately lifted and lowered in a movement that made him believe he lay on the breast of some immense creature whose breathing was so deep, so enormous, that it filled all time and all space.

For the first hours he had listened to the passing ships, some so near that he could feel the vibration of their screws in the cold water, some so distant that the airborne sound of them was like the soft grumble of thunder over his native Yorkshire dales.

The cold had swiftly stopped the bleeding of his sliced face, but the same cold had tortured him as his breath sucked and gurgled through his ravaged mouth.

In the fifth hour he could no longer see clearly. The salt had crusted his eyelids and burned his eyes. The stars shining through the gaps in the black overcast had dimmed and vanished. He had felt himself shivering no longer, because the cold water robbed him of sensation. In that same hour his pain had become something quite apart from him: he felt it still, but distantly, the way one might feel the pain of a stranger with whom one had some empathy. His ability to feel anything through the normal channels of the body had dissolved as he floated on the surface of the blue-black sea. Now, in the ninth hour, he was at last, with great weariness, beginning to lose some of his grip on life. It was too much, he thought vaguely, too much to expect anyone to live on in this cold, dark limbo.

A searchlight's beam struck him like a bolt of silver lightning. The brilliance exploded in his head. His salt-burned eyes closed against the glare in a reflexive defense, but the light came through the thin, fleshy lids in a battering wave of pain. He made a wet, croaking sound, which came from his grossly deformed mouth like the cry of a brutalized animal. He heard voices, American voices shouting.

"There! Right there! Keep the light on him."

Feebly, he tried to turn his face from the agonizing light and in doing so immersed himself in the sea. The salt water stopped his throat and sent him into a spasm of choking.

One of the voices said, "Take it easy, Mac. Easy, for Chris-sake! *Easy!* We have you."

He felt hands on him, turning, lifting.

"She-it, look at his face."

"He's a Brit. He must be from the can that went down last night."

He felt the slightest stirring of petulant anger. He wanted to say, "She was *Ramsey* and she was a bloody bitch, the way you Yank bastards built her." But what he heard was only gobbling, throaty noises, no words at all, just idiot's sounds coming from a mouth that was all ripped flesh and exposed teeth and tongue. He screamed, and that sound was no different from the others he was making. No human made noises like that, he thought.

He was pulled into a boat and wrapped in blankets and he heard the boat's engine rumble. The movement made him retch and spew sea water and bitter bile. He felt it, slightly warmer than the sea, running horribly from the corner of his new mouth under his ear and down his neck into the blanket.

Someone wiped his eyes with fresh water. Suddenly he was consumed with thirst and he struggled to raise his hands, cupping them around his face so that he could drink, choking and gagging, but getting some of the fresh water down his raw throat.

"Go easy, sailor," someone said gently. "You're going to be okay now."

He made sounds in reply, holding his face together with his numb fingertips. When he opened his eyes, there were men near him, holding him. He could see a vast, shining cliff of glaring white. It loomed above him, miles into the sky. The lights shining on that vast vertical wall were like spear points in his eyes, but he forced them to stay open despite the pain.

The white cliff moved. It was marked in red, black. He threw his head back to see the top of it.

The cliff wasn't moving; it was the boat. And it wasn't a cliff at all, rising so insanely from the black sea depths. It was the enormous hull of a white-painted ship—a hospital ship. It blazed with lights. Lord, he thought, it must be visible for a hundred miles.

Huge red crosses marked the ship. In black letters twelve feet high was her name: *Solace.* Her upper works were brilliantly lighted, and from her bridge deck searchlights swept the sea around her. She had other boats in the water, looking for survivors from *Ramsey* and who knew how many other ships that might have been sunk during the long night.

They won't find any, Cummins thought. I'm the only one. He wanted to weep, but he could not. He could only stare with mingled hope and dread, at the enormous bulk of the USS *Solace*, exposed and vulnerable in the black night on the black sea.

He felt the corpsmen and sailors in the boat easing him into a wire stretcher and then he was rising, prevented from spinning by guidelines, along the sheer, snowy topsides of the hospital ship. From time to time he glimpsed other searchlights on the sea. Perhaps the support vessels were passing now: the supply ships and the transports carrying the rear-echelon troops needed to consolidate the beachheads and turn them, the way Yanks did, into ports through which they could pour the mountains of matériel they used so lavishly in war.

When his stretcher reached a port on the weather deck, he found a helmeted head before his eyes. He could make out no features, only the glint of spectacles. A deep, reassuring voice said, "You're going to be all right, son. You're safe now."

Behind the doctor Cummins was amazed to see a woman—a nurse in starched white, glints of gold at her collar, face framed by a stiff white cap. It seemed impossible.

He barely felt the bite of a hypodermic needle, but he knew what it was and suddenly he was near to panic. He did not want to sleep on this great bright island in the dark sea. When the Japs came again, did these people actually think that they wouldn't sink this arrogant, merciful white ship?

Before he could protest, he was being carried below, through companionways as bright as the weather deck, past white steel walls, down a short shaft, and into a large white compartment filled with narrow empty beds. As he was lifted and placed in one of them, the morphine took effect, and Seaman Albert Cummins, the first battle casualty of Operation Coronet to be brought aboard a U.S. Navy hospital ship, passed out.

Now there were lights in the sea. Corporal Saigo Noguchi, stumbling among the beach obstacles of Kujukuri, stopped and stared, wondered if he had really gone mad at last.

The long Pacific swell made a soft, sighing sound that could be heard in the short intervals between the rumblings of the shells falling inland. Each send of the sea presented a sloping face to the beach, and there, just under the surface, Noguchi could see tiny moving lights. At first he told himself that what he was seeing was the reflection of the stars of early morning. But the sky was not clear. The low clouds were breaking, it was true, as dawn approached, but what he saw in the water was not a reflection of the few pallid stars he could detect in the breaks in the clouds. There were lights, shining on their own, and they were moving.

The legends told of dragons in the sea round the Land of the Eight Islands, dragons commanded by Amaterasu Omikami. Noguchi felt his teeth chattering with mingled cold and fear. He wondered if he was in the presence of some mythic manifestation of evil. Had he become a witness to something no human being should see? His head ached and throbbed and he knew that he was not thinking clearly. No one believed in dragons now. Japan was part of a modern world—as terrible, perhaps, as any world of legend, but one without spirits and dragons.

What he was looking at, he told himself, was a thing caused by men, by the enemy. Frogmen were at work on the underwater obstacles, and what he was seeing was their tiny working lights as they swam beneath the surface of the gently sending sea.

Despite his conviction that the lights were the doing of the enemy, he was caught by their fairy beauty. Like fireflies in some deep night, they glowed and moved and winked, making halos on the water's surface. The halos were pale green, sea green tinged with silver.

A star shell, fired by some Japanese gun behind the beaches, burst high in the air above the water. By its harsh light Noguchi could see, far out, the glistening shapes of black rubber boats and, beyond them, the low, sleek shapes of several small warships. Immediately a storm of firing broke from the Japanese positions inland: fireballs wobbled overhead, tracers cut fiery streaks in the darkness. Shells began to fall among the enemy boats, raising plumes of water stained with the yellow color of explosives. The warships at sea returned the fire, and the horizon flickered with lightning, an angry, flashing dancing where the darkness had only just begun to give way to a thin line of daylight, the precursor of the day that was sweeping across the immense space of the Pacific toward the islands of Japan.

Inland, where the bombardment was falling, the Japanese guns faltered, and though they did not fall completely silent, the volume of their fire steadily diminished.

Meanwhile, the lights in the sea still moved in a graceful, mysterious dance among the underwater obstacles.

Noguchi walked unsteadily to the water's edge. The waves, uncaring and unaware of the man-made storm above them, lapped his feet. The sensation brought back memories of childhood, of wading in the tidal pools of Kitagi-shima, his native island in the Inland Sea. There was a shrine there, he remembered, a torii standing in the shallows, to which the fishermen could come to ask for good catches. At night they fished with fires in iron baskets on the prows of their boats. In the distance on warm summer nights those fires, too, cast dancing, sea-green circles on the water.

As he stood swaying with each wave that rushed around his calves, Noguchi became aware of something moving between himself and the fairy lights in the sea. A shape was rising out of the gentle surf, something black. As it rose, it was wreathed in sea foam, which outlined it against the deeper darkness of the water.

An enormous black man was coming out of the sea: stepping ponderously on great finned feet. Noguchi had never seen a man so large. The black skin wrinkled and shimmered in the faltering light of the falling star shell. The flat goggled eyes reflected the last of the glare as the terrible gaze turned on Noguchi. Just before the star shell fell into the water, he could see that the monstrous man carried a white square affixed to a thin metal rod. He dropped it at the water's edge and bent down to pull a long knife from a sheath affixed to one massive leg. Then the light was gone, and Noguchi could see only the advancing black shape. He stood paralyzed until he felt a hand close over his. It was immensely powerful, but it was a human hand and not that of some creature from the deep. He struck out and felt his knuckles hit the edge of the round metal-framed eyes. Then he took a frightful blow across the side of his head, and the pain of his already fractured bones exploded in agony. He felt himself falling to his knees. One of the great finned feet smashed across his jaw and sent him down into the shallow wash of a wave. The black man loomed, bent over him, the knife coming to life like a flame as another star shell—nearer, this time—burst almost overhead.

Five hundred meters from Noguchi and the man risen from the sea, Superior Private Hotaka charged his machine gun, aimed toward the sea, and pulled the trigger. His ammunition handler, a boy conscript more stricken than Hotaka himself, mishandled the belt-feed, and the weapon jammed after firing a five-round burst.

Noguchi, lying face upward in the water and waiting, paralyzed by the pain in his head, heard four rounds strike the rubber-suited man. The impact of the bullets made four distinct noises, like the sounds made by fists against flesh. He felt a spray of hot liquid across his face. It was blood, blown from the man's chest as the bullets burst from him. Without another sound, the man fell across Noguchi, a leaden weight from which blood pumped in hot, gushing spurts.

Noguchi screamed. The sea tried to stifle him, and he scrambled in terror to free himself from the rubber-suited corpse.

167

He managed it and pulled himself along on his hands and knees, away from the sea where the dead man rolled in the gentle surf.

Up the beach, Hotaka bloodied his knuckles in a futile attempt to clear the stoppage in his gun. He had made an almost miraculous shot, but there was still something moving on that strand where there should be no living thing. They were coming! They were here!

His companion, sensing Hotaka's terror and totally panicked by the stoppage of the gun, bolted, running away from the sea. Hotaka rose to his knees to shout at him and swiftly succumbed to the same panic. He abandoned the jammed machine gun and ran for the jumbled and shattered forest behind the beach. He had not gone fifty meters when he heard the sharp rap of an officer's pistol.

The officer in the spider hole was obeying orders: "No one shall retreat." The command has been delivered in writing, under the seal of the Imperial Chrysanthemum, to the units defending this section of Kujukuri-hama. As Superior Private Hotaka ran past his position, the young officer fired again.

Noguchi crouched on his knees in the wet sand, retching. Only thin bile dribbled from his mouth. His head pounded with waves of pain. Dark blood flowed again from one ear. His vision blurred with tears. He crawled along the beach, the half-blind binoculars that had belonged to Lieutenant Fuchida dragging through the sand.

His hand struck something hard, angular. He retained enough of his soldierly instinct to freeze, thinking that the object on which his hand rested could be a mine.

It was not. It was the white rectangle on a spike the frogman had carried ashore. Something was written on it, but he did not read English, so he abandoned it and crawled on.

The sign, now rolling slightly as each small wave washed over it, read:

WELCOME TO JAPAN 6TH ARMY

COURTESY 3765TH UD TEAM

0430 Hours

Lieutenant Commander Masao Kunamoto, commander of the I-class submarine *Anemone*, rested his arms and forehead on the damp metal of the periscope housing and longed for a cigarette. The boat was cruising, at a depth of thirty meters, 150 kilometers due east of the place where the *shinyos* of the Mikura-jima Special Surface Attack Force had been set adrift the previous evening. The second I-class boat, the *Sea Lotus*, had followed *Anemone* only twenty of those kilometers before turning north to lie in wait for the invasion fleet off the Kashima Sea beaches.

The shortage of submarines in the Imperial Navy had been critical for months. The Americans had improved their anti-submarine techniques to such a degree that a war patrol was now tantamount to suicide. The numbers were a closely guarded secret of the Imperial Navy, but Kunamoto believed that the once-formidable underwater fleet now consisted of fewer than five I-class boats and perhaps 100 two- and three-man midgets. For the last desperate weeks, under almost continuous air attack, the naval shipyards had devoted themselves to the exclusive production of *kaitens*, human-guided torpedoes—a weapon Kunamoto regarded as useless to the point of futility.

Anemone's mission, after towing the boats of the Special Attack Force to sea, was to locate the American Fast Carrier Task Group that Imperial Naval Headquarters believed to be sailing well to the east of the main fleet.

Kunamoto, a disciplined and proficient officer who had, in the glorious early years of the war, accounted for nearly a half-million tons of Allied shipping, resented having been ordered so far to the east of the known track of the invasion fleet. It was plain to him that the war was lost and that he and his crew and his boat would not survive the battles of the next few days. He accepted this with some regret, since he was newly married and soon to become a father. But such were the fortunes of war, and one must meet one's fate with the proper Yamato spirit of Bushido. Still, he thought, it would have been pleasant to see his son one time before dying. It never occurred to him that Kimiko might bear a daughter.

He raised his eyes to the chronometer fixed to the bulkhead. Above him, on the surface of the sea, the first light of dawn would be breaking. It was time for a sweep with the periscope.

The narrow compartment under the conning tower was crowded with sweating, half-naked men. He had been ordered to travel submerged as much as possible, even through the hours of darkness (which was a measure of how valuable the last of the I-class boats had become). In consequence, the air in the boat was foul with the stink of men, stale food, and machinery. He longed for a breath of clean sea air.

Resting on the handles of the retracted number-one periscope, he delayed. The problem was airplanes, he thought bitterly. He remembered his days as a cadet at the Naval Academy. He had been sorely tempted to request aviation as a specialty. Many of his classmates had done so. In those days Japan had been a leader in naval aviation, far outstripping the Americans, even though they had invented the concept of sea-borne air power.

But Kunamoto had come from a family of naval traditionalists. And as much to please his father, a retired naval captain, as for any practical reason, he had applied for duty in submarines. Now all of the classmates who had chosen to become aviators were dead. Half of them had died in one furious immolation when the carriers *Kaga, Soryu, Akagi,* and *Hiryu* had been destroyed off Midway. The rest had died in ones and twos, blasted from the air by the hordes of Grummans that had begun to appear in 1943.

Lieutenant Nemuro, the executive officer, appeared at his elbow and cleared his throat politely. Nemuro had been recently promoted to lieutenant and was new to the boat. He did not know Kunamoto well, and so behaved with great formality and diffidence. A well-set-up young man, ten years Kunamoto's junior, he was not as well trained as Kunamoto would have liked, but training standards were not what they once were. If Nemuro were to live longer, he would eventually discover that Kunamoto was not the disciplinarian he appeared to be and that life in submarines was conducted with much less *urusai*, arrogance, than on surface ships. It was unlikely, however, that Nemuro would be granted the time to make that delightful discovery. Tragic, Kunamoto thought, but we can do no more than accept our karma.

"*Shirei-dono*," Nemuro said, bowing, "we have something on the hydrophones."

Kunamoto shed his weariness and looked more alert. "The carriers?"

"No, *Shirei-dono*. A single ship. Traveling at high speed."

"Bearing?"

"Seventy degrees relative. Range 6000 meters. Her course will bring her straight across our bows."

Kunamoto frowned. High-speed screws meant a warship. But a single ship, traveling alone? American warships seldom traveled alone these days. They had no need to.

"We'll have a look," he said. "Bring the boat to periscope depth."

"*Hai, Shirei-dono.*" Nemuro gave the necessary orders in a Naval Academy shout. The deck canted underfoot.

At a depth of twelve meters the boat leveled. *Anemone* was a taut, well-handled ship, and her performance always pleased Kunamoto.

"Up periscope," he said quietly.

As the scope rose he stooped to peer through the eyepiece.

When the head of the instrument broke the surface of the sea, he signaled a halt in its rise. "There. Hold steady."

Squatting to see comfortably, he moved the scope through a complete circle, sweeping the sea around the boat.

The surface was dark, but the eastern horizon was now sharply defined by the growing brightness of the coming dawn.

There were no ships in the immediate vicinity. He changed the angle and swept the sky. It was difficult to be certain, but there appeared to be no aircraft in sight.

"Where now?" he asked.

Nemuro queried the hydrophone operator and reported, "Bearing sixty-five degrees relative, *Shirei-dono*. She's closing the bearing fast. She must be doing twenty-five knots." His voice betrayed his excitement. This was his first patrol, and to encounter a single, fast-moving warship this way made him tremble with anticipation.

"I have her," Kunamoto said. He studied the distant ship carefully. "Not a sign of a zigzag," he murmured. "She is in haste to meet her destiny, perhaps. Get the recognition book."

Nemuro shoved his way through the crewmen, found the book in the rack over the attack table, and hurried back to the periscope with it.

Kunamoto rubbed his eyes and returned to the eyepiece. The oncoming ship was silhouetted sharply against the horizon. As she moved from the semidarkness in the south across *Anemone*'s intended track, her outlines became clearer against the brightening sky.

Nemuro was aware of the tension in the compartment. The crewmen at their stations were unnaturally silent, the sweat beading on their broad faces. He opened the book and said, "Destroyers, *Shirei-dono?*" Even in this tight situation he could not bring himself to abandon that formal manner of addressing a ship's commander.

Kunamoto, squatting at the eyepiece grunted, "Cruiser."

A sibilant murmur ran through the compartment. Nemuro

leafed through the book to the list of known American cruisers.

Kunamoto said, "Length approximately 180 meters. Main battery nine guns in three turrets. Two funnels. Small tripod mast forward of number-two funnel. I can't make out how she is painted. The light is behind her."

Nemuro, who had excelled at ship recognition at the Naval Academy, ran a finger down the list of ships. "Either *Portland* or *Bethlehem*, Kunamoto-san." His excitement finally broke through his disciplined formality.

Kunamoto slapped the periscope handles shut and stood. "Down periscope. Full ahead. Come left ten degrees. Hold present depth." His black eyes gleamed eagerly. He could not imagine what the cruiser's captain was playing at, sailing alone at high speed and failing to zigzag. Well, he would pay for it dearly.

He waited until the boat settled down on her new course and then ordered, "Up periscope. All the way." It would be taking a chance to let the head of the periscope rise even a meter above the surface, but he needed good observations. When the instrument was up, he swept a full circle again to make certain that the American cruiser was indeed alone. She was—and much nearer now. She was steaming at close to her maximum speed, and her course would take her directly across *Anemone*'s bow. It would be a textbook attack.

Ensign Kunisaki, the only other officer aboard the boat, and Petty Officer Hadachi were at the attack table. He focused the periscope on the cruiser, centering the reticle with easy precision. "Bearing," he said. "Mark."

"Forty-one degrees relative," Nemuro said. The attack table whirred and clattered as the information was fed to the machine.

"Range. Mark."

Nemuro read the setting from the etched scale on the periscope ring above his head. "Range 5200 meters," he said. The attack table whirred again.

Kunamoto straightened, removed his grimy naval cap, and

wiped his forehead. "Anything on the hydrophones?" he asked.

"Only the target, *Shirei-dono*," the hydrophone operator reported. "Nothing else."

"She really *is* alone," Nemuro said breathlessly.

Kunamoto favored him with a feral smile. He returned to the eyepiece for another look. "Bearing. Mark."

Nemuro consulted the scale below the range markers. "Forty degrees relative."

Kunisaki cranked the handles of the attack computer.

"Range. Mark."

"Range 5180 meters."

"Down 'scope." Kunamoto spoke into an intercom. "Torpedo room."

"Torpedo room, aye." The voice of Superior Petty Officer Hita came through the screened speaker.

"We will fire a spread of four fish. Set depth for twenty-five feet."

"Hai, Shirei-dono."

To Kunisaki at the attack table, Kunamoto said, "Make ready for final readings."

"Hai, Shirei-dono."

"Up periscope," Kunamoto ordered.

The instrument rose from its well in the deck. Kunamoto opened the focusing handles and pressed his eye against the rubber collar of the eyepiece.

The cruiser was much nearer now. He must take care not to underestimate her speed. Her captain must be in a furious rush to join the invasion fleet, he thought. Well, that was a worthy reason, but a foolish action. It was going to cost the unknown Yankee his ship. "Bearing. Mark."

"Bearing thirty-seven degrees relative."

"Range. Mark."

"Range 4900 meters." The range was closing fast as the two vessels converged.

"Ten-degree spread."

Nemuro passed the information on to Hita in the forward torpedo room.

"Angle on the bow ten degrees left."

Kunamoto heard the torpedo room acknowledge. He took one last look through the periscope. The cruiser was limned against a streak of golden light between the dark sky and the darker sea. In only moments now, the sun would be rising, touching the rim of darkness with a glorious burst of brilliance. The clouds, well broken now, were turning from gray-blue to pink, as though they had been delicately brushed by a master artist.

Kunamoto clamped the handles against the housing of the periscope and said, "Down periscope." Then: "Fire one. Fire two. Fire three. Fire four."

On the bridge of the American heavy cruiser USS *Bethlehem*, the officer of the deck, Ensign Donald Eyvanns, stepped in off the starboard bridge wing and noted the hour. It was almost time to awaken the captain and call the ship to General Quarters. As the light grew, so did the possibility of Kamikaze attacks.

Bethlehem had completed the run from San Francisco to Tinian in record time. At Tinian, she had delivered a number of mysterious cases to the Army. Now the cruiser was rushing northwest to join the fleet. The captain was determined that *Bethlehem*, despite her pacific name, would not end her war service as a messenger for the strange civilians who seemed to have gathered on Tinian. No; the captain intended that the ship should participate fully in the Big Show (the captain's own words) now taking place off the coast of Honshu.

Eyvanns, an aging regular promoted after years of service as a warrant officer, agreed absolutely with the captain's decision to rush to the sound of the guns.

He had spent the last ten years of his naval life in cruisers, and he loved *Bethlehem*. She was a fast, sea-kindly ship, swift and sensitive as a race horse. She was a happy ship and an efficient one. It troubled him that she was now traveling at high speed without escorts, though he understood the captain's urgent desire to join the war.

The Old Man had demanded—and received—permission to join the Main Force off Kashima, at his own speed. *Bethlehem* could do thirty-two knots, and the captain would have ordered it if such a speed would not have burned her fuel bunkers dry before reaching the fleet. He *had* ordered twenty-two knots, and that was what she had been doing through the night.

Bethlehem was fast for a ship laid down in 1932, but she became increasingly hot when closed up for maximum watertight integrity. Therefore, the captain had permitted her to be driven at her cruising speed with selected watertight doors and hatches open to make life more bearable for her hard-working crew. There were 700 men aboard *Bethlehem*.

No matter how hard she was being driven, Eyvanns thought, *I* would have ordered complete watertight integrity. That was what it said in the book. But perhaps, he told himself as he opened the door to the bridge, it was all right to bend regulations a little to get your ship into action against a fast-fading enemy.

Eyvanns entered the bridge and raised his hand to touch the intercom connecting the bridge with the captain's sea cabin.

His finger never touched the switch.

Two of *Anemone*'s torpedoes missed *Bethlehem*'s raked stem. They were never seen by any man on board.

The next two struck her together, twenty and thirty feet abaft the bow. The explosion unseated her forward turrets. It penetrated the armor belt that was intended to protect the magazine and the hoists that fed powder to the cruiser's guns. The magazine blew up in a cataclysmic flash that opened the entire forward hull to the sea.

With most of her bow ripped away by the blast, and propelled by 107,000 horsepower and the inertia of her 14,000 tons, the cruiser drove down into the placid sea. Great rams of water, as solid as steel beams, crashed through open hatchways and watertight doors. Men were crushed by the impact of the jets of water that skewered through half her length. Bulkheads collapsed as though made of paper. Pistons of sea water found her engineering spaces, exploding boilers and quenching live steam and oil fires in seconds.

With a roar of venting air and steam, *Bethlehem* quite literally drove herself into the depths. Her screws were still spinning at nearly full rpm as her stern lifted at a shallow angle. In little more than the 600 feet of her own length, her mass and speed carried her under.

The time that had elapsed between the instant the first torpedo struck and when the sea closed over her was exactly one minute and six seconds.

The men of *Anemone* broke into cheering when they heard the double explosion of the torpedo hits. Controlling his own elation, Lieutenant Commander Kunamoto silenced them and ordered the periscope raised.

When he put his eye to the instrument, he was momentarily dumbfounded. The sun had touched the eastern horizon, and he thought that the spears of light that were blinding the periscope were hiding his victim. But when he swung the sun filters into place and swept the sea, he found nothing but a boiling patch of bubbles and black oil, some debris, and a few rafts bursting out of the depths.

The ship he had killed, he realized with a thrill of sudden horror, was gone. The rising sun made a golden path on a vast and empty ocean.

0440 Hours

For Major Matsuru Immamura the journey down the coast from Sendai had been, and still was, a nightmare. Though the Americans had been shelling the coast north of Hitachi only intermittently, the passage of the convoy along the disintegrating coast had been difficult, dangerous, and frustrating.

The twenty trucks Immamura commanded were in bad repair, fuel was short, and the 200 men of the Special Chemical Attack Brigade were hungry, ill-clothed, and, despite all that the officers could do to raise morale, terrified of the cargo with which they shared the brigade's transport.

Though Immamura was not a professional soldier, he had realized soon after leaving the battered city of Sendai that to travel in daylight was to court disaster. American airplanes roamed freely over all of Honshu, shooting at anything that moved. A convoy of trucks, as Immamura discovered on the first day of the movement, drew Grummans like bees to honey.

General Kushiro, the newly appointed commander of the 11th Home Army, had given Immamura his orders personally. And he had made it plain that the plan was approved by Premier General Tojo, himself, and therefore by the Emperor.

It required such a weight of authority to convince Immamura that what he was engaged in was a legitimate act of war and not a war crime. Even so, his conviction rested on fragile reasoning and his doubts contributed a great deal to the general difficulties of bringing his command south from Sendai to the Kanto.

Immamura was a relatively young man for the position he had held before the war, that of professor of chemistry at Tokyo University. His training had, quite naturally, led him immediately upon induction into the Imperial Army to the Chemical Warfare Department, where he was assigned to the experimental laboratories at Shiogama, a small city near the headquarters of the Sendai Military District.

For three years he had remained at Shiogama, working mainly on defense against chemical and biological warfare. He was aware that Japanese forces had used chemical weapons in China and Manchuria, and he was also aware that the use of such weapons was specifically prohibited by the Geneva Convention and a number of other international agreements. But Japan had never signed any of these protocols and was therefore not bound by them. With his conscience protected by this reasoning, and isolated by great distances from the early battles of the war, he had tolerated military life and immersed himself in his work, which he had come to consider humanitarian, since his task was to develop defensive, rather than offensive, measures.

But as the war swept over Japan, it began to occur to Immamura that no weapon, no matter how horrible, was going to be held back from use in the defense of the home islands.

By the time Kyushu was in enemy hands, defensive research at Shiogama had come to a halt, and all the members of the laboratory staff were hard at work to produce the greatest possible quantity of the most effective chemical agent in the inventory.

The result was in the trucks Immamura had guided into the Kanto Plain: brown-banded canisters and mortar rounds of cyanogen chloride gas, a nerve and blood poison whose effects—which he had seen in laboratory animals—were both horrible and fatal.

Immamura had heard rumors that the new CC gas and other, even more repulsive, toxins had been tested in great secrecy on prisoners of war. He preferred not to believe this, though the stories persisted and gave him a number of sleepless nights.

His instructions had been clear and precise. The troops of the 11th Home Army could not be wasted on a futile defense of the northern Kanto, because the defense planners felt that the main thrust of the invasion would be directed at Tokyo proper. Yet the members of the Imperial General Staff were certain that the beaches of the Kashima Sea area would not be ignored by the Americans; they were too inviting to be passed up. Therefore, rather than mount an active defense north of Choshi, the 36th Army would be ordered to fight a retreating action there, interdicting the advance of the enemy inland, until they could be reinforced by such units of the 12th Home Army in the west as could be spared from the general battle for Tokyo and the southern Kanto Plain.

The 12th Home Army consisted largely of raw conscripts and civilians, untrained and poorly armed. Such troops were unlikely seriously to impede the Americans as they strove to close the ring around Tokyo from the north. So the men and chemical munitions of Immamura's Special Chemical Attack Brigade were to be sent into action. Imperial General Staff Headquarters believed that the Americans had such a horror of poison gas that a mere 200 men and 2,000 kilograms of cyanogen chloride might hold the Kashima Sea area against the six divisions of the United States Tenth Army.

Immamura, who had known a number of American academics before the war, very much doubted it. If the attack on Pearl Harbor had, in the words of Fleet Admiral Isoroku Yamamoto, "roused a sleeping giant," the use of chemical poisons was likely to enrage him to new excesses of savage fury.

The coast road between Taira and Hitachi had been, in its best days, a graded two-lane highway surfaced with gravel. The number of private automobiles in prewar Japan had been small, and industrial transport had been almost exclusively by Honshu's excellent system of railroads. But the heavy raids had, by early

1946, reduced the railroads to a twisted shambles, making it necessary to use the primitive road network. This, in turn, had attracted the attention of the American raiders, and each day hundreds of kilometers of road were made impassable by bombing from the air and shelling from the sea. Nightfall brought out the members of the Volunteer Defense Force to patch the bomb and shell craters. The darkness swarmed with ill-nourished villagers moving earth and rock to make the roads usable again.

Since the fall of Kyushu, the Americans' smaller warships based at Kagoshima maintained a regular patrol just off the eastern shores of Honshu, sending in a constant harassing fire intended to keep the repair crews from working. Casualties among the villagers were heavy, but their will never faltered. It was said along that coast that the roads were patched with equal parts of Japanese earth and Japanese blood.

It was along this coast road that Immamura now led his convoy of trucks loaded with chemical ordnance. When shelling began, he would order the trucks to be driven off the road and hidden, and the men to take cover underneath their vehicles. So far he had been lucky. Two men had been slightly wounded by shell splinters, but no trucks had been hit.

Ten kilometers south of Taira, Immamura's luck began to change.

Seated beside Superior Private Izuhara, the driver of the lead truck, Immamura had, since leaving the ruins of Taira, occupied himself with trying to get some useful information on the radio. The instrument was both bulky and balky, the batteries were low, and the set was intended for use in a fixed position. Moreover, neither Immamura nor any member of his command understood the proper tuning and use of the set. It had been put aboard the lead truck at Sendai, at the last minute, in the hope that it would function well enough to keep Immamura informed about the rapidly changing battle situation. It had not, though he experimented with it constantly. What he received through the crackling static and the interference caused by the unshielded spark plugs of the truck's engine was a jumble of broken, cryptic sounds and a few, very few, intelligible words. The single bit of coherent information the tired set had given him was a report that the invasion fleet had been sighted approaching the east coast of the Kanto. Even that alarming bit had been left unconfirmed, or if confirmation had been given, the news of it had been blocked out by the whinings, scratchings, and cracklings that emerged from the headset.

In disgust, Immamura threw down the earphones and looked out to sea. The road here ran near the high-tide mark, and it was possible to see the eastern horizon. The sky, he noted, had grown much lighter. The line between sky and sea was sharply defined. There were no beaches on this stretch of coast. The incoming tide made small, breaking waves on a jungle of rocks offshore. In the dawn twilight, the white froth looked ghostly and gray swirling about the dark, volcanic outcrops of rock.

The convoy had been driving without lights since leaving Taira, and progress had been painfully slow. Immamura felt shamed that he had not been able to keep the unit on schedule. There had been a thousand difficulties, of course, none of which had been properly foreseen by Kushiro's staff. But that did not absolve him from his responsibility. He and no other had been appointed commander of the Special Chemical Attack Brigade, and it was his duty to follow his orders to the letter. Driven to the realization that he was not, after all, a professional soldier, he often repeated to himself the most well-known words from the Emperor's Rescript for Soldiers and Sailors: "Be resolved that duty is heavier than a mountain, while death is lighter than a feather." Of death, so far, Immamura knew little. But that duty was indeed heavier than a mountain, he was beginning to understand.

"Izuhara," he said abruptly, "the lights. Turn them on."

Izuhara looked startled. "The lights, *Shosa-dono?*"

"Yes, the lights, the lights," Immamura said irritably. "Turn them on and speed up. We are far behind schedule."

"But Immamura-san," the officer protested, "it will be daylight soon. The Americans—"

Immamura cut him off angrily. It seemed to him that discipline was faltering in the Imperial Army. Or was it that Izuhara and all the other enlisted men recognized the fact that their commander was not really a soldier, but a bookworm, a college professor? In the circles in which Immamura moved before the war, his claim to the learned title *sensei* had carried far more weight than any military rank. But times had changed—and not for the better, he thought.

"Izuhara," he said firmly, "I order you to turn on the lights and increase speed. I wish to be in Takahagi before sunrise." In that small seaside village—or what was left of it—the trucks could be hidden and camouflaged until darkness made it reasonably safe to proceed south.

"*Hai, Shosa-dono,*" Izuhara said, and turned the headlights to bright. He put his foot down hard on the accelerator pedal and gripped the wheel tightly as the truck increased speed, jolting over the hastily repaired patches in the road. This convoy, he thought rebelliously, was a suicide mission. Not all Japanese wished to die so quickly. Who ever heard of a Kamikaze truck driver? Professional officers were always harsh and often brutal, he thought darkly, but at least they knew what they were doing. This schoolteacher will kill us all—and for nothing.

From 5,000 feet in the air the coastline of eastern Japan and the sea itself lay in total darkness. The light of dawn was spilling over the horizon and touching the high cirrus clouds in the stratosphere with delicate shades of mauve and pink, but the day always began in the heights, long before its light reached into the depths.

First Lieutenant George Showalter was an artist by profession, and these moments of transition between night and day always filled him with pleasure. Gently, he banked the twin-engined P-61 Black Widow to port and then to starboard so that he could look down into the pooled darkness below.

He was a night-fighter pilot by choice. He loved flying under the stars, in the moonlight, through the soft darkness of cloud with only the glowing green dials and the questing beam of the radar repeater for company in his narrow cockpit. The images of flight and those of night were pleasing; he had discovered them early, in basic training, when he first took a Vultee trainer into the air at night. When he was graduated from the twin-engine Advanced Flying Training School at Williams Field in Arizona, he had applied immediately for night-fighter school. He had never had cause to regret his choice. While others of his class were sent here and there to fly bombers and twin-engine fighters in flak-marred skies in daylight, he performed his wartime duties patrolling the night, alone except for his radar operator, untroubled by the harsher realities of war.

Showalter, a member of A Flight of the 1007th Night Fighter Squadron based on Iwo-jima, had never had to fire a shot at an enemy. Other members of his squadron had actually made kills (though not many, because the Japanese seldom flew at night any more), but Showalter had not. He pretended to be unhappy about this, even in conversation with Howie Teeple, his radar operator. In truth, he hoped to be able to finish his war without ever having been responsible for the death of a fellow human being.

Showalter and Teeple had left Iwo at 0200 hours with instructions to fly as far north as Morioka and then down the coast to Hitachi. Their duty was to detect and, if possible, intercept any Japanese airplanes that might be attempting the flight down from the north to the invasion beaches. Intelligence reported that there were more than 15,000 usable aircraft available for Kamikaze attacks in Japan. Many of these were supposed to be hidden in the north of Honshu.

Showalter's patrol had been uneventful. The appearance of a Black Widow in the night over the towns of Iwate Prefecture had not even drawn any antiaircraft fire. Teeple suggested that the Japs had somehow managed to ship all their artillery south to meet the invasion. And if there were secret fleets of potential Kamikazes in the north, no attempt had been made this night to move them to the Kanto.

The Black Widow, capable of flying in patrolling configuration for ten hours, was now heading for its base on Iwo. The course down on Showalter's plotting board showed a wide detour to the southeast at Hitachi, intended to keep the returning night fighter well clear of the Coronet fleet and its undoubtedly trigger-quick gunners.

Showalter squirmed in his seat to ease the numbness in his buttocks caused by hours of sitting on a hard parachute pack. His gloved fingers rested lightly on the control wheel, feeling the almost imperceptible turbulence caused by the rising air currents at the edge of the land and sea. The repeater scope in the center of his flight panel was dark, in the stand-by mode. From time to time Teeple activated the main scope, in his cockpit behind and slightly above Showalter's. When he did so, a reasonably accurate representation of the coastline below was painted fleetingly on the CRT. The P-61's radar was not intended for navigational use, but it performed that function well enough so that it was common practice for R/Os to check the pilot's navigation with it.

Teeple's gloved hand appeared at Showalter's shoulder holding a cup of hot, bitter black coffee with just a tang of brandy in it. Boozing while airborne was frowned upon, but a taste of liquor in the coffee was tacitly approved for the night-fighter crews, who flew long hours in cold darkness.

Showalter, married and, at twenty-eight, older than the other pilots in his squadron, was near to being a pacifist. The son of devout Episcopalian parents—his father was a deacon of the church and a student of the Catholic theologians—he had considered long and deeply before enlisting in the Army Air Forces. He had even toyed with the notion of claiming exemption as a conscientious objector. In the event, it was his father who influenced his decision to fight. "Saint Thomas tells us," the elder Showalter had said, "that a man must respond to the call of duty in a just war. Even our own church has been militant in the service of God and man."

As a commercial artist, Showalter had been offered duty with the Air Technical Command at Wright-Patterson Field, where writers and artists produced the technical orders issued to the squadrons with each new airplane. But having chosen to fight, he had stayed with his decision to become a night-fighter pilot. So far, he had no reason to regret his choice.

In the radar observer's cockpit, Second Lieutenant Howie Teeple sipped at his coffee and watched the sky overhead slowly brighten. From time to time he gave his attention to the dark earth below, searching for some activity that would justify this tedious mission.

He was four years younger than his pilot and the son of a career naval officer. It was one of his deepest regrets that he had been unable to follow in his father's footsteps at the Naval Academy. But at the time he had applied for admission a slight imperfection in his vision had caused him to be rejected. He had regretfully gone to the University of North Carolina, where he had acquired, in addition to his bachelor of science degree, an ROTC commission in the Army. Eventually he had found himself applying for pilot training, but the defect that had kept him out of Annapolis remained. Refused admission to pilot training, he had been offered an opportunity to become an R/O. He had accepted it eagerly.

Thus far his combat duty had been a disappointment to him. His father, on the staff of Admiral Raymond Spruance, had seen an enormous amount of action, and Teeple considered his own failure thus far to confront an enemy somehow shameful. He had, he feared, arrived in the Pacific too late. The war was nearly over, and it seemed that he would never have an opportunity to perform his family duty of killing at least one of his country's enemies.

He sighed heavily and pulled at the hanging oxygen mask attached to his helmet to ease the pressure of the rubber earpieces. He stretched his legs and finished the last of the coffee, stowing the cup and Thermos in the rack beside his seat.

Overhead the colors of the morning were becoming stronger: pink shading through gray to a delicate cornflower blue. The earth below was still deep in darkness.

He switched on the CRT and allowed the radar to make two sweeps of the track ahead. The device was intended to locate target aircraft, and the readings that came from the irregularities of the terrain had to be carefully interpreted to be meaningful. But Teeple's skill at the radar console was almost legendary in the squadron. He sometimes wondered if the other crews thought he used that skill to avoid combat for George's sake. It was an unworthy thought and he tried to put it aside. He knew that his pilot didn't lack courage; it was a long run of luck (good for George, bad for himself) that had left them without so much as a single kill.

The glowing picture on the radarscope showed the relatively unindented coastline and the scattered return that indicated a town below. He snapped on a map light and inspected his chart. The town—a village, really—was Takahagi. The Black Widow, on this course, would be over Hitachi in three minutes, at which time Showalter would make a change in heading to take them around the fleet.

Teeple tried to imagine what was happening at this moment to the south. The squadron's Intelligence officer had briefed the crews on what could be expected when the Coronet force began to land the troops. Japanese resistance, he said, would be heavy. Teeple tried to imagine what 3,000 ships all in one place might look like. It was almost impossible to envision.

There had been rumors on Iwo that the Russians might soon be taking action against northern Japan. The enlisted men and junior officers were all enthusiastically hoping that this was so, that the goddamned Russkis would finally begin to pay off their enormous debt for the help they had received from the United States. But the senior officers seemed less eager for this to happen. Teeple didn't understand this and frankly regarded the whole thing as an academic problem. The last battles of the Pacific war would be fought the way most of them had been, by Americans.

Showalter eased the P-61 into a gentle S-turn, and Teeple pressed his cheek against the plexiglass of the canopy to see below. Suddenly he sat bolt upright and reached foward to tap the pilot heavily on the shoulder. *"George. A light."*

Showalter banked the Black Widow more steeply, circling to the right.

Teeple said, "There. A truck. A *bunch* of trucks."

Showalter said, "You'd better contact Iwo control and report them."

Teeple strained to see more. Yes, it was a convoy. Ten trucks on the road, at least. Heading into Takahagi. "Come around again," he said.

Showalter put the big, black-painted fighter into a steeper turn.

"Christ," Teeple said excitedly. "Look at the bastards. Lit up like Christmas trees."

"Call Iwo," Showalter said.

"What the shit *for*, George? They're right *there*. Let's hit them."

Showalter felt a strong, but momentary, hesitation. The Black Widow's task was not ground attack and strafing, though it was certainly well enough armed to do it. In the turret behind the R/O's cockpit there were two forward-firing fifties, and in pods on either side of the radome in the nose there were four more. What possible excuse could he give for not doing what Teeple suggested? This, after all, was what they were here to do—attack the enemy. Yet he hesitated. "Those might be civilian vehicles," he said doubtfully.

"Jesus H. Christ, Showalter," Teeple said. "That's a military target if I ever saw one. Let's get it, man! What the hell's the matter with you?"

Showalter studied the lights below for another moment and then made his decision. "All right, How," he said. "Here we go."

He shoved the wheel yoke forward and retarded the throttles slightly. The big fighter dropped out of the dawn sky in a spiraling dive. He flicked the gun switches on and lighted the sight reticle so that the circle showed dimly on the thick armor glass in front of him.

As the altimeter unwound, he found himself hoping that the lights below would vanish, leaving him without a target. They did not. At 1,000 feet he began to level the airplane, flying down the coast road, which he could not see, but which he knew was there. At 800 feet the lights were centered in the gunsight. His thumb rested on the firing button in the wheel. Behind him he could hear Teeple saying encouragingly: "Closer, George. Closer. *Now!* Right on."

Showalter pressed the firing button.

Neither Major Immamura nor Superior Private Izuhara ever saw the aircraft attacking them. Their truck, at the head of the column, had just reached the center of Takahagi when the sky erupted into a shower of meteorlike tracers.

Immamura's vehicle was struck by a half-dozen fifty-caliber rounds. One shattered the windshield and removed Izuhara's left arm at the shoulder. Four others slashed through the canvas covering of the truck bed and killed three soldiers outright. The inch-long bullets punctured two gas cylinders and ripped open a third. The ruptured containers, driven like rockets by the pressure of the escaping liquid, spun like pinwheels, spewing a heavy mist of cyanogen chloride gas. They smashed two soldiers into jelly against the steel sides of the truck bed before ripping through the tattered canvas weather cloth to clatter insanely from side to side of the narrow street, spinning and bouncing and spraying gas under high pressure.

The few soldiers with enough presence of mind to understand what was happening screamed warnings and tried to put on their gas masks. None succeeded. The heavy concentration of cyanide gas snuffed them like candle flames in a wind. Most were in convulsions or dead before they could untie the tapes on their gas-mask containers.

The truck behind Immamura's escaped damage, but the driver, startled by the fiery shower of tracers apparently from nowhere, twisted his steering wheel so sharply that his heavily laden truck overturned, spilling soldiers and gas cylinders into the street. Two of the cylinders fractured and began to leak and spin, banging against the wood-and-paper buildings lining the narrow way.

The truck next in line collided with the overturned vehicle, severely injuring the driver and the sergeant seated beside him. But neither the driver, nor his companion, nor the soldiers lying and crawling in the street suffered for long. The bouncing, spinning cylinders spread their gas with terrible efficiency.

Behind the crashed truck, the rest of the convoy had come to a skidding halt. Only one other vehicle was struck by the night fighter's gunfire. It was heavily laden with live chemical mortar rounds. The tracers ignited these, and the truck volcanoed into a column of fire. Chemical shells were blown high into the air, some exploding there, others falling as far away as a half-kilometer from the main blast amid the buildings and courtyards of Takahagi.

The stalled trucks spilled terrified soldiers into the road, where they were swiftly overtaken by the spreading pool of cyanogen chloride gas. Within seconds, a carpet of writhing, dying men dotted the narrow village streets. Faces turned a cyanotic blue at the first inspiration of gas. The second started the convulsions and involuntary flushing of bowels and bladder. The third brought brain death, though bodies continued to twitch and tremble for several minutes longer.

Immamura, shocked by the sight of his driver's arm exploding into bloody tatters almost in his face, was further stunned to see Izuhara's face darken, his eyes bulge as he struggled to breathe. The primary effect of the cyanide gases was, he well knew, the destruction of the blood's ability to carry oxygen. The victim's lungs ceased to function almost instantly, and he reacted like a man being garroted. Izuhara's tongue appeared in a gaping, gasping mouth. Spasms sent the private's legs and one remaining arm into wild swimming motions. The last coherent message that reached Immamura's poisoned brain was the horrid smell of feces—Izuhara's or his own, he never knew.

• • •

190

The villagers of Takahagi, some of them, were awakened by the roar of the night fighter and the noise of exploding mortar rounds. Those who did not awaken were overwhelmed in their *futons* by the rolling, spreading cloud of gas. All war gases were heavier than air, and the gas that spread through Takahagi was heavier still, owing to the extremely rich concentration spread by the cylinders, in which the gas had been contained in liquid form and under high pressure.

The gas filled the shallow cellars and shelters the villagers had so laboriously dug for themselves in the rocky, volcanic soil.

Not all the villagers were asleep. The village prefect died kneeling behind his wife's pale round buttocks. He had awakened in the night feeling amorous—a great rarity in these times of long working hours and insufficient nourishment—and he had shaken her out of her heavy sleep to announce his need. Naked, ready to couple, they had been overcome by the smell of bitter almonds in the night air: the distinctive odor of the cyanide gases, though they did not know it.

In the village schoolhouse, the schoolmaster had been awakened by a brown-banded canister crashing though the shoji into his sleeping room. He heard the children, twenty of them sleeping in the shallow shelter below, begin to stir, and he shouted at them to get up and run from the building. He imagined the canister was an American incendiary bomb of the sort that had nearly burned Tokyo to the ground.

The mortar round was sputtering, its damaged fuse sparking and scorching the tatami. He started for the door, then stopped and returned for the Emperor's portrait, the sanctity of which it was his duty to protect.

The chemical round exploded, shredding the paper walls and filling the house with gas. Neither the schoolmaster nor the orphan children of the village ever emerged from the burning house.

All over the village, people came out of their houses to be met by the gas. They fell as they stood, as they ran, as they shouted to one another, as they cried out in terror. Cats, dogs, birds, even mice died with terrible swiftness. Farmers on the outskirts of the village who had risen early to work for an hour or two on their own rice paddies heard the splashing fall of chemical mortar shells around them. Explosions showered them with mud and gas. They stumbled and fell in the shallow paddies, not knowing what was killing them, knowing only their terror and pain. Some drowned in the brown water; others drowned in their own blood as their lungs filled with gas.

Of the 922 work-worn villagers of Takahagi, thirty were under the age of ten. These had been sleeping in shelters below ground level. All of them died. Ninety villagers survived, with massive brain damage caused by oxygen starvation. One hundred villagers survived unhurt through freak circumstances, irregularities in the terrain and in the light land breeze blowing at the time of the attack. The remainder died, as did all the men and officers of the Special Chemical Attack Brigade.

The gas persisted until sunrise, when the warmth began to disperse it. The land breeze carried the weakening concentration out to sea in sufficient strength to cause a gas-attack alert—the first one of the Pacific war—on a *Fletcher*-class destroyer on station ten nautical miles offshore an hour and a half after the horror at Takahagi. There were no casualties aboard the destroyer, and the officer of the watch noted in the log that quite probably the new chemical detectors recently installed aboard the ship were faulty and had caused a false alarm. The incident was swiftly forgotten in the welter of radio reports beginning to come in from the main invasion fleet, which was now in position off the Kanto beaches.

As Lieutenants Showalter and Teeple headed their Black Widow out to sea on course for Iwo, the R/O made a notation in the aircraft's Form One: "0440 hours: Made one pass at suspected truck convoy on Takahagi-Hitachi road. One vehicle probably destroyed or damaged."

0500 Hours

In flag plot aboard USS *Midway*, the staff officers of three services crowded around the map table. They had, at this moment, unconsciously arranged themselves in groups of their own kind—Army, Navy, and Marine Corps. All avoided the uncommanded, but powerfully felt, space around the two five-star officers in the compartment.

The general, dressed in worn khakis, his famous gold-braided cap low over his cold eyes, removed the unlighted corncob pipe from his mouth and slipped it into his pocket. "Well, Admiral?" he said.

Chester Nimitz, silver-haired and soft-spoken, rested his knuckles on the chart and drew a deep breath. This was the moment he had been waiting for all these long years of war, and he savored it grimly. He regarded Douglas MacArthur with a bleak, barely perceptible smile. They were not friends, these two men, and would never be. But they had a deeply felt understanding of, and regard for, one another.

"On time, on schedule, in place, General," he said.

"Let us proceed," MacArthur said. Made by any other man, the statement would have sounded pompous. From MacArthur it sounded right. The general was given to making historic pronouncements in just the right way. He had spent a lifetime refining that talent.

Nimitz spoke to his communications officer, Captain Leo Davis. "Signal to *Alaska*, Leo." In a quiet voice he gave the order that he and half a hundred other commanders had given again and again since Guadalcanal. "Land the landing force."

On the foredeck of the attack transport USS *Portola*, Lieutenant Harry Seaver and the men of his Ranger platoon stayed clear of the sudden flurry of activity. Boats were being derricked over the side, and men were swarming out of the troop compartments.

The Rangers squatted or sat on the deck, laden with their battle gear and weapons, watching as the soldiers of the 11th Airborne Division prepared to take to the nets and clamber down into the LCIs and Amphtracs rolling in the long, oily swell.

The sun was low on the eastern horizon, an oblate disk distorted by atmospheric refraction, and so brilliant that it dazzled the eyes. The low clouds were dispersing, leaving a sky that had, in minutes, turned from blue-gray to a hard bright blue streaked with silvery cirrus and the condensation trails of hundreds of airplanes. The Combat Air Patrols from the Fast Carrier Task Groups far to the east were crisscrossing the sky in their angry search for any sign of Japanese air opposition. So far there had been none.

From his position forward, Seaver could see other ships in the squadron. These were, like *Portola*, disgorging soldiers in a great olive-drab migration that brought to mind the movement of lemmings.

The shelling by the capital ships on the eastern flank of the operation had stopped momentarily, and the morning air was filled with other sounds: the clatter of heavy equipment, of winches and davits, the low murmuring of the moving troops, the occasional sharp commands coming through the ships' public-address systems, the shouts of the coxswains maneuvering their boats against the sides of the transports.

Portola and her sisters lay hove to a mile and a half from Beach South Sheridan. Seaver could see, in the clear morning light, a thin white line of sand against the darker low-lying land: Kujukuri-hama. He had never seen it from this offshore vantage point. It looked strange, alien, menacing.

Between *Portola* and the shore a seeming confusion of LSTs and LSMs circled, awaiting the orders to head for the beach. To the south, the lines of AKAs were arranging themselves in their assigned positions, each transport surrounded by a swarm of smaller boats. Landing craft of all kinds were being launched in such numbers that Seaver could not make an accurate estimate of how many there were. Hundreds, certainly. Perhaps thousands.

To the northwest, his vision was restricted by *Portola*'s forest of derricks and masts and yardarms. But he could see the upper works of other transports. The sea seemed carpeted with ships and men in small boats. Destroyers sliced through the crowded sea, their guns silent but turned inshore, signals flying from their flag hoists.

North of *Portola* another squadron of attack transports lay off North Sheridan, disembarking the 40th Infantry Division, while to the east, still almost hull down, the ships bringing the men destined for the fifth and sixth waves, were preparing to maneuver into their assigned places. In addition to the initial assault forces of the 40th Infantry and the 11th Airborne, three Army Corps, I, IX, and XI, were on the move toward Beach Sheridan. It would take most of the day to land the eight divisions of the Sixth Army on that thin stretch of beach Seaver could see from *Portola*'s deck.

Farther north, beyond Cape Inubo, lay the Kashima Sea beaches code named North and South Grable. There, other units of the Coronet fleet must be landing the infantry and armor of General Stilwell's Tenth Army. To the southwest, below Katsuura, the Eighth Army, commanded by General Eichelberger, was going ashore on North and South Hayworth, while on the scattered beaches of Suruga and Sagami bays—Sims and Lamour on the combat maps—the six Marine divisions of III and V Amphibious Corps must be already on the beaches.

195

Seaver wondered if the Japanese were resisting in the areas north and south of Sheridan. So far they had not fired a shot at the massed ships off Kujukuri.

A sound like a train passing overhead made the men of the Ranger platoon duck involuntarily. But it was not incoming fire. The air overhead was suddenly combed with rocket trails. Twenty small transports converted to carry banks of rocket launchers were steaming southwest, firing as they went. The Rangers watched the missiles exploding on the beach. It reminded Seaver of the crackle of fireworks during Boys' Festival. The beach was momentarily obscured by sand and dirt clouds. The rocket-firing ships loosed a dozen salvos before moving slowly on.

Corporal Joe Buie, a self-avowed socialist and an admirer of all things Russian, said to no one in particular, "The Red Army invented those goodies. They call them Stalin Organs." He raised his voice to shout, "Yo! Pour it in there, you babies!"

Jim Tanaka, crouched beside Seaver, muttered, "Stalin Organs, shit. I'd like to take Stalin's organ and split it down the middle, the double-dealing bastard." The Russians' refusal to commit themselves completely to the war against Japan inflamed his staunch anti-Communism. To Seaver he said, "Where's that famous road the colonel wants us to clear? Can you see it from here?"

"No," Seaver said. "It's around that point to the southwest." He indicated on his map the bulge of the coastline marked "Katsuura."

Tanaka studied the beach as the rocket explosions walked steadily south, flinging debris and shattered trees into the air. "What the hell are they waiting for? Why aren't they shooting back?"

"Give 'em time, Lieutenant," Sergeant Hardin said. "They'll wait until the first assault wave is committed and then concentrate on the boats."

Major Vanzetti came crouching along the deck wearing his steel helmet, flak vest (a cumbersome new piece of equipment most of the troops ignored), and flotation gear. Seaver estimated that the weight of the major's equipment would just about overcome the buoyancy of his life vest.

Vanzetti searched among the Rangers for their commander. With faces blackened and no insignia of rank showing, it was not a simple matter. "Seaver?"

"Here, Major."

"There's been another change. We may be able to put your platoon ashore sooner than planned. You're to stand by."

"Any idea how long, Major?"

"I'll tell the loading officer as soon as we hit the beach."

"You're going in with the first wave?"

"The colonel's idea. The whole staff goes. With Dog Company." He sounded breathless and apprehensive.

"We'll be here," Seaver said dryly.

"Okay. Stay on your toes," Vanzetti said, and scuttled back through the files of troops forming to go over the side into the LCIs.

"Where are the Kamikazes?" Tanaka demanded. He sounded offended at the nonappearance of the suicide planes.

Seaver squinted at the sky, which was glazing into a brittle pale blue. High up, and glinting in the sun, a squadron of P-51s passed over the fleet.

The boats circling between *Portola* and the beach were sorting themselves out, forming a ragged line astern. They were constantly being joined by other boats filled with men, tanks, vehicles. Seaver was impressed by the enormous complexity of the task of simply keeping track of the craft milling about on the softly rising and falling swell. The beachmasters and their people must be out there somewhere in that first wave. They would have to establish themselves on shore within moments of the time the first boats grounded. From then until the beachheads were secure, their word would be absolute law. No one, regardless of rank, could overrule them as they directed the flow of troops and matériel.

Portola's boats were joining the assault wave. As each craft filled with men, the coxswain pulled away from the ship and headed for the line of departure, which Seaver now noted was marked with buoys flying yellow pennants. It was like some immense, insane regatta, he thought, with boats jockeying for position and milling about waiting for the starting gun.

Each time he looked it seemed that the number of ships and boats had doubled. There had to be thousands in view now—destroyers, attack transports, LCIs and LSTs, and even rubber outboard-powered inflatables loaded with frogmen returning from their assault on underwater obstacles.

The circling boats maneuvered into columns. Each Landing Craft Vehicle/Personnel carried thirty-six infantrymen. The larger LSTs carried eighteen Sherman tanks each. The gradients at Kujukuri would allow the tanks to move directly from the ships onto the beach. In other, more shoaling, waters, where the LSTs could not go all the way to shore, the tanks wore huge flotation collars and went ashore under their own power for the last few hundred feet. Seaver had lost a friend, a tank commander, in such an operation at Okinawa. There had been no attempt by the Japanese to stop the Iceberg landings there, but Seaver's friend had been drowned in his Sherman when the flotation collar had collapsed.

With the columns well formed, the landing craft began to churn toward the beach. Amphtracs from other attack transports were moving up to the line of departure, and a section of LSTs loaded with infantry instead of armor passed close aboard *Portola*'s bows.

A squadron of Corsairs had begun to buzz the beach, the Marine pilots ready to begin strafing the moment the Japanese betrayed their positions by gunfire.

The men of the Ranger platoon were veterans of the Okinawa landings, and it was against that huge operation that they measured Coronet. Corporal Angelo Tangelli, the heavy-weapons specialist, kept trying to count the number of ships in sight, but lost track with each realignment. He gave up in disgust and thought that when he wrote to his old man about this, he would just have to make up a number. Any goddamn number he could think of was probably too fucking small. Not even at Buckner Bay, where *Portola's* squadron of AKAs assembled, had he seen so many ships.

The sun was well clear of the horizon now, and in the bright morning the sea was deep blue, shading swiftly to turquoise as it shoaled toward Kujukuri-hama. Seaver found that he was using the beach's Japanese name more often in his mind than the approved code name South Sheridan. There was a smell coming off the land with the slight westerly breeze. It was the scent of growing things, damp earth, flooded paddies. From time to time the odors of the land were overcome by the acrid stink of cordite, a hateful smell.

Between the ship and the shore the landing craft had begun to comb the shading sea with white wakes. The scene before Seaver was beautiful, unreal, frightening. There was a bustling excitement and a sense of overwhelming power here, but there was a frightening tension, an apprehension that could only build and build until the enemy's first violent reaction came.

The clouds that had darkened the night at sea were gone, shredded by the morning's land breeze and dispersed into patches whose tops burned silvery in the low, brilliant sunshine. The day would be completely clear, Seaver thought, perhaps even warm under this burning Pacific sun. Unconsciously, he let himself relax, slip back into remembered ways. "The Way of the Warrior is found in death," said the *Hagakure* of Tsunetomo Yamamoto. How many young men his own age were quoting that line to themselves over there on the silent battered beach? There was a sort of tangy irony that it was the Way he had learned as a child that now sustained him, protecting his courage. He was aware that some of the men called him the White Samurai—sometimes the White Jap. He glanced at Tanaka's blackened face under the rim of his steel helmet. Few Americans could read Japanese faces, but Seaver could. Tanaka's expression exactly matched that of the others, the white men of the Ranger platoon. If I told him what was going through my mind now, Seaver thought, he would believe I was insane. Possibly even disloyal. But the *Hagakure* seemed right for this moment.

He looked at the sky overhead once more. The contrails criss-crossing the pale blue made a pattern that could have graced a shoji, brush strokes gently drawn across the limpid sun-bright heights. Spring was a variable time in Japan. There were days of rain, and sometimes in the mountains even late snowfalls, but when the sky was clear it was really so, free of the haze and mist that made the horizons in other seasons less pure and clean. This was going to be such a day, with mountains etched against the sky. If it came to it, he thought, this would be a good day to die.

For a moment he reacted to the thought of death like a good Japanese, almost with eagerness. Then his Western heritage commanded him, and he rejected the reaction with violent suddenness. Death was anything but beautiful—and there would be too many deaths today, and tomorrow, and all the days after tomorrow until this damned war was finished. The thought revolted him. I hate this fucking war, he said to himself bitterly. I hate the fear, I hate the waste and the fatigue, and most of all I hate the killing.

"Yo, Rangers! You want we should reserve you some geishas before they're all booked up?"

The Dog Company soldiers, now going over the side into the assault boats, began to yell derisively at the immobilized platoon of Rangers.

"Sit tight, you darlin' boys. Don't get your fuckin' feet wet."

"Hey, Rangers, ain't you gonna help us win the fuckin' war?"

"Nah, they're gonna wait and go ashore with Doug."

"The fuckin' heroes are gonna stay here and play pogie with the swabbies!"

The Ranger platoon responded with catcalls and obscenities.

Hardin called to his opposite number, in Dog Company's First Platoon. "Hey, Gruver, you kraut bastard." He displayed an enormous middle finger. "Sit on this, krauthead. When you reach my elbow, twirl."

Gruver, a snarling smile white on his battle-painted face, responded with a conventional obscenity reflecting on Hardin's and all Rangers' masculinity.

Seaver raised a hand in salute to the company commander, Rufe Kizer, as he clambered stiffly over the steel bulwark and onto the landing net. Seaver knew that stiffness, that awkwardness that plucked at a man's legs as he left the transport to descend to the assault boat. No matter how often one did it, the aching, suppressed fear made movement difficult. Kizer waved. Then his helmeted head disappeared below the bulwark.

Colonel Bolton and his staff were in the line with Kizer's people. Vanzetti looked miserable. Dog Company and the staff would hit the beach at the tag end of the first wave—a bad time, because the defenders would be fully in action when the last boats in the wave grounded.

A geyser erupted suddenly between *Portola* and the next AKA in line. Then another. The Jap guns had finally begun to fire.

The Corsairs patrolling the beach began to wheel and dive. The men in the boats could hear the flat, popping sound of their guns.

The last of *Portola*'s assault craft was in the water, and the sailors were now at work releasing the lashings on the supply and support boats stowed athwart the foredeck. An officer, babyfaced beneath his gray-painted helmet, was shouting orders.

"What about our boats, Lieutenant?" Hardin asked. The changes in the Rangers' landing schedule had disturbed Hardin, a long-service soldier who liked things to be done by the book.

"Don't worry about them, Sergeant. They'll be available when we need them," Seaver said. He made an effort to sound more certain than he actually was. The organized confusion on *Portola*'s deck was enormous. The level of noise was rising as more landing craft were derricked off their chocks and over the side.

"Incoming!" One of the Ranger scouts yelled a warning.

The Jap round whirred overhead with a sound like a fan with a broken blade. The soldiers on deck ducked instinctively. A tall splash appeared a hundred yards beyond *Portola*'s starboard side.

The boats of the first assault wave were nearing the beach. Machine-gun fire made patterns of white in the water around them. Seaver wondered how it was possible that any Japanese at all remained alive on the dark land beyond the beach. All officers of the landing force had been carefully briefed about the preparatory bombardment. The inshore areas had been pounded for over a week by the battleships of the Third Fleet: *Idaho, Mississippi, New Mexico, West Virginia, Missouri, Colorado,* and even the British *King George V.* The weight of explosives pumped into this short stretch of the Honshu coastline was beyond Seaver's calculation. Yet somehow the Japanese had managed to protect their guns and enough men to fire them. It was astonishing—and ominous.

The fire from the beach was growing in intensity. But from *Portola*'s deck could be seen a line of heavy cruisers. One of them must be the *Alaska,* Seaver decided. The command ship for all of Coronet was contributing to the rising level of violence by firing her twelve-inch guns at some unseen targets inland.

The assault boats had reached the beach, and Seaver could see men splashing through the surf onto the sand. At this distance they looked black and antlike as they scattered, ran, formed into groups, died. Tanks from the grounded LSTs were fanning out right and left on the beach, firing over open sights at something above the high-tide line. In a matter of minutes, it seemed, Kujukuri-hama was crowded with men, thousands of them. Amphtracs churned out of the surf and plowed straight across the sand and into the shattered forest beyond, following the tanks. The Corsairs, too, had moved inland, still wheeling and diving like gulls as they strafed.

The water between *Portola* and the shore was no longer blue. It had been combed into white by the wakes and the incoming fire. As Seaver watched, an LCI was hit by a shell. The explosion threw men and parts of men high into the air. The boat rolled over and grounded in the shallow water, lying there like a killed sea monster. Dead and wounded men bobbed in the water around it.

"Incoming!"

Another large-caliber Jap shell whirred overhead and struck the fantail of one of the AKAs in *Portola's* squadron. Boats and men and fragments rose, black blemishes against the sky. The transport began to burn and turned out of line as her crew went into action against the fire.

Seaver looked at his wristwatch and was shocked to discover that it was only an hour since he and his men had been ordered out of the troop compartment. The sun felt hot on his back, yet the air seemed icy cold.

The beach line was littered with grounded boats. Some were backing away from the landing areas to make room for others. Men continued to swarm onto the beach in a flood. The Japanese fire was beginning to slacken. Seaver could hear shells passing overhead again, but this time toward the land. From somewhere to the east came a rolling, steady sound like thunder. The big ships were firing again.

Portola's antiaircraft guns began to shoot. The quad forties on either side of the bow were firing at a high elevation, the gunners shouting bearings at one another.

Tanaka shook Seaver's shoulder and yelled in his ear, "There! Two Zeros."

Two Japanese airplanes had suddenly appeared. They were flying high, and the air around them was instantly pocked with a plague of black shellbursts. The ship's public-address system came to roaring life. "All guns! All guns! Air action port! Air action port!" *Portola's* three-inch gun on the afterdeck began to fire. Seaver could feel the vibrations in the steel plates under him.

Beyond the two Zeros a formation of enemy airplanes appeared. They were hard to see because they were very high: black dots against the sky that mingled with the bursts of antiaircraft fire. The sky guns of all the ships around *Portola* were in action now, and the noise was deafening.

From out of the sun came another line of black dots, Mustangs or Hellcats of the Combat Air Patrol. They mingled with the distant Japanese planes, and Seaver saw two long trails of black as the Americans sliced through the ragged Japanese formation.

But the two Zeros in the lead continued to approach. How was it possible, Seaver wondered, to fly through that curtain of exploding steel untouched? It was a terrifying miracle. Then quite suddenly the lead airplane shed one wing and began to tumble wildly, spewing fire and oily smoke. It spun into the sea a thousand yards from *Portola*, spreading burning gasoline and spray over a fifty-foot area already churned into froth by gunfire from a dozen ships. The gunners in the tubs cheered, and their officers raged at them for having momentarily interrupted their fire.

The second Zero passed low over *Portola* and banked steeply. It appeared intact despite the storm of fire it was drawing. Seaver could see the scratched camouflage paint on the fuselage, the red suns on the wings, the numbers on the triangular tail. The pilot had the canopy pushed back, and Seaver could make out the brown face, the *hachimaki* wound around the flying helmet, the fluttering silk scarf. The pilot was looking at *Portola*, it seemed, as his wing tip struck the sea and his airplane cartwheeled, disintegrating and flinging pieces of metal, a landing wheel, a drop tank, and a bomb into the air. The wreckage struck the water again and vanished in a smear of flame.

"Jesus," Tanaka breathed.

Seaver raised his eyes to watch the air battle developing high overhead. It was impossible to make sense of it. The black dots maneuvered and circled and fell, burning, into the sea. From time to time one dot would detach itself from the melee and dive toward the fleet. It would be followed by another, and the sun would glint on the unpainted wings of the American and there would be another long streak of fire and smoke trailing into the sea.

One of the Corsairs that had been attacking the beaches appeared at low altitude, white smoke streaming from its long nose. It immediately drew a storm of fire from the gunners on the ships despite the repeated orders from PA systems to "Hold fire! Hold fire!" The Corsair, struck a dozen times by American guns, lost all power and crashed into the sea. It floated for a moment, tail high, and then disappeared.

Enemy fire from the shore had almost ceased. Plumes of black smoke rose from the forested area above the high-tide line where flamethrowers were at work on the Japanese bunkers. The stream of boats between the ships and the beach continued as thousands of men and tons of matériel were ferried to the narrow strand.

Portola's deck force worked steadily, hoisting the laden landing craft over the side. Weapons, ammunition, artillery, vehicles, bulldozers, food, medical supplies, spare clothing, portable shelters, fuel, even toilet paper and grave markers—all that was needed to maintain an army in the field was disgorged from the cargo holds and sent on its way to the men on shore. For an hour and a half the Rangers waited, watching *Portola* empty herself. From where they were, they could not judge the amount of opposition being met by the soldiers on the beach. It appeared that casualties were few. The boats returning from the beach with wounded seemed lightly laden as they passed *Portola* and headed out to where the hospital ships waited.

For some time now Japanese doctrine had been to oppose landings lightly and to draw the invaders inland to some more convenient killing ground before launching heavy counterattacks. But they had reverted to the old ways during Olympic. Perhaps, Seaver thought, the fact that aliens were, for the first time in Japanese history, actually putting their feet on the sacred soil of the homeland had made them react with banzai charges and even suicidal attacks by civilians and volunteer forces.

Since they had not managed to hold Kyushu that way, perhaps they had now chosen to revert again, allowing the men of Coronet to advance against token opposition until such time as they could bring to bear all the power that remained to them.

The air battle had momentarily ended. Except for the two Zeros shot down near *Portola*, no Kamikaze had managed to penetrate the Combat Air Patrol. Seaver unlimbered his binoculars and studied the sky to the northwest. The Mustangs were still there, but he could make out no Japanese airplanes. Higher, leaving condensation trails behind them, a large formation of B-29s was passing over Inubo. He guessed that their mission was to bomb the roads and the remains of the rail system, interdicting any attempt by the defenders to bring the northern armies into action.

The public-address system came to life. "Rangers stand by to join the landing force."

Seaver stood stiffly and moved along his men, inspecting equipment. When he was satisfied, he said, "All right. Let's saddle up."

Tanaka, whose task it was to oversee the Navy's off-loading of the inflatables, gave the order to put the boats over the side.

The shelling by the battleships offshore had increased in volume again. They could hear the heavy rounds passing high overhead. A squadron of long-fuselaged P-47Ns from Kyushu had taken over from the Marine Corsairs. They were making repeated bombing passes behind the beach over toward Katsuura, where the enemy was supposed to have emplaced some salvaged naval artillery.

A messenger from the bridge ran up to Seaver. "Lieutenant? Captain says you are to report to the beachmaster, South Sheridan. His name is Commander Jorgensen."

"What about Colonel Bolton?"

"Your colonel has been killed, sir."

Tanaka looked across the water at the land, his black eyes filled with hatred. "Bastards," he said.

Seaver thought: In the States today the papers will say that American forces have landed on the island of Honshu and are advancing against token resistance. The correspondents loved that phrase, "token resistance." He closed his eyes. He had no particular love for Bolton. He was a commander much like any other commander. But for an instant or two he felt what Tanaka was feeling: sheer, weary, angry hatred.

The men were standing ready, looking at him.

"All right, Hardin," he said. "Let's haul ass."

The men began to go down the landing nets. Seaver looked again at the sky. He could see nothing but contrails now, and the high, thin, silvery cirrus shining in the morning sun.

He became conscious of Tanaka standing near him. "Welcome back to Dai Nihon, Harry," Tanaka said.

0600 Hours

As the first rays of the rising sun touched the shojis on the eastern side of the villa, Katsuko Maeda roused herself from her kneeling meditation.

There was a heavy rumbling in the air, similar to, but louder than, the noise of the shelling to which the occupants of the villa had become accustomed. The air hummed with the sound made by the enemy airplanes flying back and forth, like birds of prey, over the beaches below the mountains of the Boso Peninsula. From time to time the sound became so strong that it rattled the shojis in their frames. Outside in the gardens, the three old servants left on the estate were chattering to one another fearfully, and Oyama, the ancient cook, could be heard lamenting and complaining that the terrible Yankees would soon be here to murder the men and rape all the women. Katsuko could not imagine the Americans raping Oyama, who was more than seventy years old, but the old woman was only repeating what everyone had been told would happen if the enemy was allowed to defile the homeland.

Katsuko felt tired from her sleepless night and emotionally drained by the farewell with her brother. She wondered if she would ever see him again. It was doubtful, she knew. Kantaro would stay with his men and they would fight the invaders until they were killed.

She straightened with an effort. The night chill was in her bones: the delicate kimono she had worn in honor of Kantaro's farewell gave her no protection from the early-morning cold and damp.

For a time she regarded the *wakizashi* Kantaro had left in her care. The lacquered scabbard gleamed with a deep luster in the light from the eastern sky that was finding its way into the austere room. Calmly she pulled the blade from the scabbard and looked at it. It was a beautiful thing, made by a master sword maker in another time. The steel billet had been forged and folded many times, so that the resulting blade was composed of thousands of paper-thin layers of metal. No other people on earth had ever learned to make swords like these. The cord wrappings of the hilt were of silk, almost as ancient as the sword itself. The guard was of bronze, fashioned in the shape of the double hyacinth leaf of the Maeda *mon*.

Holding the *wakizashi*, she felt a deep satisfaction in knowing that the senior sword of the *daisho* was at Kantaro's side wherever he might be.

She considered using the short sword. She even wrapped the blade with a piece of silk from her costume and held it so that the point pressed lightly against her throat. She could feel the sharpness of it touching her carotid pulse. Her hands did not tremble at all, and she was grateful for that.

Actually, the *wakizashi* was not the preferred weapon for an act of seppuku. For that one should have the *aikuchi*, the short dagger without a guard. But family legend had it that the Saotome short sword she now held in her hand had been used by a Maeda who found himself on the wrong side of the battle of Sekigahara in 1600.

She closed her eyes and tried to imagine what it had been like for that long-dead ancestor who had faced defeat with such courage and style. It was said that Iyeyasu Tokugawa himself had ordered the return to the Maedas of the *daisho* of which this blade was a part.

The lamentations of the servants were a disturbing influence.

Obviously, they were near to panic. A samurai woman of ancient times would never concern herself about such people. But Katsuko's Westernized education had separated her from the old traditions. She had the rebellious thought that there were no true samurai left in Japan now. All that had gone when the empire had joined the modern world. Japan had chosen to fight a modern war, with modern ways and modern weapons. And she had lost it. That was the bitter truth of it. Nothing anyone—even Kantaro—could say would change that.

She lowered the sword and wiped the blade carefully where the point had touched her skin. The steel must always be unsullied, she knew. Even the slightest touch of skin to the elegant metal could damage it. Unless, of course, the blade could be wiped with blood.

She remembered that once, long ago, she had heard Kantaro and Harry-san being instructed in the care of weapons by their *kendo* master. Harry's pale eyes had grown round and wide when that particular bit of lore had been imparted. A faint smile touched her lips as she sheathed the *wakizashi* in the lacquered scabbard.

She stood and opened the shoji. The sky that she could see through the overhanging branches of the red pines was now a delicate shade of blue. It was crisscrossed with feathery condensation trails left by the American airplanes. The rumble of heavy gunfire from the coast was like thunder rolling across the mountains.

"Oyama-san," she called.

The lamentations from the kitchen wing ceased, and the cook appeared, her weathered old face streaked with tears. "*Hai*, Katsuko-sama."

"We have no time to waste in weeping," Katsuko said. "Who is still left at the villa?"

The old woman seemed confused. The muttering of the distant guns made her flinch and cringe. "Who, Katsuko-sama?"

"Yes," Katsuko said patiently. "Who has not run away? Have any of the men remained?"

"There is Konishi-san, the second gardener. And Yukinaga-san, the porter. I think that is all, Katsuko-sama."

"Have we any food left?"

"Food, Katsuko-sama?" The old woman's terror made her succumb to the irritating habit of repeating everything that was said to her, but Katsuko remained patient. "Yes, Oyama-san. Food. Have we any rice? Tea?"

"Yes, Katsuko-sama. We have some. It is not good rice. The authorities adulterate it with heaven knows what these days, but yes, we have almost one full barrel." Voicing her complaints against the Kempetai, who had recently taken over all distribution of food, seemed to steady her considerably. She sounded petulant and quarrelsome, which was better, Katsuko thought, than sounding terrified all the time.

"Very well," Katsuko said. "Is there fire in the kitchen?"

"Fire, Katsuko-sama?"

"Yes, Oyama-san. Fire. For cooking. Is there any?"

"There are some coals still in the *sutobu*, Katsuko-sama."

"Good. Take all the rice we have left and cook it."

"Cook the rice, Katsuko-sama? But—"

"Cook it all, Oyama-san. And make tea. As much as you can with what we have left."

"But, Katsuko-sama, the tea we have is for the *chanoyo*."

Katsuko said, "There will be no more tea ceremonies, Oyama-san. Make the tea and cook the rice. Then tell Konishi-san and Yukinaga-san that we will be carrying it down the mountain to my brother's soldiers, who are guarding the road."

The old woman made gestures of protest. The thought of common soldiers drinking tea fine enough to be used for the *chanoyo* clearly scandalized her. For the moment, at least, her senile fears were forgotten.

"Do it, old woman," Katsuko said sharply. "Do it now."

Oyama shuffled off, muttering to herself, her geta scuffing the pebbles once so carefully raked daily by a staff of outside servants, but marked now by the tire tracks of the trucks that had taken Kantaro and his men down the mountain.

Katsuko went into her own room and knelt before a cedar-wood chest. From it she took her national uniform, the ugly, shapeless coveralls issued by the quartermasters of the Volunteer Defense Force.

She stood and unwound the obi from her waist and slipped the kimono from her shoulders. The cold bit into her as she finished stripping. She wished momentarily for the comfort of a hot bath, but the *ofuro* was cold and there was little time. She stood naked before the small mirror on her dressing table. Her breasts were full, but flat. The nipples stood distended by the cold in the room. Her hips were not broad; her legs, though short by Western standards (had Harry-san actually said something like that once? She had difficulty remembering) were well shaped. Her belly was, like her breasts, rounded but flat. The dark triangle at her crotch was sparse. She remembered seeing an Occidental girl, a schoolmate, naked once. Western women, like their men, were not only larger everywhere, but hairier. Would the American soldiers really be aroused to rape by what she saw in her mirror? Everyone said so. She could not imagine what it might be like to be raped, violated and taken against her will. Yet that was what happened to women in war. Kantaro said so. In China, Japanese soldiers had raped thousands—perhaps millions—of Chinese.

Shivering, and not only from the cold, she dressed swiftly in the mud-colored uniform. The belt was too large. It almost went twice around her slender waist. She fastened it in a knot and slipped the *wakizashi* though it.

She put on a pair of Western walking boots and tied her hair into a plain *kubimaki*, making sure that the cloth covered it all. She could not hide the fact that she was a woman, but there was no need to advertise it.

When she had finished dressing, she opened the shoji at the rear of the house and hurried alone up the path to the shrine.

This time she did not clap to awaken the *kami*. She did not pray at all. Somehow it seemed to her that Shinto was failing Japan. The gods no longer listened to prayers offered beneath the hemp-draped torii. If they had ever listened, she thought, and wondered if the Christian Americans felt the same from time to time. Religion was a thing she and Harry-san had never discussed seriously.

From the ridge she could look far out to sea, and what she discovered there froze the breath in her throat. As far as it was possible to look, from the sea cliffs around Katsuura to the eastern horizon, the ocean was covered with ships. There had to be thousands of them, she thought. Ships of all sizes, ships of all kinds. From time to time the most distant vessels were obscured by smoke and, after what seemed a long time, the rumbling of their guns reached the spot where she stood. Smaller boats criss-crossed wakes everywhere. She could make out no sense or pattern to what they were doing, but those approaching the shore were dark with men; those departing were empty, or nearly so.

Apparently a great deal of the Americans' attention was focused on the hidden beaches of Kujukuri-hama, beyond the bulge of the coast at Katsuura. There were boats moving toward the scattered and isolated beaches south of Ohara. Several ranges of small mountains hid the actual shoreline from her, but she could hear a crackling sound coming from there that she realized was the noise of distant gunfire.

A formation of blue-painted airplanes appeared from the north, oddly shaped things with wings like those of a gull, but inverted. They flew by along the face of the mountain, almost exactly at her level. She could see the pilots inside their transparent half-shells. The white stars painted on the bodies of the airplanes were scratched and chipped. The machines must be very old and hard-used, she thought. She had imagined that all the Americans' war machines would be sparkling new and freshly painted.

She watched for a few minutes more and then hurried down the path to the villa. She went into the kitchen, where Oyama-san was cooking the rice.

Katsuko called the two old men and ordered them to fill buckets with the grayish rice. When that was done, she instructed

Oyama to fill four large jugs with the freshly brewed tea. Grumbling, the old woman did as she was told.

Ten minutes later Katsuko led her small party away from the villa and down the mountain. The two old men and the old woman and the young one each carried a bamboo yoke across the shoulders. Laden with what food and drink they could carry, they trotted like coolies down the mountain road to make the lot of Kantaro's soldiers waiting to die more pleasant.

Katsuko Maeda had abandoned all thought of suicide now. She felt, she told herself, almost like a soldier of the Emperor.

The pilots of the Takasaki Special Attack Squadron had been awake and waiting for two hours when the bugle called them out of their bunkers to the assembly area in a revetment covered by camouflage netting.

Breakfast had been a handful of gritty rice, some watery tea, and a cigarette. Some of the older pilots had complained, asking how they were expected to fly properly and destroy American ships on such rations. But Kendo Matsumoto understood that food was scarce and that what there was should properly be used to feed the infantrymen and tankers of the various 56th Army positions nearby, men who would be called upon to exert themselves physically as soon as they were ordered into action on the beaches. Ensign Yoshi Kashiwahara, the flight commander, had explained all this to the men of his section.

The pilots, released at last from the confinement of the shallow bunkers in which they slept, crowded through the hidden trench connecting the sleeping area with the squadron operations revetment laughing and talking excitedly. A number of them, aware that today was Matsumoto's sixteenth birthday, had offered their congratulations and wishes for success, and even Kashiwahara had taken note of the fact that this was an auspicious day for Matsumoto.

Most of the pilots who were to fly the squadron's Akatombo open two-seat trainers had dressed themselves in their bulky cotton-quilted flying suits. Matsumoto had done so, too. The suits made the young men resemble bears, he thought, but the youthful, unlined faces detracted somewhat from the desired appearance of ferocity.

The day was going to be clear and cool, perfect for flying. The low clouds that had covered the valley in which the squadron had been hidden had dispersed, leaving a sky that was white and silvery. Far to the west there were contrails: long, straight paths of vapor left behind by the supercharged engines of the American bombers flying high and fast. Matsumoto tried to imagine what it would be like to engage one of the dreaded *Bi-ni-ju-ku* in combat. He had heard that the enormous silver airplanes bristled with guns and that they moved so swiftly that it took a Shiden fighter to catch them. Not that he, or any of his squadron mates, would ever fly a Violet Lightning. The new fighters were few and they were all in the hands of the most experienced pilots, who were required to fly escort for the Kamikazes. How humiliating that must be, Matsumoto thought dutifully, to be denied the honor of carrying the attack directly to the Americans.

As he jogged along the trench with his mates, Matsumoto repeated to himself the words of the Emperor's Rescript for Soldiers and Sailors: "Be resolved that duty is heavier than a mountain, while death is lighter than a feather." The words were a source of great comfort to him and helped to reassure him that when the time came for him to make his death dive he would do it correctly and without faltering.

As the pilots had sat in the semidarkness of the bunkers eating their breakfast, there had been much talk about the writing of wills and the need to save a few hairs or nail clippings to be sent home to one's parents. Matsumoto had considered writing a will, but had decided against it. He had no possessions of any value except for his military equipment, which would, of course, be redistributed among the pilots of the squadron not chosen for today's sortie.

He had actually attempted to write a death poem, which was a proper thing to do. But unfortunately he lacked sufficient talent and education to do it well, and he had abandoned the idea.

Everything he had tried to write had sounded foolish or, worse, familiar. He did not wish to have it said that he had stolen his death poem from the works of better, more seemly young men. It would be a serious reflection on his *makoto* and make him appear trivial. One did not wish to present oneself at Yasukuni laden with such blame. He had simply written a short note to his sister, Ochacha, asking that she take care of their parents when they grew old and requesting that she make, in future, a visit to Yasukuni Shrine whenever convenient, so that his spirit might rejoice in her company.

When the pilots had all assembled under the camouflage netting, they were called to attention by Ensign Ozawa, the squadron operations officer, and addressed by Lieutenant Commander Chita, the squadron commander.

Saburo Chita was a man of twenty-eight with one eye and one arm. He had participated, it was said, in the Battle of Midway as a Rei Sentoki, Type Zero fighter, flight commander and had been shot down by two Grummans. Wounded in the face and right arm, he had floated on a raft for six days. The submarine that had rescued him had not carried a medical officer, and the resulting neglect of his injuries had brought him to his present crippled condition. Chita was a bitter man and a harsh disciplinarian. It was his inability to fly and do his proper duty, the pilots knew, that made him so. And it was understood that when all the pilots of the Takasaki Squadron had done *their* duty, he intended to fly one last time.

Chita fixed the assembled aviators with his single eye as they bowed. He returned the courtesy with an inclination of the head and said, "You may stand easy—but be silent."

The pilots, most of whom were enlisted men or naval aviation cadets, relaxed very little.

"You will be pleased to know that the Americans have finally nerved themselves enough to attempt landings on this island," he said.

There was an involuntary murmur from the group, and Chita frowned. Silence was re-established swiftly.

"This morning several large convoys have begun attempting to put troops ashore at Kashima, Kujukuri, and on the beaches of Sagami and Suruga bays. These convoys are under fierce attack by our coastal defense forces and naval units, and their losses are very heavy."

He began to pace angrily, as he always did when considering the imminence of a battle in which he would not be permitted to participate.

"The Takasaki Special Attack Squadron has been honored by the Imperial high command. Although it is well understood that most of you are relatively untrained and unworthy, the squadron is to be allowed to join in the attack upon the American fleet."

Though expected, the news caused another slight stir among the attentive pilots. This time, Chita, whose knuckles were pale as he gripped the sword at his side, did not rebuke them. So obvious was his envy that Matsumoto actually felt a pang of pity for him.

"The squadron is to participate in the largest *tokko* attack yet made by the forces of the Japanese Empire. I hope that all of you are aware of what an honor it is to be chosen to be a part of it." He stared at the faces surrounding him as though challenging anyone to suggest that what he was saying was anything but the absolute truth. "This war," he said, "has been long and hard. Japan has paid a heavy price. Many of our best men are already spirits at Yasukuni. These men are now watching all of you." He paused, and Matsumoto was moved to see that his single eye was wet with tears. "Not all of you have been born to the samurai tradition," he said harshly. "Many of those who were have already sacrificed themselves for the Emperor, and their places in the ranks have been given to persons of lesser birth. This has been necessary." He seemed to Matsumoto to be looking straight at him. "Very well, then. Let the spirit of Yamato support you. Bushido is not only for the born warrior. It is for all subjects of the Emperor. Let it fill you and strengthen you to do your duty." The tears were plainly visible on his brown cheeks now, and his voice cracked with emotion. He raised his sheathed sword and shouted: *"Banzai! Tenno banzai!"*

The assembled pilots broke into cheers.

Chita regarded his men with trembling lips. Hoarsely, he said, "Ensign Ozawa!"

"Hai, dono!" the officer shouted.

"Take over here." He turned and walked swiftly from the assembly area toward his quarters, his back rigid, head held high.

"All right, all right," Ozawa said over the babble of excited voices. "Attention to orders. These are the target areas for today."

Fifteen minutes later the pilots filed past a table on which stood several bottles of sake and a number of *soma*-ware cups. In groups of five and six they drank a toast to success and to the Emperor and then trotted out to the revetments where their aircraft waited.

The morning had begun to take on a dreamlike quality for Matsumoto. From moment to moment he had to remind himself that this day was destined to be his last on earth. But at sixteen the *feel* of death and dying was beyond him. He could accept only the concept, and that was without real substance.

He went across the landing strip to the revetment where Seaman Misato, his mechanic, stood by the delicate Akatombo Red Dragonfly.

Misato, a young man two years Matsumoto's senior, had spent the last inactive weeks working on the trainer, and it showed the loving care he had lavished on it. Somewhere he had managed to obtain fresh paint for the Rising Suns on wings and fuselage. The tiny tears and damaged places in the fabric had been painstakingly repaired and painted. The *katakana* symbols on the tail had been redone and, Matsumoto was delighted to note, his own name had been carefully inscribed under the rear cockpit's rim.

Since it was in this same aircraft that Matsumoto had made his perilous crossing of the Sea of Japan from Korea, he felt a deep and possessive affection for the slow and clumsy machine.

Between the struts of the fixed landing gear, an armed 250-

kilogram bomb had been mounted. There was no way to release the missile from inside the airplane. Such a refinement, Matsumoto thought with a slight, sudden chill, was unnecessary.

Though it was not strictly required by naval etiquette, Misato came to attention and saluted Matsumoto just as though the younger man were a full-fledged officer instead of merely a naval aviation cadet. Matsumoto returned the salute precisely.

"*Ohayo, Sojusha-san,*" Misato said politely. He used the word "pilot" rather than make any reference to Matsumoto's probationary rank. He felt that the young man was entitled to such a special courtesy on this of all mornings.

"Good morning, Seaman Misato," Matsumoto said formally. "Is everything ready?"

"She is fully loaded with fuel, *Sojusha-san.* I have tested the engine. It runs well." He hesitated, regarding the childish face under the flying helmet with the earflaps raised (in the manner of true fighter pilots, he remembered, in other days). On the boy's *hachimaki* the Rising Sun had been painted, and there were inscriptions composed by his comrades inked on the cloth. "May I offer you my most sincere congratulations, *Sojusha-san?*"

"Thank you, Seaman Misato." Matsumoto started to collect the parachute that was neatly stacked atop Misato's toolbox and then stopped himself, smiling sheepishly. "That will not be needed today," he said. He looked at his watch and saw only his bare wrist. He had presented the timepiece, the only possession of any value in his care (it was naval issue), to Naval Aviation Cadet Watanabe, who was one of the few pilots remaining behind today. Watanabe's Akatombo was unflyable, and the disappointed pilot had been left in the sleeping bunker in tears.

"May I know what the target is, *Sojusha-san?*" Misato asked.

"The Americans are attempting to land at Kashima, Kujukuri, and in Sagami and Sugura bays. The Takasaki Squadron is honored to attack the transports off Kujukuri-hama." His voice trembled slightly, but it was, he hoped, with excitement rather than with fear.

From the direction of the command area came the sound of a

bugle. Matsumoto fastened the open neck of his flying suit and said, "It is time, Misato-san." Then he remembered the cigarette he had been given at breakfast and he reached into his shirt pocket and extracted it. He offered it to Misato, who accepted it graciously. "Thank you sincerely, *Sojusha-san*," he said, bowing.

Matsumoto, in his bulky gear, climbed onto the Akatombo's wing stiffly. On impulse he offered a hand to Misato, who took it and squeezed it. Then Matsumoto climbed into the cockpit and, with Misato's help, fastened the shoulder harness.

The mechanic dropped to the ground and ran around the wing tip to climb up on the portside landing wheel. He applied a crank to the inertia starter and wound it until the flywheel was spinning at high speed. Then he dropped off and stood back. "Clear!"

Matsumoto snapped over the magneto switches and engaged the engine. The fixed-pitch propeller jerked into action. It swung through two revolutions before the engine came to life with a puff of flame and black smoke from the exhaust stack. He adjusted the throttle and mixture controls until the engine idled smoothly.

Out on the field a member of the ground staff was signaling the trainers into line with a flag. Matsumoto raised a hand and waved the chocks away from the wheels. He began to taxi out of the camouflaged revetment. Misato bowed again, deeply, as the Akatombo moved out into the sunlight.

Ensign Yoshi Kashiwahara, dressed in flying gear, stood on the wing root of his shabby Zero at the head of the grassy strip. He watched the trainers trundle clumsily out of their hiding places under the camouflage nets and into a straggling line at ninety degrees to the takeoff run. He suppressed his irritation as Petty Officer Kanada allowed his airplane to approach too close to the craft ahead. The steel propeller came perilously near to sawing the tail off Cadet Mitsui's airplane, but Kanada managed to get his Akatombo stopped in time.

The plain fact was that the pilots of the Takasaki Squadron were poor stuff, inadequately trained and probably not naturally gifted fliers in any case.

Kashiwahara glanced across the field in the direction of the operations area to see if Commander Chita had noticed the near accident. The members of the ground staff were lined up ready to cheer the flight away, but Chita did not seem to be among them. He had probably retired to his quarters to get drunk. Chita drank a great deal these days. Kashiwahara did not approve, but he sympathized with the squadron commander. It was a bitter thing to be denied the privilege of participating in the *ketsu-go*—the decisive battle.

Kashiwahara was twenty-five years old and he had been a naval aviator for six years. He was, he realized, an anomaly: a survivor. Almost all the members of his class at the Naval Academy—certainly all those who had been selected as airmen—were now dead. Most of them had been lost in the great carrier battles of 1942 and 1943. It had been a policy of the naval high command to keep the best pilots in combat continuously, rather than rotate them as the Americans did. The result was that attrition had destroyed the flower of Japanese airmanship, and the quality of the forces available for battle had steadily deteriorated. Now, he thought bitterly, all that remained to defend the empire were pilots capable of nothing more than suicide attacks.

Kashiwahara, as an escort pilot, had seen many *tokko* attacks. Though he had never said so to anyone, he seriously doubted that they were really effective. It was true enough that many American ships had been destroyed by Kamikazes, some of them large and powerful vessels. But "many" was a relative term in dealing with the Americans, who had thousands of ships.

He had done his best to make the technique effective, coaching the inept youngsters who were assigned to the special attack squadrons to which he had been posted. But diving an airplane onto the deck of a moving ship was not, contrary to what many nonfliers seemed to think, a simple matter. An airplane was not a bomb. It had to be flown, even in a suicide dive. And too many of the *tokko* pilots were insufficiently trained to perform the maneuver properly.

And that was not the worst of it. To reach a target, the Kamikazes had to run a ferocious gantlet of antiaircraft fire and enemy fighters. Few actually managed it.

He watched the Akatombos deploy themselves for takeoff with pursed lips. Trainers, he thought, primary trainers. The Grummans and Mustangs that would be hunting them were 200 kilometers per hour faster and could climb at five times the Red Dragonfly's rate. It was one thing to sacrifice one's life in exchange for a ship and 500 Americans. It was something quite different merely to die to no purpose.

Kashiwahara realized that his opinions on this were not necessarily shared by most Japanese. "We are a people," he once told a trusted friend, "convinced of the nobility of failure."

One day—and soon; perhaps even today—he would make his own death dive. That was the inevitable fate of all Kamikaze escort pilots. But when he performed it, it would be done with skill, precision—*and* success. Kashiwahara did not believe in noble, futile gestures.

He wound the white silk scarf around his neck and put on his flying helmet. He signaled to the lead Akatombo to take off and to the others to follow him at the prescribed interval. It was risky to loiter here exposed on the ground. There were far too many American fighters about.

He shouted for his mechanic, a grizzled old aviation machinist's mate named Kuritsu, to stand by the starter. This was a geared, battery-powered motor with a notched shaft that mated with the Zero's propeller shaft. He settled himself in the cockpit and set the engine controls for starting.

The airplane was war-weary and showed it, but Kuritsu had done his best to make it fit for battle. In 1940, when Kashiwahara had first reported aboard the aircraft carrier *Kaga*, the Mitsubishi Type O had been the best naval fighter in the world.

Its 950-horsepower Nakajima Sakae 21 radial engine, two 7.7 machine guns, and two 20mm wing cannon had made it a fearsome weapon.

With a Reisen like this one, Kashiwahara had shot down a dozen American Wildcats and Devastators. But that had been long ago and, it seemed, in another war entirely.

Kashiwahara had been injured in a deck-landing accident aboard *Kaga* in May of 1942. Because of this, he had not sailed with the fleet sent to attack the island of Midway in June. The battle had been a Japanese catastrophe, resulting in the loss of four carriers, of which *Kaga* was one.

Kashiwahara had spent eighteen months in various hospitals in the homeland and when at last he was deemed fit to fly again, the character of the Pacific war had changed drastically. For Japan it had become a slow, painful process of retreat.

Because his injuries had come as the result of an accident rather than in battle, and despite his brilliant early record as a fighter pilot, Kashiwahara was never promoted, never given command of a squadron. In 1944 and 1945 he had managed to wrangle combat assignments, first in the Philippines and later on Okinawa and Kyushu. Still flying the by then obsolete Zero, he had contrived to shoot down another American fighter and one crippled B-29.

In January of 1946 he was notified by 11th Air Fleet Headquarters that he was to be, henceforth, an escort for special-attack missions. He had accepted the posting without complaint, as a naval officer should. But he was growing weary of watching the steady toll of youngsters rising while the Americans accepted the damage they were able to inflict and came steadily on.

The mechanic Kuritsu, who had originally been part of the crew of one of the new carriers, which had been sunk at her moorings in the Inland Sea even before her sea trials, had been grateful to be assigned to the Takasaki Special Attack Squadron. Many of his mates had been impressed into the Naval Landing Force units that were now distributed among the commands of the 56th Army. To have been given away to the Army would have entailed an enormous loss of face for a man who had spent most of his adult life in the Imperial Japanese Navy.

To show his gratitude, Kuritsu had done his very best to make the tired Reisen assigned to Ensign Kashiwahara the best possible fighting machine. He had even taken the pains to paint fourteen American stars on the fuselage. "It will give the young pilots confidence to see their escort's battle record," he told Kashiwahara.

The Akatombos were all airborne and circling the field in an uneven line astern when Kashiwahara shoved the throttle open and climbed into the air to join them. None of the trainers had radios, and it took Kashiwahara almost twenty minutes to round them up and signal them into some semblance of a formation.

There were seven trainers formed up on the Zero. The mission had originally been scheduled for nine, but two of the Akatombos had been unflyable owing to lack of vital spare parts. The parts were in the Army's possession, because the airplanes had originally been Army trainers. But the Army had refused to supply the parts required because, the supply officer at Nagoya said, a new training program for Army aviators was about to begin and the bits and pieces would be needed. This absurd excuse had so enraged Commander Chita that he had complained to 11th Air Fleet Headquarters, who in turn replied that there were many similar examples of interservice rivalry and that all such cases would be discussed at the next regular meeting of the Imperial General Staff.

Chita, Kashiwahara, and all the officers of the squadron were familiar with the lack of co-operation between the Army and the Navy. They had spent their service careers with it—contributing to it, in fact. But to discover that the rivalry continued at a time when invaders stood poised to strike at the heart of the homeland filled them with angry despair. They assigned the blame for it, of course, exclusively to the Army.

Kashiwahara pulled the plotting board out from under the

224

instrument panel and fastened his chart to it. Only he carried a chart. None of the Kamikazes on this mission had the skill to navigate the formation into the proper position. Kashiwahara had been briefed to fly straight east to the coast, at which time he would lead the formation down to an altitude of approximately ten meters and fly southeast 100 kilometers before turning back toward the coastline. It was assumed that this would allow them to make contact with the American fleet out of the sun and from the seaward flank, where, presumably, they would not be expected.

"The Takasaki Squadron is only one of several squadrons attacking this morning. Squadrons from Suwa, Kadoma, and Kamakura will attack from the west," Ozawa had explained, marking the routes on the chart. "We believe there will be three Army squadrons from Yatabe also participating in the first strike."

The Suwa and Kadoma squadrons were equipped with some of the new Oka—Cherry Blossom—suicide attackers. These were small flying missiles powered by three solid-fuel rockets. The warheads contained 700 kilograms of explosive, and the devices were to be carried into battle under the wing of a Mitsubishi G4M2e twin-engined bomber. They had been tested during Operation Ten-go, the massed Kamikaze attacks on the American fleet invading Okinawa, with indifferent success. The engineers who had designed the Oka now claimed that the missiles were much improved. "Of course," Ozawa had said wryly while briefing Kashiwahara, "it is difficult to obtain test-pilot reports."

Takasaki lay near the head of a broad valley abutting the mountains of central Honshu. The valley, through which ran the Karasu River and a braided complex of rail lines and roads—all heavily bombed—opened out onto the Kanto Plain, the high command's chosen "killing ground" for the invading American armies. From 2,000 meters, Kashiwahara and his *tokko* pilots could see little, but the ensign, at least, was aware that the entire plain had been honeycombed with lines of fortifications and strongpoints. Around the edges of the Kanto, the high command had situated more than 150,000 regular soldiers, 2,000 tanks, and all the artillery remaining in the inventory of the Japanese armed forces. In addition to this power, the Kempetai, working closely with the 12th Home Army, had organized almost a million civilians into the Volunteer Defense Force, armed with what weapons the military could spare, with hunting guns, with farm implements, and even with sharpened bamboo spears. It seemed to Kashiwahara that he and his fledglings would actually be doing the Americans a service by pinning them to the beachheads and preventing their advance into the Kanto. He had heard that the Americans had been stunned by the civilian resistance on Okinawa and Kyushu. That resistance was insignificant compared to what awaited them on this broad and seemingly vulnerable plain.

He gave his attention to the trainers flying in a ragged vee behind him. He had kept his Zero throttled back to a mere 140 kilometers per hour so that the Akatombos could stay with him. At this speed the controls of his fighter felt mushy, and he hated to think what would happen to him and to his charges if they should be surprised by any prowling Yankee fighters. So far he had seen nothing of the Americans except for the distant trails left in the sky by their bombers. Obviously they were concentrating their forces over the beaches. With luck he could lead his inept little band of warriors around the invaders to take them from the sea with the sun behind him.

One of the Red Dragonfly trainers was straggling more than the rest. He recognized it as the airplane flown by Cadet Matsumoto. He waggled his wings to signal Petty Officer Kanada to take the lead and dropped out of the formation. He banked under the vee of trainers and came up on Matsumoto's wing.

The youngster was flying tensely, making corrections for the light turbulence of the air with movements of the controls that were unnecessarily abrupt. In addition to this, he was staring straight ahead, his eyes fixed on the man on whose wing he was supposed to be keeping station. To fly like that when there might be Mustangs or Hellcats around was suicidal. Kashiwahara recognized the irony in that observation.

He eased the throttle forward until he was slightly ahead of Matsumoto's aircraft and waited for the boy to realize he was there. When he did, he was startled, and the trainer reacted to his surprise with a sudden drop in altitude.

Kashiwahara opened the cockpit canopy of his Zero and made a calm straight-ahead gesture with his gloved hand. He smiled at the boy to reassure him, nodding encouragingly. He clenched his fist and made advancing movements with it. The cadet nodded back and opened his throttle wider, reducing the space between himself and the formation. Kashiwahara decided to fly here for a time, at the end of one wing of the vee, where he could look out for other stragglers and herd them back to their proper places. He glanced ahead to see the gleam of the sea. Kanada was doing a fair-enough job of keeping the formation on course. When it was time to make a change, Kashiwahara decided, he would take over the lead again.

The sun stood low on the horizon, but clear of it. There was a path of brilliant white-gold on the water. He studied the air above the formation. They were crossing the line of contrails, though far below them. When he looked to the northeast he could see an occasional glint of light in the sky as the sun flashed on the polished aluminum skin of one of the *Bi-ni-ju-ku*. The bombers were flying at 12,000 meters or more, so high that few Japanese fighters could reach them, let alone engage them in combat. A Shiden Violet Lightning might manage it, or one of the even newer Raiden Thunderbolts. But Shiden were difficult to come by now that the Kawanishi assembly plant at Nagoya was in ruins. And only Chita, of all the pilots of the Takasaki Squadron, had even seen one of the pigeon-chested Raiden, which so closely resembled the American fighter-bomber called by the same name.

He looked down as the formation crossed the coast near Hitachi. There were wakes in the sea some two or three kilometers from shore. A pair of American destroyers was steaming south at flank speed, but if they saw the squadron's formation at all, they paid no attention to it. To the south Kashiwahara could make out some air activity, far away. To the north on this coast lay the village of Takahagi. He vaguely remembered that one of the squadron ratings, perhaps it was his own Kuritsu, was originally from that sleepy fishing village.

He waved to Matsumoto and swung again under the formation, inspecting it from below. It was sad and ragged, but it was obviously the best the pilots could manage. He remembered with nostalgia the skill and sharpness with which his old squadron aboard *Kaga* had flown at the Emperor's review of the fleet in 1941. What pilots we were, he thought. How beautifully we flew. But they were all gone now, all dead, the old comrades. He thought of the military anthem that began with the words "If I go away to sea, / I shall return as a brine-soaked corpse. . . ."

But the truth was that few corpses ever came home, brine-soaked or otherwise. In the beginning of the war, the honored dead's ashes were returned in boxes so that families could mourn as was proper. But since the defeats in the Philippines and Okinawa and Kyushu that was no longer done. This is not the war we thought we were going to fight, he told himself. It has become an *American* war, not a Japanese war. They set the rules now, which means that there *are* no rules.

A sudden flash alerted him. It was a wobbling fireball passing through the formation. It was followed by another. One of the destroyers below had circled and was firing at the formation. Kashiwahara advanced the throttle and climbed ahead of his *tokko*, waggling his wings for them to follow him away to the north. The group managed to stay together, but the vee quickly became a crescent, spread out across half a kilometer of sky. The Akatombo piloted by Mitsui began to lose altitude, a thin mist of gasoline trailing behind it. A shell from the ship below, fired at extreme range, had made a lucky hit on the trainer's nonself-sealing fuel tank. Kashiwahara banked hard and came up beside

Mitsui. He signaled with a hand that the boy should turn back to the coast. The round face under the helmet and *hachimaki* looked blank and uncomprehending. Kashiwahara opened his canopy and signaled again, vehemently, for the cadet to turn back.

Mitsui shook his head. He was refusing to return, refusing to be dishonored. Kashiwahara felt a sudden thickness in his throat, a mingling of pride and frustration. There was no way Mitsui could keep up with the formation; he had no chance whatever of completing the mission.

Kashiwahara flew in close and studied the damage to the Red Dragonfly. The fuel tank was punctured and there was damage to the exhaust collector ring. Flashes of flame appeared with each firing of the cylinder nearest the tear in the exhaust system. The danger of fire was acute.

He stared for what seemed a long time at the youthful face of the pilot. How old was Mitsui? he wondered. He had not troubled to ask. But he was surely not more than twenty.

He banked slightly to the right and pointed down at the destroyers below. They were almost lost in the glare of the sun and out of gun range now. He clenched his fist and then pointed again.

Mitsui's mouth opened as though he were shouting something. What? Kashiwahara wondered. Banzai! Of course. *Tenno Banzai!*

The Akatombo nosed over into a dive, heading for the swiftly retreating destroyers. Kashiwahara followed, his eyes wet with tears. The Akatombo's dive steepened, and quite suddenly the misty trail behind it was not white, but red-orange. The destroyers had not begun to fire again. There was no real need. Mitsui's dive became vertical. Flame driven by the slipstream engulfed the airplane from nose to tail. A wing came adrift and was left behind to circle down like the blade of a paper fan, scattering tiny black bits in the air. The other wing folded back against the burning fuselage, and Mitsui fell like a burning star into the sea.

Kashiwahara circled the place where the Akatombo had disappeared, but there was nothing to be seen there except a few bits of floating wreckage—very little, even of that.

He lifted his goggles and wiped at his eyes with gloved fingers. Cadet Mitsui had struck the sea no more than a kilometer or two from the rocky shoreline. Perhaps, the ensign thought, in this case the sailor would, indeed, "return as a brine-soaked corpse."

He advanced the throttle, closed the cockpit canopy, and climbed seaward to gather his scattered flock and continue the mission.

0640 Hours

Sergeant Ed MacCauley hunched low against the side of the pitching amphtrac, protecting his M-1 as best he could from the spray. The vehicle was crowded with Marines, all of them in some variation of MacCauley's low-profile position.

From where he crouched, he could see the APA the battalion had just left, surrounded by the geysers of water raised by a heavy and accurately aimed barrage of fire from the shore. The air was filled with the sound of rounds passing overhead in both directions. The noise could be heard clearly even over the sound of the amphtrac's engine.

In the forward end of the troop compartment, Lieutenant Scowcroft, still wearing his array of lethal equipment, sat with his helmet pressed hard against the steel flank of the splinter shield. He looked pale and wan, his lips colorless and his eyes wide with terror. MacCauley's dislike of the officer fought with his sympathy. A first assault was a frightening thing under the best of circumstances. And these circumstances were clearly not the best. The resistance from the shore was much heavier than had been expected, and the beach on which the battalion was supposed to land was smaller than it had appeared to be on the battle maps prepared by V Amphib Intelligence.

The target area looked deadly, in fact: a narrow strip of beach surrounded by sheer rock cliffs and broken volcanic ground. A road ran along the face of the cliffs, a narrow track that had been blasted from the rock. Beside the road there had apparently been some sort of electric rail line, though both road and rails had been cut by the bombing and shelling in several places. The most threatening aspect of the shore was that the road apparently ran through a series of tunnels here on the edge of Suruga Bay, and these tunnels had been strongly reinforced. From a number of archways in the tunnel wall came a withering fire from mortars and artillery pieces protected by huge slabs of reinforced concrete that had plainly withstood the preparatory bombardment.

Lieutenant Colonel Cleghorn, the battalion commander, had called in air support, and a dozen Corsairs and P-47s were making repeated bombing runs at the tunnel openings. Their bombs were raising smoke and splinters, but as far as anyone in the amphtracs could see, they had failed to make any real impression on the well-protected defenders.

As the line of amphtracs closed to within a thousand yards of the beach, MacCauley noted that they were converging, narrowing their front dangerously. The Japs on shore were beginning to fire air bursts from their howitzers on either flank. At each burst, the sea was lashed to froth by the shower of shrapnel. Mac-Cauley tried to swallow the dryness in his throat. Though he tried to think of something—anything—else, the memory of Pelileu kept coming back.

The faces of the other men in the amphtrac were as familiar to him as his own—Smith, Gracey, Kavanaugh, Angostino, Carpenter—yet they seemed total strangers. At a time like this, he thought, every man is alone.

Someone said, "Jesus, I'm gonna be sick." MacCauley felt a gripe of nausea himself, partially due to the motion of the amphtrac in the sea, but mostly due to the cold fear that had a solid grip on his guts.

A shell struck the water nearby, drenching the men and peppering the steel sides of the amphtrac with splinters. Scowcroft closed his eyes, and MacCauley thought he saw the officer's lips move in silent prayer. One couldn't blame the bastard for that, he thought. He wished that he could seek that sort of comfort, but, not for the first time, MacCauley realized that he did not believe in God. What sort of bloody-minded deity would let the creatures he created indulge in something like this?

Feeling himself to be frozen to the side of the troop compartment, he forced himself to straighten and raise his head above the splinter shield. He could just see the coxswain's head above the rim of his tiny steel box. The gray eyes beneath the blue-gray helmet looked flat, opaque, as though they had been painted on the white face.

It was not something he really wanted to do, but MacCauley forced himself to take a good look at the amphtrac's destination, Beach West Sims.

Shit, he thought. Ginny Sims wouldn't be pleased by the beach that had been given her name. Sims, the sweet-singing vocalist for Kay Kayser's band, was one of MacCauley's favorites, and it was no compliment to have given her name to the narrow, rock-bound, and vulnerable stretch of volcanic sand now some 400 yards from the advancing amphtracs. It lay almost directly beneath that damned tunnel and would be subject to plunging fire the minute the Marines hit the beach.

Above the road and ruined rail line the mountains seemed to shoot straight up, row on jumbled row of them, and beyond them he could see the snow-capped cone of a broad, symmetrical mountain. From the deck of *Sarasota* it had been obscured by the clouds and mist over the land, which were now being dispersed by the freshening onshore wind. It took MacCauley a moment to realize that he was looking at Fujiyama. There it suddenly was, like a postcard image, its snowy slopes tinged with the roseate light of early morning.

The sight hit him like a fist in the belly. *Japan.* Not just another stinking Pacific island, but the *last* island.

He felt someone pulling at his webbing and he crouched again. Gunnery Sergeant Peltzer said, "Head down, asshole."

"I saw Mount Fuji," MacCauley said.

"Congratulations. You've never seen a fuckin' mountain before?"

"Not *that* mountain, Gunny." He remembered the mountains of his native Colorado, which were so different from these jumbled peaks. These did not seem to lie in proper ranges at all, but appeared to sprawl around Fuji like the corpses of rocky giants. No wonder the Japs thought the mountain was holy. It rose over the land like a spectral pyramid built by Titans.

The fire from the shore increased in intensity as the waves of amphtracs approached the northern curve of the bay. The landing force was taking a heavy enfilading barrage on both flanks. The amphtrac next abeam was hit by a large shell, not less than a fifteen-centimeter mortar round, MacCauley's experience told him. It vanished in a cloud of fire, black smoke, steel fragments. Bits and pieces of steel and unidentifiable shreds of meat and bone and smoldering cloth pelted the men in his amphtrac. Private Kavanaugh, a thin, pale eighteen-year-old from San Diego, stared at what appeared to be a human tongue in his lap and immediately vomited into the bilges. Peltzer snatched up the bloody object and threw it over the splinter shield into the sea. Scowcroft turned his face against the bulkhead.

The amphtracs on the port flank were grounding on the dark volcanic sand, and Marines poured out of the vehicles and scuttled up the narrow beach in search of cover.

MacCauley felt the prow of his amphtrac strike the sand, and without conscious thought he found himself splashing through the shallow surf onto the pebbly beach. There were Marines everywhere, crowded shoulder to shoulder. The amphtracs were massed almost solidly from one end of the crescent-shaped strand of West Sims to the other. The front was not more than a thousand yards and it was suddenly swarming with men.

To his right a fire team was setting up a mortar. Ahead of them a BAR was already in action. Amphtracs were trying to back away from the beach to make room for the next wave, which consisted of LSTs loaded with more men and equipment.

MacCauley ran up the beach to a line of volcanic rocks above the high-tide mark. He turned and signaled his recon squad to follow. A line of bullets stitched the sand between him and his men, and he saw something pluck at Angostino's boondockers like an invisible hand. Angostino fell face down and did not move. The others of the squad crawled swiftly by him and crouched breathlessly beside MacCauley.

Some twenty yards away, Captain Freeman was setting up the Fox Company OP and yelling into the radio for some supporting fire from the warships offshore. "We're pinned down on the beach. Get some heavy stuff in here fast."

MacCauley turned over on his back so that he could see the uneven line of boats landing the second wave of Marines. It seemed to him that there were thousands of them, all crowding onto tiny West Sims.

Far down the beach a mortar shell exploded, sending men and pieces of men into the air. There were shouts: "Corpsman! God-damnit, corpsman!"

Kavanaugh lay next to MacCauley, his face dead white, his boondockers smelling of vomit. He clutched his M-1 so hard that his knuckles were whiter than his face.

"All right?" MacCauley asked.

"I'll be okay, Sarge," Kavanaugh said. "I just didn't think it would be like this."

MacCauley suppressed an angry impulse to ask Kavanaugh what he *had* expected—battle ensigns and the Marine Hymn?

Scowcroft came scuttling across the sand. The sharp volcanic particles had shredded the knees of his carefully tailored pants. His eyes were as blank and staring as they had been in the amphtrac, but his voice was remarkably steady as he said, "What's holding us up, Sergeant?"

MacCauley raised his head and pointed up the cliff face at the section of road tunnel directly above them. From the cavelike opening came the distinctive, flat popping sound of a Japanese Nambu machine gun. MacCauley's movement attracted the attention of the gunners, and bits of reddish volcanic rock flew from the boulders just above their heads as a burst of 7.7mm rounds fanned across the recon squad's front.

When the gunners realized that the squad was in defilade, they swung the machine gun to the right, and two Marines working on setting up a mortar sprawled, one of them holding his thigh and yelling for a corpsman, the other leaking blood from a hole just above the bridge of his nose.

"Let's get that Nambu," Scowcroft said.

"Yeah, shit, Lieutenant," Private Gracey said. "How?"

"Grenade."

Gracey pulled a grenade from his musette bag and hooked the safety pin out with a finger. He threw it in an arc from a supine position. It fell a good five yards short of the cave opening above the squad and clattered down through the rocks. The Marines hugged the ground until it exploded just on the other side of the boulders behind which they were sheltering.

"Jesus Christ, you fuckin' asshole," Corporal Carpenter screamed at Gracey.

Above them the Nambu continued to fire, sweeping the narrow section of beach behind the squad. They lay pinned, listening to the rumble of incoming naval shells, which burst somewhere off on the flank, where the Japs had that fifteen-centimeter howitzer working.

Scowcroft said, "We have to move, Sergeant. We can't stay here."

MacCauley knew the officer was right, but he could not bring himself to do what he knew was necessary. Elsewhere on the beach, Marine fire teams were beginning to climb the jumbled slides of volcanic boulders. The Nambu fired again, and Mac-Cauley saw a Marine slump among the broken pieces of lava.

"All right, Sergeant," Scowcroft said in that calm, dead voice. "Try to give me some covering fire."

He wriggled between two boulders and began to climb the slope toward the Nambu on his hands and knees.

MacCauley rolled into a prone position and fired a clip from his M-1 at the opening in the tunnel. "Gracey," he said, "see if you can get a BAR up here."

Kavanaugh, too, began to fire his rifle up the slope. The machine gunners traversed their gun once again, and the bullets sent bursts of volcanic sand flying. Scowcroft continued to crawl steadily toward the gun.

MacCauley kept firing until he could see that Scowcroft was almost in position to throw a grenade. He held his breath, expecting the officer to move, but he did not. Instead, he seemed to be crawling back, retracing his path down the slope.

"Well, *shit!*" Carpenter muttered. "What the fuck is he *doing?*"

Scowcroft now seemed to be groping around among the broken rocks, searching for something.

Gracey reappeared, crawling on knees and elbows, and flung himself into the cover of the rocks. "Freeman will get us a BAR as soon as he can, Sarge. They're all busy now," he said. He rolled over and looked up the slope. "What the hell is Chauncey doing, for Chrissake?"

Scowcroft was still fumbling about among the boulders. From time to time the Nambu would loose a burst at him and he would flatten himself against the ground. But as soon as the gun was silent, he would renew his groping.

"Jesus," MacCauley said. "Cover me." He left his M-1 propped against the rocks and crawled through the opening that Scowcroft had used. He climbed on his belly with a terrible metallic taste in his mouth. The hairs on the back of his neck stood like spines as he anticipated the bullet that would kill him. His helmet felt unbearably heavy, yet terrifyingly thin and fragile. Each time the Nambu fired, he had to tighten his sphincter to keep from fouling himself.

After what seemed an incredible number of seconds, minutes, even hours, he reached Scowcroft. He yanked the lieutenant's webbing to attract his attention.

"What is it?" he whispered. "Are you hit?"

Scowcroft said, "I lost my grenades."

"You *lost* your fucking grenades?"

"Yes. You said I shouldn't carry them on my webbing, you remember. So I had them in my pocket and I must have dropped them crawling up here. Have you got one?"

MacCauley wondered if he was hearing right. "Yes," he said. "Here."

Scowcroft's face was no longer pallid. It was flushed and sweaty from the effort of climbing the steep slope on his elbows and knees. "Do you want to throw it, Sergeant?"

MacCauley shook his head, unbelieving.

"All right, then," Scowcroft said. He took the grenade, carefully removed the safety pin, then opened his hand to make certain that the fuse was alight.

"*Throw* it, for Chrissake!" MacCauley hissed at him.

Scowcroft got to his knees and lobbed the grenade into the tunnel opening. One of the Jap gunners uttered a screeching shout and then the grenade exploded.

MacCauley lay back against the rocks with his eyes closed. He could feel his chest shaking, convulsing with hysterical laughter.

"Sergeant? You okay?" Scowcroft's moonish, immature face was filled with concern.

"Oh, sweet Jesus," MacCauley breathed. "Yes, Lieutenant, I'm fine. Just fine." He sat up and raised his clenched fist in a pumping motion to signal the remainder of the squad. "All right, Marines, get your asses in gear and let's *go!*" And then, without really thinking, he dipped into his store of Marine lore and yelled at his men. "*Move* it, Marines! You want to live forever?"

Below, at the edge of the beach, Carpenter yelled back: "Your fuckin' A we do, Sarge!" and began to lead the squad up the steep slope toward the road.

0700 Hours

Marquis Koichi Kido, Lord Privy Seal and close adviser to the Emperor, took his place at the head of the long table and bowed to the men gathered in the teahouse.

The shojis were closed so that no one would be subjected to the depressing sight surrounding the building. Though the grounds of the Imperial Palace had not been bombed, the fires that had razed the city outside the moat had blackened the ancient stone walls and fortifications and blighted the gardens. Dead pines stood in groves, their needles brown or scattered on the ground. The pools and fountains were either dry or filled with stagnant water. There was the ever-present smell of death and burning in the air.

The men at this secret emergency meeting near the Imperial Palace were four: Admiral Soemu Toyoda, the chief of the Imperial Navy General Staff; Lieutenant General Torashiro Kawabe, deputy chief of the Army General Staff; Shigenori Togo, the foreign minister; and Kido himself.

Outside the teahouse, Kawabe had posted as guards six selected officers of the 7th Tank Brigade, older men whom he believed to be reasonable and who could be trusted.

It was Kido who gave the signal for the meeting to begin. "General Kawabe," he said, "please give us your appreciation of our situation."

Kawabe, his face deeply lined and pale, referred to a sheaf of battle reports he had taken from his briefcase. "Our situation, *Koshaku-dono*, is quite simply disastrous. The Americans have begun to come ashore at Kashima, Kujukuri-hama, and in the Sagami and Suruga bay areas. They are attacking us with what appears to be a force of forty-two divisions. We have not identified them all, but we know that General Stilwell's Tenth Army is involved in the Kashima Sea area landings, General Krueger's Sixth Army is leading the assault on Kujukuri-hama, and General Schmidt's V Amphibious Corps is leading the force attempting to establish a beachhead on the northwestern shore of Suruga-wan. We have tentatively identified one more, the III Marine Amphibious Corps, consisting of three divisions."

The old soldier's voice shook as he continued. "Though our ability to gather intelligence is severely curtailed by the enemy's complete domination of the air, we believe that the United States First Army, redeployed from Europe, is standing in reserve and will be brought ashore as soon as the major beachheads are secure." He regarded Toyoda bleakly. "Unless the Navy is prepared to prevent it." When the admiral quietly shook his head, Kawabe went on. "It is General Tojo's belief that we have sufficient military force to engage the enemy here on the Kanto Plain and inflict upon him such heavy casualties that he will agree to a negotiated peace with terms advantageous to us."

For a moment everyone was silent. As suspected members of the peace party, each had been in serious danger during the Crimson Dawn Coup. It had been only the regard in which they were all known to be held by the Emperor that had saved them from the vengeful *gumbatsu*. And each realized that by meeting now, secretly, they had revived that danger a hundredfold.

Kawabe said evenly, "General Tojo is wrong. Or at least mistaken." It offended his sense of propriety to make such a flatly negative statement about a member of his own class and profession, but it was something that had to be said.

"You will all recall that last June, before the loss of southern Kyushu but while the Americans were reducing Okinawa, the

Supreme War Direction Council issued a statement, Basic Policy for the Future Direction of the War, which resulted in the formation of the *ketsu-go* battle plans. We now know that although Tojo was at that time in retirement, he was influential in the formation of that statement. I would like to refresh your memories about one part of the statement, which in light of later developments shows how inaccurately our situation was presented to the War Direction Council and therefore to the Emperor." He took from his briefcase a copy of the document bearing the title *Saiko Senso Shido Kaigi Tsuzuri* and began to read.

" 'Changing tendencies in the world situation will be exploited through the pursuit of an active and aggressive diplomacy, especially toward the Soviet Union and China, with a view to furthering the prosecution of the war.' " He looked steadily at each man in turn and then said, "By that one may suppose that the War Direction Council chose to believe, even at that late date, that the American resolve to force us into unconditional surrender could be ignored." He looked reproachfully at his listeners. "Some of us were members of the council at that time and we allowed ourselves to be convinced that this statement represented a realistic view of the war situation. I myself was guilty, and I have long considered how I might best apologize to the Emperor for my failing." The men in the teahouse knew exactly what sort of apology Kawabe had considered. For an officer and a samurai the choices were limited—and bloody.

"Let me remind you of the conclusions of the statement of June 1945," the general continued. He adjusted his eyeglasses and read on. " 'On the home front, all necessary preparations to enable the nation to fight unitedly in the decisive battle of the homeland will be rushed to completion in thorough conformity with the spirit of a people's war. In particular, the Government will lay stress in all its measures on the replenishment of the nation's material strength with special attention to securing food supplies and augmenting the production of special weapons as well as boosting fighting morale and consolidating national unity, with the formation of people's volunteer units as the backbone of the program.' " He paused and then said, "Please note, gentlemen, 'as the backbone of the program.' We are all aware—are we not?—of what that 'backbone' is to be made." He removed his glasses and wiped at his eyes with a handkerchief. "When the *gumbatsu*'s coup overturned the government of Premier Suzuki—despite his promise to defend the homeland according to this very plan—the young officers demanded the return of General Tojo as prime minister and minister of war. Only he, they told us, could lead the nation in these terrible times. Lead the nation to what end, gentlemen? The statement speaks of replenishing the nation's strength. From what sources? I ask. We are already cut off from our own southernmost island. It speaks of special weapons. What weapons, gentlemen? Bamboo spears, *kaiten* torpedoes that must be piloted by the last of the Navy's brave sailors, Kamikaze bombs and airplanes that are taking the best of Japan's next generation to death, packs worn by women and children to be exploded under American tanks. I don't need to go on. We all know what is meant by a 'people's war.' As we sit here there are tens of thousands of civilians preparing to throw themselves into battle against the Americans, with sticks and farm tools and bare hands, if need be. General Tojo has massed the last of Japan's Army, 150,000 soldiers, to engage the Americans here in the Kanto. The *ketsu-go* that is about to take place will be a *Götterdämmerung* more suited to Germans than to the people of the Eight Islands. When it is finished, when we have taken the blood price from Americans, how much of a nation will they leave us?" He stood stiffly erect, his lined cheeks wet with tears that were now flowing copiously. Like many Japanese, General Kawabe was a severely disciplined man, but a deeply emotional one. "You asked me, *Koshaku-dono*, what our military situation is. It is bad and soon to become much worse. Right now there are at least 100,000 American troops within 150 kilometers of the Imperial Palace. There are half that many within 100 kilometers. By tomorrow, they will have broken out of the northern beachheads and they will be racing toward Tokyo. Before anything else is decided, we should

---

242

implore the Emperor to evacuate the Imperial Palace and take refuge in the mountains."

Kido said, "That is out of the question. The Emperor refuses to leave his capital. I have spoken to him as recently as last evening. He is resolved to remain."

Togo stood and bowed to Kido. "*Koshaku-dono*, we should consider removing the Emperor and his family by force if necessary. Such things have been done before."

"Impossible," Toyoda said, frowning. "The Emperor is the symbol of the nation. He must remain here at Edo." He used the ancient name of the city and the palace grounds deliberately, to remind the others of the absolute need to prevent the Americans from desecrating this shrine of Japanese nationalism with armed men. Whatever was done must be done before the Western soldiers reached Tokyo and this great park, which had once been, in the time of the Tokugawa shoguns, Edo Castle.

"I agree," Kido said. "The Imperial family must remain here, but they must not, under any circumstances, be taken prisoner. I cannot imagine the terrible results of such an event." He signaled Kawabe and the foreign minister to be seated. Then he unfolded his spare frame and stood looking somberly at the others. "It is not surprising to me that our military situation is desperate. Japan has done all that any nation could do in the course of this terrible war. Our people have made enormous sacrifices. Our soldiers and sailors have performed with all the courage, all the Bushido, that our long history demands. But there comes a time to call an end to the destruction and the death." He opened a lacquered box that rested on the table before him. From it he removed a document whose cover bore the Imperial Chrysanthemum seal. "I have prepared a draft of an Imperial rescript which, if I have your approval, I shall present immediately to the Emperor. Allow me to read it to you."

The men at the table bowed their heads respectfully because they were about to hear words that, once signed by the Emperor, would become *his* words.

Kido opened the document and began. " 'To Our good and

loyal subjects: After pondering deeply the general trends of the world and the actual conditions obtaining in Our Empire today, We have decided to effect a settlement of the present situation by resorting to an extraordinary measure. We have ordered Our Government to communicate to the Governments of the United States, Great Britain, China, and the Soviet Union that Our Empire accepts the provisions of their Joint Declaration. . . .' "

At the mention of the Joint Declaration of Potsdam, a statement demanding unconditional surrender, Kawabe allowed his hand to close on the hilt of the ancient, razor-sharp *aikuchi* secreted under his tunic. As a soldier, he knew that what Kido's draft rescript contained was necessary if Japan was not to be obliterated as a nation, and he approved it. But once the decision was taken and approved by the Emperor, Kawabe fully intended to disembowel himself on the bridge over the moat protecting the holy precincts of the Imperial Palace, as countless samurai who had failed their Emperor had done.

Kido's voice broke several times as he read, for he was now as emotional as his companions. To plot peace was one thing; to plot surrender was something else again—though necessary. These men, Kido knew, and others to whom he had spoken secretly were agreed. Japan *must* end the war.

" 'Despite the gallant fighting of the officers and men of the Army and the Navy, the diligence and assiduity of Our servants of state, the devoted service of Our one hundred million subjects—despite the best efforts of all, the war situation worsens from day to day. Moreover, the general world situation is not to Japan's advantage. . . .' "

Admiral Toyoda was weeping openly; his posture was correct and rigid except for the shaking of his shoulders.

"Let the nation continue as one family . . . with unwavering faith in the imperishability of Our divine land. Cultivate the ways of rectitude—' "

Kido's reading was interrupted by a burst of machine-gun fire outside the teahouse. There followed shouts and pistol shots, then another burst of machine-gun fire. The men at the table got to their feet as the shoji was smashed to tatters and a dozen young officers carrying automatic weapons burst into the room, their faces contorted with fury.

Kido and Togo, both men in their late seventies, made no move to escape. They knew that their karma was upon them. But the admiral and the general, though not much younger, drew their swords and confronted the young fanatics. Kawabe realized bitterly that these were all youthful Guards officers, Japan's best remaining soldiers.

Five of the young men dropped their automatic weapons and drew their swords. They charged the old men and cut them down. Kido they beheaded. The others they mutilated with such ferocity that the inside of the teahouse was spattered everywhere with blood.

When they had done what they came to do, one of the Guards officers found the draft of the rescript Marquis Kido had prepared. He set it alight and used the burning document to set the teahouse on fire.

Murder done, the officers dispersed through the half-ruined grounds of the Imperial Palace park. The smoke of the burning teahouse rose straight into the still air and blended with the lasting smoke from the fires of last night's raid by American bombers.

Colonel Kantaro Maeda huddled against the sandbagged rim of the OP, conscious of the men around him but unable to force himself to raise his head to ascertain accurately how many of the battalion staff remained in the observation post.

It was not lack of courage that kept him in an almost-fetal position against the burlap-and-earth wall. His fear had been pounded out of him hours ago by the continuous blasting of the artillery that had begun to fall directly on his unit's position two hours ago and continued unabated as the day grew brighter. But he had found that the constant shocks had frozen him in his crouching position, almost literally stunning him into immobility.

245

The noise and repeated waves of stinking hot air that assaulted him and the others prevented them from raising their eyes to the level of the parapet to observe the activities of the enemy on the beach below.

The battery commander's binocular scope, a device that ordinarily made it possible to observe without being observed because of its periscopic construction, had long ago been smashed by shell splinters. At the beginning of the barrage on the position, Captain Takeda, the battalion's second-in-command, had been almost decapitated by a steel fragment, the radio had been perforated and put out of action, and Lieutenant Genda, the young artillery observation officer, had been badly wounded. Genda now lay propped against the sandbags with his life slowly oozing in a foul-smelling red-and-brown slime from a deep wound in his belly. There was nothing anyone in the OP could do for him, and no one tried. In the momentary lulls between the fall of shells, he could be heard sobbing softly.

The observation post had been established days before, on a shallow rise in the ground above the high-tide mark, on a small point of land almost exactly halfway between the now almost nonexistent villages of Katsuura and Ohara. Maeda's battalion of Imperial Guards, far understrength and long ago reduced by casualties and special postings to hardly more than the size of a prewar company, held a front of 900 meters. On their left flank, facing the southernmost part of Kujukuri Beach, a regiment of the 147th Infantry Division, reinforced by a squadron of the 3rd Independent Tank Brigade, was absorbing the impact of what appeared to be a full American infantry division—the 11th Airborne, to judge by the soldiers' shoulder patches.

Earlier in the morning, before the Guards' position had come under direct fire from the cruisers offshore, an observer at the northern edge of the 147th's sector had reported that the soldiers coming ashore belonged to the Americans' IX Corps and that their tanks were being disembarked in great numbers. He had asked for artillery to stop the flood of armor from the LSTs, but there had been none to give him. The Shermans had smashed through the defensive positions and were by now driving inland in the direction of Togane, a village at the junction of the Mobara-Choshi and Togane-Chiba roads. Once the tanks began to roll toward Chiba, on the western shore of the Boso-hanto, the entire peninsula would be cut off.

Maeda's position was not so strategically vital to the Kanto's defense. The makeshift force, stiffened by the Guards battalion, was intended to inflict casualties on the flank of the Americans' Kujukuri beachhead. But apparently the planners at Imperial General Staff Headquarters had underestimated—yet again—the resources available to the Americans. To the southwest of Maeda's battalion, what was being reported as an American brigade, possibly even a full division, was already ashore on the narrow beaches of the southern tip of the peninsula. What was worse, before the radio was destroyed a report had reached Maeda's position that the division storming ashore on his right flank was only the advance element of a much larger formation. Units of the X and XIV Corps had been identified. If the information was accurate, it meant, Maeda knew, that the veteran U.S. Eighth Army had chosen to land not more than twenty kilometers from where his understrength battalion huddled under the naval bombardment.

The fortress area behind the battalion's forward position sheltered nearly 2,000 troops and contained some fifty assorted artillery pieces. But the galleries and tunnels had taken a week-long pounding from the warships offshore, and Maeda was not confident that it could take much more. Covering his face against the almost continuous rain of foul-smelling earth thrown up by the shelling, he thought bitterly about General Shibata and the staffers from Tokyo who had come down to the Boso Peninsula with their Kyoto geishas. It was difficult enough to keep up the morale of the men under these conditions without asking them to fight while their superiors disported themselves in the safety of the command bunker with women and sake.

Colonel Ogaki, Maeda's immediate superior, and a Guards officer, had allowed Maeda to choose his own positions for the battle—the battle that would one day be called, Maeda supposed, the Battle of Katsuura or Ohara or even the Boso Peninsula. If anyone was left in Japan to read of such a battle, he amended bitterly.

Rather than seek the dubious protection of the laboriously constructed fortifications, Maeda had situated his men in the broken volcanic-rock formations between the fort and the high-tide mark. There was no beach directly east, so the Americans could not use their superior numbers and fire power to make a frontal assault. To the north of the battalion a much-cratered, but still-passable road ran from the fort's eastern gallery down a steep slope toward the small series of beaches abutting the vast sweep of Kujukuri-hama, where the Americans appeared to be making their most determined effort. The road had been heavily mined and was protected by tank obstacles and wire: its coordinates had been registered with all the artillery units within the fort whose guns could be brought to bear.

But none of the engineers and planners could have foreseen the incredible power of the bombardment to which this entire sector of coast had been subjected. The American *Iowa*-class battleships, reported by Intelligence to be 45,000-tonners or larger, had cruised this coastline for weeks firing their batteries of nine sixteen-inch guns at almost point-blank range. The result had been to reduce the defensive works everywhere around the Katsuura-Ohara fortifications, and the fortifications themselves, to impotence. The road had become a solid river of churned earth, a ramp of rubble ready to accept the American tanks whenever they chose to make use of it. The guns inside the fortress galleries had been dismounted and smashed, except for the smaller pieces that the men were able to withdraw from the openings to safer positions within the mountain.

Maeda cursed the decision that had resulted in so many useful troops being held inside the largely useless concrete works. The fate of the Maginot and Siegfried lines should have taught the Japanese planners something about the worth of so-called impregnable positions, where troops might shelter, but from which they could not fight effectively.

Maeda's positions were being shelled by smaller ships now. Apparently the invisible cruisers had handed off the target to the racing destroyers that churned back and forth importantly a few thousand meters offshore. The intensity of the bombardment appeared to be lessening, and he forced himself to raise his head over the sandbagged parapet so that he could look to the northeast, where the Americans' activities were just visible beyond the point of land dividing his area from the beaches near Kujukuri.

A number of landing craft had veered away from the beachhead beyond the point and were heading in Maeda's direction. Some boats had apparently already landed, because he could see a score of heavy tanks and amphtracs moving toward the battalion's positions. The armored vehicles were accompanied by large numbers of infantry.

He staggered to his feet and called for a runner. When the soldier, as disoriented from the shelling as Maeda himself, appeared, he instructed him to return to the fortress and warn the garrison that the Americans were on the move in their direction. He wrote the order on a pad and gave the co-ordinates of the head of the American column, hoping that there was enough functioning artillery to bring the enemy under fire.

The soldier disappeared, crawling through the rocks and climbing toward the entrance to the fort's east gallery.

Next, Maeda checked the field telephone connecting his OP with the battalion's various mortar and machine-gun positions. Half of the communications net had been disrupted by the shelling. He could not reach his troops on the seaward flank by phone, so he sent runners to warn them to prepare for action. The other positions, those between himself and the churned-up road, he was able to alert. Only then did he allow himself the luxury of calling for a medical corpsman to attend to Lieutenant Genda, who still sat moaning softly, his hands over his belly wound.

The medic appeared quickly, disregarding the by now fitful fall of a shell fired by the destroyers offshore. When he had examined the young officer, he straightened and shook his head.

Maeda knelt beside Genda and tried to think what he might do to comfort him. There was nothing. Genda had been a student at Kyoto University only a hundred days ago. He had told Maeda quite seriously that he had been tempted to leave the university and enter a monastery to become a Buddhist monk. Since he was not a Shintoist, he could not be soothed with stories of the marvelous afterlife awaiting the heroes of the nation at Yasukuni Shrine in Tokyo. Maeda himself had begun to have some serious doubts about that roseate future among the shades of the millions of samurai under the protection of Amaterasu Omikami. When last he had seen Yasukuni, the grounds of which abutted the avenue on which stood—or *had* stood—the Kudan-shita railway station, the shrine had been in ruins. The wooden buildings had been savaged by the fire raids. The great gates bearing the Imperial Chrysanthemum seals were down, scorched. The great toriis were lying in shards and splinters.

One did not openly question the power of the gods, but Maeda had seen and experienced too much of war to remain a true believer. Colonel Ogaki had once said to him, "In war if one is to keep one's ideals, one should die young."

Well, Lieutenant Genda was young, and he was surely dying—dying in agony. Maeda could only place a hand gently on the boy's damp forehead and hope that it did not take too long. He did not relish the thought of giving him the *coup de grâce*—a thing he must do rather than let him fall dishonorably into the hands of the Americans still alive.

Genda's eyes were flat black, opaque. A trickle of bile and blood had dried at the corner of his mouth. He stared at Maeda unseeing. His breathing was shallow and rapid.

Maeda's orderly, Sergeant Koga, who was watching the Americans' advance through Maeda's binoculars, said, "*Taisa-dono*, they are in battalion strength."

Maeda took the binoculars and examined the advancing line

of armor and infantry. Koga was right. As he watched, two more Shermans rounded the point on the narrow spit of sand. They were followed by a pair of self-propelled 105mm howitzers. Maeda studied the armor and artillery hungrily. What couldn't *we* accomplish with equipment like that, he thought.

"Airplanes, *Taisa-dono*," Koga said. Maeda lowered the field glasses and squinted into the morning sun. From the sea were coming a dozen or more gull-winged Corsair fighter-bombers. They flew low over the water, almost in line abreast. Against the glare it was difficult to make out details, but he could see the externally racked bombs and rockets. Even as he watched, the first element fired missiles at the openings in the fort's eastern gallery. As the airplanes roared close overhead, the men in the OP fired at them with their Arisaka rifles, but if there were hits, the Corsairs gave no sign of it as they climbed steeply and vanished over the ridge line to the west.

Another formation of American airplanes was approaching from the south. They were P-47s, the Thunderbolts: big single-engined machines with gracefully shaped elliptical wings and massive bodies. Survivors of the battles on Kyushu had reported that these airplanes, apparently brought to the Pacific from Europe, could carry very heavy bombs and many more rockets than the Corsairs.

As the medic squatted beside Genda, the wounded man's fingers clawed at his sleeve. The medic, tired and frightened, pushed the groping fingers away. Maeda glared angrily at him. What could it cost, he thought, to treat the dying man with consideration? If not that, with common politeness. He kicked the medic away. Genda's lips were moving. He was trying to speak, perhaps to voice some protest. Maeda said, "Yes, Genda-san. Yes, what is it?"

Genda made beckoning gestures with his fingers. Maeda lowered his face, braving the terrible smell of offal that clung to the dying man. Genda struggled to speak.

Maeda put his ear to Genda's lips, and Genda said: *"Naze?"*

Maeda controlled an exasperated expletive. Why? How could

251

one answer such a question? How could a Japanese soldier ask it?

Genda seemed to be staring straight up at the sky. He had stopped breathing. Maeda closed the blank eyes with thumb and forefinger. He felt a wave of the most profound melancholy. He had had no particular regard for young Genda, who had been an indifferent officer at best. But somehow it seemed wrong that he should be dead.

"*Taisa-dono!* Look!" Koga shouted. He was pointing excitedly back at the tunnel that led into the fort. Maeda stood, rigid.

Soldiers were pouring out into the open, running and leaping like a river of people. They carried their rifles high, the harsh sunlight glittering from fixed bayonets. Officers were mingled with the torrent, samurai swords waving. All of them were shrieking like demons. Maeda, horror-stricken, recognized General Shibata running heavily at the head of the column: fat, breathless, stumbling over the churned, uneven ground that had been the road down to the shore. Beside him ran Captain Azumi, his sword held over his head in both hands as though ready to strike a blow. And Colonel Ogaki, Maeda's own regimental commander. And Major Higashi, the headquarters company commander. All of the men who had been at the sake party in the command bunker were in that surging mass erupting from the fort. There were so many running toward the shore that the road could not contain them and some tripped and stumbled and fell down the steep talus. It appeared that all of the 2,000 men who had been in the fort, from Shibata to the lowliest second class private—every man, in fact, who could carry a weapon—were joining in a mad, tumultuous charge at the beach. Maeda could hear the fortress bugler's instrument making brassy, disconnected noises as he ran.

The Americans stopped, and their tanks and tracked artillery formed a massed front. The charging Japanese saw this and interpreted it as some kind of victory, because they ran on, screaming and waving their weapons.

Maeda's own men were caught up in the madness and the

wild exhilaration. They began to shout, *"Banzai! Tenno banzai!"*

Koga, a Guards soldier with twenty years' experience, was halfway up the sandbagged parapet, screaming as loudly as any of the recruits in the flood of men erupting from the cover of the fort. Maeda tried to find his own commander in the crush, but Ogaki had now been swallowed up by the human wave rushing toward the Americans.

The tanks began to fire over open sights at the Japanese charge. Because the men had emerged from a single tunnel in the fortifications, and because they had had to run down a narrow road toward the beach, they were massed shoulder to shoulder. The fire from the tanks began to cut swathes in the river of humanity. Great bloody trenches appeared in the crowd. As the shells exploded, they were almost smothered by the press of the bodies they were shattering.

Maeda's men were leaping up and down like children, screaming encouragement to the men who were charging. Then by ones and twos, and finally in a flood, they began to abandon their positions and join the attack. Maeda shouted at them to halt, to remain where they were and serve their weapons so that the American fire power could be interdicted, but they ignored him and ran screaming down the rock slope to join the others.

Maeda saw Shibata just once again. The general had run, clumsily and drunkenly, to a spot on the shoreline where several large volcanic boulders prevented him from running farther. He stood there on a rock, waving his sword, until a shell from one of the massed American guns struck him, shearing the top half of his fat body from his legs. Streamers of bluish entrails, blood, and bone blew out behind him. His sword, spinning and glittering in the harsh sunlight, fell into the sea. Maeda could see no more.

The P-47s appeared, flying low over the water and firing rockets into the mass of running soldiers. The explosions seemed to walk up the road right to the tunnel mouth, blowing men and pieces of men high into the air.

The charge continued for perhaps five minutes more before

253

the guns fell silent. Maeda could scarcely believe what he saw. Not one Japanese soldier had reached the American line of advance. The nearest was an officer who sat stupidly on the ground, without legs but still holding his sword, watching his blood run in a torrent into the ground. Back from that spot, some twenty meters from the nearest American tank, lay a carpet of dead and dying men, broken weapons, bloody limbs, limbless torsos, headless bodies, and men simply so torn that they could do nothing but await their dying. They lay piled on one another; in places the shells had stacked them seven and eight deep. The road was no longer the color of the volcanic soil. In those few places not covered with men and parts of men, the soil was bright red. Blood ran down the slope between the rocks. There was a kind of mass, swarming movement, as those who could do so attempted to crawl into whatever cover they could find. It was as though some mythical dragon had been minced into segments and yet found time to protest its own slaughter.

Maeda's stomach griped with sudden nausea. He had seen charges before, had even participated in some. But this was butchery on a scale beyond his experience. In no more than seven minutes, the Americans had killed or wounded most of the garrison of the only fort on the Boso Peninsula. Thanks to General Shibata's drunken bravado, 1,000 men lay dead, another 800 nearly dead, and a few, finally, had run away. They were being cut down by an occasional burst from the enemy.

Even as he watched, hand grenades exploded here and there among the injured as men blew themselves to bits rather than be taken alive.

The explosions brought another sharp storm of fire from the American column. The battleground was tumbled and harrowed with more steel for three or four minutes. Then the American infantry began to advance again, cautiously, holding their weapons ready to blast any sign of movement in the charnel house they had created.

What he had seen, Maeda thought, was no longer war. It was something quite beyond that.

"Taisa-dono?"

Startled, he turned to face a heavy-featured young private who had crawled from somewhere into the almost deserted observation post. "What shall we do, Maeda-dono?"

The confusion of the conscript peasant reminded Maeda of his responsibilities. For a while he had wished simply to die—not to die a hero, charging the enemy like the others—but simply to die alone and at once. But the dazed soldier wakened him from that peaceful dream.

"How many are left?" he asked.

"Up there—" the soldier indicated the slopes where, an eternity ago, Maeda had so carefully sited his machine guns—"fifteen or twenty, I think." He paused uneasily. "We almost joined the charge, *Taisa-dono*, and perhaps we should have. But we had no orders—" He broke off helplessly.

"You did the proper thing," Maeda said. He turned back to see that the American column was advancing steadily, though slowly and cautiously, through that hideous harvest of corpses and sobbing wounded. "Follow me," he said. "We will gather whatever is left." And carefully he led the way over the wall of sandbags and began to work around the fortress's crumbled remains. "We will fall back and make a stand in the mountains," he said.

Second Lieutenant Lloyd Hansen dreamed that he was lost in the mountains of Wyoming. There was a cold, silent wind and snow on the ground and he was walking, walking, but the scenery never seemed to change. The sky was a terrible dead white, and in the far distance he could see a dark line of pines that never came any closer. They were ugly pines, strangely naked of needles—just the skeletons of pines, stark against the white land and sky. The shuddering cold penetrated deep into him, and he held his belly muscles as tight as he could hold them, trying to save some of his body's warmth. But he was losing the fight and from time to time he would slip out of himself and look down at a frozen shape in the snow, a shape made of glazed ice that he somehow knew was himself, dead.

He opened his eyes with a start to find that he was still in the place where his captors had confined him. They were civilians, farmers probably, ageless—because the unlined faces were so expressionless that he could not judge their years—and totally alien.

They had marched him for hours along dikes between paddies, prodding him with their bamboo spears and from time to time bursting into fits of screaming at him. His bare feet had become bloody and muddy, and his legs had sometimes refused to carry him farther. When he fell to his knees, the Japs had poked and prodded and beaten him with their damned sticks.

From the place where they had captured him, they had turned back toward the east, into the growing light of the morning. But with the sun had come very little heat. He had the terrible feeling that he would never again be dry or warm. He was hungry, too, with a dull aching hunger. They had taken everything from him except his shirt and trousers. Once, he had nerved himself to protest that they should give him food and water before marching him further, but his protest had died almost instantly in a storm of shouting and flailing bamboo sticks.

They had led him between the rice paddies and along unpaved roads into a flat country of marshes and lagoons. He tried to remember where on his chart he had seen those reedy lakes, but he could not. They had taken his chart, of course, along with his watch and the pistol he had been carrying.

Perhaps even bringing the pistol along on a mission had been a mistake. What had he expected to do with it? Setting the Norden to fly the airplane and drop the bombload was another sort of thing entirely. It killed people, yes, but it wasn't like firing a pistol at someone you could see.

He had tried to make the farmers understand that he was an officer, a prisoner of war. There had been not the slightest indication that they had any idea of what he was saying. There was no indication, in fact, that they *wanted* to know. They had simply whipped and prodded him along, screaming and shouting at him whenever he faltered, until they reached this farm. He guessed it was a farm. At least there was a house with a tiled roof and some outbuildings, one of which was this foul-smelling barn where they had confined him.

It was too small to fit his idea of a barn, but at some time animals had been kept here. There was dung dried and hardened on the stamped earth floor. There were places that resembled stalls and a pit where once, long ago, there might have been a fire. Thin white daylight came through the spaces in the walls. He could hear vermin moving in the thatch overhead. Occasionally he could hear voices outside, and once a man had opened the door to stare at him where he lay tethered to one of the posts supporting the roof. He had held up his hands and asked to have his wrists untied, but if the man understood he gave no sign of it.

Hansen tried to organize his thoughts and consider the problem of capture in the way he had been taught back at Miyazaki. "You are soldiers," Colonel Rivera had told the aircrews. "If you should be captured, remember that you are entitled to proper treatment as prisoners of war." There had been a great deal more about not giving the Japs any information, only name, rank, and serial number. And then some Nisei from Oregon had tried to teach everyone some Japanese phrases, such as: "You must treat me well. It is the law" and "Soon the war will be over and we will all be friends." But from Hansen's present perspective none of that made much sense. Even if he could remember the phrases in Japanese, which he could not, they didn't seem to be the sort of thing one said to a bunch of hostile, stocky men pushing at you with sharpened sticks.

The inside of the barn was freezing cold, and Hansen huddled against the post trying to stay warm. Sometime much earlier in the morning he had heard what sounded like a long column of armored vehicles passing on the road through the paddies. Tanks, most likely, he thought, because of the squeaking and clanking. They had been coming from the west and heading God knew where, but he assumed their destination to be the coast.

By this time the invasion must be well under way, he thought. Unless it had been postponed, which would have been just like the fucking Army. The rumble of the shelling was a sound to which he had become so accustomed that he no longer heard it or even thought about what it might mean.

He wondered what had happened to Sergeant Stansky after that one awful howl of pain he had heard in the early-morning dark. There was no way of knowing. No way, either, to guess whether or not anyone else had made it out of "The Cornhuskers" when she was hit.

Hansen shivered and tried to keep his spirits up. After all, if the troops were coming ashore right now, it couldn't be too long before he would be liberated. The Japs were strange and frightening, but they didn't have things like concentration camps, the way the Germans had. And some aircrews in Germany *had* been sent to concentration camps, to a place called Mauthausen, where the fucking Krauts worked them to death in a quarry. It had been in *Stars and Stripes*, the whole dirty story. So things could definitely be worse. A guy had to keep remembering that.

He heard more shouting outside and the sound of an airplane flying low overhead. The familiar quarrelsome roar of a Rolls-Royce or an Allison made his heart leap in his chest. But the sound faded and the Mustang did not return.

A few minutes later he heard another engine, this one a truck of some kind. It came to a stop outside with a squeal of brakes, and there was more shouting. Didn't the Japs ever speak in a normal tone of voice? he wondered. They were always yelling and screaming as though they were constantly in a rage.

There were scrambling noises and more shouts as another vehicle arrived to stop by the barn's heavy wooden door. Hansen heard the unmistakable sound of soldiers: the clatter of weapons and shouted commands.

The door burst open, and Hansen squinted against the wintry glare. He saw that two trucks had been backed up to the building. In the open back of one of them three Japs had set up a Nambu machine gun. They were small men in tight, ugly mustard-colored uniforms and steel helmets.

From the other truck, soldiers were prodding American prisoners, three of them. One, a lanky captain wearing a leather flying jacket and a helmet, towered over his captors. The other two Americans were enlisted men, one black, one white, in muddy fatigues and combat boots. The white man had been wounded. His left arm was wrapped in a field dressing and he carried it tucked into his field jacket. The other was unhurt, but badly frightened.

The Japs screamed and kicked at them and herded them into the barn. Then they stamped inside and prodded the black man with their bayonets, pointing back at the truck, where a fourth man lay.

"Jesus, Captain," the black private said in a cultured but trembling voice, "what is it they want with me?"

"They want you to carry your officer in here, I think," the captain said. "I'll give you a hand." He started toward the door, but his move was met by a storm of furious anger from the Japanese soldiers, who threatened him with their weapons. "Sorry," he said. "You'll have to manage alone, it seems."

The black soldier returned to the truck and half dragged, half carried, an enormous man into the barn. The wounded man had a pale face and huge limbs, and was clearly dying. His mouth hung slackly, and his head was heavily bandaged. The dressing was dark with dried blood.

The Japanese shouted some incomprehensible orders at the prisoners and slammed the barn door shut.

The tall captain—a pilot, Hansen saw from his insignia—knelt beside the large man, feeling for a pulse.

"How is he?" the black soldier asked.

The flier looked up and shrugged. "I don't get a pulse. I think he's had it, soldier."

The black stood in silence. The dying man, a first lieutenant, wore the gold double-tower badge of the Corps of Engineers on the collar of his shirt.

The soldier said at last, heavily, "He was a mean bastard of an ofay. But he took care of his men. You have to say that."

Hansen said, "Hey, how about untying my hands?"

The infantryman with the injured arm sat down on the floor. "Shit. A million-dollar wound and look where I am."

The tall pilot, who said his name was Higgins, came over to Hansen and began to work on the cord binding the bombardier's wrists. "Who are you?" he asked. "How did *you* get here?"

Hansen realized that the civilians who had captured him had stripped his uniform of everything, even insignia. He identified himself and asked for news.

The black, Private Slocum, seemed reluctant to leave his officer. "We were building a pontoon bridge," he said. "Over something called the Tonegawa." He looked up and his voice steadied. "We're Combat Engineers. We were right close to the line. The goddamn armor that was supposed to be protecting us took off after some Jap tanks and we got banzaied by a whole regiment of Slopes." He looked again at the inert figure of his officer. "They overran us. It was a slaughter, man, a slaughter—" He shook his head and muttered something inaudible.

The infantryman, Corporal Ray, had been taken prisoner in the same engagement, and Hansen wanted to know where it had happened. "How far away are our guys?" he asked.

"Twenty, maybe thirty miles," the captain said. "But there's what looks like a whole Jap division between us and them."

Hansen rubbed some life into his wrists. He walked to the door to peer out through one of the spaces between the rough-hewn planks. He could see a number of Japanese soldiers in the muddy yard. The trucks were under camouflage nets now. Some of the soldiers were setting up a battery of what looked like 20mm antitank rifles. Others were laying wire and digging spider holes in the soft, sandy earth.

"It looks like they're expecting a fight," he said.

The captain came to the door to see. "It looks that way."

"Where did you get shot down?" Hansen asked.

Higgins explained that he had been flying a P-47 in a raid on

Yatabe, a much-bombed and often repaired Jap air base a few miles north and west. He had flown too low on his bombing run and had damaged his airplane in the blast. "I bailed out just in time."

"Well, listen," Hansen said, "you're senior officer. You have to make these slopeheads treat us like POWs."

"That may not be so easy, Lieutenant," Higgins said.

The big officer, whom they had taken for dead, suddenly moaned and opened his eyes. Slocum dropped to his knees at his side. "Hey," he said. "Lieutenant. Sir. Can you hear me, Lieutenant?"

The wounded man stared blankly.

"Listen," Slocum said earnestly. "Stay awake, sir. Please." He essayed an encouraging smile and allowed a soft Southern accent to come into his voice, the broad dialect of the Alabama cotton fields. "Try to pay attention to me, sir," he said pleadingly.

The officer's eyes remained empty, dazed.

Slocum looked up at Hansen and said, "You have to speak to these Southerners in their own language. Lieutenant Yancey, here, he's from the South. He doesn't understand real English." He turned again to the wounded officer. "Come on, now, Lieutenant. You can't just lie there staring at nothing."

"He's in bad shape, Private," Hansen said.

"He'll be all right," Slocum insisted. "You'll make it, Lieutenant," he said, a note of desperation coloring his voice. "Come *on*, white man. You have *responsibilities*, man."

Yancey continued to stare vacuously at the roof. Then he made what appeared to be a feeble effort to sit up, and Slocum cradled him gently in his arms and dragged him across the floor to where he could lean against a post. The man's eyes never changed expression. If a vegetable had eyes, Hansen thought with a shiver, they would be like Yancey's.

"I don't suppose anyone's got any rations," Hansen said.

Ray reached into the thigh pocket of his fatigues with his good hand and extracted a packet of C rations—hard bittersweet chocolate. Hansen grabbed it and opened the oiled cardboard carton. "Anyone want some?"

No one spoke.

Hansen said, "I haven't eaten since yesterday afternoon." No one replied to that either. He began to gnaw on a rock-hard cube of chocolate, salivating so much that a brown smear ran down his chin.

The door burst open again, and two soldiers and an officer appeared. The officer was taller than the soldiers and he wore the three stars of a captain on his red-and-yellow collar tabs. An enormous samurai sword hung at his side.

"Officer," he said.

"Jesus," Hansen said. "You speak English. Thank God for that. Listen, we need food and medical attention for—"

The Jap officer cut him off with an angry gesture. *"Officer!"* he shouted. *"Officer!"*

His face was a pale-brown color, like coffee with milk in it, and he wore a thick, drooping mustache. His eyes were half hidden under pronounced epicanthic folds. They glittered furiously. He walked over to where Lieutenant Yancey sat, stopped, tugged at the engineer's collar, and examined his insignia. He straightened and spoke to the two enlisted men with him. *"Hai,"* he said, gesturing that they should take Yancey outside.

"The man's wounded," Slocum protested. "You can see he's hurt—"

The Jap struck Slocum across the face with the back of his clenched fist and signaled impatiently that his men should take Yancey out. Slocum staggered but did not fall. He stood in silence, blood running from his cut lip, as the Japanese dragged the heavy officer out into the courtyard.

The door slammed shut again, and Hansen rushed to peer through the crack. Outside, the two soldiers forced the wounded man into a kneeling position and steadied him there. Hansen watched in growing horror as the officer drew his sword, made one or two ritual gestures with it, and without warning brought it down on the back of Yancey's neck.

Hansen saw the bandaged head virtually leap from the kneeling body and roll across the muddy ground leaving a red trail. Blood spurted from the severed neck in an unbelievable pumping torrent, spilling over the engineer's uniform in a crimson flood. The headless body fell forward and balanced there a moment. It looked as though Lieutenant Yancey had somehow managed to bury his head in the earth. Then the knees, twitching and jerking, straightened, and the mutilated body lay shuddering at full length in the gory mud.

"Oh, my *God*!" Hansen said thickly.

Before any of the others could speak, the door slammed open again, and the Jap officer, this time holding the bloodstained sword at his side, stood against the glare, polished boots spread, his immaculate uniform speckled with blood.

"*Officer!*" he said again.

Second Lieutenant Lloyd Hansen fainted.

0730 Hours

The formation of Akatombo trainers from the Takasaki Special Attack Squadron had been flying now for an hour and a half. By this time, Ensign Kashiwahara thought, they should certainly have encountered the Americans' picket boats, but so far they had not. The problem was, in part at least, the slow speed with which the formation moved. The Red Dragonflies were not built for speed, and the heavy bombs fixed between the landing gear did not help.

Since losing Cadet Mitsui, the formation had managed to stay together and keep the remaining trainers in the air. Kashiwahara had moved his Reisen into the trailing position on the left-hand side of the straggling vee, where he could keep an eye on his charges and still search the sky for the American fighters that were certain to appear soon.

The coast of Honshu was only a thin, dark line on the horizon now. The sea was a miraculously deep cobalt blue, except where the morning sun made a path on it, sparkling gold and silver. Gradually, the formation had been losing altitude to reach its attacking height of ten meters. Kashiwahara had objected, during the escort pilots' briefing, to the plan sending inexperienced pilots in training aircraft into battle at wave-top altitude. He had risked a severe reprimand from Commander Chita for doing so, but Chita had only said that ten meters was the height ordered by 11th Air Fleet, and ten meters it would be. Others, he said, would make high-altitude attacks. Others, Kashiwahara suspected, with better chances of success.

He studied the ragged formation irritably. It offended him to see such poor flying, but there was no point in expecting better. The pilots were simply not up to it.

He searched the sky constantly, as fighter pilots who wished to live always did. To the west, and at a greater altitude, he could see a wide vee of airplanes, black and gnatlike against the bright sky. Not Americans, he concluded. The Americans no longer flew in large, cumbersome formations of vees made up of three-plane elements. Since 1943 they had learned to fly in finger-fours, a formation consisting of a flight leader and wingman supported by an element leader and wingman, so that the formation resembled the fingers of a hand extended. It was a flexible and efficient formation that allowed the four airplanes to work together or in elements of two. The Imperial Navy had never adopted this idea, and now it was far too late.

The formation to the west flew on a slowly converging course, overtaking the Takasaki Squadron. As they crossed above him, Kashiwahara identified them as Nakajima Ki-84 Gale fighters of the Army. He was surprised to see so many of them; there were twenty. It supported the rumor he had heard that the Army had hoarded at least fifteen fighter regiments and a large number of bomber regiments to use independently of the attacks planned by 11th Air Fleet. It was typical of the Army, he thought, that they should choose to act without co-ordinating their plans with the Navy. It could never have happened if Hideki Tojo had been an admiral instead of a general.

On the horizon to the south, Kashiwahara saw the first American picket, a *Benson*-class destroyer. As his formation approached the invasion fleet from the east, he saw two similar ships steaming in line. They had begun to fire their antiaircraft batteries at the Nakajimas.

Kashiwahara's inexperienced pilots saw the sky dotted with the black explosions of the American barrage, and the formation became even more ragged. He cursed and circled the wavering vee, signaling the pilots to stay together.

From the direction of the shore a three-plane element of Shiden Violet Lightnings appeared. They closed in to fly a hundred meters from Kashiwahara. They were escorts, because they carried no bombs slung under the fuselages. Kashiwahara rolled back his canopy and waved to them. The pilots waved back and took station with the Takasaki Squadron formation.

Beyond the line of destroyers Kashiwahara could see other ships, a gradually increasing number of them, and long before his unit reached the picket ships, all the pilots could see that the sea was covered with vessels of every imaginable size. The fleet stretched from horizon to the shore, and far off, where the sun's glare made it difficult to see clearly, a long line of battleships was firing at targets ashore. Transports by the hundreds lay hove to or moved at slow speed to take their turns at disembarking troops.

The Shidens pulled up in a sudden steep climbing turn. Kashiwahara swiveled to look up and back. There, dropping out of the sun, was a four-plane formation of Bearcats, diving on his Akatombos. He slammed the throttle forward and snapped hard to the left just as the lead Grumman opened fire.

The Bearcat pilots apparently knew enough to ignore the escorts. They headed straight for the Akatombos. Kashiwahara leveled the wings of his Zero and fired a full-deflection burst at the lead Bearcat. He thought he saw a hit on the thick, humpbacked fuselage, but he could not be certain. As he racked over into a vertical turn to remain between the attackers and his fledglings, he saw a Nakajima from the Army formation falling in flames. It left a trail of burning bits as it plunged into the sea.

Off toward the shore, he caught a glimpse of a flight of Mustangs closing on his formation. He ignored them for the moment and looked for his own people. The Akatombos had scattered, of course. There had never been a hope that they would maintain formation discipline under attack. One of them was already burning, spinning toward the blue sea like a falling leaf, weightless and oddly beautiful, alight with autumn colors.

A Bearcat flew by him, the sun glistening on its silver flanks. The Americans had recently stopped painting their naval aircraft blue. He turned in behind the attacker and tried to stay with him, but the Grumman was far faster than his old Reisen. It closed in on the trainer flown by Petty Officer Kanada and fired a long burst from its eight fifty-caliber machine guns. The Akatombo appeared to shred under that torrent of bullets. Long streamers of fabric peeled away from the wings, chunks of wood and metal flew, spinning, into the slipstream. Kanada attempted a sharp turn, as he had been taught, but the strain was too much for the battered air frame. The Akatombo quite literally disintegrated, the wings separating from the fuselage, which plunged like a dart toward the sea. Kashiwahara watched it, sickened and furious, as it disappeared in a splash of white.

He felt choked with frustration. A thousand targets lay on the sea, and two of his pilots had been shot down before they could even begin to make an attack.

He fired at the Bearcat that had shot down Kanada, but the range was extreme and he saw his tracers falling away. Then he felt his Zero shiver, as though it had been struck a blow with a huge hammer. A jagged hole appeared in the root of the right wing. He rolled the airplane on its back and pulled hard on the stick in a split-S maneuver as the first Bearcat's wingman flashed by him. He pulled out of his vertical dive with care, because his damaged wing was buffeting as though it might collapse.

An Army Nakajima flew by inverted, with a pair of silver Mustangs on its tail. He saw it plunge into the sea, still inverted.

He leveled his Zero out almost at sea level and looked about desperately for his pilots. To the east he saw a burning airplane, but he could not tell whether it was one of his. He began a hard climb, back up to fighting altitude.

One of the Army fighters was attempting to dive onto one of the picket destroyers. Unable to penetrate the screen of defenders, it was the Army pilot's only option. Kashiwahara watched him as he flew through a converging cone of antiaircraft fire and crashed into the fantail of the wildly maneuvering ship.

Kashiwahara felt a surge of exultation as black smoke billowed from the destroyer and he felt a touch of respect for the Army pilot. But then he saw that the destroyer had been damaged only slightly. The Nakajima had not managed a killing hit. He was tempted to dive into the destroyer himself, but he did not. Instead, he climbed back up to 500 meters and looked for his squadron. The only Akatombo he could see was the one piloted by young Matsumoto, the birthday boy. It was angling down through a storm of antiaircraft fire in a straight-line course that should have doomed it. But miraculously it continued to descend, unscathed, toward a line of ships far out on the seaward flank of the invasion fleet.

Above and behind Matsumoto's Akatombo, a single Mustang had begun to drop like a stooping hawk. Kashiwahara put his Reisen into a steep climb through the flak-dirtied sky. Disregarding the protests of the damaged wing, the Zero raced toward the Mustang in a futile attempt to intercept.

Major Richard Stanley Connel's wingman, Lieutenant Donaldson, pressed his microphone button and said, "Jesus, Major, let's get clear of this flak. The swabbies are going to cream us if we don't."

But the major did not reply. He continued to dive through a storm of bursting shells and wobbling tracers. A near burst riddled the wing tip of Donaldson's Mustang, shredding the aileron on that side. He had had enough. It was one thing to stay with this fucking wild man when he dropped down to six feet off the ground while strafing some Jap oxcart, but this was too goddamned much. If he wants to court-martial me, Donaldson thought, pulling up and away, let him. At least I'll still be alive.

In the lead airplane, Donaldson's defection was noted and filed for future reference, but Connel did not let it deter him. He had already shot down four Jap Franks—Nakajima Ki-84s—and a George—a Kawanishi Shiden—on this hunt and he was not about to stop now. It was a bloody damned turkey shoot, he thought with savage delight. A man could get fat on Japs today.

Below and ahead of him he caught sight of a lumbering Jap airplane that was unfamiliar to him. It looked like a primary trainer, he thought. They had to be close to the bottom of the barrel if they were dragging out kites like that one to be Kamikazes. He depressed the long nose of his P-51 and angled down through the flak from the ships.

The Jap was heading out toward the line of ships to the east, where the supply ships and auxiliary transports were all mixed in together. As he approached them, they concentrated their fire on him but failed to hit him. The swabbies' gunnery, Connel thought, was a disgrace.

There were several burning oil slicks on the water where would-be Kamikazes had gone in the drink. Connel looked briefly up and back to see that his tail was clear. It was. The other Japs seemed to have been wiped from the sky. Looking down, he saw a single Zeke climbing toward him. Just wait, little brother, he thought. I'll get to you next.

He had closed on the trainer to a distance at which he could make out the freshly painted meatballs on the wings and the head scarf on the pilot. Closer, Connel thought. Close enough for one short burst. Save some for the Zeke.

Cadet Kendo Matsumoto's fists were clenched on the stick and throttle. He was gripping them so hard he had lost all feeling in his hands. He looked around him desperately. He had never in his life believed that there could be so many ships. There were thousands of them, and from every one came a torrent of fire that seemed to pass within inches of his laboring Akatombo.

He had never in his wildest imaginings thought that battle would be like this. The airplane seemed to resist his efforts to control it. There were several tears in the wings, and a steel fragment had actually struck the instrument panel and destroyed most of the gauges, so that he had no clear idea of what the aircraft was doing.

He passed directly over one ship, a transport of some kind, judging by its forest of masts and hoists and yards. He had fully intended to shove the nose of the airplane down and do what he had sworn to do. But when the moment came, he was frozen. He simply could not bring himself to do it. Instead, he continued along the line of ships, all of which were moving at so slow a speed that they could not maneuver effectively to remove themselves from his flight path. He passed over another ship, and *still* could not force himself to die.

He began to weep in great racking sobs, aware of his *haji*—his terrible shame—and wondering what Ensign Kashiwahara would say of him to the others at Takasaki.

He heard a ripping sound over the noise of his own engine and he twisted in his seat to look back. An American fighter, a Mustang, was upon him. He saw the gun flashes on the leading edges of its wings, and suddenly his Akatombo began to disintegrate. Jagged pieces of metal peeled away from its wings. Half the vertical stabilizer was shot away, and, as the bullets hit, his feet were struck from the rudder pedals. The Akatombo began to fall, shedding pieces of itself.

Matsumoto realized then that he was going to die. He had thought he realized that when he was chosen to be a Kamikaze. He had thought he believed it when he had written his letter to Ochacha and tried to write a death poem. He imagined that he knew it when he departed from the grass field at Takasaki, and when he had watched, with tears in his eyes, the gallant death of Mitsui.

But he had been wrong. All of that was fantasy. This—*this moment*—was real. Now he knew that it was so.

He tried to cheer for the Emperor, but he could manage no shout from his dry throat.

A ship appeared ahead of him. It was white, with large red

crosses painted on it. He shoved stiffly forward on the control stick.

As he struck the highest masts and yards of the hospital ship, his last vision was of fire, his last feeling a desperate desire to live.

Speechless with horror and outrage, Major Connel watched the Kamikaze bury itself in USS *Solace* just behind the bridge. The bomb the Jap carried exploded somewhere deep within the ship, which was instantly wreathed in plumes of steam and fire.

Connel could hardly believe what he had seen. It was an incredible act, an act of barbaric savagery. He could not contain himself as he banked low over the white ship, now dead in the water and burning. He screamed, raging at the dead Jap.

He was brought back to sanity by a streak of tracer twisting past his canopy. The Zeke had closed in on him and was making an attack. Connel, in cold fury, aligned the approaching Zeke in his gunsight and pressed the trigger.

Ensign Kashiwahara saw the cadet's Akatombo explode on the hospital ship and he, too, was horrified, imagining the screaming wounded and dying men aboard her. But his horror was swiftly overwhelmed by his hatred of the Americans, who were at this moment defiling the sacred soil of the homeland, raping its women, butchering its soldiers. His hatred swiftly focused on the pilot of the Mustang who had so mercilessly followed Matsumoto, seeking to kill him.

"*Kill me, Yankee pig!*" he shouted as he opened fire.

The Mustang was firing, too. He felt the heavy-caliber bullets smashing home, ripping into his Reisen, exploding all around.

He had a glimpse of the sun flashing on the water only a meter or two from his wing tip. It looked like a shower of polished golden coins. He knew in that moment that the unknown American pilot was not going to take evasive action, nor was he.

The Zero and the Mustang collided head on only ten feet

above the sea. The fireball sent a shower of burning fuel and wreckage into the air before it tumbled into the water and scattered into its component parts, which bounced and skipped across the surface before the sea quenched the fire and silenced the sound.

Then what could be heard was the crackle of flames aboard the heavily damaged hospital ship and the whooping alarms of the destroyers and smaller ships closing in to offer their assistance.

Strangely, casualties aboard *Solace* were light, since few wounded had as yet been taken aboard. Among the medical staff, one surgeon, an anesthesiologist, and two nurses were killed instantly when the engine of the Akatombo crashed through their operating theater. Their patient was also killed. He was Leading Seaman Albert Cummins, the only survivor of the sinking of HMS *Ramsey*.

1000 Hours

Corporal Saigo Noguchi opened his eyes to the most horrible living nightmare for a Japanese soldier. Somehow, he had been taken prisoner. He remembered seeing the black figure arising from the sea. He remembered, too, that the huge man had tried to kill him and that he somehow had been killed instead.

Noguchi had crawled up the beach in the predawn dark and had fallen there, face pressed against the sand, and that was the last thing he remembered.

He tried to move and found that he had been bound hand and foot. He lay half sheltered by some enormous armored vehicle painted the color of mud and bearing on its flank the hated white star of the Americans.

His eyes felt swollen, his mouth dry. His head still throbbed and ached horribly. But the shelling had stopped. In its place was a most confusing medley of noises. Men shouting and talking in alien voices, the clatter of machinery, the rumble of motors. There were all the sounds of an army on the move, but an army such as Noguchi had never imagined.

He struggled to sit up, but could do nothing more than raise his head. What he saw filled him with despair.

He lay in a line of corpses, eight of them. They were the corpses of Japanese soldiers who had managed what he obviously had not: they had died honorably in battle. One could easily see that from the nature of their wounds. The Americans had stacked them here like offal, presumably because they were inconveniently placed where they fell. All around him strode American soldiers in their baggy, strongly made uniforms, their feet in splendid leather boots. No one paid the slightest attention to the corpses—of which Noguchi now considered himself one, because, though he might still breathe, he was dead as a Japanese.

He lay on raw ground, a place where some powerful machine had scraped away the wreckage of the shattered forest. He could see pines that had been splintered by the shelling. They had been carelessly shoved aside by a bulldozer to clear a path through the rubble. He could hear it working farther inland, its heavy diesel engine echoing hollowly across the ruin of what had once been a pine and bamboo forest.

The vehicle near which he lay was a half-tracked armored personnel carrier. It was dirty, but new. It still had an odor of fresh paint.

As he tried to clear his head and come to terms with his situation, he was constantly shaken by the roaring noise of tanks passing by. There were dozens of them, great Shermans with long 75mm cannon. The hatches were open, and in each a crewman wearing a strange-looking helmet rode. On either side of the tanks walked a line of infantry—big men carrying an amazing variety of heavy weapons. Their uniforms were thick and dry, and seeing this made Noguchi aware that his own was thin, ragged, and wet. He steeled himself against the cold. He might no longer be a Japanese soldier, but that was no excuse for allowing the enemy to see him trembling. They might assume that he trembled from fear. And Noguchi felt no fear, only despair.

Since he could smell the sea, he assumed that he was not far from the beach. But what had happened to the defense? How had so many Americans managed to come ashore so swiftly? He squinted at the sky. The sun was high. It was midmorning. There was still fighting going on. He could hear small-arms' fire and an occasional heavier explosion. But it was far off, a long way inland. So much for Matsuo Fortress, he thought bitterly. All the bunkers and trenches and spider holes so laboriously dug, all the guns so carefully sited, all the pounding and shelling the men of his unit and others had taken—what had it accomplished? Apparently very little. The Americans were ashore and walking inland as though they were strolling among the deer of Nara. It made him want to weep.

From where he lay near the half-track, he studied the Americans. He had seen them before, but never in such numbers or in such variety. Most of them were huge, with thick arms and legs and white faces and odd-looking eyes. Their noses were sharp and protuberant. They were singularly ugly. They were noisy, too, chattering like magpies as they walked along carrying their beautifully made weapons. Here and there were men of a sort that had to be peculiar even among Americans. He had heard that there were Americans with black skins, but he had never seen any. A file of these strange creatures was moving down the bulldozed track in large trucks laden with pontoons and steel matting.

An American wearing a helmet bearing a red cross set in a white circle came across the roughly cut road, skipping and running like a child to avoid the rumbling tanks. He was tall, like all Americans, but not as grossly made as most. His uniform was hung about with heavy canvas bags and cases. He stood looking down at Noguchi with an unreadable expression on his ruddy, freckled face. He opened one of his bags, and Noguchi wondered if it was now that he would be killed. It was well known that Americans killed prisoners, and he was grateful that it was so. Perhaps he could still find a place at Yasukuni even though he had not died actually fighting the enemy. Surely Lieutenant Fuchida would speak for him and explain to the honored dead that his failure as a soldier had not been intentional.

Then, incomprehensibly, the tall American smiled. Noguchi had never before seen an American smile. It was an unnerving experience, because he showed large white teeth, like a tiger's, and because it seemed to imply that he was not, at this moment, going to kill anyone.

The American said something that seemed to be a question and dropped to one knee beside Noguchi. From his bag he took a field dressing and broke it open. Noguchi felt a surge of dismay. The American was going to treat his head wound. He was going to try to keep him alive, prolonging his disgrace. He rolled his head and tried to push himself away by digging his heels into the raw ground.

The American spoke again, but Noguchi continued to resist him. He shook his head and called to another soldier, who appeared from behind the half-track. This one was even larger and redder of face and he did not smile. His helmet did not have the red-cross sign and he carried a well-cared-for M-1 rifle slung over his shoulder. Noguchi looked desperately at him, willing him to unsling the weapon and use it to end his disgrace. For a moment it appeared that the larger soldier was considering it. He looked down at Noguchi with a grim expression. This soldier was quite different from the medic.

He stooped and took Noguchi by the shoulders and jerked him into a sitting position. Noguchi's head exploded with pain and, despite all he could do, a moan escaped him.

The medic said something to the large soldier, who gave a short, barking laugh and forced Noguchi to bend forward so that the medic could deal with his head wound.

It was difficult to remember how, exactly, he had come by the injury. Noguchi hoped that it was a battle wound. He also prayed that it was severe enough to kill him eventually, because it was obvious that no American had enough sense of a soldier's honor to do it. He sat, hunched and shivering, like a small child in the large American's grasp while the medic worked on him.

In the distance he could hear some automatic weapons firing. The tanks and infantry continued to pour along the raw road like a torrent. Was there no end to the number of men and tanks? Now he could hear aircraft overhead. There were many of them and they flew low. They must be American as well. It had been weeks since he had seen a Japanese airplane. Now it became apparent why this was so. No matter how brave and skilled the pilots of the Imperial Army and Navy might be, it was unreasonable for anyone to expect them to prevail against such numbers.

And the equipment and weapons of these soldiers! For the first time Noguchi allowed himself to look carefully and enviously. It was no wonder the Americans fought with such ferocity. It was not their sense of honor that made them do it, for obviously they had none, or else they would have given him an honorable death. No, it was the quantity and quality of their weapons that forced them to fight well. How could any soldier, even an American, fail to fight for a government so generous and capable?

Noguchi wondered if the Americans were coming ashore in such great numbers at all the beachheads. A week ago, when he had been in the log bunker with Koriyama and Iwaka, he had heard that the Americans would try to land at Kashima and in Suruga and Sagami bays. He closed his eyes to hold back the tears. Only a week ago? He thought about Koriyama and particularly about Iwaka, whom he had treated so harshly. Yet Iwaka was already at Yasukuni, and with him was fat Koriyama, who had imagined he could one day be a sumo. Actually, he had been harsh with both of them, and now this had happened. It was possible that *they* would bar the path into Yasukuni, regardless of whether or not Fuchida was willing to speak for him.

Fuchida might say: "He did not surrender. It was not his fault."

And Koriyama, who was basically a good-natured person, might possibly agree. But Iwaka would surely say: "He struck me often without good reason. He made fun of my Aomori accent. He was a bad corporal and a worse soldier. He allowed himself to be captured—"

The big American lifted him to his feet. He stood unsteadily while the medic looked closely at his eyes and then indicated that he was to walk. He stumbled along between the two men, like a child between two adults. They were both so large, as large as Koriyama, though not so fat. He let himself be led. What did it matter?

He looked vaguely around him as the Americans took him through the enormous, orderly confusion. Once he caught a glimpse of the beach and he noted with some bleak satisfaction that the Americans had not, after all, come wading ashore like holiday trippers at the seashore.

Boats and smashed vehicles littered the beach, and there were working parties taking American bodies from the surf. It was instructive to know that the Americans honored the dead, as Japanese did, though he had been told that they buried their dead where they fell, and had therefore left a train of burial grounds across the Pacific from Australia to Okinawa.

But there were still hundreds, perhaps thousands, of ships and boats offshore, some anchored just a few hundred meters off the beach. A steady stream of smaller craft ferried men, men, and more men from the ships to the shore, and the beach was stacked with huge mounds of crates and cases, among which rumbled the tanks and vehicles splashing down the ramps of the constantly arriving landing craft.

He looked hopefully at the sky, wondering where the *tokkotai* were, the special attackers who had promised to stop the invaders before their boots touched the soil of the homeland. And what of the Crouching Dragons—of whom he and his comrades had also heard so much: incredibly skilled and brave swimmers who were to have waited on the bottom of the sea off the beaches, explosive charges on poles held ready, to blow up the enemy landing ships as they passed overhead. What had happened to them?

Perhaps they were all dead—*honorably* dead, he thought bitterly. Not like Corporal Saigo Noguchi, who pretended for many years to be a soldier, but who, in the end, was a fraud. He allowed the Americans to lead him easily, hoping as he walked through the masses of men on the beach (many of whom stared curiously at him) that his family would never discover the *haji* he had inflicted upon them.

They came to a place where there were officers. Noguchi was shocked to see that they wore the same shapeless uniforms their men did. They could be distinguished only by the insignia painted on their helmets and by the cloth representations of their badges sewn on their fatigues.

The large soldier said something to the medic and departed. The medic did not release Noguchi, but spoke to a soldier with chevrons on his helmet and sleeves. A *gocho*, just like me, Noguchi thought. Or, more properly, a corporal like I was before the calamity of capture.

The American *gocho* regarded Noguchi curiously and then disappeared into a small shelter that had been set up near the high-tide mark. Presently three officers appeared. One wore a peculiar mark on his helmet: three yellow bars surmounted by a star. Under the coveralls he wore a fine khaki shirt with the silver leaf of a *chusa*, a lieutenant colonel, on the collar. He must be a naval officer of some kind, Noguchi thought. He had seen sketches of the insignia worn by the American Navy, and the bars and star resembled what he vaguely remembered was worn by the enemy on the sleeves of their naval uniforms. But he had had little interest in the appearance of enemy naval officers. It was their army that had been of primary importance.

There were two younger officers with the naval *chusa*: a *chui*, first lieutenant, and a *shoi*, second lieutenant. What startled Noguchi and almost roused him from his despairing lethargy was that the *shoi* was Japanese. For an instant his own shame was forgotten, drowned in the flooding horror of seeing a Japanese wearing the uniform of an enemy of the Emperor. It shocked him to the depths of his being.

"What is your name and unit, Corporal?" the traitorous Japanese asked. His accent was strange; there were odd echoes of the north in his speech. Noguchi, disgraced as he was, could not bear to be spoken to by a Japanese so depraved as to join the invaders of his country. He reacted by spitting on the ground and turning his face away.

The Japanese lieutenant's eyes glittered angrily.

Then Noguchi received a second, and even more profound, shock. The *chui*, a slender young man with sandy hair and cool blue eyes, said sharply: "You forget yourself, Corporal. Are all soldiers of the Imperial Army so lacking in military courtesy as you?" The words were spoken in Japanese of great purity and elegance. Even Lieutenant Fuchida, who had lived much of his life in Kyoto, had not spoken the language with such clarity and precision.

Noguchi snapped to attention. Even though he could no longer consider himself a true soldier, it was impossible for him not to respond in a respectful and military manner to an officer, even an enemy officer, who spoke like an aristocrat.

The white officer regarded him severely. Noguchi, his head throbbing, feared he might fall and further disgrace himself.

"Speak when you are spoken to, *Gocho-san*," the *chui* said. "I asked you if discipline was dead in the Imperial Army."

"Forgive me, *Chui-san*," Noguchi said. "I lost my composure. I am ashamed." He bowed deeply despite the pain it caused him.

"For your information, *Gocho-san*," the officer said, "this officer is Tanaka-san. He is of Japanese ancestry, but he is an officer of the American Army. You will treat him with the same respect you would give one of your own officers. Is that clear?"

"It is, *Chui-san*. I apologize." Noguchi hesitated, wondering if this strange American who spoke Japanese so perfectly would understand his dilemma. "May I speak, *Chui-san*?"

"Yes. It is permitted."

"I forget myself because I am no longer a soldier, *Chui-san*." He felt his eyes fill with tears. "I am nothing."

The white officer looked annoyed. "That is a foolish and impolite thing to say. One may become a prisoner and still remain a soldier."

Noguchi's heart sank. Obviously the fact that this strange officer spoke Japanese was no reason to assume that he was honorable. Otherwise he would not have made such a shameful statement.

The white officer seemed to read his mind. That was a capability officers of whatever army seemed to have. He said quietly, "I know that you have been taught that to be taken prisoner is to cease to be a Japanese. This is a wicked and selfish thing. I remind you that to endure shame and the scorn of your own people with courage and dignity is the act of a samurai. I remind you, *Gocho-san*, of the Forty-seven Ronin, who endured much in order to serve their lord. Are you deserving of better treatment than they?"

Noguchi's opinion of the white officer began to improve. Who would have expected to hear an American speak so understandingly of the Forty-seven Ronin, who were folk heroes of the Divine Race?

"Answer me, *Gocho-san*," the *chui* said, frowning.

"Of course not, *Chui-sama*," Noguchi said quickly.

"Then behave like a soldier," the officer said. "Endure the unendurable." He indicated the naval officer beside him. "This is Jorgensen-dono; he is a *kaigun chusa* of the American Navy. Presently he will have you taken out to one of the ships lying offshore. There you will be fed and your wound will be cared for. In return for this kind treatment, you will remember that you are a soldier, a noncommissioned officer, and you will do as you are ordered to do by those in authority. Is that clear to you, *Gocho-san*?"

"*Hai, Chui-sama*," Noguchi almost shouted. It felt wonderful to be spoken to in this manner. It was a marvelous thing to know that one remained a soldier, and to be told this was so by an officer.

The *chui* relaxed slightly and, for the first time, smiled. "Now tell us your name and unit, *Gocho-san*."

"I am Corporal Saigo Noguchi, *Chui-sama*. My unit is the 3rd Battalion of the 15th Regiment of the 147th Infantry Division. I was a member of the garrison of Matsuo Fortress." Noguchi found nothing whatever wrong with imparting this information. He was quite ready to impart more. The Americans had only to ask. Since Japanese soldiers were assumed to be incapable of surrender, there had never been, in their long military tradition, any provision made for withholding information from an enemy while a prisoner of war. In Japanese military doctrine, prisoners did not exist and therefore it had never been thought necessary to provide soldiers with a code of conduct.

"Very well, Corporal Noguchi," the white officer said. "*Shoi-san* Tanaka and I must return to our unit now. It is unlikely that we will meet again. But I remind you that while you are the guest of this *kaigun chusa*, you are to conduct yourself like a soldier and a Japanese."

Noguchi looked respectfully at the tall, gray-haired naval officer. He had not imagined that he would be considered the guest of the *kaigun chusa*. He had never in his life been the guest of so high-ranking an individual. It astonished him that he would be treated as a person of some importance. He felt a deep gratitude toward the blue-eyed young man who spoke so like a member of the Divine Race, and an educated and highly placed one, at that. He hoped that the Japanese-American had forgiven him his irresponsible breach of good manners. He bowed deeply to the white officer and then again to the Japanese, who still looked unfriendly. "I apologize most sincerely, *Shoi-san* Tanaka," he said. "I did not understand that you were an American despite your appearance."

The blue-eyed officer seemed to suppress a grin, and Noguchi hoped that he had not again committed a shameful act. It was confusing to deal with white men who seemed Japanese and Japanese who were American.

"Very well, then, *Gocho-san*," the first lieutenant said. "Hard work." It gave Noguchi a genuine thrill of pleasure to hear the officer bid him farewell with the expression used by all Japanese soldiers as a familiar greeting and dismissal.

To Tanaka-san, the *chui* said, "We will rejoin our troops, Honorable Second Lieutenant." There was a broad grin on his face as he spoke, but the Japanese-American did not seem to find it amusing. Obviously, Noguchi thought, he was a humorless man with less understanding than the white lieutenant.

The two officers saluted the *kaigun chusa*, and Corporal Noguchi bowed again as they departed, walking side by side across the cluttered beach toward the bulldozed road.

1600 Hours

Captain Charles Beardsley, commanding officer of USS *Midway*, stood on the flybridge of his ship surveying the vast expanse of flight deck. The Bearcats scheduled to relieve the Combat Air Patrol now circling over the task force were stacked at the stern, wings folded, but with pilots in the cockpits and deck crews standing by.

The helicopters had been brought on deck, and they stood now like odd insects, their rotors turning, ready to take General MacArthur and his staff ashore.

Beardsley was unfamiliar with helicopters. The machines were new, relatively untried in combat situations, and they were ugly. There was something faintly comical about an aircraft that resembled a cross between a dragonfly and a child's toy. One could understand the aerodynamic principles involved and still have a gut feeling that the damned things would never get off the deck.

Though Beardsley had not been present in flag plot when the discussion arose, the scuttlebutt was that the admiral disapproved of MacArthur's decision to establish himself on the South Sheridan beachhead so soon. The original plan had called for Supreme Command to go ashore on Y + 3 or even later, when it was absolutely certain that the beachhead was secure. But the battle reports from South Sheridan had been so favorable that MacArthur had decided to move at once. Beardsley suspected that the general wished to remove himself from the Navy's care as soon as possible. He was the sort of man to whom that would be an important consideration.

Midway was cruising at reduced speed; no more than ten knots of wind blew across her deck. To both Beardsley and his air boss, Commander McElderry, who stood beside him, it seemed all wrong, somehow, to launch aircraft at such a speed. But the helicopters were fragile, and the AAF commander of the three-chopper section had made their requirements clear most precisely. It would be best, he had told Beardsley, if *Midway* was brought to a complete stop. But he understood that this was not a prudent thing to do while there was any chance of enemy action, so ten knots would have to do.

Beardsley, who had participated in many of the carrier actions fought early in the war, before the U.S. Navy had swept the seas of Japanese submarines, was made uneasy by the low speed. To allow his beautiful ship to loaf along at a pace that any Jap I-boat could easily exceed took a concentrated effort of will.

The *Midway*'s speed seemed to upset her escorts, too. Five destroyers that had been assigned the task of protecting the carrier steamed about her in a wide circle at twenty knots. Just now the escort command ship, *Stevenson,* was churning by *Midway* at 2,000 yards, flashing interrogatories with a signal lamp on her bridge. Beardsley heard the signalman behind him speaking to the officer of the deck. "*Stevenson* wants to know how much longer, sir."

Beardsley suppressed his annoyance. *Stevenson*'s captain was a newly made commander named Rutledge, a Southern aristocrat with excellent connections in Washington. He was a first-rate officer, but he tended to take liberties. He heard his own executive officer, a not-at-all aristocratic Mustang named Reilly, tell the signalman to order *Stevenson*'s captain to confine himself to operational messages. He smiled slightly at that, imagining Rutledge's flushed anger at being peremptorily reprimanded.

"Well," McElderry murmured, "he's got a point. What's holding things up? Is Doug putting on his make-up?"

It was an unfair criticism of the general, Beardsley thought, but one he brought upon himself with his theatrical ways: the battered gold-braided Philippine field marshal's hat, the corncob pipe, the dark glasses. Around General MacArthur one never mentioned such things as hair dye, age, costumes—or Harry Truman. The general despised the President of the United States. Someday, Beardsley thought, if they both live long enough, there's going to be a confrontation.

Some of the general's people were emerging from the island now. Beardsley recognized Colonel Charles Willoughby, the general's senior aide, and two of the younger military secretaries. They hurried along the deck to the waiting helicopters.

"Tell the OOD they're coming now," Beardsley said. "Have someone stand by the general's flag." He glanced up at a yard from which flew two five-starred flags, one blue, for Admiral Nimitz, the other red, for MacArthur. The general's flag would be lowered the moment his helicopter left *Midway*'s flight deck. And the general would be watching, too, from his chopper. He was intensely aware of these military niceties and would remember them.

The fact was, Beardsley thought, that Douglas MacArthur was far more than simply an American original. He was a military genius, and that was a truth that no one could reasonably deny. His style and manner did create public-relations problems in some circles. There was the Dugout Doug business, for example. Beardsley did not like MacArthur; few people did, though those who loved him did so with great intensity. But *Midway*'s commander knew real courage when he saw it, and any suggestion that MacArthur was overly concerned with his own safety was grossly unfair.

Beardsley knew, or thought he did, why the general was choosing to go ashore on Honshu on the first day of the invasion. It was at least partially a result of the stories and rumors that had flown from unit to unit about his staged landing on Leyte. The talk was that the famous picture of MacArthur wading ashore had been taken days after the actual landings, when all danger had ended.

The truth was something less simple. MacArthur had come ashore on Leyte while the beach was still under fire and jammed with men and equipment. A harried beachmaster had refused to allow the general's LST to dock at one of the temporary piers the engineers had constructed. Perhaps the man had not realized who was aboard the landing craft. Perhaps he really had not, in his overworked condition, cared. Beachmasters, in theory at least, outranked even five-star generals.

So MacArthur, impatient as always, had ordered the boat beached, the ramp dropped, and he had waded ashore like any infantryman. One of the staff photographers who went everywhere with him had snapped a picture. Later, when the photo was developed, some public-relations genius on the staff—perhaps Willoughby—had seen in the poorly composed and lighted shot a genuinely dramatic picture, one that every newspaper in the States would run on the front page.

He had pleaded with the general and convinced him to make the landing again, this time on a beach and at a time of day that would allow the photographer to produce a really memorable portrait of the great general returning to the Philippines. That was the picture the United States and all the Free World had seen.

Only MacArthur, Beardsley thought, would become a party to such a blatantly self-serving deception. But the original wade to shore had been genuine, and under fire.

More of the general's staff had appeared on deck. Only the senior members would make the flight in the helicopters, because space was limited. Beardsley was pleased to see that Tech Sergeant Arceniega, a Philippine Scout who went everywhere with the general, had been included. He carried a Thompson submachine gun slung over his shoulder. MacArthur never carried a weapon.

The OOD's voice cracked an order, and the PA system blared: "Attention on deck!"

Beardsley and McElderry straightened to attention as Mac-Arthur, wearing an old-style Army Air Corps leather flying jacket, and Admiral Nimitz, in shirt sleeves, appeared on the flight deck.

To port, *Gillespie*, one of the escorting destroyers, set her siren to whooping in salute. *Gillespie*'s commanding officer was a young reservist, whose name escaped Beardsley for the moment, but he could remember a ruddy, cheerful, *civilian* face. MacArthur, at any rate, seemed to appreciate *Gillespie*'s boisterousness. He raised a hand in salute as the can slipped by *Midway*'s flank.

McElderry raised his eyes to check on the position of the Combat Air Patrol. It would not do to allow those ungainly helicopters to travel a single mile without a heavy escort of fighters. Too many senior officers had died already in this war, and it would be a disaster if anything were to happen to MacArthur. The ambush of Admiral Yamamoto by Lamphier and his P-38s was something an officer charged with the security of commanders was unlikely to forget. But *Midway*'s Bearcats were close at hand, flying low across the carrier's stern and waiting for the choppers to get themselves airborne.

Beyond the picket line of destroyers, the men of *Midway* could see a squadron of light cruisers steaming in line astern—*Wilkes-Barre*, *Birmingham*, *San Diego*, and *Brooklyn*. Far out on the horizon, fifteen miles from *Midway*, a division of Task Group 38.1, which included *Bennington*, *Lexington*, *Hancock*, *San Jacinto*, and *Belleau Wood*, was in action, the nearer ships launching strikes against the Japanese concentrations behind the northern beachheads, while others could be seen recovering aircraft. But information had a way of seeping through the fibers of a ship, not always along the chain of command. Both men were aware that the assault was successful at North and South Grable, where the Tenth Army was already expanding the area it held, and at North and South Sheridan, where the Sixth Army was in action. They were also aware that the Marines of V and III Amphibious Corps, who had been given the nastiest part of Operation Coronet, along the rocky coastlines of Sagami and Suruga bays, were running into heavy opposition and had not yet been able to expand their beachheads appreciably. Casualties were high and they were increasing. The Eighth Army, which had hit North and South Hayworth, on the southeastern shore of the Boso Peninsula, was also having a difficult time of it. Ships of the Support Group, which should by now be landing supplies for the Marines and the landing force, were still standing offshore and experiencing repeated attacks by Kamikazes and suicide boats. So far, no major ships had been sunk, but a number had been hit. And there was an angry rumor making the rounds that a hospital ship attached to the Sixth Army's Support Group had been severely damaged by a Kamikaze.

Of more immediate concern to Beardsley was the safety of the party on the flight deck. He had no intention of becoming known in the Navy as the man on whose ship the two allied supreme commanders were lost.

The bosun's pipe twittered as MacArthur exchanged salutes with Nimitz and climbed into his helicopter. The crew backed away as the rotors on the three ugly machines began to turn. "Goddamn eggbeaters," McElderry, a career-long naval aviator, muttered.

Beardsley noted that the red five-starred flag was being lowered at the precise moment the wheels of the general's helicopter lifted from the flight deck. Nimitz and his people were hurrying back to the island, hunched against the windstorm caused by the helicopters.

The three choppers backed for the first ten feet of altitude and then lifted their tails like sexy insects and moved slowly off the bow. Beardsley watched them with a feeling of relief. Slowly at first, and then with increasing speed, they veered away to the southwest, staying low over the water.

"Well, that's done, thank God," Beardsley said. "Let's get the CAP's relief up." He turned to speak to the men on the bridge. "Thirty knots," he said to the officer of the deck.

Midway began to throb as her turbines increased rpm to bring the ship to proper speed for launching aircraft.

The men on the bridge stepped back respectfully as their captain came in and climbed into the high chair welded to the deck.

The executive officer stationed himself behind the captain's chair. Both remained silent but watchful as the officer of the deck gave the helm and engine orders. It was gratifying, Beardsley thought, that so many reservists had managed to learn enough ship handling and seamanship to fill out the Navy in this war. It was nearly over now, and that thought brought with it mixed relief and regret.

Beardsley stared through the heavy glass at the sea. The water had gone from blue to gray-blue because the sky was clouding over. The met officer reported that a tropical disturbance was filling in from the south. Not a storm, but enough of a low to bring rain and, farther north, possibly snow flurries. The weather in the western Pacific was always unsettled at this time of year. One day bright and clear, the next wet and blustery. God pity the people ashore if several days of rain should set in over the Kanto.

"Stand by to launch aircraft." The PA system alerted the deck crews. Signal flags broke from the yardarm above the air boss's station.

The bridge telephone buzzed, and the junior officer of the watch answered. He listened and then said, "Right." He spoke to the captain directly—a slight breach of naval etiquette.

"*Stevenson* says they have a large Jap formation on radar, sir. Bearing 270 degrees true, range nine miles."

"Very well," Beardsley said. "Sound General Quarters." To the deck officer he said, "I'll take the conn, mister." Simultaneously, the general alarm echoed through the ship. To McElderry, who had just entered the bridge, he said, "Get those fighters up or get them below."

"Stand by to launch aircraft," the PA system said again, and then: "Launch aircraft! Launch aircraft!"

Even through the noises made by the ship and the buffeting of a thirty-knot gale streaming by the open door to the bridge, Beardsley could hear the roar of the Bearcats taking off in swift succession. The four-plane formation formed up as it climbed.

Beardsley allowed himself a moment's concern about the fate of the painfully slow helicopters flying shoreward. But there was nothing he could do about them now. He picked up the bridge phone and said, "Flag plot."

The reply was swift. "Flag plot, aye."

"Please tell the admiral that we have a large formation of Japs coming in."

"Very well." The reply was calm and distant. Both flag plot and CIC were like other planets on *Midway* when Nimitz was on board. He insisted on an atmosphere that was almost academic.

A watch officer reported, "Twenty-four Japs. Range seven miles. Speed 200 knots. Bearing unchanged."

To the west Beardsley could see flak dotting the sky as some of the picket ships began to shoot at the oncoming Japanese airplanes.

He listened grimly as the various departments reported their readiness. He was remembering the day *Yorktown* was hit. It was early in the war, and he had been a very green lieutenant commander, a squadron commander of scout bombers. The Japs had hit *Yorktown* badly, and some of the pilots had had to ditch, because they could not land and they could not reach another American carrier. Beardsley had seen *Yorktown* ablaze. It was a sight he would never forget. A carrier was the most powerful ship afloat—and the most vulnerable.

"Enemy bearing unchanged, still 270 degrees."

The Japs were coming straight in, taking whatever they would have to take to get at his ship, Beardsley thought.

On the open gunnery control platform, the air defense officer gave the command to the sky guns: "Air action port. Fire when ready."

Beardsley said, "Hard right rudder. All ahead flank."

Midway heeled as her 45,000 tons carved a white path in the sea. When she straightened on her new course, the antiaircraft guns began to fire, adding their shell bursts to the leprous sky over the Task Group. *Gillespie*, racing alongside the huge carrier, was firing her 40mm pompoms at the advancing Japs. The cruisers to starboard had also opened fire. The sky was filled with the black dirt of exploding shells.

Beardsley accepted his helmet from an orderly and stepped outside. He looked up to see a four-plane formation of Bearcats slash through the straggling vee of Japanese. Three of the enemy began to burn and fall toward the sea. The Japs were Betties. That was unusual.

He saw two *baka* bombs separate from their bombers and begin to arch down toward the ships. There were men in those damned things, he told himself. He watched the longish cylindrical craft try to maneuver. The wings were stubby, the control surfaces small. The pilots really had little command of the things that were carrying them to their deaths. One of the *baka*s lit off its rocket engines, but something went wrong immediately. There was a small popping explosion, and the horizontal stabilizer separated from the body of the craft and fluttered away. The rest of the flying bomb began to tumble. It continued to go end over end until it fell into the sea 2,000 yards off *Midway*'s stern quarter. There was no explosion.

A squadron of Hellcats from one of the Task Group's carriers was among the Betties. Beardsley saw two of the Jap airplanes collide and disintegrate in a brilliant explosion. Debris and flaming fuel rained down in twisting curlicues of black, oily smoke. The banging of *Midway*'s own sky guns was deafening.

A Betty, smoking from one engine, banked toward the carrier. It looked misshapen because it had not yet been willing or able to launch its *baka.*

Beardsley called in to the bridge: "Right fifteen degrees rudder." He had to grip the splinter shield to steady himself as the ship heeled to port.

The Betty was driving now. It flew at the apex of a cone of fire as every gun on *Midway*'s starboard side opened up on it. As it was hit repeatedly, Beardsley could see pieces being blown away from the wings and fuselage. The smoke from its crippled engine was laced with fire. But still the Jap pilot came on.

At a range of less than 1,000 yards, the *baka* separated from its mother ship. It seemed to be flying straight at the spot on the bridge where Beardsley stood. Through clenched teeth he muttered furiously, "Get away from my ship, you Jap bastard."

"Hard left rudder." His voice sounded strange to him, as though it were the property of another.

Midway heeled again as Beardsley held onto the splinter shield with white-knuckled hands.

The *baka* bomb pitched downward and seemed to pass within feet of the antennas and flag hoists atop the island. It missed cleanly and drilled into the sea, its 1,100 pounds of high explosive going up in a tall spout of fire-laced sea water.

The blast shook *Midway* so severely that Beardsley was thrown off his feet. A watchkeeper was at his side instantly. Beardsley shoved him away furiously. The gunners on the starboard side were all cheering. He stepped into the bridge and seized the microphone of the PA system. "This is the captain speaking. The next gunner who cheers when he should be shooting is on report!"

The volume of gunfire increased immediately.

The Betty that had dropped the *baka* had flown down the carrier's port side, engine blazing fiercely now, one wing tip perilously close to the water. But the pilot managed to bring the clumsy bomber to a level position as every gun that could bear fired at him.

He gained a few feet of altitude and headed straight for *Stevenson*. The destroyer heeled immediately in a sharp turn, but the Betty persisted. More shells ripped into the airplane, and an explosion tore the right-hand engine away. It fell, twisting and burning, into the sea. The Betty's wing dipped again, and Beardsley thought it would surely cartwheel into the water. But the Jap pilot leveled his airplane for an instant before it slammed hard into the water. It struck nose high and skipped into the air like a flat stone thrown by a schoolboy. The wings broke off and flew high in the air. The center section and fuselage struck the sea again exactly at *Stevenson*'s water line.

There was a fireball that engulfed the destroyer's midsection, and the ship went dead in the water, blazing amidships. There was no explosion at first, because the Betty had carried only the *baka*. But as the fire spread through *Stevenson* in a river of blazing gasoline, it swiftly reached the main magazine. There was a deep, thudding sound as the destroyer's bottom was ripped out of her by her own exploding ammunition. There was a geyser of fire and steam as her innards turned to white-hot wreckage. In the next moment *Stevenson* rolled over, as though desperate to quench the fires in the cold sea.

Beardsley watched, sickened, as her red-painted bottom came uppermost. There was a jagged opening half her length in her hull, and it streamed water and steam as her speed fell off to nothing and she settled swiftly.

There were men in the water, perhaps a quarter of her crew, as *Stevenson*, still blowing steam through her ruptured hull, vanished beneath the sea.

Beardsley watched as *Midway* swiftly left her astern. Then he raised his eyes to the sky and was surprised to see it clear. The Japs were gone, though there were smoky trails marking the paths they had taken to their deaths. As quickly as it had begun, the battle had ended. He removed his helmet and wiped his sweaty forehead, feeling twice his forty-two years. He spoke to the white-faced yeoman carrying the message pad. "Signal to *Gillespie*, Yeoman. Assume command escort. Detail *Nicholson* to pick up survivors."

The Imperial Navy submarine *Anemone* was sixty-five kilometers northwest of the island of Sumisu when the wake of her periscope was seen by a crewman of the Catalina flying boat "Royal Flush" patrolling the eastern flank of Operation Coronet's Support Group 12.

"Royal Flush" was flying just ahead of a weather front moving swiftly up from the south, and there was a discussion between Lieutenant Willy Harper, her pilot, and Ensign Ted Rothermel, her copilot, about the advisability of attempting to stay with the unidentified submarine until her nationality could be established. There were, the pilots knew, a number of American boats in the general area. Moreover, they were four hours from base, at Ariake Bay, Kyushu. Because of this and the deteriorating weather, Harper and the navigator, Ensign Macmanus, decided to send out a sighting report and hand the problem over to others.

The position and sighting were sent routinely, and "Royal Flush," at the end of her patrol leg, turned southwest for Ariake.

When the radio report was received by Coronet Operations, at Buckner Bay, Okinawa, an immediate check was run to discover whether or not any American boats were operating in the area where the sighting was made. There were none. The submarine was tagged "Enemy" and a warning was radioed to the Coronet fleet.

With most of the available carrier aircraft engaged in attacking shore targets, the submarine sighting was given to Task Group 30.2, a British force consisting of the battleship *Duke of York*, two destroyer escorts, *Whelp* and *Wager*, and the light carrier *Unicorn*. These ships had been steaming in company with Task Group 30.1, consisting of USS *Missouri* and her three escorts, the destroyers *Taylor*, *Nicholas*, and *O'Bannon*.

Rear Admiral Raymond Forbes Sawkins, the British commander, had been chafing under the domination of his American allies. His force, formidable by British standards, had been all but submerged in the multitude of American fighting ships cruising Japanese waters. The submarine sighting gave him a momentary diversion and an opportunity to take independent action.

Accordingly, he ordered *Unicorn* to fly off a section of six Hellcats and one of Avengers loaded with depth charges. The aircraft had difficulty finding the *Anemone* because, although Lieutenant Commander Kunamoto was unaware of the rising interest in his boat, the weather had grown steadily worse.

One hour after arriving at the place where the American Catalina had reported a sighting, the six Hellcats were forced by diminishing fuel supply to turn back. The Avengers, American torpedo-bombers modified by the British for the Royal Navy, remained to continue looking.

After a square search of the area lasting two hours, the Fleet Air Arm pilots were ready to dismiss the sighting as an American fantasy. Pilots and crews of patrol bombers tended to relieve their boredom from time to time with fanciful reports.

The leader of the section, Lieutenant Alan Hobhouse, regarded the low black clouds and the line of rain squalls closing in between his flight and the course back to *Unicorn*. Fuel would soon be running low. He decided that it was nearly time to follow the Hellcats back to the ship. The notion of jettisoning a round dozen depths bombs into the sea was distasteful, but he could not allow his section to land on *Unicorn*'s deck so heavily laden with explosives.

He pressed the intercom button and spoke to his observer/navigator, Sublieutenant Maclean. "You are quite sure of the position, are you, Ian?"

The voice in his earphones was slightly aggrieved. "Of course I'm bloody sure, skipper."

"This is our phantom Jap's farthest-on then."

"As near as makes no difference," Maclean replied.

Hobhouse searched the darkening gray sea. There were whitecaps now. Occasionally the TBMs flew through low bits of scud, losing sight of the surface of the sea.

"Ten minutes more then," Hobhouse said, and informed the other planes that they should begin working out a course back to the ship.

Kunamoto was weary. He leaned heavily against the shaft of the retracted periscope and studied the chronometer fixed to the bulkhead.

Anemone had been submerged now for twelve hours, and the air in the boat was almost unbreathable. The men in the control room were wet with perspiration and their eyes were heavy. They breathed through open mouths. The oxygen cylinders had

296

not been fully packed when the submarine left Mikura-jima with the *shinyo* boats in tow because the facilities on the tiny island had not included oxygen separators. In addition to the foul air, *Anemone* was now being plagued by low batteries. It was imperative that she surface soon to recharge the batteries and air out the stinking interior. Yet while it was still light on the surface, it would be too dangerous to go up.

It would be a shame, Kunamoto thought, to be kept from returning to Kure to report *Anemone*'s destruction of an American cruiser. Such victories were too rare these days to go untold. He had come to the conclusion that his victory over the foolishly racing cruiser had distorted his judgment slightly. He had assumed that the American ship had been the vanguard of one of the Support Groups for the invaders attacking Honshu, and he had stationed himself in a place where he thought it likely that he could expend his remaining torpedos on rich, fat targets: American transports and heavily laden cargo vessels. But none had come his way. Each time he had raised the periscope, he had swept only empty sea.

The last time he had searched the horizon he had seen the dark clouds moving up from the south. All the bad weather in this part of the Pacific came from the south. The great typhoon that had almost decimated Kyushu during the American assault had come from the south. He closed his eyes and uttered a short supplication to Amaterasu Omikami. The Divine Wind that had smashed Kublai Khan's great invasion fleet in the twelfth century had come swiftly, like the typhoon of last November. If only it would come again and catch the enemies of Dai Nihon exposed on the beaches.

He caught himself quickly. Fantasizing was a symptom of carbon-dioxide poisoning. The air in the boat was becoming dangerous.

"Periscope depth," he ordered. He watched the depth gauge move until the needle leveled off at eight and a half meters. The depth of water under the keel could not be recorded on the instruments *Anemone* carried, because the submarine was cruising over the Japan Trench, an abyss in the sea that began near the Bonins, turned west to hug the coast of Honshu, and extended as far as the Kuriles. The average depth was 11,000 meters. Even for a submariner, such a black abyss was daunting.

"Up periscope," Kunamoto said.

When the instrument was extended, he swung it in a quick search of 360 degrees. All it revealed was a darkening, empty sea and a sky filled with low, racing rain clouds.

He made a swift decision. "Surface," he ordered.

Lieutenant Nemuro repeated the order, and the men on the buoyancy-tank controls reacted with grateful swiftness. The deck canted slightly, and *Anemone* broke the surface of the gray and turbid ocean.

The section of TBMs, flying in two three-airplane vees, emerged from the rain squall at an altitude of 1,000 feet.

Sublieutenant Evelyn Forsythe, a young Londoner only recently assigned to *Unicorn*, was the first to catch sight of the I-boat broaching. He squeezed the microphone button on the TBM's throttle and shouted, "Tally ho! Submarine at two o'clock!" His voice trembled with excitement.

His observer/navigator, a long-service lieutenant from Edinburgh named MacTavish, twice his pilot's age and given to dourness, said, "We don't use that Battle of Britain chat out here, Sub. Just say what and where."

Forsythe refused to be put down. He had never before seen a Japanese submarine—or, for that matter, a Japanese warship of any kind. He had arrived in the Pacific long after the Imperial Navy's glory days.

"I see him, Mr. Forsythe," Hobhouse said. "Section, form right echelon on me. Now."

The TBMs assumed a stair-step formation, and Hobhouse turned toward the Japanese submarine. Obviously, no one aboard the boat had yet seen the Avengers as they emerged from the squall. It was almost too good to be true, Hobhouse thought. A sitter, by God. Targets like this were hard to come by, and he didn't intend to give the Jap commander a chance to wake up to his danger.

"We will attack in line astern," he said calmly. "Everything on the first run. He won't sit forever." He peeled his Avenger away and down, flying straight along the submarine's wake. He saw the hatch in the conning tower open and a man emerge. It was like watching a piece of film in slow motion. The Jap clambered out and started to climb the periscope housing to the starboard lookout's platform. As he turned, he caught sight of the line of Avengers closing. Hobhouse imagined the terror, the sudden shock. He felt no pity, none at all.

Hobhouse's depth bombs were fused for ten and twenty feet. They dropped in a perfect straddle and exploded, bulging the surface of the sea on either side of *Anemone*. A harsh yellow light flashed in the deep. The submarine heaved upward, her pressure hull shattered by the swiftly consecutive explosions.

She settled into the boiling water heavily as, in rapid succession, the remaining Avengers dropped their depth charges around her. None came as close as Hobhouse's had, but each added to the mortal wound he had given her. Air and oil bubbled up from the frothing water as the submarine began her last dive, the long, deep death that was her karma.

Inside *Anemone* all was darkness and screams and rushing water. Kunamoto felt the angle of the deck steepen beneath his feet. In the pitch blackness he clung to the oily shaft of the periscope as the bow dropped swiftly until the boat was vertical in the sea. The water boiled up around him, driving away the fetid air. His last thought was not, as he had always imagined it would be, of the Emperor. It was of his wife. His last emotion was regret that he would never know whether she would bear a son or a daughter.

Like a smooth black stone, the Imperial Navy submarine *Anemone* dropped into the abyss. It would take her seven full minutes to reach the cold, sunless bottom, where she would lie on her side in the darkness for a thousand years.

1900 Hours

At seven in the evening, under a swiftly darkening sky threatening rain, the leading elements of the 7th Infantry Division, XXIV Corps, U.S. Tenth Army, entered the rail-junction city of Ishioka.

The men of the 1st Platoon, Able Company, 231st Infantry Regiment, approached the ruined city center in two single files supported by a section of Sherman tanks from the 2nd Armored Regiment.

The breakout from North Grable beachhead had been accomplished with surprisingly little difficulty. Rather than fight on the beaches, the defenders—regular soldiers of the Imperial Army's 116th Independent Mixed Brigade—had fought a sporadic rearguard action as they retreated swiftly around the north end of Kasumiga Lake.

Captain Daniel Wallace, company commander, was a veteran of the European theater, more familiar with the hedgerows of France than the rice paddies of the central Kanto. The flat open country, with its lattice of foot trails between flooded paddies, made him distinctly uncomfortable. It limited maneuver and made the tanks useful only as mobile artillery. But the Japs had not chosen to make a stand at any of the seemingly suitable places between the beachhead and Ishioka. There had been a half-dozen sharp fire fights, but as the American spearhead advanced, the Japs continued to fall back, leaving a few dead, some burning vehicles, and little more.

Ishioka was the 231st Infantry's Y-day objective, and Wallace was both pleased and suspicious of how easily it had been attained.

As he walked through the smashed and bombed city center behind a Sherman, he felt the first sprinkles of a cold spring rain. The day that had been so clear and bright had deteriorated into a chill, damp dusk.

It was at Ishioka that the armor was due to refuel. Ordinarily Wallace would have been unwilling to call a halt and bivouac in a place where the rubble and shattered buildings offered so much cover for possible enemy activity. But Able Company's point squad had radioed back that they still maintained light contact with the retreating Japs, and that they were running, as Sergeant Fahnhorst reported, faster than the point squad could chase them. It was a typical report from the sergeant, who was convinced that the dire tales of suicidal Jap resistance were only war stories told by Pacific veterans to frighten the new men from Europe.

By the time full darkness descended, Able Company had established a bivouac in the ruins near the rail yards, a tangle of twisted rails and burned buildings that allowed Wallace to establish a reasonably secure defense perimeter. The Shermans were parked in an open area near the remains of the main railway station—a thing Wallace would not have permitted if it had been his decision to make—and were being refueled by their crews from fifty-gallon drums brought forward in armored personnel carriers.

The rain was falling more heavily now, and the troops huddled in their ponchos eating K rations. At 2300 hours, Easy Company would pass through Able's position and become the spearhead. At 2330, the column would begin to move again toward the 231st's Y + 1 objective, the town of Oyama, on the east bank of the Omai River.

It had surprised Wallace that his men had encountered almost no civilians in their advance from the Kashima Sea beaches to Ishioka. The farmhouses—those still standing—had been deserted, the villages empty. The rice stood in the flooded paddies unharvested. He had been told that the Kanto was not only the heartland of Japan, but also the most heavily populated area on Honshu. Where the hell were the people? he wondered.

He ate his rations fitfully, conscious of the rain leaking down his neck, of his muddy boots smelling of the paddies, of the weariness of the long march from the coast.

First Sergeant Isaacs appeared with hot coffee in a canteen cup, and Wallace accepted it gratefully. He offered the sergeant a cigarette, and they sat smoking, protecting their cigarettes against the rain in cupped hands with the practiced ease of experienced infantrymen.

Morris Isaacs had been with Wallace since the dash across Germany to the Elbe. The two men were accustomed to one another and habitually spoke in dirt soldier's shorthand.

"Check the outposts?"

"Done," Isaacs said.

Wallace stretched, wishing there was time for a few hours' sleep. It had been a long day; they had hit the beach at North Grable at six in the morning. But there wasn't time for sleeping.

"What's going on down south?" Isaacs asked.

Throughout the day Able Company's radios had been picking up spotty transmissions from the beachheads. Weather was interdicting close air support, and the troops were having trouble finding main-force Jap units that could be cut up with naval gunfire.

"The Jarheads are having trouble at Suruga Bay, but the people at Sheridan are going all right," Wallace said.

Isaacs looked around at the dark, rain-slick ruins surrounding Able Company's bivouac area. He took a last pull from his cigarette and sent it in a sparking arc with a flick of his forefinger.

"Problem, Ike?"

"I don't know, Captain. It doesn't *feel* right."

"It doesn't, does it? Where in hell are all the *people*?"

"Remember what they told us about Okinawa and Kyushu?"

Wallace said, "There are two million people in the Kanto. Two million don't commit suicide."

"I guess not," the sergeant said. He stood. "One more look at the outposts."

"I'll come with you." Wallace stood and buttoned his poncho. The night was not only wet, it was also growing cold.

Together the two men made their way through the jungle of twisted rails and rubble. They exchanged passwords with the men in the first foxhole. Wallace checked their weapons, exchanged a few words, and moved on.

They were halfway along the company's 200-yard front when Isaacs stopped. "Listen," he whispered.

From somewhere in the darkness of the ruined city came a soft susurration, a strange shuffling sound. Then a single voice was heard, high-pitched, shrill, and strange, almost certainly a woman's voice. Immediately there was the noise of gunfire from the outposts: the flat crack of M-1s and the deeper, more authoritative thumping of a BAR.

Wallace and Isaacs immediately unslung their carbines and began to run back toward the command post near the wreckage of the railway station. The volume of firing increased. It was all American fire. The pop of Arisakas and Nambus was totally missing. Somewhere, an American screamed in fury or pain.

"Able Company! Take cover!" Isaacs shouted as he ran.

Wallace yelled, "Mortars! Get some flares up!"

He could hear the sound made by people running, a great many people, and padding noises, with an occasional defiant shout. He saw movement off to his left but held his fire because he did not want to risk hitting any of his own men.

A mortar coughed, and immediately a parachute flare started to burn high in the air, bathing the rubble with a cold blue-white light. Wallace saw the faces first: pale, moving like masks suspended against the darkness. The firing grew in intensity, but the faces only seemed to multiply. He realized that he was watching a wave of human beings running straight toward Able Company's position. The flashes of gunfire were like yellow tongues in the uncertain light. The running Japanese carried sticks— *sticks*, by God, he thought.

"God damn," Isaacs said breathlessly. "How many of them are there? What do they think they're doing?"

The mob had begun to utter sounds Wallace had never heard before: guttural noises, gasping, sucking sounds, and thin, wailing screams.

"They're civilians, by God," he shouted. To his men he called, "Cease fire! Cease fire!"

The first wave overran the outposts easily, trampling their own dead without slowing down, running over those of their own first rank who stumbled. They ran shouting and crying, their voices massed into an inhuman, wailing choir.

Isaacs leveled his M-1 and screamed at Wallace, "Shoot, Dan! *For Chrissake, shoot!*"

The human wave overran Wallace, impaling him on a half-dozen bamboo spears. Isaacs's M-1 fired until the barrel grew too hot to touch, but when he paused to change magazines, he, too, was trampled and spiked to bloody tatters by old men, women, even children stabbing at him with their bamboo weapons. The human tide ran on, straight into the fields of fire from the hastily resited heavy machine guns and mortars of Able Company. Bodies exploded, ripped to rags by bullets. Yet the wave of people ran on. They climbed over the piled dead to plunge into the American positions, shrieking and stabbing. The moment they reached the clearing where the tanks were parked, they were hit by the 75mm cannon in the Shermans' turrets. Great bloody paths opened in their ranks. The mortar flare was down, and for a time the darkness was broken only by muzzle flashes and explosions. One of the Japanese civilians managed to reach the fuel dump with a satchel charge. It blew the Japanese nearby into bloody bits, but it ignited the fifty-gallon drums in the APCs as well, and a towering column of flame topped by a swiftly rising fireball turned the night to hellish daylight.

Some of the tank crews managed to get their Shermans moving away from the fire. They were swarmed over by maddened civilians who poked in frustrated fear and rage at the openings in the armor, wounding some tankmen. Bodies were mashed under the treads of the retreating tanks. The clearing had become an abattoir.

The survivors of Able Company, formed by their platoon leaders into a defensive perimeter, poured gunfire into the finally faltering human wave.

Fifteen minutes after the attack had begun, it was over. The rubbled streets around the burned-out railway station of Ishioka were littered with bodies. Bamboo spears lay about like scattered matchsticks. Two Shermans and an APC had been destroyed; 1,500 gallons of gasoline had been burned—still burned in the streets and gutters. Able Company had lost its commanding officer, first sergeant, and sixty-two men killed; twenty-two were wounded or injured in some way by the Japanese spears. The attack by the Volunteer Defense Force of Ishioka had resulted in the death of 1,800 civilians, 200 of them women, 50 of them men over the age of sixty, 170 children between the ages of ten and fourteen. There were almost no surviving wounded among the Japanese. Those few who had been given hand grenades by retreating soldiers used them to commit suicide. Others committed a crude form of seppuku with their bamboo spears or household knives.

The shocked Americans reacted in various ways. Some were angry enough to shoot any wounded they found. Others simply stared at the carnage in sickening disbelief. Not one of them would ever again doubt the warnings they had received about the Japanese determination to resist the invasion to the last man, woman, and child. For the first time since the dark days of the early battles on Guadalcanal, some Americans wondered about the cost of the ultimate victory.

Y-day plus 14
15 March 1946

On the strength of its advantageous geographical position and the undying loyalty and solidarity of its people, the Empire will prosecute the war to the end in order to preserve the national polity and protect the Imperial Homeland, thereby securing the foundations for the future development of the race.

> *Saiko Senso Shido Kaigi Tsuzuri*
> (Basic Policy for the Future Direction of the War)
> Proceedings of the Supreme War Direction Council

After clearing the beach zones, our advancing forces will encounter strongly organized defensive positions blocking the approaches to the heart of the [Kanto] plain. The most important sectors will be occupied by Army divisions, the less critical areas by relatively immobile but numerous volunteer defense units. Resistance will be determined and bitter; any penetration of the organized areas will be met by prompt and vicious counterattacks by local reserves, possibly accompanied by small tank units. By the time these forward positions are fully developed, our attacking forces may be opposed in the northeastern area by 35,000 to 45,000 troops; in the central eastern area by 40,000 to 50,000, and in the southwestern area by 45,000 to 60,000.

> Staff Study Operations: "Coronet"
> General Headquarters
> U.S. Army Forces in the Pacific

307

0800 Hours

Lieutenant Harry Seaver lay on the steep hillside and watched the Jap strongpoint through his field glasses. The carpet of cedar needles under him was wet, and the cold rain dripped steadily from the boughs of the gnarled old trees. It had been raining steadily now for thirteen days. Sometimes the wind would blow and squalls would race across the mountainous peninsula, but mostly the rain had fallen in a steady spring downpour, turning the road into a quagmire and sending freshets tumbling down the steep, forested slopes into the rushing Koito River far below.

It was mainly the weather that had made the platoon's progress so slow. The tanks the new battalion commander had insisted on sending up the mountain with the Rangers slipped and struggled in the mire, and each time the patrol encountered a barricade of felled cedar trees it had been necessary to back the Shermans into cover before the infantrymen could move forward to clear the obstructions with satchel charges.

Whoever was conducting the retreating defense of the road knew what he was doing, Seaver thought. He knew the countryside, too. The obstacles and strongpoints the Rangers had kept having to assault were brilliantly sited. Wherever a steep embankment made attack difficult, wherever a sharp turn in the road put the lumbering Shermans at a disadvantage, there was certain to be a defensive position.

The Rangers had taken heavy casualties. There were ten dead and twice that many wounded left along the road from the coast for the medics to find. Two of the five Shermans that had left South Sheridan with the Rangers were mired down behind them, helpless until the tank retrievers could be moved up. And God knew when that might be, Seaver thought.

He wiped the drops from the lenses of his glasses and studied the new strongpoint. It was constructed of heavy cedar logs and packed earth. The firing slit was beautifully placed to give the occupants of the bunker a wide field of fire. The next half-mile of road was steep, twisting, and naked of cover on the side commanded by the bunker. The lead Sherman was 1,000 yards down the road with its crew and a squad of unhappy Rangers trying to free its right-hand tread from a trough of mud cut across the road by the seeping water from the steep embankment above. It was going to take the men at least an hour to free it. Until they did, it would be impossible to move the following tanks past.

Through the glasses Seaver could see only darkness in the firing slit of the bunker. Yesterday they had run into a fire fight at a similar strongpoint, and the tank detachment commander, Staff Sergeant Schuster, had been chastened when it developed that the Japs had an old Model 38 37mm antitank gun, in addition to the customary Nambu machine gun, hidden behind the cedar logs. One of the Shermans had taken two hits, which unseated the turret and made it impossible to traverse its weapon. After the tank had made an ignominious reversing retreat, Seaver had had to send Tangelli and a squad in with the flamethrower.

But then something had gone wrong with Tangelli's big Zippo, and here was another damn log-reinforced earth bunker. Seaver's compressed lips felt rough and chapped. He was tired and hungry and sick to death of this patrol—and the day had only just begun.

Jim Tanaka appeared, crawling up the slope to the ridge. "What's the holdup?"

Seaver handed him the glasses.

"Shit," Tanaka said, studying the bunker.

Seaver looked at his watch. It would take a squad the better part of an hour to climb down into the ravine and then up to the next ridge, from which the bunker could be safely attacked—*if* it could be safely attacked. He had lost a man and had taken a graze himself in just such a maneuver two days earlier. He had neither the men nor the time to reduce each bunker in the conventional way.

"How are they doing with Schuster's Chrysler?" The Sixth Army's Sherman tanks had all come from the Chrysler factory in Michigan. It was a long way to bring them to be made scrap on a mountain road in Chiba Prefecture, Seaver thought.

"Ten, maybe fifteen, minutes more," Tanaka said. "But Schuster is antsy. He's afraid he'll get another scratch on it."

"One more bog-down and I'm sending the Shermans back," Seaver said. "They aren't worth a damn up here."

Suddenly, some imprudent movement on the road where the platoon waited alerted the Japanese in the bunker. A Nambu began to fire, probing the hillside blindly. Bullets clipped the cedar branches overhead, sending down a few needles and a great deal of rain water.

"That's torn it," Seaver said angrily. "Go back down there and tell the troops to take cover. I'm calling in some artillery."

Tanaka bobbed his head and scuttled down the slope, his M-1 held low. The Nambu clattered irritably, but hit nothing.

"They know we're here, don't they, Lieutenant?" Buie said.

"They know, all right," Seaver said. "See if you can raise Battalion."

Buie, the heavy radio on his back, jammed himself against the wet trunk of a tree and spoke into the handset.

Radio communications had been growing more difficult between the platoon and Battalion. The distance from the beachhead was less than twelve miles air-line, but the terrain was rough and the beachhead was now in radio defilade.

Seaver returned to his scrutiny of the bunker. It was as well constructed as all the others had been. Whoever had planned the

311

defense of this road was good, no doubt about it. He shivered slightly in his damp clothes and wished for a cigarette. He did not light one.

Presently Buie stopped talking and shook his head. "Sorry, Lieutenant. No can do."

Seaver turned again and raised his glasses to look back through the overhanging branches at where the sea should be. He could see nothing because of the rain and mist. He took his map from inside his combat jacket and studied it carefully. Then he referred to his notebook. "Call—" He ran a grimy finger down the list of code names and assignments for March 15. "Here it is. CL42 is Rifle Six. Call her," he ordered.

Somewhere, cruising not far from shore, the USS *Savannah* had the duty—if she wasn't ducking Kamikazes, Seaver thought.

Buie spoke again into the handset. "Rifle Six, this is Trigger Nine. Do you read?" He listened for a time and then said: "Stand by one, Rifle Six." He handed the radiophone to Seaver.

"Rifle Six," Seaver said, "this is Trigger Nine. Could you give us a little help?"

The voice from the cruiser came back cleanly, free of interference. The operator in the ship's CIC spoke with a pronounced New York accent. "Affirmative, Trigger Nine. Standing by." The word "by" came through "boy." New Yorkers are the Tohokujin of America, Seaver thought.

He said into the radio: "Target is stationary, Rifle. A rammed-earth-and-log bunker. Some troops, number unknown. Bunker controls our road." He referred once again to his notebook and map. "Grid blue, repeat blue. Co-ordinates X-ray 7.1, repeat X-ray 7.1; Yoke 4.70, repeat Yoke 4.70."

"Trigger Nine, we read blue X-ray 7.1, Yoke 4.70. Your posit?"

Seaver judged the distance between the bunker and his own soldiers on the road. "Rifle Six, we are clear by 900 yards. Our posit X-ray 6.80, Yoke 5.1."

"Trigger Nine this is Rifle Six. Roger. Stand by."

Seaver rested his helmet against the earth, squinting up at the gray sky through the cedar branches. On the cruiser, Trigger Nine was cut into the battle circuit so that Seaver could spot the fall of the shells.

"Trigger Nine, this is Rifle Six. Spotting salvo coming up."

Seaver keyed his radio and spoke to Schuster's radioman in the lead tank down on the road. "You getting this?"

"We're on, Lieutenant," the tanker said. "Understand fire support coming. You all keep your heads down up there, heah?"

Twelve miles away, the cruiser's turret would be turning, the guns elevating.

Soon a shell struck the steep hillside a hundred yards below and fifty yards to the left of the bunker. Bits of a shattered tree spun down the mountainside, and the sound rolled through the ravine.

Seaver spoke into the radio. "Rifle Six, this is Trigger Nine. Up 100, right 03."

Presently the voice of the cruiser's guns said: "Stand by to spot, Trigger." A pause. Then: "Spot."

The shell struck the long wall of the bunker's glacis. It ripped the cedar to splinters and unseated the lintel over the firing slit. Once again the sound rolled down the wet ravine.

"Rifle, this is Trigger," Seaver said. "Right on the money. Pour it on."

"Coming up, Trigger. Service with a smile."

Seaver grimaced—at the gunners on the ship and at himself. How gaily we play at this game, he thought. Is it because we might keep horrors at bay with smart-alecky talk like this?

Shells began to fall around the bunker, yellow explosions tearing at the earth and splintering the trees and the heavy cedar logs of the bunker itself. Seaver watched through the field glasses as the distant gunners ripped the strongpoint to rubble. There was no indication that the bunker was, or ever had been, occupied by human beings. There was only the steady rain of high explosives and the singing of steel shell splinters scything through the trees.

Seaver spoke into the radio. "Rifle, this is Trigger. Check fire. Check fire. Let me take a look."

In the sudden silence a bird called out, a branch sagged and fell. Around the pile of churned earth and wood that had been the bunker, nothing stirred.

"Rifle Six," Seaver said, "this is Trigger Nine. That's done it. Our thanks."

"Ah, Trigger Nine," *Savannah* said, "your battalion CP heard us talking to you. Can you raise them?"

"Negative, Rifle," Seaver said. "Can you patch us through or relay?"

"Roger, Trigger Nine. Wait one."

Seaver spoke to Buie. "Leave the radio here and go down to the road. Tell Sergeant Hardin I want a recon of that bunker."

Buie slipped off the radio harness and scuttled down the rain-slick hillside to the road. Seaver waited. A deep stillness had settled over the forest. Even the rain seemed to fall silently. The air was frigid and growing colder. The mountains of the Boso Peninsula were not high, only steep. But in early spring the freezing level could sometimes drop to 1,000 feet or less as sudden masses of cold air swept over southern Honshu from Siberia. He remembered the Maeda villa with the gardens hidden under snowbanks, the ponds and waterfalls frozen into mirrors, and twisted filigree spikes of icicles hanging from the *onigawara*, the demon tiles edging the fancifully curved roofs.

He examined his feelings about being so close to that well-remembered place in these present circumstances and found that they were not at all what he had expected they would be. The dozens of Japanese he had dispatched to Yasukuni stood in the shadows behind him. It was his karma never to be free of those reproachful spirits; their sad presence was the price of having become, however inadvertently, a *bushi*, a warrior. The old swordmaster who had taught him had once said, "The *bushi*, when he takes up the sword, incurs obligations that can never be fully repaid." He had understood the *sensei* imperfectly then. He understood him better now. Because he had been taught to think like a Japanese and because he was not Japanese, the purity of the concept of *gimu*, the obligation that can never be repaid, even in a lifetime, had become soiled. For a true Japanese the fullness of *gimu* consisted of *chu*, duty to the Emperor, *nimmu*, duty to one's work, and *ko*, duty to parents and ancestors. Because he was, and would forever be, a *gaijin*—literally, one from outside—for him there was only *ko*, duty to his ancestors, to his blood. It was this narrow definition of *gimu* that had brought him back to Japan as an invader, unrepentant, and anxious only to do what must be done to end this endless war.

"Trigger Nine, do you read?"

"Trigger Nine. Go ahead, Rifle."

"We have you patched in to your battalion CP, Trigger Nine."

There was a pause and then a fainter, different voice came on the radio circuit. "Seaver? This is Kizer. Do you read?"

"I read you R4 S3, Kizer. Go ahead."

"Harry, all hell's broken loose on the beachhead. The Japs are counterattacking in division strength. Harry? Did you read that?"

"I read you, Kizer," Seaver said. "What do you want us to do—pull back?"

"Negative, Harry. We're holding them all right here. But the Jarheads on the other side of the mountains are pinned down. They are looking at two full divisions supported by armor. We can reinforce them, but we need that road, Harry."

Seaver considered before replying. Somehow, the Japanese had managed to concentrate large units of their 52nd Army and were counterattacking under cover of the bad weather. Without command of the air, the American forces were incredibly vulnerable, with large formations striking inland and others still aboard the transports or packed into the beachheads. The fact that he was talking to Kizer, the senior captain in the Ranger Battalion, rather than the new commanding officer, suggested that the battalion was taking casualties.

"What is your position, Harry?"

Seaver gave Kizer the map co-ordinates. The platoon was only one-third of the way across the peninsula. The tanks had slowed down the Rangers' advance almost as much as had strongpoints they had been forced to reduce one after another. At this rate, it would take them a week to reach the mouth of the Koito River. He estimated the distance to the Maeda villa as twenty miles. If they could take the tanks that far and leave them dug in there to protect the approaches, he estimated he could cut the time to the Koito delta in half.

He explained his situation to Kizer. "The road is clear to this point," he said. "You can send anything you want up behind us. We'll need another flamethrower squad and a couple of backup companies."

"You got 'em." The radio transmission began to break up. Before it faded completely, Seaver heard Kizer say, "Kamikazes are trying to get the mulberries." These modular piers at Kujukuri were duplicates of those built on the coast of Normandy.

Seaver wondered why the Japanese could fly when the Americans couldn't. Then he remembered that the Japanese pilots were making one-way trips. The lowering weather would actually help those it did not kill.

A four-man patrol, led by Corporal Angelo Tangelli, the slope-shouldered Sicilian, had crossed the narrow draw. Now the men were climbing the slope to the shattered bunker. Seaver listened to the radio for another minute, but transmission had stopped. If the beachhead was under attack again, *Savannah* probably had her hands full protecting the unarmed transports, which by now must be lined bow to stern at the prefabricated piers assembled for use until Suruga and Sagami bays were secure.

Tangelli stood and waved from atop the jackstrawed logs of the strongpoint. He pointed at the wreckage around him and yelled, "Sukiyaki, Lieutenant. Jap stew."

Seaver signaled for the squad to return to the main body, shouldered the radio, and made his way back to the road.

When he reached the damaged Sherman, he called the squad leaders and said, "The Marines are having trouble on the other side of the peninsula. Division is sending more tanks up this road. We'd better move faster." He indicated the crest of the next ridge. "I want to be up there tonight." He looked angrily at Schuster. "If that beast of yours breaks down one more time, or gets stuck in the mud, we leave you to wait for the reinforcements from South Sheridan. You got that, Sergeant?"

Schuster's soft Southern drawl was mournful as he acknowledged the warning. He had lived the first twenty years of his life in Meridian, Mississippi, and had never before seen a Jap. Now he had two to deal with, one white and one yellow. It was enough to make a man despair. He wished he was back in Fort Hood instead of accompanying these crazy Rangers into places where his beloved tank didn't belong.

The columns began to move again, and Seaver stood by the side of the road until Tanaka, marching at the tail of the column, came along. He dropped in beside him.

"Battalion says the Japanese are counterattacking all the southern beachheads," Seaver said. "We have to make better time. They want this road."

Tanaka regarded Seaver expressionlessly. "And you're going to give it to them."

"Something like that," Seaver said. "What's eating you, Jim?"

"This platoon doesn't need two officers. I'm a fifth wheel."

Seaver marched with his eyes on the forest. "You know the Army."

"Sure," Tanaka said. "I know the Army."

He's uncomfortable here, Seaver thought. He thinks the troops don't trust him. And he doesn't really trust me. He was too wet and tired to think deeply about it, but plainly Colonel Bolton had been wrong to think that his "two Japs" could work well together. There was nothing Japanese about James Monroe Tanaka except his face.

"Take the point," Seaver said.

Tanaka looked startled. "*Hai, Chui-san,*" he said, and hurried past the lumbering Shermans to join the head of the column. Seaver watched him, perplexed. Then quite suddenly he realized that he had spoken to Tanaka in Japanese.

He passed a hand over his eyes. He was very tired. He had not been sleeping well, and when he did, his dreams were all of the childhood he remembered in this place, among these familiar cedars and steep mountains. What's happening to me? he wondered.

Lieutenant Isao Hideyoshi sat shivering in the icy, wet cockpit of his *kaiten* somewhere near the mouth of the Uraga-suido, the narrow channel connecting Sagami and Tokyo bays. His fifteen-meter-long craft lay awash in the sea, the sharp chop breaking completely over the low enclosure covering the cockpit. His eyes were no more than six centimeters above the surface of the water, and the movement of the cylindrical hull was making him miserably seasick.

The *kaiten*, named for the mythical Sea Dragon, was one of only a half-dozen remaining to the Special Naval Attack Force that had been stationed at Yokosuka.

The approved technique developed for *kaiten* attack on enemy shipping was for the human torpedo to be carried to sea on the casing of an I-class submarine and launched at close range, allowing its pilot to guide the 1,500-kilogram warhead to its target.

For Hideyoshi and the two *kaiten* pilots who were now supposed to be following him out into the waters of Sagami Bay, a proper opportunity to perform their duty had never come. Repeated attempts had been made to mount a proper *kaiten* attack against the American warships crowding into the bay, but the submarines that carried the *kaiten*s to sea had never returned. One of the pilots with Hideyoshi had actually begun an attack, but had been forced to abort it when his *kaiten* began to take on water and sank to the bottom of the bay. In ten meters of water, Ensign Fukuoka had managed to escape from his machine and make it to shore. Hideyoshi had never forgotten the reception Fukuoka had received on his return to Yokosuka. It had been a terrible object lesson to all of the *kaiten* men who remained.

Commander Tonosho, the group's commanding officer, had stood Fukuoka before all the others, including the enlisted sailors and civilian laborers. "You are the first pilot of a *kaiten* ever to return," he had said icily. "Others of our flotilla have willingly pursued their missions to the very end, even though they may not have been fortunate enough to sink any enemy ships. Clearly, they were ready to meet death when they departed happily to serve the Emperor. But you, you were incapable of preparing yourself to do your duty. And so you have returned pleading mechanical failure. You are a contemptible coward, Fukuoka. It is in my mind to reduce you to the ranks and send you off to the infantry, who might perhaps know what can be done with you. You have disgraced the memory of those who have gone before you, and you have demoralized this unit. I put you under arrest until further notice." The commander had then ripped off Fukuoka's collar tabs and, trembling with fury, had slapped the terrified officer repeatedly across the face. It had been a scene of such incredible shame that Hideyoshi's cheeks burned at even the memory.

It had frightened him almost as much as it had Fukuoka, because he had begun to hope—silently, of course—that with the loss of the last submarines there was a chance that the remaining *kaiten* pilots might survive. Fukuoka's disgrace had swiftly disabused him.

When the Marines had landed on the Miura Peninsula between Sagami and Tokyo bays, they had advanced swiftly across the base of the peninsula to the very edge of the Yokosuka Naval Base. There the advance had stalled, and their leading units had been pushed back by armored columns of the 2nd Independent Tank Brigade. Rather than pleasing Tonosho, this had infuriated him. He became enraged at the thought that his tiny command had been saved from destruction by the Army. It was then that he had ordered the last of the *kaiten* prepared for sea and informed the pilots that he himself would lead a sortie into Sagami-nada in search of American shipping. "The weather is bad, the visibility poor," he said. "That will work to our advantage. Our *kaiten*s will be towed to sea by our sailors in rowboats. Once out in the channel, we will divide into two divisions. I will lead one and Lieutenant Hideyoshi will lead the other. We will find the enemy and totally destroy him."

Hideyoshi did not risk exchanging glances with Fukuoka and the other pilots. Plainly, the honorable unit commander was not thinking clearly. To tow six *kaiten*s any distance in the rough waters of the Uraga-suido was an almost impossible task for men in rowboats. Yet there was no fuel for the launches, and, with the submarines gone, there was no choice at all except to do what Tonosho was ordering done.

Accordingly, six *kaiten*s had been shoved down the ways and secured with towing hawsers to the rowboats in the predawn dark. The rain and the wind, in addition to the darkness, had separated the individual units almost immediately. And as a dirty gray light came with the gusty, squally morning, Hideyoshi found himself rolling and wallowing in a choppy sea, long since deserted by his rowboat, somewhere near the mouth of the Uraga Narrows. He hoped that the other members of his division were with him, but he had no possible way of knowing whether or not they were. Where Tonosho might be was an even greater mystery—one that Hideyoshi had no wish whatever to solve. He had begun, guiltily, to be sure, to think about survival once again.

The cockpit of the *kaiten* was narrow: a box of black-painted steel containing the simple controls and a magnetic compass. A tiny glass cover, similar to a fighter plane's canopy, projected from the cylindrical hull. The entire device was a development of the Mark X torpedo, modified with a weak electric motor for simple maneuvering and with two compressed-air tanks capable of driving the screws for perhaps two minutes—a time considered sufficient by the Imperial Navy planners to make a final, high-speed attack.

A short periscope projected from the weapon's cockpit so that the final run in could be made below the surface if that seemed likely to produce success.

No one at Yokosuka knew for certain whether or not any *kaiten* had ever destroyed an American ship. It was said that successful attacks had been made on the ships used by the Americans at Okinawa and Kyushu, but even Tonosho stopped short of claiming any confirmed sinkings.

Hideyoshi's mouth tasted of bile. He had already vomited in the cockpit, and the stench in the tiny space was nearly overpowering. The clumsy machine rolled sluggishly in the chop; some of the movements so violent that he feared it might capsize.

The waves breaking over the glass canopy made it impossible to determine his surroundings. According to the chart he, as leader of the second division, had been issued at the briefing, he should be some few kilometers off Miura, on the south shore of the peninsula. Coast watchers there had reported that two American cruisers had sailed into Sagami-nada to give fire support to the American Marines attacking Hiratsuka. It was not possible to say if these reports were accurate. Aircraft were no longer being used to observe enemy fleet movements. The entire Army and Navy inventory of airplanes had been assigned to *tokko* units.

For a time Hideyoshi considered the possibility of running his *kaiten* ashore. It was a shamefully disloyal and cowardly thought, and it troubled him that he would even consider such a course of action. But he had come to the conclusion that he was nearly helpless, bobbing about in his fifteen-meter steel coffin with little idea of where he actually was and little ability to travel more than a few short kilometers.

The air—what he could discern through the water sluicing over his craft—was misty. The temperature had been dropping for several days, and at five in the morning, when the *kaiten*s had been towed to sea, there had been snow flurries. The bad weather was preventing the Americans from using their tremendous air superiority. Surely there was some significance to that? Could it be that once again the Divine Wind was going to save the homeland? As much as he would like to believe that, he found it unlikely.

He looked at his chart again, holding the tiny flashlight he had been issued over the soggy paper. The shape of the peninsula drew his guilty attention. It was still, as far as he knew, in Japanese hands. He allowed himself a delicious fantasy. If he could beach his *kaiten* safely, perhaps he could make his way north to Kawasaki and from there to the isolated mountain town of Nagano, where he had been born and where, if they still lived, his family waited for his return. Surely Nagano would be safe from the invaders. It was there that the Imperial General Staff had prepared a retreat for the Emperor.

The dream evaporated in a grinding, jolting shock. His heart felt as though someone with icy fingers had squeezed it. He twisted desperately in his confinemnt, trying to see what it was that the *kaiten* had struck.

Through the salt-smeared canopy he caught a glimpse of something large and black in the sea. For a moment his panic made it impossible to think. Then he recognized the shape of another *kaiten*. He had collided with a member of his own division.

The impact had caused the two *kaiten*s to separate by a few meters and they lay side by side, nose to tail. Hideyoshi caught just a glimpse of the pilot watching him through the thick panes of the other cockpit. It looked like Fukuoka, but it was impossible to be certain. Whoever it was stared back at him across the intervening space with terror on his face. Then the other *kaiten*'s warhead rose from the water and towered over Hideyoshi as the stern settled in the sea. The *kaiten* assumed a vertical position that made it look like a great black finger pointing up out of the depths. Swiftly, it sank.

Hideyoshi shivered uncontrollably. Once again, Fukuoka was riding a defective *kaiten* to the bottom. But there would be no escape this time. The water in this part of the Uraga-suido was not ten meters deep, but 200.

USS *Alaska* cruised at reduced speed across the head of Sagami Bay. In CIC, Bertram Temko's radar limned first the point of Cape Tsurugi and then the bulkier mass of Cape Nojima at the tip of the Boso Peninsula. The officers in the center watched with interest. Firing support missions by radar was a relatively new technique.

Alaska had recently been liberated—Lieutenant Potkonsky's phrase—from her duties as command ship. All the generals were ashore with their troops on their assigned beachheads, and *Alaska* was now free to assume more mundane tasks, such as giving fire support to the Marines who were having a difficult time of it at North Lamour.

Temko's radar fixes provided the base for the solution of the fire-control problems, and it pleased the men in the CIC that the Japs would be taking a beating from *Alaska*'s guns in weather that made it impossible for anyone on the ship to see the shore.

The voices on the battle circuit were flat, unemotional. Nothing in their impersonal tones suggested that they were sending death through the misty snow flurries.

Throughout her 800 feet, the shock of the *Alaska*'s guns could be felt. Ten thouand yards away, the shells from turret one landed. The fall of shot was observed and correction called for by the fire-control party ashore—in this case, a naval officer and two Marines.

"All turrets. Continuous salvo fire. Commence firing."

Great tongues of yellow flame turned the air to steam. On the bridge, Captain Weed sat alertly in the high seat welded to the deck. He disliked bringing his ship into these restricted waters under conditions of almost zero visibility, but that, he realized, was simply a shipmaster's reluctance to approach any unseen shore. Actually, the radar navigation was going well. The ship's position was precisely marked on the chart and, from what he could hear on the battle circuit, the Marines ashore were getting what they needed. Because he liked his best men on duty when there might be a need for tight maneuvering, Lieutenant Commander Steinhart was general-quarters officer of the deck. "Tell *Trenton* we'll be coming about in three minutes, John," he said.

The OOD relayed the message to the old light cruiser steaming behind *Alaska*. *Trenton* had been scheduled for transfer to the Russians, but Coronet's need for fire-support ships had canceled the transaction. Weed took a grim satisfaction in that. The *Trenton* had been commissioned in 1924, and she was as obsolete as any ship in the fleet. But giving ships to the Soviets was poor policy, he thought. Almost a full year had passed since the German surrender, and there was no sign that the Russians were prepared to support the invasion of Japan. They had snatched the Japanese conquests on the mainland, so it could be said they were at war with the Japenese, but apparently they were interested only in what they could steal at little or no cost.

Alaska's commander stared moodily out at the foredeck. The rain continued to fall, mixed with some softly frozen snow. The met people had warned all the senior officers that weather this unsettled could be expected in Japan in March, but the reality was depressing.

The Carrier Task Groups had withdrawn to some 200 miles off the coast of Honshu, because it was impossible to carry on deck landings and takeoffs with less than a sixteenth-mile visibility. All air activity was being conducted by the AAF and the Marines based in eastern Kyushu. The soldiers and the Marines refused to admit that the weather was making it all but impossible to fly close support for the armies attempting to encircle Tokyo. And they were paying a price for it. The last Intelligence summary distributed to fleet and unit commanders showed a sudden skyrocketing of the accident rate among the tactical air squadrons.

For the first time Weed could remember in this Pacific war, he found himself less than optimistic. Not that there was any doubt whatever about the final outcome. No, the Japs were beaten—or nearly so. But Coronet was not running on schedule, or ahead of it, the way Operation Olympic and others had done.

The weather was part of it, of course. The entire operation had been conceived as one in which the participants could, whenever they chose, call in thousands of airplanes in support of ground operations. This reprise of winter was making land operations far more difficult than they should be.

That was not all that troubled Captain Weed. As a professional naval officer, he had spent his life preparing to fight against other professionals, or at least against other soldiers and sailors. But he had been warned that Operation Coronet might meet with a different sort of resistance. He had seen Japanese civilians die by the hundreds on Okinawa. By the tens of hundreds on Kyushu. Now, it appeared, they were willing to die by the thousands—perhaps, God forbid, by the millions. The Intelligence report on the incident at Ishioka had been a shock. The entire population of a good-sized town had apparently gone completely mad, attacking a company of infantry supported by tanks. With *sticks*, Weed thought. This sort of thing had happened at a number of places now, always with some casualties among the invaders and enormous losses among the civilians of the so-called Volunteer Defense Force. What sort of government demanded such suicidal behavior from its citizens?

He drew a deep breath and took a cigar from his shirt pocket. He did not light it but clamped it between his teeth. He keyed in the battle circuit through his communications unit. He heard the order: "Cease fire. Cease fire. Come to the ready and stand easy."

The fire mission was now complete. It was time to bring *Alaska* onto a reciprocal of her present course and work her down the western shore of the Boso Peninsula.

Weed stood and walked out onto the bridge wing. The air was soggy and cold; sleet puddled on the steel deck. He shivered and went back into the bridge. "Come right to course 189, Quartermaster," he said, and, to Steinhart, "Tell *Trenton* we'll be moving to quadrant X-ray, John."

The OOD gave the order to the signalman.

Somewhere, back there in the murk, Weed knew, the old light cruiser followed her newer, stronger consort in a wide turn.

"Bridge, this is forward port lookout."

"Bridge, aye."

The lookout's voice was sharp, hurried. "Something in the water about a hundred yards off our port bow. Looks like a *kaiten*!"

Weed flung the bridge door open and rushed to the port splinter shield. There! He could see a dark shape bobbing in the chop, a long, cylindrical thing. He caught the glint of a cockpit. Goddamn, he thought, it *was* a *kaiten*—and right under his bow. *Alaska* had nearly run the filthy thing down.

The only guns that were of any use at all at this minimal range were the quad forties in the tubs abaft the bridge. They began to fire immediately, and the water around the *kaiten* boiled with a storm of shells.

The warship was almost upon Lieutenant Hideyoshi before he saw it. It had appeared out of the rain and mist like a steel mountain on the sea. The size of it, so near, so powerful, almost caused him to faint from terror. In that single, dreadful moment he knew that he was a fraud, that he could not perform his duty to the Emperor, that he could not willingly die—not like this.

The guns along the cruiser's side were spewing fire. He heard fragments whine off his sloping steel flanks. His cockpit glass was pocked, but did not break, though water oozed in through cracks.

He struggled to open the hatch so that he could throw himself into the sea before the *kaiten* dispatched itself swiftly—as so many others had—to the bottom. But the latches were jammed. He began to moan with overwhelming fear.

As the cruiser drove through the water less than thirty meters from his wildly rolling craft, he could feel the vibrations of its screws. He caught just a glimpse of the white water frothing under her fantail before the *kaiten* spun as though it had been caught in a whirlpool. All he could think about was escape. Snapping on the electric motors, he rammed the rheostat full forward, trying to regain control.

He had just managed to establish steerageway when a second steel mountain materialized out of the spray, directly in front of him. He twisted the wheel hard over, but it was too late. The *kaiten*'s way was insufficient to make a sharp turn. It is doubtful that the device could have done so even under ideal circumstances.

The nose of the *kaiten* struck *Trenton* at the water line abaft the engineering compartment.

There was a screeching howl of metal as the cruiser's speed drove her onward. The fuse in the *kaiten*'s warhead was damaged enough to cause a two-second delay. The *kaiten* was dragged up out of the water for a third of her length before the 1,500 kilograms of toluol exploded.

Of the 600 men that made up the crew of the old cruiser, *Alaska* was able to pick up 310. Fifty more actually reached shore by clinging to rafts and wreckage. They were met by soldiers of the 37th Mixed Regiment of the Tokyo Defense Army and machine-gunned as they emerged from the sea.

1300 Hours

Sergeant Ed MacCauley marched by instinct alone, each step automatic, feeling the weight of his body and his equipment only as a numbness in his legs and feet, a vague awareness of discomfort by now almost completely deadened by cold and fatigue.

The column of Marines stretched along the wreckage of the Tokaido Road, led by a detachment of armored personnel carriers in which, from time to time, members of MacCauley's squad were privileged to ride with the wounded.

For two solid weeks, V Amphibious Corps had been in constant contact with the enemy. There had been upward of a dozen sharp fire fights each day; MacCauley had long since stopped counting anything but casualties. The Japs were retreating, but theirs was a retreat in strength, and the Marines had paid in blood for each mile of the miserable Tokaido they had taken.

The road, in its best days, had not been much by American standards. Though it was one of the two main routes connecting the Kanto with western Honshu, it had never been properly paved. It was a graded gravel road of the sort MacCauley associated with the mountain roads he remembered from his childhood. By now, shelling and bombing had reduced it to a pitted, rubbled track. Rain had filled most of the holes and frozen. There were men and equipment in and under the ice: hands and feet and broken vehicles and weapons lay like insects in amber.

The Marines no longer noticed these grisly relics of the battles they fought and left behind.

MacCauley's recon squad was part of the column's spearhead laboriously moving across the base of the Izu Peninsula through the Hakone Mountains.

Since Y-day, the battalion had lost 30% of its effectives. The Japanese, moving in swift and mobile units through the mountains, striking and running and then striking again, were taking a heavy toll from V Amphibious Corps. MacCauley's squad had lost only Angostino on Y-day, but there had been a steady attrition since then. Private Gracey had been killed on Y + 3, along with eight Marines from the battalion headquarters company, when a Jap unit from the 234th Division had charged down out of the hills behind fifty light tanks. Intelligence had assured the troops that there was no Jap armor in the Hakone Mountains, and Intelligence had been dead wrong.

In thirteen days, the corps had advanced twenty miles, from Kambara—where Lieutenant Scowcroft had distinguished himself in the attack against the positions in the tunnel—to Mishima, the battered wreck of a town just ahead of the column. This put them way behind schedule. Mishima should have been taken four days ago, and they should now be past Odawara and ready to leave the coast to strike inland toward Yokohama and Tokyo.

The clouds lay thick on the mountains. Occasional snow flurries came knifing down the steep valleys. Though hidden by the low ceiling, the breath of the snowfields on the slopes of Mount Fuji lashed the weary, wet Marines as they marched.

For a week they had not seen a friendly airplane. From time to time they could hear the sound of engines above the clouds, but the close support on which they had learned to rely was simply unavailable. Once before in recent operations American ground forces had had to fight without their air support: Bastogne had been heroic, but it had been bloody.

"I don't understand this weather, Sergeant." Scowcroft, his childish face stubbled and drawn, so that he looked like a plump, aged baby, marched alongside MacCauley. Since the business of the grenades at Kambara, he had attached himself to the sergeant, using him as a sounding board for absurd ideas and as a source of all the arcane information that—Scowcroft was certain—was taught to enlisted men, but never to officers.

"It's almost *April*, for goodness' sake. And just look at it. It keeps trying to *snow*." He seemed to be personally offended by the inhospitable quality of Japanese weather.

MacCauley, who had slept only ten hours in the last three days, wondered irritably where the man got his energy. And where in hell did this fat Ivy Leaguer find the enthusiasm to babble on so constantly?

"The captain says the Japanese used gas up north," Scowcroft said.

MacCauley had heard the rumor, and so, apparently, had General Schmidt, commander of V Amphibious Corps. For the first time in the Pacific war, Marines had been ordered to go into battle carrying their gas masks and protective gear.

MacCauley said, "Is that confirmed?"

"I think so," Scowcroft said, shifting the weight of his M-1 from one shoulder to the other. "A Marine from Able Company says it was pretty bad. Lots of casualties."

MacCauley walked on in silence. The truth was that there was more scuttlebutt and less hard information in this campaign than in any he had experienced before. The island fighting had given plenty of proof that the Japanese didn't believe in the same set of rules Westerners did, so nothing should come as a surprise. He allowed himself to wonder what he might do if invading armies were marching through the United States. He doubted that any set of "rules" would deter him from doing whatever seemed effective against them.

"I don't believe one should behave like a savage even in war," Scowcroft said primly.

Macauley sighed and slogged wearily on. Near the head of the column, the APCs rumbled as they climbed the piled rubble on the road. Their tracks ground the icy puddles into mush.

MacCauley caught sight of some men from the point platoon

running back toward the head of the column. The gunners in the APCs covered them with their fifty-caliber machine guns, but there was no firing. A Marine called, "Mr. Scowcroft and Sergeant MacCauley, up front!"

MacCauley stirred himself into a jog; Scowcroft ran breathlessly along beside him. Whenever the plump officer had to exert himself, he puffed like an old man. But he always arrived in better shape than anyone else in the platoon. Perhaps it was something in the genes, MacCauley thought sourly.

When they reached the head of the column, they found that Lieutenant Colonel Cleghorn, the battalion commander, had signaled a halt.

"Scowcroft," he said, "I have a job for you."

Scowcroft almost saluted, but caught himself in time. Back near Kambara, one of the other officers in the battalion had saluted the colonel and had had a strip torn off him for doing it. You could get senior officers killed that way.

"I want you and MacCauley's squad to take the point as we approach Mishima. It looks quiet enough, but I'm sending one of the APCs along to give you support."

MacCauley signaled for the recon squad to move up, and the six remaining members of the team jogged forward to form a circle around the colonel.

"It looks as though the Japs have withdrawn from Mishima, but we have to be sure. If they have, fine. If not, I want to know what they've left behind," Cleghorn said.

He waved an APC forward. "Keep buttoned up until you're sure." For MacCauley, the admonition was scarcely necessary. His two weeks in Japan had left him suspicious of everything that moved and much that did not.

As the squad moved out in company with the APC, Scowcroft said, "What bothers me, MacCauley, is—well, where are the civilians?"

What the officer implied was true enough. It seemed as though most of the civilian population—of Shizuoka Prefecture, at least —had vanished. The Marines had encountered only a number of old people paralyzed with fright. Someone in the battalion who spoke some Japanese, or claimed to, had told MacCauley that they expected to be killed, ground up for dog food, and shipped to the States in cans. It was so grotesque a fear that it occasioned great, and tasteless, mirth among the Marines of the landing team.

Perhaps now, MacCauley thought, as the battalion approached the southern edge of the Kanto Plain and the ruins of Yokohama, Kawasaki, and Tokyo, there would be more civilians to deal with. The 3rd Marine Division staff, he had heard, had already begun to make plans for civilian hospitals and food-distribution centers. The few people MacCauley had seen since Y-day were badly in need of food and medical services.

The squad advanced down the Tokaido in open order on both sides of the APC. On the right the shore of Suruga Bay lay within a few dozen yards of the road. Breakwaters of volcanic stone had been laboriously built out into the waters of the bay, presumably to protect the fleets of fishing boats that had once worked along this shore. Of these, only a few burned ribs remained.

As the squad approached Mishima, they moved through a landscape of violent desolation. There were no houses left standing, only burned stones and tiles. Here, even the ubiquitous rice paddies were abandoned, with no growing thing to be seen in the squares of half-frozen mud. Then, in the distance a single standing building was seen, a one-room affair whose brick construction had apparently saved it from the fires. A sticklike figure in a black suit appeared from the building.

Corporal Carpenter unslung his M-1 and thumbed off the safety. "Lieutenant."

"Hold your fire," Scowcroft shouted. "That's a white flag." He turned to MacCauley for advice.

MacCauley shrugged. There hadn't been many white flags on Honshu, but this could certainly be one. There were Japanese hiragana characters on the long, narrow cloth, which fluttered on a bamboo staff as the man waved it enthusiastically.

Scowcroft studied the Japanese through his field glasses and then handed the binoculars to MacCauley. "What do you think, Sergeant?"

The civilian was well past middle age, MacCauley judged. The suit he wore was greenish with age and hung on him loosely. The sunken cheeks and deep-set eyes were those of a starving man.

As he watched, the man called to someone in the brick building, and from the door came a dozen or more children, boys in the quaintly archaic nineteenth-century uniforms worn by Japanese schoolchildren, girls in black skirts and middy blouses.

"That's a school," MacCauley said.

"Let me see." Scowcroft took the glasses back. The children were, he estimated, between eight and twelve years old. The tallest of them was not five feet in height. The schoolmaster, watching the Americans, bowed deeply. The children did likewise. Scowcroft noted that all but the smallest wore knapsacks.

He lowered the glasses and signaled the squad to advance slowly. "Private Kavanaugh, front and center."

Kavanaugh gave MacCauley a look to indicate what he thought of the Lieutenant's attempt to give orders like a Marine, but he dropped down off the hood of the APC. "Yo, Mr. Scowcroft."

"Are there any rations?"

"Some Ks in the APC."

"Get them."

"They're our dinner, Mr. Scowcroft."

Scowcroft appealed to MacCauley. "They're starving, Sergeant."

"Yeah, sure, Lieutenant," MacCauley said. He had seen it, too. The children were almost wraithlike in their frailty. "Get the chow, for Chrissake, Kavanaugh," he said.

"Okay, Sergeant. If you say so."

Kavanagh climbed back into the APC, and he and the gunner at the fifty threw four rucksacks loaded with K rations over the steel side. Kavanaugh got down again and looped the sacks over his shoulder.

"Let me have a pack," Scowcroft said.

Kavanaugh handed one over, and Scowcroft opened it. He slung his M-1 and advanced with the pack in his hand. The squad followed at a distance, curious to see what these strange creatures would do when offered food by the horrible Marine devils. Scowcroft stopped some twenty feet from the files of children. He held out the ration pack.

The children did nothing. One, a small girl as delicately made as a porcelain doll, was crying softly. The schoolmaster—the Marines could see now that he was an old man, almost as frail as his charges—had lifted his bamboo flagpole. He began to speak to the children rapidly. The little girl stopped weeping, but continued to sob.

Scowcroft made eating gestures and took several steps forward, offering the ration pack encouragingly.

MacCauley studied the children intently. There was an atmosphere of fantasy in this scene, with Scowcroft, plump and well fed, if grimy and tired, offering the squad's rations to a group of starving children. Then he straightened with shock. Each one of the children who wore a haversack held a cord. The cord was attached to the backpack. *"Scowcroft! Back off!"* he screamed, and unslung his M-1 at the same time.

Scowcroft had walked nearly up to the little girl and was about to put the ration pack in her hands when the schoolteacher uttered a cry of "Banzai!" and simultaneously brought his white banner down in a commanding arc.

The little girl ran to Scowcroft. She was sobbing again. As he reached out to pick her up, she yanked hard on the cord in her hand and exploded.

MacCauley dived for the ditch by the road.

Chauncey Scowcroft was lifted into the air, his uniform scorched, his chest and abdomen eviscerated. The little girl's head, all that was recognizable as human, rolled crazily along the road and under the APC.

Two of the children ran for the APC. One of them made it,

and the subsequent explosion flashed through the lightly armored floorboards and killed the driver and the gunner.

MacCauley fired a half-dozen rounds at the old schoolteacher, blowing him backward like a bloody rag doll. Kavanaugh and Carpenter unleashed a fusillade at the running children. Small bodies were smashed and dismembered. Several of the satchel charges exploded, one after another.

"Cease fire! Cease fire, goddamn it!" MacCauley heard the hysteria in his own voice but was unable to control it. The firing trailed off, raggedly.

MacCauley rose to his feet unsteadily and walked over to what was left of Lieutenant Scowcroft. Strangely, his fat, stubbled face was untouched. There was a look of stupid surprise frozen there. MacCauley lurched away from him and stood looking at the old man he had killed, the dead and dying children.

"Ah, God," he said, holding his weapon tight against his heaving belly. "Ah, Jesus *God.*"

The other members of the squad gathered around him, looking at the carnage in shock. "They're kids," Kavanaugh said in a cracked voice. "Little *kids.*"

The sound of tanks awakened them, tanks and incoming mortar fire. From the direction of Mishima a line abreast of Japanese light tanks surrounded by trotting infantry with rifles and bayonets had appeared.

"Fall back," MacCauley said hoarsely. "Fall back."

They retreated down the Tokaido Road toward their own forces, jogging, with their weapons held low. As he ran, MacCauley realized that he no longer cared whether or not he survived this war—or even this terrible, frigid, bloody, insane day.

A Douglas C-54 of the AAF Air Transport Command emerged from the thin cloud cover over Iwo-jima flanked by two flights of P-51 Mustangs. A third flight of fighters kept station 2,000 feet above the descending transport—a shiny new aircraft with the name "Independence" freshly painted on its long nose.

In the cockpit Colonel Thomas Vano, the recently assigned commander of the 1000th Base Unit—the President's Flight—signaled for the seat-belt sign to be turned on. He picked up his microphone and said, "Sergeant Claussen, make sure the President is in his seat and buckled down." Harry Truman was a restless air passenger and he had an unfortunate reluctance to respond to such admonitions as seat-belt signs. The flight from Washington by way of the West Coast, Hawaii, Wake Island, and Guam had been long and tedious, and Truman had begun it in an angry mood. Claussen, the steward, had reported that neither the President nor Secretary of State Byrnes had slept more than an hour or two the entire trip. General Benny Myers, the President's military aide, and his people had spent the long hours in the air playing poker and drinking bourbon. They were all asleep now, sprawled about in the main cabin.

Vano nodded to his copilot, Captain Bill Foy, who spoke into his microphone. "Iwo, this is Army 010 for landing instructions." The call for "Independence" was simply the last three digits of her serial number. There was nothing that would indicate to a potentially hostile listener that her passenger was the commander in chief of all the armed forces of the United States.

Vano banked the big Douglas around in a wide turn over the volcanic island. God, there wasn't much to the place, he thought. Nothing to suggest what it had cost only eleven months ago. Probably not one of the casualties would now recognize the place. The Seabees had begun work even before the island was cleared of entrenched Japs, and the old Japanese airfields had been expanded and improved into a major U.S. base. For the last six months of 1945, the island had served as a fighter base, with thirteen air groups stationed on it, and as a bomber's way station, a haven where the B-29s damaged in the raids on Japan could land safely. Now, the fighters were mostly gone, operating from new bases on Kyushu. What remained on Iwo was a mixed bag of B-29s, night fighters, and several hundred ATC Douglas transports, which were to be used to ferry personnel and priority cargo to the still-newer bases captured on Honshu by the Coronet invasion force.

Iwo had already taken on the bustling, but nonthreatening, air of a stateside AAF base. The last attempt by the Japanese to attack the island had come on the night of March 24, 1945, when a squadron of Betties had tried to bomb the new facilities. They had been intercepted by P-61 Black Widow night fighters and shot down. Since that time the Black Widows stationed on the island had been assigned to intruder missions over Kyushu and, more recently, over north and central Honshu.

The tower operator at North Field came on the radio with landing instructions. The voice was that of a young WAC, and Vano could detect a note of anxiety. People tended to sound that way when they knew that they were speaking to the airplane carrying the President of the United States.

Vano took over communications and asked, "Has Marzipan landed?" He wondered who in MacArthur's Intelligence section had come up with that fanciful name for the general's airplane. Quite possibly he had done it himself. He was said to have a quixotic sense of humor from time to time.

"Ah, negative, 010," the tower operator said reluctantly. "But we have him on radar."

Vano felt a flush of anger. "Well, tell him to land," he said sharply. What was MacArthur thinking of? Was it his intention to keep the President waiting while he made a grand entrance? He searched the gray horizon to the north for MacArthur's Lockheed Constellation, one of the few aircraft of that type in service with the Army Air Forces overseas. But there was nothing.

His irritation grew as he continued to fly in a wide circle around the island. The sea below was gray, reflecting the sky. Of course, it was possible that the general's flight had been delayed getting off because of the bad weather over central Honshu. MacArthur and his staff had actually helicoptered ashore on Y-day—a bit of bravado that had made Truman's normally tight mouth even tighter when it was reported to him. By now all of the aircraft assigned to MacArthur's headquarters—and there were plenty of them, Vano thought sourly—were at a former Jap air base called Imba, which was only about two dozen miles from the front. Facilities there were primitive, and flying in and out of the place in a great bloody Constellation could not be easy. This would be offset, however, by dispatches datelined "an advanced air base in Japan," which would look just fine in Republican newspapers stateside. Vano was nothing if not totally loyal to President Truman, and no one around the President ever lost sight of the fact that 1946 was an election year and that in 1948—day after tomorrow in American politics—the country would be choosing a new president.

The country was susceptible these days to the appeal of successful generals. Dwight Eisenhower was safely engaged in the occupation of Germany and the rehabilitation of Europe. George Marshall was too austere and duty-bound ever to be a threat to the political establishment. But Douglas MacArthur? Who knew what Dugout Doug might have in mind. Vano had never met the general, but if the President said he was a prima donna and an arrogant son of a bitch, that was plenty good enough for Tom Vano.

"Army 010, this is Iwo. Marzipan is holding fifty miles out. They say they are having some communications problems. Marzipan suggests you land first."

Vano studied his fuel gauges with restrained temper. The bastards knew he'd be short after a flight from Guam.

The intercom bell pinged.

"Tom, this is Benny. What the hell's going on? The Boss wants to know why we're circling."

"Marzipan hasn't landed yet, General," Vano said.

"Where the hell is he?"

"Holding fifty miles out."

There was a long silence while some conversation took place in the passenger cabin. Then Myers came back on the intercom loop. "Jimmy says go on in. We can't outwait the bastard, can we?"

"Not really, General. I don't want to cut it too fine."

"All right, then. Score one for the Great Man. It won't matter. He won't like what he's going to hear today anyway."

"Roger, General." Vano nodded to Foy to lower the gear. He had been in the Army and around the brass long enough to know that Myers or Byrnes would take whatever heat there was for allowing MacArthur this petty triumph.

He watched the fighter escort peel away and head for South Field, then he brought the big transport neatly onto the base leg of the pattern for North Field, where a VIP area had been cleared and was being isolated under heavy guard. This visit by the President to the Pacific theater was supposed to be top secret, but there was about as much chance for it remaining so as a snowball had in hell. By tomorrow, he thought grimly, the correspondents clustered hungrily around the PIO's office would be filing stories about how the President of the United States flew 15,000 miles to ask General Douglas MacArthur's permission to win the war.

As the large silver Constellation taxied up to the line to park beside the "Independence," a wiry, angry man in a gray suit out of place in the soggy weather stood stiffly at the door of the Quonset that had been fitted out as a meeting place. The members of his staff surrounding him could feel, almost physically, the fury that filled Harry Truman.

He watched, narrow-eyed, as the hatch in the airplane opened and the general stood at the top of the boarding ramp surveying the scene.

As always, General of the Army Douglas MacArthur was dressed in his well-worn khaki uniform, shirt open at the neck. The only insignia on his uniform were the miniature five-star circles on his collar points. The familiar braid-bedecked cap, the gold tarnished to a greenish hue, was worn low over the dark aviator's sunglasses. Myers, who secretly admired MacArthur's ability to manipulate his own image, noted that the famous corncob was not in evidence. But I'll bet some ADC is standing by with it, he thought, just in case there is a photo opportunity.

General Baker, the base commander, and a youthful full colonel in a raunchy cap stood rigidly at attention at the foot of the stairs. As MacArthur started down, they hit a smart salute—smarter, it seemed to Myers, than the one they had given the President.

He glanced covertly at Byrnes, wondering if the old pol had the same feeling he had: that they were visitors in a private satrapy, a land of ruffles and flourishes populated by worshiping military subordinates. The problem was that MacArthur deserved the adulation he received from his lieutenants. He got the job done. He always got the job done. When the republic had desperately needed a hero, he had given it one. Now it was up to plain Harry Truman to remind the great commander that even though the occupant of the White House was no longer a New York patroon but a failed haberdasher from Missouri, that occupant was still president of the United States—at least, Myers thought wryly, until someone convinced the American people to send him packing.

Truman was so agitated that he seemed to shift his weight from one foot to the other. He said to his people as MacArthur reached the concrete ramp: "Stay put." His voice was tight and nasal and his eyes seemed sunken in his head. He walked swiftly out to the airplane.

Before MacArthur could acknowledge his presence, he said to Baker: "Leave us alone, General. Right now."

Startled, the general and his airdrome officer complied, uncertainly joining the members of the President's party standing before the Quonset.

Truman looked directly at MacArthur and said in his harshest Missouri twang, "General, if you ever keep the President of the United States waiting again for so much as ten minutes, I'll relieve you of your command."

MacArthur regarded Truman with an expression of mild surprise. He touched the peak of his cap in a most informal salute and said, "Would you really, Mr. President?"

"I suggest you don't try me."

"It is customary in military circles, sir," MacArthur said, still in that faintly condescending tone, "for the senior to lead. I am sorry if you did not understand that, Mr. Truman."

"Don't give me lessons, General," Truman said evenly. "I didn't come here for that."

"And why, exactly, did you come, sir?"

Truman glanced up at the airplane. "Where are your staff people?"

"I came with only my senior aide, Colonel Willoughby, Mr. President," the general said. "More seemed unnecessary until I have some idea of what has prompted this visit."

Truman regarded the general with less anger now and more appraisal. A lifetime spent in politics signaled him that this was a man without a true politician's ability to dissemble and accommodate. He began to feel better about his own relationship with this larger-than-life creature. It could easily be, he thought, that MacArthur entertained political ambitions. But this was a man who would never develop the one quality essential to any American who aspired to the highest office. MacArthur was an American aristocrat, an American *military* aristocrat. He was the product of a society in which rank, order, and, above all, discipline prevailed. Right now he was a hero to the man in the street at home. In peacetime, he would swiftly become what he had always been: an American version of Coriolanus. Truman was not a brilliant man, but he had an unerring instinct for the political jugular. MacArthur's pride, elegance, and arrogance would forever keep him from rising higher than he stood at this moment.

Realizing this, he began to feel better. He even managed to bestow a wintry smile on the other man. "All right, General. Let's go talk." He led the way swiftly into the Quonset.

. . .

Forty minutes later, General MacArthur's outward composure remained unbroken, but he was angry. This little man, he thought, has in effect brought me an ultimatum. Either I agree to what he proposes, or I will find myself relieved of command.

The general knew that if he was relieved, the political consequences for Truman, and his people in Congress, would be severe. A triumphant return to the States now could stir up enormous resentment against the man and the party who broke a long string of victories to spite the man who won them. But the war would still be going on, victories would still remain to be won—and others would win them while General of the Army Douglas MacArthur spent his days addressing Rotary Club conventions and the American Legion.

The plain fact is, he thought bitterly, that this ward politician, who learned his trade from the bosses of Kansas City, *is* the president of the United States.

He sat at the table in the sultry air of the closed and guarded Quonset and looked from Truman to Byrnes and back again. Would it do any good, he wondered, to tell them that he sincerely thought them wrong? That what they proposed was a thing better left undone, for fear of what it might mean to all nations for all time to come? Couldn't they see what it would mean to the alliance and, above all, to future relations between the United States and the Soviet Union? He hated the Bolsheviks with a deep and abiding passion, but this did not preclude his understanding what their reaction to the proposal, and the secrecy surrounding it, would be.

"Mr. President," he said, "I ask you to reconsider. This monstrous weapon is not needed. We are winning without it."

He—one of the few, most senior, officers of the Army and Navy who had read the reports on the Manhattan project and who had seen the motion pictures of the February test in New Mexico—was convinced that he did not want that *thing* exploded in his theater of war.

Last summer, when he had heard of the failure of the first attempt to detonate an atomic device, he had been relieved. He was, after all, a soldier born in the nineteenth century, with all the accompanying notions of valor and gallantry. What the scientists had attempted to do in that New Mexico desert was to take war out of the hands of the warriors and deliver it to the ideologues. When they failed, he had hoped they would not try again, even though that was a forlorn hope.

Then when Coronet was ordered at last, he had imagined that the threat, the mushroom-shaped nightmare, had passed.

But he had reckoned without the imperatives of politics. Now here was the President telling him, in effect: "General, our casualties are already too high and they will be much higher if Coronet takes a year to defeat the Japanese. The voters won't like it. Ergo—"

"Mr. President," he said again, "I warn you that if we do this thing, the time will come when we will regret it. There may come a day—and soon—when enemies, knowing it can be done, will do it themselves and threaten us with it. I ask you to consider most carefully."

"General," Truman said intently, "how many men, how many American soldiers, have we lost in the two weeks since Coronet began?"

"Our casualties as of today are 75,000 men, Mr. President. Of those, 14,000 have been killed in action, the remainder are wounded or missing. I do not minimize these numbers. I warned you when Coronet was being planned that the cost would be high."

"Very high, General. And how many Japanese have been killed? Civilians, sir."

"We estimate something in excess of 200,000, Mr. President. That was factored into the planning as well."

"Of course it was, General," the President said. "But hasn't our war aim from the beginning of this year been to bring Japan to accept the conditions of the Potsdam Declaration? Of course it has been. How are we going to deal with these people if we continue to kill civilians in such numbers?"

"Civilians, yes. Not noncombatants, Mr. President."

Truman regarded the general shrewdly. "Yes, we have been hearing about that, General. I understand that there was a massacre of civilians at some place called—" He reached for a paper handed to him by Byrnes. "Ishioka. Yes, Ishioka. I even understand that an American officer is facing possible court-martial because he could not control his men."

MacArthur's eyes hardened. "That is not quite the way the matter stands, Mr. President. Officers of the Tenth Army staff have investigated the Ishioka affair and they report that a forward position of their 231st Infantry Regiment was overrun by more than 1,000 members of the civilian Volunteer Defense Force. They were severely mauled, but they held their ground and repulsed the enemy."

"In other words, they had the choice of dying at the hands of a mob or perpetrating a massacre. And, not too surprisingly, they chose the second alternative," Truman said, almost gently.

"That is true, Mr. President," MacArthur said coldly.

"And how often has that kind of thing happened in the time since our troops went ashore on Honshu, General?"

"It has happened more than once, yes. That was predicted."

"Was the effect on our own men also predicted? And on the people at home? Letters have been getting though the censorship, General. The Chicago *Tribune* is calling for an open congressional investigation on the conduct of the war. Did you know that, General? Do you have any idea what that would mean to the war effort?"

"Mr. President, *all* the possibilities were discussed at length during the planning of Coronet. We had the experience of Operation Iceberg and Operation Olympic to draw on and we made it very clear that we would be facing what amounts to suicidal resistance on Honshu. I beg of you not to avoid the hard realities simply because of the possible political consequences of a long campaign in Japan. The alternative you offer, Mr. President, is too uncertain, too likely to have unforeseen consequences." He paused, seeming to be engaged in an uncharacteristic search for words. "Mr. President, we have both seen the films of the Febru-

344

ary test. What you are proposing to do is to change the nature of war for all time." He regarded Truman steadily, and for the first time it seemed to the men seated opposite him that Douglas MacArthur was an old man. "You will change, too, the nature of warriors, Mr. President. Neither of us will like the soldiers of the new age. Consider that."

Truman spread his hands on the table to signal that the conference was at an end. "Very well, General, I will think about it." He stood. "Thank you for coming to see me. I will let you know my decision."

Once again aboard the "Independence," Truman sat moodily watching the empty sea far below. The fighters had peeled away as they reached the limit of their range, and the big Douglas was alone in a vast and empty sky.

It had been a serious risk to make this flight, particularly in company with the man next in line for the presidency. But the decision to be taken was so vital that Byrnes had to be present at the meeting with MacArthur.

Sergeant Claussen entered the compartment carrying a cup of hot bouillon. Truman would have preferred a stiff bourbon-and-branch-water, but he accepted the cup and thanked the steward with the old-fashioned courtesy of which he was often capable.

"Shall I make up a bunk, Mr. President?" the sergeant asked. "It's going to be slow going all the way home. The colonel says we're bucking headwinds."

The President allowed himself the wry thought that he was in no real hurry to get back to Washington. Each hour's delay was one hour of grace before having to decide what he must do now.

"No, thanks, son. Just ask Mr. Byrnes to join me, will you?" he said.

When the secretary of state appeared and took the seat opposite, Truman said, "Well, Jimmy?"

"The general is an arrogant man, Mr. President."

Truman suppressed his impatience. "Of course he is, Jimmy.

He is also a greedy, ambitious son of a bitch. I don't need any-one to tell me that. He wants to be president."

Byrnes put on his Supreme Court face and said, "But there may be something in what he says. It isn't as though we are in any danger of losing the war at this late date."

"Jimmy," Truman said, "when Oppenheimer promised that *thing* last summer, I had already decided to use it. I believed it could end the war. Then when the whole thing fizzled, I had to let the Combined Chiefs go ahead with Olympic and Coronet. Now the decision has to be made again. Only this time we know almost exactly what Coronet is going to cost us. Seventy-five thousand casualties in two weeks, Jimmy. Fourteen thousand killed. Those aren't estimates on some brass hat's piece of paper. Those are American boys dying, Jimmy."

"The Japs can't go on, Mr. President," Byrnes said.

Harry Truman regarded Byrnes bleakly. "What the hell makes you think so? Look at the numbers, Jimmy, the *numbers*. On Okinawa, Intelligence says there were 120,000 Japs engaged. And *that*'s how many casualties they took—or near as makes no difference. One hundred percent, Jimmy. We're still trying to add up the civilians who killed themselves or died trying to fight our troops. And on Iwo—my God—they lost 6,000 killed. Two hundred and twelve were captured. Most of those were taken wounded or unconscious. Do you know how many actually sur-rendered? Twenty-two. Jesus Christ—*twenty-two* out of *6,000.*"

"But those were all soldiers, Mr. President. Fanatics."

"What does that mean, fanatics? Don't talk like a lawyer. By MacArthur's own estimate, there are a million and a half fighters on the island of Honshu. We'll have to kill all but 45,000 of them if they act like the bastards on Iwo did. What is that going to cost *us* in lives? Have I the right to accept casualties like that if there is any chance to shock the sons of bitches into quitting?"

Byrnes looked out the window past the airplane's wing at the flat, featureless sky. He wished that the President would make up his own mind about this thing. It was a purely presidential duty to decide. Didn't he claim so proudly that "the buck stops here"?

He said carefully, "I see it as a political decision, Mr. President."

Truman scowled. In a sense Byrnes was right, of course. He had accepted him as a political necessity, but Byrnes was a loyal Democratic party wheel horse and his judgments on what the American voter would and would not accept were almost always accurate. Was this a decision an American president could make simply on that basis? As much as he despised MacArthur, he sensed that the general's objections to the introduction of the new weapon were genuine. The old son of a bitch, thinking he was going to live forever, was already worrying about a time when he might have to fight the goddamn Russians. And who could say he was wrong? Potsdam had been a bitter revelation. As much as Truman had loved FDR, he had realized at that meeting in Germany that the Old Man had made a terrible error in agreeing to the protocols the Big Three had signed at Yalta. Half of Europe had been swallowed up. Was the United States prepared to allow that to happen in Asia?

Goddamn it, he thought, *no*. The problem was how to prevent it. MacArthur thought it could be done one way—the slow, bloody soldier's way. General Leslie Groves and the scientists had the idea not only that the war could be ended at one blow, but also that *all* war might be ended with the *same* blow. Somehow that seemed a naïve notion. What if they were right, however, and MacArthur was wrong? The general did not know that all the German scientists who had been working on a nuclear bomb for Hitler had scattered, some to the west, but most to the east, to Russia. Was it reasonable to assume that they would refuse to try to build a weapon for the Bolsheviks? The goddamn Krauts seemed willing to work for anyone, anywhere. For that matter, American scientists were not exactly models of patriotic loyalty. They seemed to think that if a thing *could* be done, it *would* be done, and devil take the hindmost. No, a president of the United States had to think about what it would mean if it was the Soviets and not one of the Western powers who first produced atomic bombs in quantity. And the bastards would do it, Truman thought. They would do it now if they could. It was a

---

chilling thought to have to live with—yet there it was, like the ghost at the feast.

Byrnes worried about the political cost of continuing with Coronet, and well he might, the President thought. The people were getting tired of the war, tired of casualties and shortages and dead sons and husbands. It was a bitter irony that the most costly part of the long battle should come so near the end. The Joint Chiefs had warned that Operation Coronet would chew up a million American lives. To judge by the battle losses of the last two weeks, that estimate had been optimistic. One more factor to weigh in the balance.

Who would the voters turn to in November if the battle for Japan remained in doubt when they went to the polls? The prospect of a Republican Congress, hostile and recalcitrant, filled Truman with loathing. I am a politician, not a statesman, he thought. Statesmen go the way of Winston Churchill when war-weary populations want a change, any change.

"Mr. President?"

Truman passed a hand over his gray-stubbled cheeks. Suddenly he was very tired. "Jimmy," he said, "no matter what I decide, some son-of-a-bitch historian is going to say I decided wrong, and for all the wrong reasons. That's the history of the presidency. And that brass-edged bastard MacArthur will second-guess me no matter what I do. We're going to come to it one day, that son of a bitch and me. Count on it." He leaned his head back against the seat cushion and closed his eyes. "Now I need some sleep, Mr. Secretary. Give me an hour or two and then tell Benny and his people to get the cards and be prepared to lose some money at seven-card stud."

The secretary of state rose and prepared to leave the compartment. As he did so, the President asked, without opening his eyes, "Is it getting dark outside?"

Byrnes bent and looked through the window at the sky. The airplane was rushing toward the oncoming night at 300 miles an hour. "Not yet, but soon, Mr. President."

1500 Hours

By midafternoon, the major counterattack by the main body of the Japanese 36th Army, led by the massed Model 97 medium tanks of the 4th Armored Division, was fully developed. Attacking from the south, where the division had been concentrated in the outskirts of Tokyo, two regiments of tanks supported by infantry units of the 1st Imperial Guards Division, detached from the Tokyo Defense Army, had completed the encirclement of the American bridgehead on the south bank of the Tonegawa.

Field Marshal Shunroku Hata, the officer who had until recently commanded the 2nd General Army, with headquarters at Hiroshima, had stripped the western commands of men and equipment in order to strike at the American Tenth Army spearhead with all the power he could collect. One of the oldest serving officers in the Imperial Army—he was a 1912 graduate of the Imperial Military Academy—Hata was also one of the most dedicated. This developing battle was, he believed, the start of the true *ketsu-go*—the decisive battle on which all Japanese strategy for the defense of the Kanto depended.

With great difficulty he had contrived to mass a force of 70,000 men south of the Tonegawa. He was conscious of the good fortune that had made this possible, and as he paused at the roadside shrine near the village of Noda and stood surrounded by the respectful officers of his staff, he gave thanks to heaven for the heavy rains and the cloud that had so effectively grounded the Americans' aircraft. The fourteen days free of harassment by fighter-bombers had made it possible for him to complete his concentrations and move his new command to the Tonegawa.

He had received command of the 36th Army directly from the Emperor, and the old soldier was strongly aware of the honor.

"Our situation is critical," the Emperor had said, taking the field marshal completely into his confidence. "The Kwantung Army is lost—surrendered, so the Americans claim, to the Chinese. In the two weeks since the invaders landed on this island we have lost 5,000 aircraft and pilots. We have inflicted monstrous casualties, but still the Americans advance on our capital. In this extreme hour, we turn to our most loyal warriors."

Hata had opposed the Navy's decision to attack the Americans at Pearl Harbor as unnecessary and unwise. He and his more conservative friends had been certain that the Greater East Asia Co-prosperity Sphere could be established without war with America. He had even written a monograph for the Imperial General Staff on the wisdom of moving into Southeast Asia by carefully measured steps, presenting the Americans with a *fait accompli* at each stage. With their eyes firmly fixed on the European war, the Americans, he had believed, would have blustered and complained, but they would never have attacked the flank of the Great Move Southward.

Well, that was then, he thought. And it mattered not at all that he had probably been right. The nation had taken its fateful course, and what remained now was to mount a decisive battle that would so bloody the Americans that they would abandon their insane insistence on unconditional surrender.

Standing in the rain, he bowed deeply to the *kami*. An unimportant little shrine this was, but at this terrible hour in Japan's history, no spirit living in the land should be considered unimportant. Colonel Obata, his ranking aide, draped his thin shoulders with a rain cape. On the road, the tanks of the 4th Armored Division were moving nose to tail toward the river. Once again he gave thanks to Amaterasu Omikami for the blessed weather.

If it continued this way—and the meteorologists promised that it would—he would, by nightfall, have sufficient force massed at the Tonegawa to smash the American bridgehead and begin to collapse the American position along the entire central front.

Captain Victor Mendelsohn, forward air observer assigned to the Tenth Army's 27th Infantry Division, huddled shivering in his foxhole in the center of the Tone River bridgehead. At nightfall yesterday, the rising waters of the river had smashed the engineers' bridges, isolating the troops of the spearhead on the south bank of the river from the main body of the XXIV Corps, which had been leading the advance all the way from the Kashima beaches.

For a day, observers on the few bits of high ground within the river beachhead had watched as the Japs massed armor in the surrounding countryside. Calls for support by divisional artillery had been met, and they had produced some effect among the Japanese, but the advance inland had been too swift for most of the self-propelled 155mm guns. Half of them had been left behind, bogged down in the unexpected mire caused by the heavy rains.

Somehow or other the Japs had managed to do what the divisional artillerymen had not. They had found it possible to bring their own guns to bear on the bridgehead. Since noon the 27th's point had been subjected to increasingly intense shelling.

At 1300 hours, Mendelsohn had established direct contact with a patrolling Superfort Pathfinder from 20th Bomber Command and explained the situation. He disliked radar bombing even as an aircraft commander. It was often inaccurate and always dangerous to troops in the field. Hunched with his radio operator in a soaking, muddy foxhole on the Tone River, he liked it even less, but the situation was growing desperate.

At 1530, Brigadier General Fritz Jowett, the divisional commander's deputy, who had made a perilous crossing of the swollen Tonegawa in a rubber boat, appeared at the post. A dapper officer, sporting a pencil-line mustache and a burnished helmet, Jowett was a man given to swift, and sometimes risky, decisions. He dropped into Mendelsohn's hole, followed by the miserable figure of Lieutenant Collis Doré, a young officer whose social connections had led him almost inevitably into the job of a general's aide, and who at this moment wished he had never seen Jowett or Operation Coronet or the island of Honshu.

"Well, Mendelsohn? What's happening?" the general demanded.

"It's on, sir," Mendelsohn said. "But—"

"But what, Captain?"

"Nothing, sir. It's just that radar bombing isn't all it's cracked up to be."

Jowett favored him with a white smile redolent with menace. "The whole fucking Air Force isn't what it's cracked up to be, Captain. It just happens we don't have any choice at the moment. Make your contact."

Mendelsohn drew a deep breath and held out his hand for the radio. Sergeant Obledo, a Californian who had begun his military career as an aviation cadet only to wash out of flight training and end up in an FAO unit, complied.

Mendelsohn keyed the microphone and said, "Keystone, this is X-ray Peter Tare."

Jowett helped himself to one of the earpieces to listen to the reply.

"X-ray Peter Tare, this is Keystone. Go ahead."

"Are you ready to give us a Santy Ana?" Mendelsohn asked. A Santy Ana, so pronounced by airmen who had trained in Southern California, was the name of a hot, dry wind that blew across the Los Angeles basin in spring and early summer. It was also the code name for a technique of mass area bombing through heavy cloud cover by radar. The method had been used in many of the B-29 raids on Tokyo and other Japanese cities, and Air Force planners were convinced that it had utility in battlefield situations.

"We have fifty birds on station, X-ray Peter Tare," the unseen bombardier said. "Give us the co-ordinates and hold on to your socks."

Mendelsohn bridled at the light-hearted tone. He understood well enough that the men of the B-29 squadrons were actually getting bored with the war. For the last six months there had been almost no opposition to their milk runs over Honshu. There were men in the B-29s overhead who had never been shot at, had never even seen a Japanese fighter. For the last three months the squadrons had had difficulty finding targets worth bombing at all. They had spent most of their time, as they themselves put it, "rearranging the dust."

"What is your altitude, Keystone?" Mendelsohn asked.

Jowett asked impatiently, "What the hell difference does that make, Captain?"

"It will affect bombing accuracy, General."

"We are orbiting at angels twenty. The soup is up to our bellies," the bombardier said. "How's the weather down there?"

Jowett snatched the microphone and said, "This is General Jowett speaking. Who am I talking to?"

The voice of the airman changed tone. "This is Captain Matthew Whalen, General. Lead bombardier, 315th Bomb Wing. Sir."

"Well, Captain, it is raining down here. It is raining rain and it is raining Japs. Now let's get the hell on the ball." He handed the microphone to Mendelsohn and spoke to Doré. "Take that smart-ass officer's name, Collis."

Doré produced that single most important piece of an aide-de-camp's equipment, a notebook, and wrote down Captain Whalen's name for future attention.

Mendelsohn clicked the microphone and said, "Keystone, this is X-ray Peter Tare. Stand by for bombing co-ordinates." He lifted the flap on his map case and studied the military grid overlaid on the map of central Japan. For this kind of work, what was needed was a large-scale chart, but none had been issued to him. It had not been thought that any FAOs would have to call in massive air strikes so near their own unit perimeters.

He carefully grease-penciled the squares of the grid he thought could be bombed without risking the troops in the bridgehead. Jowett, watching over his shoulder, made an angry sound and took the map. He shaded the grid squares much nearer their positions. "For God's sake, Captain. We need support, not distant fireworks. That's the whole fucking Jap 36th Army out there looking down our throats. Now call those numbers in and quit screwing around."

Mendelsohn studied the map and swallowed hard. For a man who never had a decent word to say about the "flyboys" and "zoomies," Jowett was expecting a great deal from the crews in the B-29s, most of whom were kids in their teens and twenties with a couple of hundred hours of four-engine time. Radar bombing took precision flying and accurate navigation. An error of a sixteenth of a mile—meaningless under ordinary conditions—could completely foul up a radar mission.

"That's very tight, General," he said.

"Obey your orders, Captain," Jowett said frigidly. "Collis?"

"Yes, sir," Doré said wearily, and wrote Mendelsohn's name in his notebook.

Mendelsohn, despising himself for not sticking to his objections—he was, after all, the division's forward air observer and the final authority, theoretically, on what the AAF could and could not do for these paddlefeet—picked up the microphone. "Keystone, this is X-ray Peter Tare. Mark grids Oboe, Peter, and Queen. Also grids Charlie, Dog, Easy, and Fox. Have you got that?"

"Roger. Keystone reads Oboe, Peter, Queen, Charlie, Dog, Easy, and Fox. That's a big sweep, X-ray Peter Tare."

It was, as the bombardier in the B-29 leading the mission said, a big sweep. It covered no less than four square miles in which the Japanese had concentrated their armor, confident that they were safe from air attack. It also meant that the 500-pounders that would rain down from 20,000 feet would be falling within a few hundred yards of the outposts of the Tone bridgehead.

"X-ray Peter Tare, we will start on grid Fox and bomb from northwest to southeast in six minutes. Keep your heads down, you guys. Keystone out."

Mendelsohn looked at Jowett and wished him in hell, but the general only lighted a cigarette with a gold Zippo and settled himself down in the foxhole, burnished helmet low over his eyes, to wait.

The Boeing B-29A Superfortresses of the 315th Bombardment Wing, Twentieth Air Force, flying over the central Kanto were an assorted mix from five bombardment groups. Three of them had recently been transferred to the 315th, and many of the crews were fresh from training fields in the States, replacing crews rotated home. General Curtis LeMay, commander of the Twentieth Air Force, had objected vociferously to the continuation of the rotation policy this late in what he was pleased to call "the Battle of Japan," but the policy was continued on the direct orders of General of the Army H. H. Arnold, who had been made aware of the possible political repercussions of any change by Secretary of War Robert Patterson himself.

As the lead aircraft, commanded by a lieutenant colonel from the wing staff who had flown only a half-dozen missions of any sort, made its final turn onto the bomb run, the formation began to straggle. In addition to the fact that the crews were unaccustomed to flying together, the aircraft were heavily loaded with 12,000 pounds of bombs each and, at a gross weight of 135,000 pounds, tended to fly sluggishly at 20,000 feet. A formation of fifty aircraft is a difficult unit to maneuver under the best of circumstances. Now, there was a strong southerly wind at flight level. The heavy undercast had made it impossible for the lead navigator in the colonel's airplane to observe the ground and correct for drift. The radar set on which the wing was relying gave an indefinite picture of the ground, which was relatively empty of strong topographical features except for the Tone River.

The formation, thus handicapped, completed its turn to the southeast over the town of Kasukabe, seven kilometers from the river. Below them the men of the 121st Antiaircraft Artillery Battalion, commanded by Colonel Yasunobo Higuchi, had managed to get their faulty audio-detection system into action long enough to detect the large formation overhead. Without the listening devices, the gunners would never have heard the B-29s, but hear them they did, and they managed to fire a hundred rounds into the overcast. Most of these fell far short, exploding harmlessly well below the aircraft. A dozen shells did manage to rise above the cloud cover to burst in the pale sunlight to starboard of the formation.

Unaccustomed to even such token opposition, the pilots of one group allowed the interval between themselves and the lead group to widen.

At 1543 hours, the lead navigator informed the lead bombardier that the formation was now over the edge of grid Fox. Bomb-bay doors were opened, and a rain of 500-pound bombs began to fall.

The first bombs began to strike the Japanese units on the left flank of the 36th Army. Since the bombers could not be heard and were not expected, the troops were caught in the open as the 500-pounders began to burst among them.

Like a tsunami, the wave of high explosives saturated the concentration areas where the Japanese armor and infantry had massed for the assault on the bridgehead. The torrent of explosives and steel from the sky rolled along the southern bank of the Tonegawa at the rate of six miles a minute, shattering vehicles, weapons, and men. In less than three minutes, the fifty B-29s unloaded 600,000 pounds of high explosives on the soldiers and vehicles of the 36th Army. Eleven thousand men were killed, 19,000 were wounded, another 3,000 were never to be found alive or dead.

Field Marshal Hata had just left the roadside shrine and was mounting his command car when the rumbling wave of bursting bombs rolled over him and his staff. Hata was blown to fragments and, of his senior staff officers, only two survived, both badly wounded.

He was not the only high-ranking officer to die.

In the bridgehead, the Americans heard the approaching roar of the falling bombs. To Captain Mendelsohn, a New Yorker, it sounded like a thousand subway trains approaching. To Sergeant Obledo, his radioman, who had been a child in Long Beach, California, in 1936, it sounded like an onrushing earthquake. To General Jowett and Lieutenant Doré it was like the crackling roar of a thousand massed cannon.

A vast wave of darkness seemed to roll over the bridgehead, darkness shot through with yellow lightning. Each blast pushed ahead of it a hot, searing wind laced with singing steel fragments.

Mendelsohn burrowed into the muddy earth, knowing that the airmen had managed to do this all wrong, that he had let the general overrule him, and that now they were all going to die. He felt the repeated shocks in the earth, the heat in the wind, the stinging pain of steel slicing into his body. For an eternity he tried to make himself a part of the ground, gasping for breath in the hot, stinking air.

Then, as swiftly as it had come, the rumbling wave began to recede toward the southeast. Mendelsohn was shocked to discover that he was still alive. He huddled, shivering, head hunched between his shoulders, unable to move. He heard the voices of the wounded, the screaming calls for medics, the soft sobbing of Obledo beside him.

He opened his eyes and looked about. Jowett crouched nearby in the hole, but his burnished helmet was gone, and so was the top of his head. Above his eyebrows there was nothing. Doré sat staring stupidly at the stump of his right arm, which was pumping bright blood into the mud at his side. Obledo was staring blankly at the mangled ruin of the radio set he had been carrying on his back. A steel fragment had demolished it, reduced it to a tangle of wire and bits of steel and glass. It had saved the sergeant's life.

When Mendelsohn moved, he felt a deep ache in his chest. He looked down to see a steel fragment shaped like a dagger protruding from his left breast. Without thinking, he grabbed it and pulled it out. The metal seared his hand, and he dropped it into the wet mud, where it lay hissing. He looked dumbly at the blisters swiftly rising on his palm. Quite suddenly he loved the pain in his hand, delighted in it, because he knew that it meant he was alive.

The last bombs dropped from the Superforts fell on an abandoned farmhouse surrounded by neglected rice paddies. There, a small detachment of Japanese infantry had established itself under the command of Captain Matsu Yaruyama, to whom the endless procession of defeats for Japanese arms had become a personal affront.

In prewar days, Yaruyama had been fencing champion of Chugoku Army District and a master swordsman. As the war became a tragic series of catastrophes for the Imperial Army, his personality began to change radically. Never a lovable commander, he had taken to chastising his soldiers with his scabbarded sword, often screaming at them that he wished all enemies of the Emperor had but one head so that he might destroy them with a single stroke.

The B-29s of the 315th Bombardment Wing put an end to Yaruyama's fantasies of samurai glory. Two 500-pound high-explosive bombs landed among the soldiers of his tiny command, killing seventeen of them. Among those killed was the captain himself, neatly eviscerated by a red-hot fragment of bomb casing.

The blasts also churned up the earth behind the now-flattened barn, blowing from their shallow graves the corpses of three American officers: Lloyd Hansen, a lanky fighter pilot named

Higgins, and an engineer officer named Yancey. Two more bodies were blasted from their uneasy resting places, one white, one black. Because they were not officers, Ray and Slocum had not been considered worthy of Yaruyama's sword and so were not beheaded as the officers had been.

The survivors of Yaruyama's detachment found it strange—perhaps the work of some malevolent *kami*—that the captain's body was found, after the attack, surrounded by those of his victims. His family sword, a blade of indifferent quality, had been shattered by a bomb blast.

Aboard the attack transport USS *Portola*, returning damaged and laden with wounded to Kagoshima Bay, Corporal Saigo Noguchi lay on a bunk in the sick bay under guard, trying to understand the motives of these strange people who had first nearly killed him, then destroyed his Japanese honor, then made an enormous effort to heal him, and now had begun to convince him that all of the ideals by which he had lived were to be reconsidered.

He had been taken from the beachhead at Kujukuri-hama with other wounded—Japanese as well as American, he had been amazed to realize—to one of the ships in the harbor. That in itself was cause for wonderment: never before had there been a harbor at Kujukuri, but the Americans, drawing on their wonderful and seemingly unlimited sources of supply and ingenuity, had built one there in a matter of hours after their landing.

On board the ship he had been given medical treatment and food; had been interrogated by another American Japanese, this one a *gocho* like himself with whom he could be more nearly at ease; and had then been confined in a guarded, but sinfully comfortable, compartment with a half-dozen captured Koreans.

Being billeted with the Koreans had at first undone much of the good feeling he had begun to develop toward the Americans. For the first day he had refused to speak with the Koreans, of course, and with the Japanese corporal as well. It should have been immediately apparent to any person of sensitivity that to confine a Japanese soldier with Koreans came perilously close to being an insult.

The American Japanese *gocho*, whose name was Atami, and who said that his parents had come from Hanoura, on the island of Shikoku, explained that the white Americans had meant no insult. "It is because in the United States it is considered bad manners to dislike any person because of his race," Atami said. "Of course, this does not mean that such things do not happen, because even in America there are many persons who have such bad manners. But it is considered even worse among Americans for one member of a minority race to dislike another."

"But surely," Noguchi had said, perplexed by these peculiarities, "it is known in America that Koreans are an inferior and unworthy people. It is a thing that is understood everywhere."

"Not everywhere, *Gocho-san*," Atami had replied. "And I suggest that you rethink this matter. The *shosa* to whom you will be remanded when the ship reaches Kagoshima is a very liberal man, who will take it badly if you display unseemly manners to the Koreans with whom you may be confined."

The idea that he might eventually be confined as a prisoner was a thing that Noguchi had begun to come to terms with; he had, after all, allowed himself to be taken. But the suggestion that he might find himself in a compound with Koreans was a thing he found distressing.

Perhaps, he thought, the head wound that had broken his skull (for that, the American Japanese corporal had explained, was what had happened to him) had affected his ability to think clearly. He had begun to wish that he might in some way be of service to these odd Americans who had displayed such strange magnanimity to a disgraced one-time Imperial soldier. Was it possible, he asked Corporal Atami, that he could be allowed to escape confinement in a prisoner-of-war compound? Perhaps by performing some useful service to the new rulers of Japan?

Atami had said that he would consider Noguchi's request and

had even discussed it with the white officers of the Military Police and Intelligence branches, whom Atami had the honor to serve.

On the following day, twenty-four hours before the ship departed from Kujukuri-hama for Kagoshima, Atami-san had arranged for Noguchi to be confined in another compartment, away from the Koreans and among several soldiers of his own division who had been taken prisoner while unconscious and who still remained so.

The voyage to Kagoshima was a nervous time for Noguchi, who had seldom traveled on a ship and who thoroughly disliked doing so. It seemed to him that since his disgrace and rebirth as a non-Japanese (for he could no longer consider himself a true member of the Yamato race), he had become a more tentative and uncertain person. Plainly, he was no longer the proud soldier he once had been. When he thought of Lieutenant Fuchida and the men of his own mortar section, he was filled with a great sadness. They were surely all awaiting him at Yasukuni Shrine, unaware that he would never join them. He thought perhaps that it was this sadness that made him the indecisive individual he seemed to have become. Of course, he told himself, it could be something as simple and straightforward as the effects of the broken head he had suffered in the shelling of Matsuo Fortress. He had seen men with such injuries, and they often underwent personality changes.

He resolved to improve himself as much as he was able before meeting the *shosa* at Kagoshima who would decide the fate of the prisoners.

He fasted for a day, though he found it shamefully difficult to do in view of the fact that Atami-san had arranged for the prisoners to be fed a proper Japanese diet—one that was, for Noguchi, almost voluptuous, and unlike anything he had eaten in the Army for the last two years.

Though the deprivation should have been good for him, he found that the fasting weakened him further. The movements of the ship, like those he remembered of the ill-smelling *maru* that had brought him home after his first tour of duty in the southern ocean, made him queasy and left him trembling. Atami grew concerned and instructed him to cease fasting at once. "Contemplation and deprivation are all right for a priest or monk," he declared, "but not for a wounded soldier."

Noguchi reminded him that, strictly speaking, he was no longer a soldier, that he was no longer even a Japanese, but such statements seemed only to irritate Atami. The *gocho* certainly had a Japanese face, and he spoke the language of the Eight Islands, but he was as perplexingly American as the large white soldiers and sailors who filled the other compartments of the ship.

In the late afternoon of the day *Portola* was expected to enter Kagoshima harbor, Atami appeared to take Noguchi on deck for his once-daily excursion into the fresh air. Ordinarily, such a privilege was reserved for the Koreans on board, since they enjoyed the somewhat anomalous status of persons believed to have been impressed, rather than willingly enlisted, into Japanese service. But the naval doctor who had undertaken to treat *Portola*'s one ambulatory Japanese POW had prescribed at least ten minutes each day on deck for Noguchi, together with limited exercise. X-ray examination had shown a mildly depressed fracture of the frontal bones of the skull, causing the doctor to suspect that the Japanese had suffered some damage to the dura. Under different circumstances, complete bed rest would have been prescribed. The doctor had served with the Marines in the worst days of the battle for Guadalcanal, however, and it was not in him now to pamper a damned Jap soldier, even a confused wounded one.

Atami had found that he had some feelings of sympathy for Noguchi. The Japanese was so obviously disoriented by his experiences, so plainly consumed with melancholy, that the Nisei had decided he would make the man's captivity, if not pleasant, at least no more unpleasant than was absolutely required by the circumstances. Except for his parents, Noguchi was the only native-born Japanese Atami had ever met, and he did not intend to return home to tell his mother and father that he had been in any way responsible for unnecessary cruelty to a prisoner of their—and his own—blood.

As Noguchi followed Atami out onto the weather deck, he could hear sounds of shouting and laughter coming from aft. The words and the manners were indisputably Korean, loud and offensive. What possible excuse could the Koreans have for such merriment on board an American ship en route to an American prisoner-of-war stockade? he wondered.

The air was cool, almost cold, but the front that had so afflicted the weather was passing. Then, too, the ship had traveled some distance to the south, and Noguchi saw with pleasure that the sky was clearing. A bank of low clouds in the west still obscured the sun, but from time to time the southerly wind would make an opening in the cloud cover, and at such times a brilliant golden path would appear on the water.

The decks were wet, either from the recent rain or from having been sluiced by the sailors of the crew, some of whom lounged at the weather rails watching the Koreans, who had been assembled on the fantail for bathing under the ship's pressure hoses. Naked, they disported themselves in a loose and typically uncouth manner. Noguchi was offended and looked away. He remembered the two officers he had encountered on the beach at Kujukuri—the Japanese *shoi* and the white *chui* who spoke the elegant Japanese of the aristocracy. The *chui* had commanded him to conduct himself with humility and the dignity of a Japanese soldier. That, certainly, he had tried hard to do since entering the strange world of the *gaijin*. But it was difficult to maintain one's dignity in the presence of a mob of naked, laughing Koreans who did not seem to be aware that they were participating—unwillingly, perhaps—in a great tragedy for Nihon.

Noguchi forced himself to think of other things. With the air so clear and the clouds so near to the western horizon, he decided that tonight there would be a sunset of great beauty, one worthy of viewing with seriousness and appreciation. He resolved to ask Atami-san if it would be possible to remain on deck until the sun went down.

The Americans apparently had taught the Korean laborers a number of expressions—expressions of great vulgarity, Noguchi was sure—which they were shouting at the laughing Americans lounging about the ship. The lack of discipline this showed caused Noguchi to flush with anger. Obviously, the Americans found it all hilarious, but to a Japanese soldier their behavior was offensive. He watched them through narrowed eyes, his head suddenly aching again.

The Koreans had seen him come on deck with Atami-san, but, rather than come to attention as they should immediately have done, they slouched about in their nakedness, looking at him and making filthy comments in their own debased language.

It seemed to Noguchi that he once again heard the words of the white *chui-san* speaking of dignity in adversity being the mark of a Japanese *bushi*. Almost without conscious volition, he found himself among the Koreans, addressing them stingingly in his best parade-ground manner. "Stop this at once. Come to attention and behave like soldiers!"

His orders brought forth only laughter, and, what was worse, smiles from the Americans. Even Atami-san seemed to find his attempt to instill discipline amusing.

One of the Koreans, an evil-looking fellow almost as large as Koriyama-san had been, stared insolently into his face and said, in abominable Japanese: "Go and fuck your father's wife, Japanese pig. No one has to obey you any longer."

Noguchi's temper exploded. Never in all his time in the Army had a subordinate ever said such a thing to him. And to hear it from a garlic-eating Korean was more than his composure could bear. He did what came naturally to him as a noncommissioned officer of the Imperial Army. He slapped the man across the face with all the strength he could muster.

The big Korean's black eyes went opaque with hatred. All the loathing of an oppressed people for a master race was in those eyes. The heavily muscled man took a stance that Noguchi recognized as the attack position of *tai-kwan-do*, the most deadly of the Korean martial arts.

Before the Americans could intervene, the man struck an upward blow at Noguchi's neck. It was a blow with the hand's edge intended to shatter the carotid artery, and it missed. The rocklike edge of the hand caught the base of Noguchi's skull with enough force to knock him completely off his feet. The blow's impact traveled through the bones of his head and so jarred the already fractured skull that the arteries of the dura began to hemorrhage violently.

Noguchi found himself lying on the steel deck looking up at the sun through a blurred montage of shapes and faces. As blood filled his eyes it seemed to him that the sky was turning red, a fantastically beautiful color, shot through with silver. The sun is setting, he thought. Why don't the fools step aside and let me view the sunset? He heard the singing of the blood in his veins, the rustle of his breathing, the fluttering of his own heart.

What a foolish thing had happened, Saigo Noguchi thought. And yet how very beautiful it was to die.

2200 Hours

Lieutenant Tanaka completed his tour of the outposts and stood under a gnarled cypress, listening to the steady dripping of the rain on the thick carpet of needles underfoot. When he looked up he could see a few stars through the cloud cover, and in the west a waning gibbous moon hung low over the mountains. From time to time, at this elevation, the Rangers had caught sight of the snowy slopes of Fujiyama, seventy miles away across the remaining ridges of the Boso Peninsula and the darkness of the Sagami Sea. The great mountain was like a ghost that appeared briefly and then faded in the mists.

Tanaka was a worried man, and he was not the only one in the platoon who was. They had engaged in a number of sharp, short fire fights in the afternoon as they encountered first one and then another of the ambushes that had been laid along the mountain track. They had killed a number of Japanese infantrymen, all of whom wore the insignia of the Imperial Guards Division. The platoon had lost four men killed and six wounded. The wounded had been detached and sent back toward Ichinomiya with the one tank that Schuster and his men had been unable to repair. The dead had been left beside the road wrapped in ground sheets to await the graves registration people, who would be coming with the main body of troops following the Rangers at a slower pace.

It was not the engagements they had fought or the casualties they had taken that worried Tanaka. It was Harry Seaver.

Something very strange was happening to the platoon leader. Tanaka was not an imaginative man, nor was he given to intellectual or emotional puzzles. But it was growing increasingly obvious that it had been a mistake to send Seaver to this particular place.

Earlier in the afternoon, Sergeant Hardin—a man Tanaka was sure had no particular liking for him—had approached him uncertainly. That in itself was cause for alarm. The platoon sergeant was seldom unsure of himself. He was a man who relied completely on the military verities. If the answer to a problem could not be found in a field manual or in Army regulations, then the problem had no reason to exist. Yet the sergeant had sought him out and had spoken uneasily, refusing to look directly at him, as though there was some shame in what he was saying.

"It's about Lieutenant Seaver, sir," he said. "Did you hear him when he charged that last strongpoint?"

Tanaka had indeed heard Seaver—and watched him, too. He had charged the last twenty yards like a man possessed, firing a Thompson he had taken from one of the tankers and screaming in Japanese.

"Well, Sergeant, it shakes up the enemy when someone comes in yelling at them in their own language," he said.

"I understand that, Lieutenant," Hardin said restlessly. "That's why he's here." He glanced almost furtively at the Nisei. "I guess that's why you're here, too."

"You got it, Sergeant," Tanaka said dryly.

"But hell, Lieutenant," Hardin said. "After it was over, and Tangelli's squad was cleaning up, he started giving the wop orders in Japanese. He didn't seem to realize he was doing it."

"I see," Tanaka said. But he didn't see, and that was what was worrying him. Seaver hadn't been sleeping since the platoon had entered these mountains. As they had moved deeper into the hills, as the places had become more familiar, he had seemed to

---

367

become more silent, more reserved, as though something was happening inside him.

"Listen, Sergeant," Tanaka said. "Lieutenant Seaver is tired. We're all tired. Maybe we're all a bit Jap-happy." He essayed a mirthless smile. "Even me, Sergeant."

Hardin inspected the breech of his M-1 without looking at the Nisei officer. "I guess maybe that's it, sir. It confuses the men, that's all."

Hardin had returned to the column of march leaving Tanaka profoundly unsettled.

Then there had been the incident of the *kami*.

An hour after clearing away the Jap roadblock, the track had entered a series of sharp switchbacks, all perfect places for another delayed action by the retreating Japanese. Yet there had been no ambush. Seaver, walking with Tanaka ahead of the last remaining Shermans, had looked about him like a man waking from a dream. It was difficult for Tanaka, who had grown up in the agricultural Santa Clara Valley of California, to realize that these mountains of cypress and red pine were once as familiar to Seaver as the flat fields south of San Francisco Bay were to him.

"There is a shrine not far from here," Seaver had said suddenly. "A rock path and a torii and a stone *kami*, where the spirit lives."

Tanaka had never understood—nor wished to—the intricacies of Shinto worship. This odd business of reverence for the spirits in stones and trees and ponds seemed both foolish and slightly barbaric to him. His own parents had been Buddhists in Japan and they had converted to Christianity with some fervor when they emigrated to the United States. He had not been captured by their Baptist enthusiasms, but he had gone through the approved motions while he was growing up, and enough of the church's teachings had stuck to him to make him intolerant of Shinto.

The column had been moving up the mountain toward the ridge in the deepening afternoon. The weather remained cold, and here and there were patches of snow on the ground under the trees. The radio was functioning again—not well, but well enough for them to make occasional contact with the main column moving along the road several miles behind them. Battalion had sent along a weather report that promised the front would move over the peninsula by evening, leaving clearing skies for tonight and thereafter. That meant the fighter-bombers would be out soon, and the Japanese counterattacks that had so badly mauled the beachheads would turn into retreats.

There had been some sort of major battle to the north, along the Tone River. The reports were difficult to sort out, but Tanaka had the impression that a large counterattack by the Jap 36th Army had been blunted, and the American XXIV Corps was beginning its encirclement of Tokyo.

But that was the Big War, Tanaka thought as he walked beside Seaver. The platoon's war was here, in one after another minor ambush and skirmish, on the way through these mountains where Seaver had played as a child.

"There," Seaver had said. "Up that little draw, between the trees."

"There what, Harry?"

"The shrine," Seaver had said. "The *kami* is old. Who knows how old? Oyama-san used to say it was put there by a priest of the Ashikagi, a thousand years ago."

"Oyama-san?"

Seaver had given him a curious look. "Sometimes I forget you weren't born here, Tanaka-san," he said in Japanese. "Oyama-san was an old servant woman at the Maeda villa. She used to say the Ashikagi stole the *kami* from the main shrine up on the Maedas' ridge, and that they put it down here for the convenience of the *sohei* who had the task of defending this road."

Seaver had half-smiled at Tanaka's confusion. "The *sohei* were warrior monks, great soldiers."

As the column approached the path leading to the shrine, Seaver had suddenly ordered a halt and sent out scouts. Tanaka disliked stopping. There was no need. "Why the halt?" he asked.

"Follow me."

He had trailed after Seaver as he started up the rocky path. The nearness of the trees and the steep high ground made him distinctly uneasy.

"There won't be an ambush here," Seaver had said.

The path twisted and became a series of steps hewn from the rock. At the top of the climb stood an old torii gate made of cedar logs. The hemp rope hanging across it was shredded and rotted. Seaver had regarded it quietly. "It's been long since this place was purified," he said in Japanese. "How very sad."

Tanaka had felt a chill run down his back. He had gone no farther, but had stood and watched while Seaver walked under the torii and approached a moss-covered stone standing near an old, fallen stone lantern.

Seaver had approached the stone and bowed. He had clapped his hands and stood with his head inclined, his eyes closed. Tanaka had felt the chill again. This detached, submissive Seaver was unknown to him. For several minutes Seaver had stood in silent meditation. Tanaka had been conscious of the sounds that nature made in this place: the soft rustle of the wind in the pines, the drip of water, the sound of the silence. He could hear the voices of the troops on the road and the rumble of the Shermans' engines, but he could hear the silence, too. It was to that Seaver must have been listening, the Nisei thought.

Presently Seaver had bowed to the *kami* again and turned. Tanaka had been shocked by the emptiness he had seen in Seaver's eyes. Or if it was not emptiness, it was a void into which he could not see and had no wish to.

Seaver had stopped and lifted the heavy stone lantern. He had replaced it reverently on its pedestal and walked back down the rock stairs.

Tanaka had said uneasily, "You look as though you believe all that."

"Believe what, Jim? That there are spirits living in beautiful places? Perhaps I do," Seaver had said somberly.

Now, standing his watch on the ridge in the night, Tanaka thought about the moment at the shrine and what Hardin had said and he wondered what strange thing was happening to Seaver.

If I were more Japanese, he thought, perhaps I would know. As it was, he could feel only the restlessness and doubt that were the hallmarks of his Occidental upbringing. Whatever was happening to Seaver, he didn't like it. It made him afraid, and a soldier had enough to fear without being confused by mystical transformations or metamorphoses.

Troubled, he made his quiet way back to the platoon command post.

Thirty minutes later, mortar rounds began to fall into the platoon's position. The unknown Jap officer whose roadblocks and ambushes had been delaying them since leaving the beachhead had finally begun his attack in force.

Y-day plus 15
16 March 1946

In the time of the Emperor Godaigo, it happened that the Regent, Takatoki Hojo, was besieged and defeated at Kamakura by the daimyo Nitta Yoshisada. Seeing that all was lost, Takatoki smuggled his legitimate wife and child out of Kamakura disguised as fisherfolk, and this having been done, led his retainers of the Bakufu out of the city into the hills that surround the capital. The procession went at night, carrying torches, so that the retainers could be clearly seen by the army of the Yoshisada as they climbed a road to a shallow cave above a steep ravine. Here Takatoki halted and spoke briefly to an old retainer who passed the message down the line. It had begun to rain and the men carrying torches now placed them upright in the earth, and this done, began to make their own preparations. As Takatoki removed his outer robe and drew his short sword, his beautiful and beloved mistress appeared among the retainers begging her lord for permission to accompany him. Since Takatoki dearly loved the girl, he placed his hand gently on her head and signalled to a retainer poised behind her, who swiftly drew his knife and cut her throat. Takatoki did not delay longer. He knelt and made the stomach-cut and then signalled by lifting a finger that he had desired kaishaku, the stroke of a dear friend. This he was given and his head rolled down the steep hillside toward the watching army of the Yoshisada. Next, half of his retainers knelt and made the stomach-cut while the other half struck off their heads. Then half of those remaining cut themselves open and were in their turn decapitated. Then half again. At the end, of course, those few who remained had to summon the strength to make the stomach-cut deeply enough not to require kaishaku. And it is said that as the rain extinguished the last torches, the astounded Yoshisada heard the sounds of severed heads slowly rolling down the hillside toward their camp, catching on a bush or rock for a time, and then rolling on. It is said, too, that on this night of the mass seppuku at Kamakura there died one woman and eight hundred and seventy-three warriors of the Hojo.

Paraphrased from
Jack Seward, *The Japanese,*
New York: William Morrow, 1972

0530 Hours

The sky over Tinian Island was clear, changing gradually from blue-gray to blue as the sun approached the eastern horizon. Aboard the ships in the harbor, a general alert had been called, and the men of the transport fleet complained about the Navy's strange ways. No enemy aircraft or surface vessel had been detected within a hundred miles of the central Marianas for months.

On the airfield, a bulldozer and work crew had prepared a large pit in the center of one of the taxiways. The technicians who had arrived from the United States by air several days earlier, civilians overseen by an extremely nonnautical Navy captain, had been fussily precise about the pit. It was required to be exactly fourteen feet long, twelve feet wide, and eight feet deep.

When the pit had been measured and found to meet specifications, the work crew was withdrawn and escorted to the field perimeter, three miles distant. There, the puzzled men of the construction battalion were ordered to remain on the far side of a new chain link fence guarded by white-helmeted military policemen carrying automatic weapons.

Those Seabees in a position to observe anything at all now watched as the tiny, distant figures signaled for the advance of a large transporter with canvas sides erected to hide the load it bore. The transporter was driven to the pit in the taxiway, where it was joined by a lifter of the kind used to change engines in B-29s.

Construction Specialist First Class Glen Porter, the only member of his detachment who had managed to liberate a pair of Jap field glasses, sat on a stack of runway matting and described what he saw to his fellow Seabees.

"They're using the lifter to move something from the transporter into that pit we dug," he reported.

An MP lieutenant, starchy in carefully pressed khakis, white webbing, and white helmet, and carrying a Thompson, stationed himself below the pile of steel matting and stared up at Porter through dark aviator's goggles. "What the hell do you think you're doing up there, sailor?"

Porter made a sucking noise through his teeth and replied in a tone finely shaded on the safe side of insolence. "I'm sittin' and watchin', Lieutenant. Any regulations against that?"

The MP, young and new to Tinian, was ready to start quoting base regulations when a Military Police jeep bearing his company commander pulled up near the Seabees. The captain beside the driver was an old Tinian hand. He had been on the island when the Seabees began to build the base, long before the arrival of the supporting troops of the Army Corps of Engineers. His relationship with the construction battalions was excellent, and he had a comfortable, air-conditioned office to prove it.

"What do you see from up there, Porter?" he asked.

"Beats the hell out of me, Captain. Looks like they're burying something in that fuckin' hole we dug."

"Old, used-up Seabees, no doubt," the captain said. He raised his hand in greeting and signaled the driver to move on along the fenced perimeter.

The MP lieutenant, Porter noted, at least had sense enough to take a hint and stop making a nuisance of himself. He, too, moved along, trying to see through the linked fence what was happening.

The members of Porter's outfit sat around smoking, drinking Cokes, and reading comic books. From time to time someone would ask for a report, but as the morning sun grew steadily hotter, they began to lose interest and drift away.

Porter remained. He lit a cigarette and, resting his elbows on his knees to steady the glasses, continued to watch.

The island was rife with rumors about the crates that had been brought ashore from *Bethlehem* a fortnight ago. It was said that some of the stuff the cruiser carried had been so secret it had actually been welded to the deck of the cabin assigned to that same Navy captain who was now out there in the morning sun directing activities around the pit.

Glen Porter was not a man to be impressed by the games the Navy played. He had built bases all over the central Pacific and had a unit citation to prove it, but in all of his experience he had never encountered such a cloak-and-dagger program as this one. It was ironic that it centered mainly around a fucking hole in the ground.

Now the transporter and the lifter were being backed away from his pit (he thought of it as his), but the canvas screens had been removed from the transporter and put in place around the hole in the ground. Porter again sucked his teeth in exasperation.

The hot sun had begun to make him sweat, so he removed his shirt. He was getting thoroughly sick of Tinian. He was, in fact, getting thoroughly sick of the whole scummy war. Everyone had thought that the moment the Marines and dogfaces hit the beaches of Honshu, the Japs would get the message that they were through. But it wasn't happening that way. The Japs still didn't know how to surrender, and the scuttlebutt around the CB base was that things were going hard up north. There was a battle going on near Tokyo, and though the Japs weren't winning it, no one seemed willing to say that the Americans were either. Shit, Porter thought, judging by the way things went on Okinawa and Kyushu, it could take years to finish the war. Golden Gate by Forty-eight was the word. Or maybe by Fifty-eight. Who knew how long those yellow bastards would keep fighting? They didn't have the sense to know when the jig was up.

377

He thought about the 6,000 bucks he had stashed away—three years' poker winnings—and his collection of souvenirs: a Jap sword, a couple of flags, one with Jap blood on it, the Nambu officer's pistol, the Naval Landing Force cap—all won or bought from Marines and dogfaces who absolutely guaranteed their authenticity. I'm ready to go home to Detroit, he thought, and be a bona-fide war hero with cash in my pockets. Instead of that happening, here he sat 8,000 miles from God's country watching a bunch of Navy and Air Force squirrels burying something in the ground. He flipped the cigarette away and lifted the glasses again.

The people out on the field were just standing around now. There were a half-dozen MPs. All were standing with their backs to the shielded pit, looking out across the airfield. What were they expecting, for Chrissake? A banzai charge by the WACs over in Operations?

A glint of reflected sunlight far off to the right near the 509th Composite Group's area caught his attention. A tractor had been hooked up to one of the B-29s and was hauling it toward the group standing around the pit.

The 509th had been on Tinian for two months now. They had arrived with two other Superfort outfits from the States. But when the others went operational against the Japs, the 509th just sat on its can, flying only training missions. They had taken quite a ragging for that from the other zoomies, but eventually the groups flying missions against Honshu had flown off to Okinawa, leaving the 509th alone on Tinian.

Speculation about the special group had died down. Rumors didn't last long on Tinian. Now everyone assumed that the 509th was on the island for engineering test work intended to improve the performance of the Superfortress. It was as good a story as any. They flew off in two- and three-plane elements. Out at dawn, back at nightfall, in their bright and shiny new Boeings. No one knew where they went or what they did when they got there. The aircrews lived in a restricted area that was off limits for everyone else on the island, and there were rumors about *that*, too. The regular old Tinian hands said that the restricted area was set up with a plush officers' club and a USO for the enlisted men, and that the whole group was made up of people who had relatives in the government pulling wires to give them a cushy war.

Porter had had a glimpse of the 509th's area. He had driven his dozer by there one afternoon and been chased away by the MPs for his trouble. But it had looked just like all the other areas on Tinian: Quonsets and prefabs, with nothing luxurious about them that he could see.

The B-29 the tractor was hauling had an arrow and a circle painted on the tail fin and the number 82 on the fuselage. He had seen it before. It was the airplane flown by the 509th's group commander, a young bird colonel named Paul Tibbets. The tractor moved slowly across the vast empty field. A jeep-load of MPs led the way, and there was a staff car following. Quite a procession, Porter thought.

His stomach growled, and he considered trucking on over to the mess hall for some breakfast. To hell with it, he decided. Powdered eggs and Spam held no appeal. He'd wait until the Transients' Mess was open and eat there. Sometimes you could wangle real ham and canned orange juice from the cooks who fed the brass passing through Tinian on the way to Kyushu. Seabees didn't live by ordinary Navy rules. They were too useful to have as friends.

He settled the glasses more comfortably against his eyes and continued to watch as the B-29 was brought toward the pit. He frowned as he watched the ground crew maneuver the huge airplane directly *over* the hole.

For a long while nothing much seemed to happen. The men standing around the airplane continued to stand around. Then someone, the crew chief probably, climbed aboard. Porter watched as the ground crew attached a battery cart. And presently the bomb-bay doors were opened. Then activity seemed to come to a halt again, and there were more conferences among the khaki-clad men, most of them officers, he could see.

The ground crew set to work once more, removing the canvas shields around the pit. The shadow of the B-29's fuselage made it difficult to see, but Porter was able to make out a black hump of some sort protruding from the pit. What it looked like, he thought, was the top of a bomb. A fat, mammoth bomb. Perhaps it was some special sort of mine. Before they flew off to Okinawa, the other groups had spent time dropping aerial mines in the Inland Sea. It was said that Japan's inland waters were so thick with the ungainly things that a guy could walk from Kyushu to Shikoku without getting his feet wet. Typical Army flyboys' talk. They made the war sound like a game of water polo.

As he watched carefully, the airplane's interior hoist began to lift the mine, or whatever it was, into the bomb bay. It had to be heavy, because the bomber settled on its oleos as it took the strain. It was interesting that just one bomb was doing that, he thought. The Superforts could carry a 12,000-pound bombload; so that thing had to weigh plenty.

Slowly, the object vanished into the bay of the airplane and the bomb doors were closed.

Porter sat watching for another thirty minutes, but nothing much happened. The staff car loaded up and drove away. The tractor remained connected to the bomber's nosewheel. The MPs remained spaced in a circle around the whole shebang. He shrugged. He had expected the aircrew to climb aboard, fire the airplane up, and fly it away. But no such thing happened. The fort just stood there, squatting on its overloaded shock-struts, surrounded by MPs.

Porter sighed, recased his Jap glasses, and put on his shirt. End of show, he thought. Time to check out breakfast. He clambered down from the pile of runway matting and started out across the concrete ramp, shimmering now with the heat.

The whole morning's operation left him puzzled. But then, much that the Army Air Forces did puzzled him. Even the airplane was a little peculiar. There was no naked chick with big tits painted on the nose—only a funny name in simple block letters.

Someone had told him that it was the name of the colonel's mother. Porter was fond of his own mother and he supposed that if he commanded a Superfort he might be prevailed upon to name it after her. But still, for Chrissake, who ever heard of a bomber named "Enola Gay"?

1300 Hours

Between midnight and noon, the Ranger platoon received 400 rounds of mortar fire and suffered no fewer than seven banzai charges by the Japanese occupying the broken ground between the ridge and the next range, on which stood the Maeda villa.

Harry Seaver had situated his men well, and they took a bloody toll from the Japanese troops attempting to stop their advance.

At dawn, after six hours of intermittent shelling, the Japanese had overrun, but failed to hold, the position where Seaver had sited the Shermans. The fighting had been hand to hand, a battle with bayonets, small arms, knives, and even fists. The Japanese managed to hang on long enough to attack one Sherman with Molotov cocktails. None of the attacking force survived the counterattack of the Rangers, but the tank had been destroyed and several of the Rangers had been killed. Sergeant Schuster and his gunner were both wounded, and the driver, fighting outside the tank, had been killed.

Twice more that morning the Japanese had made a concerted attempt to knock out the two remaining tanks, but they had not succeeded. Instead, they had left twenty dead on the tank's revetment, and several wounded were scattered here and there through the scarred forest. The Rangers could hear some of them moaning, although no Japanese made any attempt to reach them. In fact, Seaver did not hear any of them ask to be rescued.

For the last two hours the Rangers had crouched in their holes waiting for the next charge and wondering how many more Japs there were amid the densely packed pine and cypress.

It had rained lightly twice during the early-morning hours, but the sky was definitely clearing. In an hour or less it would be possible to call in air strikes and wipe out the Jap defenders with napalm. Seaver was fully prepared to do this, though he was no longer sure it would be necessary. The Japanese seemed to have spent themselves in their nightlong series of savage attacks. They had taken heavy casualties, and though they had hurt the platoon, Seaver still had forty men unhurt and plenty of ammunition. The surviving Shermans would finally be of use, on the last thrust up the ridge to the villa, because there were stretches of straight road and open patches in the forest cover.

Seaver studied the platoon's front with his field glasses. The Japanese had broken the line several times, but each time they had, the Rangers had bloodied them badly. Tanaka had killed an enormous Japanese soldier, who Seaver was certain had originated in Hokkaido, where the Ainu strain had permeated the Japanese population and produced large, pale, hairy people of great ferocity. Seaver suspected that Tanaka would not have been able to handle the Ainu if it had not been for the Japanese's surprise at finding himself locked in combat with an American with an Asian face.

Seaver lowered his glasses and signaled for his communications man. When Buie had scuttled to his side, he took the radio and called battalion to locate the head of the column behind them. He did not want to take a chance of a force of Japanese circling around and laying an ambush behind his platoon. According to Kizer, riding in the lead APC some eight miles to the rear, there was no sign of any Japanese activity between the Rangers and the battalion.

The counterattack on the beachhead had been blunted and more troops were coming ashore. Units of the First Army, until now held in reserve, were preparing to break out of the Sheridan beachhead to the north, toward the Tone River, where a large Japanese force was trying to stop the XXIV Corps from completing its crossing at Noda.

Twice during the predawn attacks, Seaver had caught a glimpse of a Japanese officer urging his troops forward with a sword in his hand. In the almost stroboscopic flashes of battle, he had found himself staring at the commanding figure with the upraised *katana,* and the sight had chilled his blood, reminding him of the nightmares he had had on the troopship.

He gave the radio handset back to Buie and raised the glasses again.

"Are they finished, Lieutenant?" Buie sounded exhausted.

Seaver shook his head. He did not know how he knew, but he did. They would come again, at least once.

He signaled for a runner. When the soldier crouched at his side, he said, "Tell Tanaka to take two squads and get up on that rise." He pointed to a rock outcrop on the right. "I want fixed bayonets, plenty of ammunition, and at least four men with grenade launchers." He looked down the staggered line of foxholes where his men waited.

"If there is a breakthrough anywhere along the front, I want flanking fire and plenty of it. And when they pull back, this time we follow them. Go."

The soldier scuttled away, crouched low and darting from tree to tree.

Seaver lowered his head until his cheek touched the sweet-smelling carpet of cedar and pine needles still wet with the rain. He had never been so tired, he thought. It was as though with almost no strain his spirit could remove itself from this dirty, aching corpse of a body he had been forced to bring up this beautiful mountain.

He shook himself awake and looked through the trees, away to the west. Mists were forming in the deep ravines, like silvery brush strokes placed by a master painter on the deep green of the pines and cedar trees. He found himself thinking of a poem

written by the Emperor Jomei, who had ruled in the seventh
century:

> Over the broad earth
> Smoke-mist hovers.
> Over the broad water
> Seagulls hover.
> Beautiful, my country,
> My Yamato,
> Island of the dragonfly.

How strange it was to come here as an invader and remember
that, a poem taught him by an old *sensei*—how long ago? A long
time, surely, since he had roamed these hills as a child and
played the games children played.

A movement alerted him, and he raised the glasses. He could
see a mass of men in mustard-colored uniforms crawling along
the forest floor. They were coming again. He hand-signaled to
the Ranger in the next foxhole as he slipped the safety catch off
his M-1—and waited.

In flag plot aboard the USS *Midway*, Fleet Admiral Chester
W. Nimitz faced his staff and read the presidential order aloud.
When he had finished, he studied their faces carefully. Not one
of them, he realized with a shock, understood the meaning of the
information he had just conveyed to them.

Ashore, at General MacArthur's headquarters, a similar scene
must be playing at this moment. The admiral wondered if the
soldiers had understood any better. Quite probably not. This was
not a thing men could grasp easily. But they would, in time. Oh,
yes. Soon, very soon.

He spoke directly to his air officer. "See to it that no aircraft of
this command flies south of 34°30′ north latitude or west of
132°40′ east longitude between 0400 and 1100 hours local time
tomorrow." To his aide he said, "Notify all surface and submarine commands that I want every unit in the Inland Sea south

of the Bungo Strait by 0600 hours tomorrow." He looked at his staff members and added, "That is all for now. Carry on, gentlemen." Then he turned to look out an open port at the long line of powerful gray ships steaming in company with *Midway*. He wondered if they would ever seem quite so powerful again.

1600 Hours

The next-to-last charge against the Rangers came before two in the afternoon. The troops Seaver had observed moving into position had attempted an encirclement of the platoon's outposts on the ridge, advancing cautiously under cover of a steady bombardment from 50mm mortars. Seaver concluded that the platoon was facing a pick-up force of perhaps 100 men and radioed for air support.

At 1520, a flight of P-47Ns appeared, flying under the low clouds. Seaver marked their targets with white phosphorus grenades, and for forty minutes the four planes made napalm and strafing passes at the Japanese positions. The result was a ring of violent fires all around the Rangers. The biting stench of jellied gasoline and burning flesh rolled down the ridge. At 1600 the Thunderbolts withdrew, and a crackling silence descended over the battleground.

Seaver signaled for the two Shermans to fire up and pull out, ready to begin the advance once more. It was then that the Japanese made their final, desperate charge, rising out of their foxholes in a screaming, furious attack. Seaver, on the line of advance, fired his M-1 until the barrel grew too hot to touch. All along the front the Americans were laying down a withering fire, and the running Japanese fell like wheat before a reaper. He could hear the tack-tack-tacking sound of a Japanese Nambu, and he knew that the platoon was taking casualties from it, but he could not locate the position of the gun. The heavier, more solid sound of a fifty-caliber mounted on one of the tanks rolled through the trees. When the attack slackened, Seaver called, "Cease fire. Cease fire."

There was a moment of pale sunshine, made golden by the smoke from the still-burning napalm. Seaver shifted position in his hole and signaled for the second squad to make ready to cover the advance of the first. Soon, now, he thought, as soon as the next wave tried to break the perimeter.

The sunlight faded swiftly, as though some spirit's hand had taken hold of the sun. A rain shower began, icy but sweet. Seaver tasted the freshness of it on his lips. He looked down at his jump boots and saw that they were caked with freezing mud. There were tiny clumps of ice frozen in the lacings. The Japanese spring, he thought, as changeable as the sea. Old General Maeda had once said that Japanese spring was a female season, and that was why it was both difficult and beautiful. What had become of him, the old samurai who wrote haiku while his troops raped Nanking?

"Lieutenant?" Tangelli was beside him, looking frightened.

"Yes. What?"

"Are you okay, sir? Are you hit?"

"I'm fine. No problem," Seaver said.

The mortar barrage had stopped. The Japanese had run out of ammunition. How many mortar rounds had each man carried up this long climbing road? he wondered. They must have loaded themselves like pack animals. But there was no resupply for them now.

"Lieutenant Tanaka wants to know if he should hold his position."

"Tell him yes. They'll try to break in once more. Then he can come down on them."

"Right, sir." Tangelli withdrew, still looking concerned. About me? Seaver wondered.

The snap of Arisakas increased in volume. The Japanese were

moving down the slope. He could see them darting from one bit of cover to the next.

"Hold fire, hold fire," Seaver called. "Wait until they come."

He looked up the road. How far now to the villa? It seemed to him that he remembered each step of the way. He could almost see himself with Kantaro and Katsuko, children running along the gravel road, waving sticks for swords and bits of bright paper for battle flags.

The Japanese started their charge, a solid wave of mustard color with here and there a brilliant patch of red, yellow, gold as the brightness of their collar patches stood out in the rain.

"Commence firing!" He began to fire his M-1: careful, aimed shots. He could see his bullets strike with a spatter of water from the wet uniforms and then the red stain of blood showing as the men he hit fell, legs drumming, to the forest floor.

The Japanese were not returning fire. They came on, their long Arisaka rifles held out before them. They used the bayonets the way the *ashigaru*, the ancient foot soldiers, had used *naginata*, halberdlike weapons. To Seaver the scene had an unreal quality, as though he were refighting the mock battles of his childhood.

The wave burst through the platoon's perimeter, and from Tanaka's position on the flank came a storm of steel. The charge broke into small groups of Japanese milling about in confusion, falling, dying. Seaver signaled for the Rangers to close with the attackers, and he ran, shooting his M-1 from the hip. He made for a stocky noncom, who turned to face him with his bayonet. He parried the thrust and smashed the man's face with the butt of his rifle. The soldier took the blow and fell. Seaver turned in time to see a Japanese lunging at Buie. He pulled the trigger, but the M-1 clicked on the empty chamber. Clubbing the rifle, he brought the butt down across the Japanese soldier's back. The man's rifle went flying, but he managed to keep his feet. Seaver swung at him again, missed, and felt the wind driven out of him by a helmeted head. He grappled, smelling the man's sweat and the sourness of his breath. The ground was slimy beneath them.

There was blood mixed with the pine needles and the mud. Seaver heard himself screaming, with the mingled fear and rage that was always part of battle. He was screaming in Japanese, though he did not realize it.

Tanaka's detachment came charging down from the slope and struck the Japanese with their own bayonets. Seaver could hear the grunts and cries, the rasping breathing of men fighting for their lives. He reached for his trench knife and drove it upward into the body of the Japanese who held him. He felt the hot wetness flood his hand and the sudden slackening as the man went flaccid. Down on the road the fifties mounted on the Shermans stopped firing, but he could hear American voices and the cracking of M-1s.

He heaved the dead man off and got to his knees in time to see a Japanese officer charging at him, sword held high. The man's uniform was bloody, his face streaked with mud. He wore no helmet. Seaver met his eyes, and a cold shock almost paralyzed him. It was Kantaro Maeda.

Time froze. He could not rise to his feet. He held the useless trench knife and waited for the fall of the sword. Maeda's black eyes were wide with the shock of recognition.

Then Seaver heard a short rattle of gunfire, and Maeda spun and staggered, his left side torn ragged, smoking and flooding red. He did not drop the sword, but braced himself on it as the burst turned him. Two Japanese Guardsmen, both of them wounded, caught him around the waist and supported him between them as they retreated.

Seaver saw them scrambling up the hill and into the forest. He lurched to his feet, dazed. As though by magic, the only Japanese in the platoon's position now were sprawled dead or dying. He raised a clenched fist and signaled for the Rangers to counterattack. Then he staggered forward after the retreating Japanese, fumbling for a fresh clip for his M-1. He was numb, shivering with inner cold, only half believing. But he led the counterattack, because that was the Way of the Warrior. What else could he do?

At the bend of the road he could see the next-to-last Sherman burning. With almost nothing left but steel and a few grenades, the Guardsmen had fought beautifully. He tried to estimate the casualties the Rangers had taken, but it was difficult because there were mingled bodies scattered everywhere across this mountain killing ground, Americans and Japanese sprawled in foxholes, around the burning tank. As he led the way up the slope after the retreating enemy, perhaps two dozen Rangers followed. Tanaka was one of them. He marched stolidly, his face pale.

The unit that had been dogging and harassing the Rangers for two weeks was broken. Seaver could see individual Japanese soldiers running down the steep mountainside, crashing through the brush and trees. His own men were firing at them, and it angered him because he wanted to find the officer. Had it been Kantaro actually, or had he imagined it?

The Rangers advanced through the patches where the napalm dropped by the Thunderbolts had left only charred ground and charred corpses—black bundles oozing cooked juices through cracks in the carboned carapaces, arms extended toward the rain, fingers like black talons grasping at nothing. Here, the smell of burned flesh was sickening, but the Rangers moved stolidly on, their senses dulled by battle.

"We've finished the bastards at last," Tanaka said.

Seaver looked at him and did not speak. He kept walking after the vanished enemy. Behind him the last Sherman fired up and began to move along the road. Back on the battleground he could hear the medics shouting to one another, but he did not want to count the dead, not yet.

He walked woodenly, the M-1 like a great weight dragging on his arm. Time seemed to be fluid, and with each step the way became more familiar. The Marines at Kimitsu and their problems, the death and destruction all around—all was as misty as the rain that had become gentle as it began to move on across the mountains.

He raised his eyes to the sky and felt the dampness on his face.

Tanaka was speaking to him. "Yes? What is it you say?" Once again, he was unaware that he had spoken in Japanese.

Tanaka said, "I think we shouldn't get too far ahead of the column, Harry."

"Oh, I know these hills," Seaver said, still in Japanese.

Tanaka frowned and looked back at the straggling platoon. They no longer looked like soldiers of a modern army. They moved in a different way, he thought, like a band of *ashigaru.* It was a thing that happened to military units in battle: they followed the lead of their commander, if he led well. But this was all wrong, as though Seaver was leading his troops, not only along a mountain road, but also backward in time. It was nightmarish, and Tanaka decided to call a halt until Seaver came out of this dreamlike state. Battle fatigue, he thought, that's all it is.

A rattle of gunfire echoed down the slope from the ridge. The troops took cover, searching for the Japanese. The volume of fire was light, but Tanaka heard Tangelli yell that he was hit and a call went up for a medic. Since the medics were behind, at the place where the platoon had stood off the repeated Japanese charges, Tanaka dropped back to see what he could do for Tangelli.

When he found Tangelli lying in the roadside ditch, he signaled for a runner to go down the road and order the tank forward. There was no point in submitting to harassing fire now, after the main body of the Japanese had been dispersed.

Tangelli was cursing and trying to fit a field pack on his leg, where he had taken a clean wound from an Arisaka. Tanaka cut away his pants leg and used his own sulfa and field dressing. "What's happening up there, Lieutenant?" the corporal wanted to know. "I thought we had it made."

"Stragglers," Tanaka said. "Can you walk?"

"I can make it," Tangelli said.

"Get back to the medics, then. And tell Hardin I want him up here. On the double."

As Tangelli limped back toward the main body of the platoon, Tanaka twisted around to look up the road toward Seaver. What he saw made the breath freeze in his chest. Seaver was upright again, walking straight up the slope toward a wooded copse of cedars. The Japanese, wherever they were, were not firing. God knew why. They could have killed Seaver easily.

"Harry! For Chrissake! Get down!" Tanaka yelled.

But Seaver continued up toward the cedars like a sleepwalker. Tanaka followed him, ready to give covering fire. Quite suddenly, someone shouted for Seaver to stop where he was. A Japanese soldier was actually giving him a warning. Tanaka raised his rifle and when he saw just a patch of mustard yellow among the trees, he fired. The soldier slumped forward over his Arisaka.

"Harry! Get back!" When Seaver paid no attention, Tanaka shouted in Japanese.

Seaver heard the shout and ignored it. He knew this place even better than he knew the road and the mountains. For Harry-san and Kantaro and Katsuko it had been one of those secret places children find and keep for themselves. He moved into the trees, almost knowing who he would find there.

Kantaro Maeda knelt on the pine needles. He had removed his uniform tunic; it lay in a bloody pile beside him. The single Imperial Guardsman who had been protecting him lay prone and motionless over his rifle.

Kantaro's left side was raw, torn, burned. In his two hands he held a bayonet, and with it he had made the stomach-cut of ritual seppuku across his abdomen. A single gray coil of intestine had spilled out across his loosened belt. Next to him lay the Saotome sword of the Maedas, sheathed but half drawn from the black lacquered scabbard.

Seaver dropped his rifle and took a step toward his childhood friend. Kantaro, his handsome face stretched and drawn with agony, raised his eyes to Harry. With an enormous effort he released the grip of his right hand on the bayonet and stretched it out beside him, the first two fingers raised in an unmistakable signal.

Seaver could hear Tanaka crashing through the brush behind him. Kantaro could hear him, too, and he looked at Harry appealingly. His white lips formed a single, soundless word. It was *kaishaku.*

Without hesitation, Seaver stooped and picked up the ancient sword. It came to his hand familiarly, another deep memory from childhood. He drew it from the scabbard, his eyes fixed on his dying friend. Kantaro leaned forward, almost falling, but held himself ready.

Seaver raised the *katana* in both hands.

Behind him, Tanaka screamed, "No, Harry, no!"

Seaver brought the blade down with all his strength.

Kantaro Maeda, his head severed perfectly but for a thin bit of skin and muscle, collapsed forward onto the sweet-smelling forest floor.

Behind him, Seaver could hear Tanaka retching. He pitied him, knowing that if the Nisei lived for a thousand times a thousand years he would never know, as Harry did now, the serenity of embracing fully and with joy one's undoubted karma.

2100 Hours

General Hideki Tojo waited uneasily in the audience room of the special concrete bunker that he had ordered built for the protection of the Emperor's person on the day after General James Doolittle's raiders had dropped the first bombs on Tokyo.

The general was tired, almost frantic with worry, and fearful of what this sudden and secret summons into the Royal Presence might mean.

In September of the previous year, when Tojo had found himself out of power and perilously close to disgrace, he had made the gesture of attempting seppuku. It had been ill-advised. No officer of the Imperial Army who genuinely wished to atone for his mistakes by committing suicide should have any difficulty whatever accomplishing his design. It was true that for a man in his late years the correct, ceremonial act might present some small difficulties. But a number of the officers responsible for the defense plans of Saipan—the loss of which had precipitated Tojo's first resignation as premier and his military disgrace—had had no difficulty whatever dispatching themselves. Colonel Shigenori of the War Plans Division of Imperial General Staff Headquarters had done the job by shooting himself in the mouth. General Ito, whose task it had been to wipe out the American invasion fleet with his air forces, had killed himself by leaping to his death from the battered Dai Ichi building in the ruins of central Tokyo. Therefore, the rather pallid attempt at seppuku by the ex-premier had impressed few persons within the government.

With the coup that had returned him to power, Tojo had impressed only those young fanatics who saw in him the remaining person totally dedicated to a final victory for Japan. Tojo appreciated their loyalty, but he had been shocked and distressed by the murder of Marquis Kido and Admiral Toyoda. Both men had been close advisers to the throne, and since their assassination, the Emperor had not been seen.

Tojo clutched the case he carried with damp hands. If the Emperor wished for an assignment of guilt for the killings that took place on the day the Americans landed, Tojo was prepared. The young officers who had committed the act were under arrest, confined in a secret barracks in Nagano. Tojo had seriously considered summary execution in order to make certain that his own connection with the act be buried with these fanatics. But with the war situation as fluid as it presently was, he had decided merely to keep them sequestered and in the hands of specially loyal units of the Kempetai. True fanatics were valuable commodities. One could never be certain when they would again be useful.

But if the Emperor wished for an accounting of the military situation, this meeting could end badly for the premier. Any one of a number of commands from the Emperor could force him into an impossible situation.

The deaths of Kido, Toyoda, Togo, and Kawabe—that traitor to the Imperial Army—had gutted the so-called peace movement in Japan. If the Emperor now commanded his chief of government to make peace with the Americans, to whom could he turn? With the Diet in permanent recess, Tojo had appointed some easily available nonentities to fill the posts of the assassinated men. But they were not men with whom the Americans would consider dealing. Nor would they ever negotiate with Tojo himself. The allies had already named Tojo a war criminal and marked him for death. Therefore, if the Emperor ordered peace, it could be interpreted only as a royal command to resign, and to commit suicide—this time effectively and conclusively. The thought of undergoing the deadly ceremony again—and sincerely—made Tojo break out in a cold sweat. He was not a physically courageous man, and the idea of self-inflicted death was repugnant, though he had never in his life admitted it to a living soul.

The room in which he waited was quite bare of furniture. The only seat was on the raised dais surrounded by rare and ancient screens on which were painted scenes from the Battle of Nagashino. The premier wondered if the screens had been selected specifically to convey a message. It was at Nagashino that the gallant Takeda clan broke itself to bloody fragments making repeated cavalry attacks against the musketry of Oda Nobunaga. It was a battle that might now be taken as a paradigm of Japan's present unhappy condition.

Only the dais was floored with tatami. The floor beneath Tojo's polished boots was of parquet laid over concrete, and it creaked as the sixty-two-year-old premier shifted his weight from side to side on weary legs.

The strategic situation was bad, Tojo admitted to himself, but not yet catastrophic. The months of work on the defense plan called Ketsu-go Number 3 were having an effect. The main battle had developed, as planned, along the line of the Tonegawa. There, he had managed to concentrate almost the entire power of the 36th Army and supporting units. It was a pity that Field Marshal Hata had been killed by American bombers, because the old man had been an undoubted tactical genius who would have spent the manpower of the 36th frugally, exacting an enormous cost in blood from the Americans. But even without Hata, there was no reason why the Tonegawa line could not be held for at least a month—and by that time, who knew what might develop? Elections were to be held in the United States in the fall, and every American soldier who died was his family's vote against the men currently conducting the war. There was a peace party forming in America, too; Tojo was certain of it.

In the southern Kanto, the situation was not so promising. A large counterattack against the Kujukuri beachheads by the 52nd Army had been repulsed bloodily. That imbecile Shibata had led most of the 3rd Imperial Guards Division out of the laboriously constructed forts along the Boso shore in a mad banzai attack and had been slaughtered. If the idiot had not lost his life in the drunken attack, Tojo would have had him summarily court-martialed and shot. But these things were to be expected in the almost hysterical atmosphere permeating the nation now.

An aide-de-camp the premier did not know personally entered the audience room and stationed himself by the door leading to the Imperial family's private shelter. Tojo straightened himself to a position of rigid attention. The Emperor came in, and Tojo bowed deeply.

Hirohito wore a black cutaway coat and a stiff collar. Tojo was secretly dismayed to see that he had abandoned the ornate military uniform generally worn for Imperial audiences. Was there something to be learned from this? he wondered.

A small man, slightly built and wearing glasses, the Emperor was not a commanding figure. But his face was ruddy and his expression angrier than Tojo ever remembered having seen it. He walked with a shuffling gait because he wore soft slippers on his feet. Reaching his chair, he settled into it, though remaining stiffly upright.

He began to speak without preamble. "We have called you here, *Taisho-san*, because it appears impossible for us to obtain any accurate information concerning our military situation. When our aides receive communiqués from Imperial General Staff Headquarters, the documents are useless."

Hirohito's dark eyes, seen through the thick lenses, looked enormous. "You have our permission to speak, General."

Tojo opened his case awkwardly because he had no place to lay his papers. He extracted a folder marked with the red ribbons and Imperial Chrysanthemum seal. "I have here a complete evaluation of the situation along the Tonegawa, Majesty. If you would examine it—"

Hirohito shut Tojo off with an uncharacteristically sharp gesture. "*Taisho-san*, the enemies of the nation are at this very moment no more than twenty-five kilometers from this spot. We do not need to read reports to know that the empire is in desperate condition. What we wish to know is what you intend doing about it."

"Majesty, the Army is loyal," Tojo said emotionally. "There is not one soldier wearing the uniform of your service who will not gladly give his life for you."

The Emperor's face grew redder, angrier. "Until fourteen days ago we had at our disposal the services of our dear friend Koichi Kido, a man we have known and loved since childhood. Now he is dead, together with all the others who might have found a way to bring this war to an end." He held himself rigid, as he had been taught from infancy to do in the presence of lesser mortals, but the premier could see that he controlled his agitation only with great difficulty. "Too many excellent men have died, *Taisho-san*. Too many men whose service the nation cannot do without." He reached into the pocket of his black coat and drew out a sheet of rice paper. "Do you recognize this? It was found among Kido-san's personal papers."

Tojo advanced to the edge of the dais and took the paper. He recognized Kido's elegant hiragana calligraphy.

"You will see," the Emperor said frigidly, "that it is a draft for a rescript he wished us to issue. A rescript accepting the terms of the Potsdam Declaration."

"Majesty—" Tojo dropped to his knees and bowed his head. "I beg of you not to issue such a document. It will mean the end of us as a nation. It will mean that we accept defeat."

Hirohito said, "What other course is open to us, *Taisho-san*?"

Tojo sat back on his heels in a position of abject submission. "Majesty, the Army is intact. We can still force the enemies of the nation to give us honorable terms." He decided to risk a shrewd thrust. "Surely, sire, you realize that the Americans are prepared to arrest you as a war criminal. The destructive effect of such a humiliation on our people is beyond my capacity to imagine. I do not rule out the possibility of suicides by the millions. It could mean the obliteration of the Yamato race."

The Emperor regarded Tojo narrowly. There was no surety about what the general was saying, yet it was not beyond the realm of possibility. One could never be absolutely certain what Westerners, with their strange ways of thinking, might do. It was well known among the people of the court that the Americans considered the Pearl Harbor attack a criminal act rather than a legitimate *coup de guerre.* Plainly, the Emperor thought, something must be done—and soon. The nation might hold out for a month, three months, even six. But military defeat was absolutely inevitable. The only thing in doubt was how swiftly it would come. For two weeks, the American advance had been slowed by the weather. That would not last. The spring was advancing. In the south, the cherry blossoms were surely beginning to open. It filled him with sadness that his writ no longer ran in the southern islands and he could not visit the island of Kyushu, where the Yamato race was said to have been spawned by the gods.

"*Taisho-san,*" he said severely, "in one week's time there will be a meeting of the Privy Council to elect a new lord privy seal to replace Kido-san. At that time we shall expect your recommendations for satisfactorily concluding this war. Is that clearly understood?"

"Sire," Tojo said, "I most earnestly beg of you not to remain in Tokyo until then. We have prepared a temporary court for you and the Imperial family in Nagano, where you will be safe."

"Are you telling us, *Taisho-san,* that you cannot guarantee our safety in our own capital?"

"Majesty, the Army will do its duty. That is understood. But the American bombers—"

"The Americans have contrived not to bomb the Imperial Palace grounds so far," Hirohito said. "Do you suggest that they are about to change that policy?"

"One cannot be certain what barbarians are capable of doing, sire."

Hirohito stood and held out his hand for Kido's notes. "It is very late to begin to worry about such things, *Taisho-san*," he said. "Leave your reports with our aide." Without further comment, he left the room.

Tojo stood for a time looking after him thoughtfully. The audience had not been as bad as he had expected, or as good as he had hoped. The Emperor had not yet come to a certain decision about the future conduct of the war, but plainly he was casting about for an excuse to end it with a stroke of his brush. If he were allowed to do that, it would be the end for Hideki Tojo. It would also mean the end of the Japanese nation; the general was convinced of that. In the final trial, he thought, there was only the Army to rely upon. The Navy was finished. The Combined Fleet no longer existed. The Air Forces were spending themselves in one last holocaust of *tokko* attacks. Since invasion day, Japanese soldiers—yes, and sailors, too—had died by the thousands. Tojo's most recent count of Japanese casualties stood at over 240,000 killed, missing, or wounded. The Volunteer Defense Forces were prepared to give that many more. Oh, yes, the nation would *fight*; there was no doubting that. Even the Americans and their allies must believe it now. Imperial General Staff Headquarters estimated that the Americans had lost almost 80,000 men since Y-day.

In the face of such sacrifices, surely the Emperor could not simply make peace. It would be too bitter.

Yet if he did, what then? Perhaps, Tojo thought, if it comes to that, I shall find the strength to make the cut deep enough to earn my way into the holy precincts of Yasukuni Shrine.

The battered Ranger platoon, no longer under Harry Seaver's command, entered the compound of the Maeda villa two hours after sunset.

Lieutenant Tanaka, not knowing what to expect in the way of opposition, advanced the column in battle formation, weapons ready for use. He was surprised and relieved not to encounter opposition. The American troops entered the *mura*, the walled area of the villa, to find that the Japanese troops who had fallen back to the villa had evacuated the place, taking their dead and wounded with them. What remained to greet the invaders were a pair of old men, an old woman, and a girl in the baggy uniform of the civilian Volunteer Defense Force. As the first Rangers entered the compound, the inhabitants awaited them in a line and, as the last soldier came through the gate, greeted them with a deep bow.

Tanaka called a halt and sent scouts to take up positions outside the walls. He detailed Hardin to conduct a complete search of the villa, but somehow he was quite certain that the sergeant would find no troops remaining in the place.

Overhead, a pale moon rode in a clear, starry sky. The courtyard had been lighted with torches. It was, Tanaka thought with a shiver, medieval.

The girl approached him, bowed again, and said, "I am Katsuko Maeda, *Chui-san*, the daughter of this house."

Seaver had spoken of the Maeda family often enough for Tanaka to know that they represented everything he had been taught to despise about Japan. It was people such as these who had made serfs of his ancestors. He did not understand them, would never understand them, had no wish to understand them. Seaver did, and look what had happened to him.

He signaled for the Sherman to enter the *mura*.

The tank moved through the gate. Seaver, erect and silent, rode on the forward armor. He had not spoken since the grotesque business after the last battle. He rode holding the sword, which no one had been willing to try to take from him. Behind him, wrapped in a groundsheet and lashed to the front of the tank, rode the body of the Japanese colonel he had killed.

Tanaka said, "Do you speak English?"

The girl bowed again. "Yes, Lieutenant."

"Do you recognize the officer on that tank?"

In the torchlight, Seaver's face looked white and drawn, the face of a man far distant from this place.

"It is Seaver-san," the girl said softly. "I know him."

"Behind him is the body of one of your officers. He would not leave it on the battlefield."

"I understand, Lieutenant," Katsuko said.

"Do you? I think it is the body of Colonel Maeda—your brother, I believe." Tanaka had no wish to spare her, but he was not prepared for the stoicism with which she accepted his statement.

"Yes."

"You can remove the body," Tanaka said roughly. "And make whatever arrangements you want." That would be what Seaver wished, Tanaka thought.

The girl inclined her head and spoke to her old servants. The old woman uttered a birdlike cry of despair, but the girl spoke softly to her and she fell silent.

Tanaka said to the tank crew, "Help them with that."

The tankers released the muffled corpse and lowered it into the arms of the old woman and the two ancient men. Katsuko knelt beside her brother's body and opened the wrappings over the face. She must see what had been done to him, Tanaka thought. When she had looked carefully, she covered the young man's dead face and stood, looking up at Seaver, who still sat on the tank, the sword across his thighs.

The girl bowed very low and said, "*Domo arigato gozimashite*, Seaver-san."

Tanaka stared, shaken and angry. She somehow knew what Seaver had done—and she was *thanking* him for it. I will never understand these people, he thought.

Seaver stirred himself into motion. Very slowly, like a man many times his age, he climbed down from the Sherman. The Rangers stood in the shadows, watching uncomfortably.

Seaver seemed suddenly aware that the officer's sword was in his hands. He offered it to the girl, bowing. Like a Japanese, Tanaka thought, exactly like any Japanese.

The girl took the weapon reverently, with just the suggestion of a strange, bleak smile for Seaver. She spoke to the old people, and one vanished into an outbuilding, returning with a narrow board. Using this as a palanquin, they put the dead colonel on it and waited for the girl's command.

She looked at Tanaka for permission.

"Yes," he said. "Go do whatever you intend doing."

Katsuko bowed again and gave a quiet order. The servants picked up the body and carried it to the gate. The girl followed them silently. Seaver watched her go.

Tanaka called for Corporal Buie.

"Yo, Lieutenant."

"Take charge of Lieutenant Seaver. See if you can find a place for him to lie down."

"Yes, sir." The corporal, with astonishing tenderness, said to Seaver, "Come with me, Lieutenant. Please?"

Tanaka shook his head in despair. Seaver was like a sleep-walker. Would he ever come out of it? He set about stationing sentries and occupying the now-deserted villa.

By 2200 he had his troops billeted in the cold, empty rooms, an observation post on the ridge, and the tank dug in to command the road down to Kimitsu. He had reported to battalion that the platoon was in position on the highest ridge of the peninsula, gave the number of casualties, and informed the commander that he, and not Seaver, was now in command.

He did not describe Seaver's incapacity. He was not at all certain that he could have even if he had wanted to. What Seaver needed was a psychiatrist, and those were in short supply among the Rangers. He decided that he would leave Seaver here with the OP team when he moved the platoon on down the Kimitsu road. The Maeda girl was an old friend—all right, let her take care of him.

No matter how he tried to understand, Tanaka could not. His loathing for people such as those who had lived in this villa was fixed. Now he knew why it was he had never liked Harry Seaver. He was like *them*; my God, he was one of them. Who else could have done what he did to that dying man? Why, he thought, it was a war crime, an atrocity! He found himself wondering what he should do about it. Marines might collect Japanese ears, and B-29 pilots might bomb civilians, but no American did what Seaver had done. It was sickening.

Sergeant Hardin reported that the Maeda girl and her servants had taken the colonel's body to a small shrine on the ridge above the house and buried it there under a cairn of stones. The formality and stoicism with which the entire affair had been handled made Tanaka shudder. But this was the way of things in this benighted country. It was obvious to anyone who came here that the Japanese were in love with death—the bloodier and more savage the better. For 2,000 years these people had been eviscerating themselves and cutting off heads. How could such a nation think itself civilized? He thanked God for his father's courage in leaving this land for the unknown promise of America. If it had not been for that, how might he himself have ended? Not as a samurai Imperial Guards colonel, that was certain. No. More than likely as some lowly, bowing, fish-sucking *nihotei*, a recruit burned to charcoal in a log bunker back at Kujukuri Beach.

He looked about him at the room in which he had settled his personal gear. Massive old cedar beams, gold-bordered tatamis on the floor that probably cost twice what that old woman—Oyama-san, was it?—was paid in a year. God damn them, Tanaka thought, God damn all aristocrats who lived by rules no sane man could fathom; and in particular damn all Japanese aristocrats who lived by rules no sane man would *want* to fathom.

Tomorrow the platoon would move on, leaving this villa to be occupied by the men of the battalion moving up. He thought that could not happen nearly soon enough to suit him. The events of this day had left him exhausted, perplexed, and filled with sullen anger.

Harry Seaver knelt on the tatami and listened to the silence. Outside in the *mura*, where the troops had bivouacked in the outbuildings, there was the soft murmur of voices, the noises soldiers made after a day of fighting and marching. But he did not listen to those sounds. He was filled with the darkness—a darkness populated with old memories. The room where Buie had spread his sleeping bag was familiar. Surely he had slept here once, perhaps more often than that, but a long while ago?

Across the space between this wing of the house and another, he remembered, there was a garden of rocks and raked sand. It was too dark to see, but he felt certain that it was there. Katsuko had once told him that the rocks were deer, like the fawns of Nara, and they were picking their way—oh, so delicately—across the river of sand and gravel that the master builder of gardens had contrived to make eternal. He almost smiled at that. How fanciful Katsuko-chan could be. Kantaro contended that the rocks were warriors rallying round their lord. The garden builder, who had come to this villa in the time of the Emperor Meiji, had, of course, never said what images his garden was intended to convey.

Seaver stared at the dark and tried to empty his mind. Images of the war kept intruding. He remembered the steaming islands; Japanese soldiers dying in flames; ships burning; airplanes falling. I killed Kantaro, he thought suddenly. No, that was incorrect. We contrived his death together. That was our karma.

He got to his feet and went to a cupboard unerringly in the dark. He took a *futon* from it. Oyama-san used to do this for me, he thought. There were many servants in this house when I was young here.

He unfolded the *futon* and began wearily to undress. He found that he was very tired. Is the bath hot? he wondered. It was too late to go and see. Morning would do. There would be many things to do in the morning.

Naked, he crept into the *futon*, shivering at the touch of the cold padded blanket against his skin. It had been a long time since he had slept in a *futon*. He stretched luxuriously and closed his eyes. Within minutes he was asleep.

· · ·

He did not know how long he had slept when the soft sound of someone nearby awakened him. He opened his eyes but did not move. There was a sweet scent in the room, and the soft scuff of tabis on the matting.

"Harry-san?"

He lifted his head and saw Katsuko, almost invisible against the cold moonlight shining through the shoji. She was dressed in a kimono and she carried something in her outstretched hands. He was filled with joy to see her. "Katsu-chan," he said.

She knelt beside the *futon*, and he felt her fingertips on his lips warning him to be silent. Gods, yes, he thought. The old general would go into a rage if he were to find Katsuko in the room of his son's guest. But how often he had dreamed of this actually happening!

Katsuko placed the *daisho* carefully on the tatami beside the *futon*. How like her to bring the swords, knowing how much he admired the ancient Saotome blades—though he could scarcely suppress a smile, thinking that a sleeping room was hardly the place and this was not the time to admire the antique weapons.

"Katsu-chan," he said again. And again she touched his lips, warning him to silence.

The filtered moonlight gave just a suggestion of illumination to the silent room. Out in the *mura* Seaver could hear the night servants moving about their tasks, preparing all that the Maedas and their guest would require when the sun touched the crest of the ridge.

Katsuko unwound her obi. She moved silently and with grace. Her kimono fell open, and he caught a glimpse of her. He wished there were more light. Then kimono and undergarments fell, and for a moment he could see her. Her breasts were small, but rounded. Her thighs white and full, and there was a patch of darkness between them.

He felt the sudden steady pounding of his heart. Though he had dreamed so often of Katsu-chan this way, he had never imagined that he would have her. He opened the *futon*, and she slipped in beside him.

He had expected her to be chilled from the night air. She was not. Her skin was hot to the touch, as though she burned with fever. He put his arms around her and put his lips to her hair. It smelled of flowers.

She wound her legs around him and spread herself so that he could feel the wet warmth of her. He covered her breasts with his hands and felt the nipples rising against his palms. She moved her hips in a circular motion, breathing in time with her movements.

He caught her with his hands spread on the small of her back and held her while she strained to spread her thighs still wider. Without any guidance, he entered her, feeling the wetness and depth of her as he thrust against her spread thighs with all his strength. He closed his eyes for a moment, but he did not want to lose sight of her face, so near his own, or her eyes, black and bottomless in the thin moonlight.

Now she responded to him with a deep, mindless, and sensuous abandon, moving her hips and grasping him with the muscles of her vagina. No Western woman ever abandoned herself so completely to the act of love, he thought. He felt the dampness of her skin against his own, the pressure of her fingers on his back. Smiling with joy, he remembered how, as children, they had read the *Shunga* together and been amazed at the wonderful complexities of pleasure between man and woman.

Like a wave, they crested, climaxed, and fell, lying together and gasping for breath in the moonlit stillness, gathering strength for the next act of love.

Hardin shook Tanaka awake, shining a flashlight in his face. "Lieutenant? Wake up, Lieutenant, for Chrissake!"

Tanaka opened his eyes and automatically reached for his weapon. "What is it, Sergeant?"

"You know those old men and the old woman? They've killed themselves."

Tanaka sat bolt upright. "When? How?"

"You know they took the guy Lieutenant Seaver killed up to

the shrine and buried him. Well, they just sat up there until about ten minutes ago. Then they all held hands and jumped off the fuckin' cliff." Hardin sounded shocked. "It wasn't much of a drop, only about fifty feet. But it was enough. I sent Buie down to take a look, and they're dead all right."

Tanaka said sharply, "You sent Buie?"

"That's right, Lieutenant."

"Where's the girl?"

"Christ, I don't know, Lieutenant. Why?"

"Come on," Tanaka said. He jumped to his feet, his M-1 in his hand, and ran out into the courtyard calling for the corporal.

When Buie appeared, Tanaka said, "Follow me." He ran toward the wing of the main house where they had billeted Seaver.

They leaped onto the wide verandah, tracking mud across the scrubbed planks. Tanaka slid the shoji aside and shone his light inside.

The light found the niche where the traditional scroll hung and the simple flower arrangement of early spring blooms. Below it lay Seaver's military gear, his clothes, and his sleeping bag. There was a neat pile of brilliantly patterned silk next to it—a kimono and obi. Tanaka swung the light across the room.

"God," Buie whispered.

The man and the woman lay naked together on the bloody *futon.* So much blood, Tanaka thought, so much *blood.* He closed his eyes and thought: I want to go home. I want to go home and never see this country again.

Y-day plus 16

17 March 1946

IV. Evacuation

1. Evacuation from the objective areas initially will be by suitably equipped and surgically staffed surface vessels. Hospital ships, APHs, converted APAs, and APAs will be utilized; the more serious cases will be evacuated in the hospital ships as practicable. In emergency, small naval assault craft or heavy cargo shipping will be utilized, but due to the limited facilities aboard these vessels, patients are not to be carried farther than the Kyushu area on these types of vessels. . . .

    b. Army commanders or commanding generals USASCOM-C, as appropriate, will be, in their respective objective areas, responsible for the evacuation from Army installations to hospitals, beaches, or air strips as appropriate. . . .

    e. Secondary evacuation from rear bases to the Zone of the Interior will be the responsiblity of commanding generals, U.S. Army forces . . . within their respective areas. Full use will be made of available ATC air lift for secondary evacuation to the Zone of the Interior. . . .

3. The commanding generals Western and Middle Pacific

Areas will make available, by prior clearing of hospital beds in their respective areas, the necessary bed credits to Y + 90 as follows:

Western Pacific Area	Y-day	10,000
	Y + 10	15,000 additional
Middle Pacific Area	Y-day	4,000
	Y + 7	6,000 additional
Kyushu Area	Y-day	10,000

Staff Study Operations: "Coronet"
General Headquarters
U.S. Army Forces in the Pacific

0430 Hours

Lieutenant Commander Saburo Chita, commander of the Takasaki Special Attack Squadron of the 11th Air Fleet, walked unsteadily out of the operations tent and stood on the wet grass looking at the brightening sky. There were a few clouds remaining from the recent storms; just how high the clouds were was difficult for Chita to judge with his one good eye, but he viewed the morning sky with satisfaction. It would be a fine day for flying.

The field was silent. There was no sound of airplane engines being tested because all the airplanes had gone. Only Chita's Reisen remained, parked in its nest of sandbags and covered with camouflage netting.

In his one good hand, Chita held a bottle of sake. It, too, was the last, and he had nursed it carefully through the night, drinking with Ensign Ozawa, the operations officer. Ozawa was asleep now. He had asked to be awakened when Chita departed from Takasaki in the Reisen, but he had been sleeping so soundly that the squadron commander had not had the heart to wake him. They would meet at Yasukuni, in any case.

All of the enlisted men except his own crew chief and a few squadron clerks had gone, dragooned into the ranks of the Army. By now they were all probably fighting the Americans along the Tonegawa. Chita did not miss them. In fact, he rather appreciated the stillness that had descended on the airfield. For a few moments there was time to view the sky and clouds, the dew on the grass, the serene shapes of the red pines growing at the end of the strip. A faint morning wind rattled the stalks of the bamboo grove in which the operations tent had been situated— *tanikaze*, a wind in the valley.

Chita lifted the sake bottle and sipped the dregs of the wine. He dropped it, empty, on the grass and walked slowly out toward the airplane his crew chief, Petty Officer Teshio, was preparing. Teshio was from Hokkaido, a taciturn northerner, but conscientious to a fault. He would not like the infantry, Chita thought, but he would do his duty and do it well. He must remember to say something appreciative to Teshio when he made his last farewell.

Chita was dressed in flying clothes. They felt strange to him, since he had not flown for a long time. The empty sleeve hung on his right, tucked into his belt. On his head he wore a sheepskin-lined flying helmet, the earflaps tucked up in the old way of Imperial Navy fighter pilots in better days.

As he walked across the field, his boots left tracks on the wet grass. The air smelled marvelously fresh and clean.

He stopped a dozen paces from his old Reisen to look at it, as one would pause to regard an old friend. He had let the last flight commander take the single Shiden out yesterday. The newer airplane belonged to Chita by right of his rank and position, but he had not wanted it. His last flight should be in a Reisen, the Type Zero that had cut a flaming swathe across the skies of all Asia for three marvelous years.

Studying the airplane in the cool light of the morning, he remembered his old mates in *Akagi*. What a marvelously carefree troop they had been, even though there had always been the rivalry between the air groups on *Akagi* and *Soryu*. The pride of the 1st Air Fleet, they were, and the fighter pilots were the pick of the fleet. It pleased Chita that they would all be waiting at Yasukuni for him. He grinned at the thought of that noisy, exuberant mob of pilots waiting there, probably improperly dressed, wearing their helmets with the earflaps fastened over the tops of their heads.

"Ohayo, Kaigun Shosa-san." Petty Officer Teshio stood before him and bowed deeply. "Everything is in order, as you wished it to be. I apologize that I was unable to run the engine to warm it this morning, but I have filled the tanks with the last of the aviation fuel. And, as you ordered, I did not fit a bomb." Chita had decided that his own last flight would be as a fighter pilot, and not simply as a brain and hand guiding a bomb. The sky was full of American fighters and bombers. He would fly his last mission against his own kind.

"The guns are fully loaded, *Shosa-san*," Teshio said. He squinted at the sky with his narrow, deep-set eyes. "It surprises me that we have seen no Americans yet this morning."

That was so, Chita realized. Ordinarily, by the time it was this light the Mustangs and Hellcats and Thunderbolts were prowling everywhere. "Perhaps they are all concentrating on the battle at the Tonegawa," he said. Last night he had considered joining that air battle, but he had reconsidered. What he really wished to do was to fight his last fight over the waters of the Inland Sea. It was there that, as a cadet and later as a trainee, he had learned his fighter pilot's craft. He had flown with great warriors, *bushi* whom a man was honored to know: Minoru Genda, who trained the airmen of the 1st Air Fleet for the attack on Pearl Harbor; Mitsuo Fuchida, who had led the strike force that glowing Sunday morning; all the others.

Chita extended his left arm and said, "Please remove my watch, Petty Officer Teshio."

Teshio did so, holding the timepiece reverently. It was a Swiss aviator's chronograph of great value, a gift to Chita from his father on the day he was graduated as a naval officer from the academy at Etajima.

"I wish you to have it, Teshio-san," Chita said. "In appreciation of the excellent service you have given me."

Teshio, overcome with emotion, could only bow. When he straightened, he was weeping.

415

"Come now, Teshio," Chita said with a smile. "You cannot join the Army with tears in your eyes. Think of the honor of the Takasaki Squadron."

"I shall wear the watch with pride, *Kaigun Shosa-san*," Teshio said in a husky voice.

"You must keep it and never give it away to a pretty geisha," Chita said jokingly. He looked again at the sky. He was hungry to fly again. A glance back toward the senior officers' sleeping bunker brought no sign of Ozawa. Let him sleep, Chita thought. He won't like the Army much either. He felt a momentary sadness, because he knew that neither Ozawa, nor Teshio, nor any of the others who had already departed would last long fighting with the Army. But that was their karma. This was his.

He walked behind the revetment to the tiny squadron shrine and stood there, trying to focus his mind on eternity. But all that he could think about was that he would soon be flying again.

He bowed and went back to the airplane, walking around it with the crew chief behind him. There was no real need to inspect the Reisen. Teshio would have it as well prepared as it was possible to be, given the sorry state of supplies and replacement parts.

He nodded his approval and climbed up on the wing and into the cockpit. Teshio had placed a parachute in the seat, but Chita did not bother to fasten the straps. It was awkward to work the switches and controls with only his left hand, but at least it *was* the left that remained to him. To have operated the throttle and propeller controls with the right would have been far more difficult.

When his cockpit check was complete, he smiled at Teshio and extended his hand. The petty officer took it in both of his and said, "It has been a very great pleasure to serve with you, *Kaigun Shosa-san*. May we meet soon."

Chita nodded agreement and closed the canopy. It was time, at last, to fly again.

At an altitude of 500 meters, Chita turned the Reisen onto a course of 230° true for the Inland Sea. The distance was 600 kilometers, at the extreme range of the Reisen, so it was necessary to conserve fuel. He throttled back and advanced the propeller pitch. The engine protested with some roughness and detonation, but it could not be helped.

He flew alone in the clear spring sky. The sun was rising, and though he could only occasionally catch a glimpse of the sea, it did glimmer like bright metal from time to time.

To his left as he flew lay Tokyo and the great battle being fought along the Tonegawa. He had no desire to turn east and see it. Instead, he flew low and steadily over the mountains of central Honshu, watching the sun glint from the patches of snow still on the ground, a pattern of pure white etched with the intricate designs of the dark pine and cedar forests. How beautiful is the land of Yamato, Chita thought, how beautiful and how tragic!

At the end of his first hour of flight, after a glimpse of the reflecting lake at Shugakuin, where the Emperor's villa stood, he was over Kyoto. The Americans, oddly, had not bombed the ancient capital. He flew low over Nijo Castle and could see the sky reflected in the waters of the moat. He could almost imagine that he could see the great golden carp that swam in the dark waters. The streets of the city were not deserted. Here and there he could see women, out early, perhaps to find what they could in the empty markets. He rolled back the cockpit canopy and waved to a girl in a kimono of red silk as he flew over the grounds of the Koruji Temple. She waved back, and he was delighted. He felt like a boy again, playing silly but wonderful games with his trainer, risking reprimands but so filled with high spirits and the joy of flying that he was willing to take such chances. On his left lay Mount Momo, with some snow on the trees near the summit.

He flew over the curving serpent of the Katsura River, and Kyoto was gone, swallowed up in the misty distance. He began to look in earnest for prowling American fighters. Since there still were none, he began to worry that he would run out of fuel before finding a worthy adversary.

After another forty minutes, the Reisen was flying over the northeasternmost islands of the Inland Sea. Even here the sky was clear of enemy airplanes. What had become of them? Chita wondered. Had they all simply vanished, returned to those places across the sea whence they had come? There was a strange serenity in the empty air, with the clear sky of early morning above and the sparkling Inland Sea below. He flew for a time with the canopy open, letting the roar of the engine fill his senses and the cold wind whip the *kubimaki* wrapped around his throat.

By 0740 hours he found himself low over the island-dotted strait between the Takanawa Peninsula and Kure. The naval base at Kure was a disheartening sight. Warships lay sunk at their moorings. The new aircraft carriers *Katsuragi* and *Amagi* capsized at their island berths were a sight that filled him with sadness.

The garrison at Kure was apparently so unaccustomed to seeing Japanese aircraft in flight overhead that they opened fire on Chita's Reisen, forcing him to turn south.

As he approached the tip of the Sada-misaki Peninsula at the southwestern end of Shikoku and saw that he had little fuel left, Chita found his Americans. High above him, at 9,000 meters or more, he saw a flight of three B-29s flying in an open vee. It had been a long time since he had seen Americans flying such loose formation. They were growing careless, he thought as he advanced his throttle and propeller-pitch control for a maximum-power climb.

The B-29s were traveling fast, but he began to overtake them as the Reisen responded to his urgings. He charged his guns and test-fired a short burst from the two 20mm cannon in the wings. His heart began to beat fast with the remembered excitement of combat. At 7,000 meters he had closed the distance between himself and the B-29s to no more than two kilometers. He was now climbing under their tails in a stern chase, the Reisen's engine laboring. He was certain that no one aboard the three bombers had yet caught sight of him. He flexed his hand on the control stick. He had closed to within a thousand meters of the bombers and still there was no sign of evasive action. The leader carried a *mon* of a black arrow.

A great and sudden silence filled his head. The struggling Nakajima engine had consumed the last of its fuel and stopped. The Reisen's speed dropped swiftly, and the aircraft stalled in the thin, high air. Chita cried out with frustrated rage and beat his fist against the instrument panel. The fighter, silent now except for the sound of the wind, fell into a steep spiral. Chita, his face streaked with tears, made no effort to level the airplane. It dove in an increasingly tight corkscrewing track toward the sea. Weeping freely, he lay his head back against the thin armor of the headrest and stared straight ahead. The blue, sparkling surface of the Inland Sea was very near. And far above, the three B-29s continued on toward Hiroshima.

0815 Hours

Mariko Sayama, the forty-year-old wife of the principal of the Normal School, left the house and clattered down the cobbled street in her geta, avoiding, when she could, the puddles left by yesterday's rain. She had heard that there was fish to be had in the marketplace, and though she had been disappointed by rumors before, she had decided to rise early and be among the first to buy if anything was really available.

The sun felt warm on her shoulders. She could feel it comfortingly through the cotton of her kimono. She swung the string bag she carried as she hurried along with her shuffling gait. She was thinking seriously about fish. Haddock, perhaps. Or maybe tuna, or even salmon. It had been a long time since there had been anything on the Sayama table other than rice and a few vegetables.

She knew that it was disloyal, perhaps even criminal, but she could not help wishing that this long and terrible war might end soon. The city had not been badly bombed, not like so many other places. But even this morning there had been an air-raid alert—caused, so Sayama-san said, by a single enemy plane snooping around over Kure. Then there had been an all clear, and now another alert. Mariko squinted up at the morning sky. Yes, there were three widely spaced *Bi-ni-ju-ku* flying over the city. Perhaps she should go to the shelter. No one else was doing so, however, and if she did, she would arrive at the market too late.

She continued to shuffle quickly toward the city center. She could see the morning sun sparkling on the river. She looked up at the Americans again. Now there was only one, and he had dropped something. She watched it fall. A parachute opened. Could one of the *gaijin* aviators have fallen out?

What Mariko Sayama saw next, she saw only for an instant. It was a light, such a light as had never before been seen in the Land of the Eight Islands.

Y-day plus 24

25 March 1946

IMPERIAL RESCRIPT

To Our good and loyal subjects:

After pondering deeply the general trends of the world and the actual conditions obtaining in Our Empire today, We have decided to effect a settlement of the present situation by resorting to an extraordinary measure.

We have ordered Our Government to communicate to the Governments of the United States, Great Britain, China, and the Soviet Union that Our Empire accepts the provisions of their Joint Declaration.

To strive for the common prosperity and happiness of all nations as well as the security and well-being of Our subjects is the solemn obligation which has been handed down by Our Imperial Ancestors, and which We lay close to Our heart. Indeed, We declared war on the United States and Britain out of Our sincere desire to ensure Japan's self-preservation and the stabilization of East Asia, it being far from Our thought either to infringe upon the sovereignty of other nations or to embark upon territorial aggrandizement.

Hostilities have now continued for more than four years. Despite the gallant fighting of the officers and men of the Army and the Navy, the diligence and assiduity of Our servants of state, the devoted service of Our one hundred million subjects—despite the best efforts of all, the war situation worsens from day to day.

Moreover, the general world situation is not to Japan's advantage. Furthermore, the enemy has begun to employ a new and cruel bomb which kills and maims the innocent, and the power of which to wreak destruction is truly incalculable.

Should We continue to fight, the ultimate result would be not only the obliteration of the race, but also the extinction of human civilization. Then how should We be able to save the millions of Our subjects and make atonement to the hallowed spirits of Our Imperial Ancestors? That is·why We have commanded the Imperial Government to comply with the terms of the Joint Declaration of the Powers.

To those nations which have, as Our allies, steadfastly co-operated with the Empire in the emancipation of East Asia, We cannot but express Our deep regret. The thought of Our subjects who have fallen on the field of battle or met untimely death in the performance of their duties, and of their bereaved families, rends Our heart. The suffering which Our nation yet must undergo will certainly be great. However, We have resolved, by enduring the unendurable and bearing the unbearable, to pave the way for a grand peace for all time to come.

Since it has been possible to preserve the structure of the Imperial State, We shall always be with you, Our good and loyal subjects, placing Our trust in your sincerity and integrity.

Let the nation continue as one family from generation to generation with unwavering faith in the imperishability of Our divine land. Cultivate the ways of rectitude, foster nobility of spirit, and work with resolution so that you may enhance the innate glory of the Imperial State and keep pace with the progress of the world.

We charge you, Our loyal subjects, faithfully to carry out Our will.

The 25th day of the third month
of the 21st year of Showa

Afterword

The province of the historian is history. The province of the novelist is fiction. It is risky business to mingle the two, but I have taken that risk with this book.

History tells us that Operation Coronet never took place and that World War II was ended by the dropping of two atomic bombs, on the Japanese cities of Hiroshima and Nagasaki, in August 1945. But the reality we know depends on an infinite number of events taking place in precise sequence. If only one event in that infinity were changed, what of history then?

Operation Coronet is genuine. It exists now only as a staff study in the National Archives of the United States. It was abandoned because it was not needed. The Ketsu-go Number 3 defense plans are also real. They can be found in the war archives of the Japanese government. Similarly, the other military documents listed among the sources in the bibliography can be found by any researcher. All have been declassified.

This novel is based on these documents. The people in this novel, with the exception of certain actual historical persons, are fictional. They exist in these pages and nowhere else.

Acknowledgments

I wish to acknowledge the help given by many individuals who contributed time and effort to assure the accuracy of this work. My appreciation goes to Matthew Bruccoli, of Charleston, who helped develop the concept; to William Emerson, of the Franklin D. Roosevelt Library, Mrs. Agnes Petersen, of the Hoover Institution on War, Peace and Revolution, Ben Frank, of the Marine Corps Historical Center, Edward J. Reese, of the Modern Military Branch of the National Archives and Record Service, Robert R. Smith, of the General History Branch of the Department of the Army, and Rear Admiral John D. H. Kane, USN (Ret.), of the Historical Section of the Department of the Navy, for assistance in locating essential documents; and to Rear Admiral Jacob W. Onstott, USN (Ret.), and Commander Edward I. Weed, USNR (Ret.), for their reconstructions of naval operations in the Western Pacific at the end of World War II. Thanks also go to Thomas Vano, of San Francisco, for enlightening a former pilot on the hazards of small-unit infantry engagements, and to former gunnery officer Julian P. Muller for an introduction to the arcana of naval artillery.

In Japan, I was assisted by Professor Sinji Sudo, of the Political Science Department of Kyoto University, by William Immerman, Political Counselor of the U.S. Embassy in Tokyo, and by Barbara Adachi, whose books on Japanese art and culture are classics in the field. Particular thanks go to Baron Masakazu Honda, Curator of the Honda Family Museum in Kanazawa, which houses one of the finest collections of Japanese arms extant. The many Japanese naval and military documents used as sources for the work were translated by Takamichi Yamamoto and his associates.

Special appreciation is due to Miss Kimiko Noguchi, guide and interpreter extraordinary, who overcame difficulties of ethnic reluctance, language, secondary roads, and pressing schedules to take me to the many now obscure places I needed to see; and to Miss Roberta Leighton for copy editing a difficult and demanding manuscript with great skill and greater patience.

A. C.

The 21st day of the sixth month
of the 56th year of Showa

Source Materials and
Selected Bibliography

Plan for the Defeat of Japan, CCS 381, Records of the U.S. Joint Chiefs of Staff, October 1943.

Conference Plan for the Invasion of Northeastern Honshu, JWPC 333/1, Records of the Joint Chiefs of Staff, June 1944.

An Outline Plan for the Invasion of the Kanto (Tokyo Plain), Records of the Joint Chiefs of Staff, June 1944.

Staff Study Operations: "Olympic," General Headquarters U.S. Army Forces in the Pacific, 1945.

"Olympic," Strategic Plan for the Invasion of South Kyushu, War Department Operations and Plans Division, May 1945.

Staff Study Operations: "Coronet," General Headquarters U.S. Army Forces in the Pacific, 1945.

"Coronet," Operations in the Kanto Plain of Honshu, War Department Operations and Plans Division, August 1945.

Third Fleet Operation Plan (Annex A), CINCPAC/CINCPOA, August 1945.

Operation Plan No. 12-45 (Annex D), CINCPAC/CINCPOA, August 1945.

COMPHIBPAC Operations Plan 11-45, August 1945.

Handbook on Japanese Military Forces, War Department Technical Manual TM-E-30-480, 15 September 1945.

The Reports of General MacArthur, Vol. II, Part II, Washington, D.C.: U.S. Government Printing Office.

Dai Niji Sekai Taisen Ryakureki Otsu (Abridged Chronicle of World War II), 2nd Demobilization Bureau.

Dairi Kushi Dai Nisenyonhyakisanjuhachi-go (Outline of Operational Preparations for Operations *Ketsu*), Imperial General Headquarters Army Directive No. 2438.

Hondo Joriku no taisuru Hangeki Sakusen Jumbi (Preparations for Counterattack Operations in Defense of the Homeland).

Ketsu-go Number 3 (Operational Plan for the Defense of the Kanto).

Koku Tokko Sembi (Battle Preparations of Naval Special Air Attack).

Sojo Sho Sambo Socho Gunreibu Socho (Report to the Throne by the Chiefs of the Army and Navy General Staffs, 19 January 1945).

Adachi, Barbara. *The Living Treasures of Japan*. Tokyo: Kodansha International, 1973.

———. *The Voices and Hands of Bunraku*. Tokyo: Mobil Sekyu K.K., 1978.

Bauer, K. Jack, and Coox, Alvin D. "Olympic vs. Ketsu-go," *The Marine Corps Gazette*. Aug. 1965.

Belote, James and William. *Typhoon of Steel: The Battle for Okinawa*. New York: Harper & Row, 1970.

Benedict, Ruth. *The Chrysanthemum and the Sword: Patterns of Japanese Culture*. New York: New American Library, 1946.

Carey, Otis, ed. *War Wasted Asia*. Tokyo: Kodansha International, 1975.

Emmerson, John K. *The Japanese Thread: A Life in the U.S. Foreign Service*. New York: Holt, Rinehart & Winston, 1978.

Hayaski, Saburo, and Coox, Alvin D. *Kogun: The Japanese Army in the Pacific War*. Quantico, Va.: The Marine Corps Association, 1959.

Ienaga, Saburo. *The Pacific War*. New York: Pantheon Books, 1968.

Livingston, Jon, and Moore, Joe, eds. *The Japan Reader: Imperial Japan 1800–1945*. New York: Pantheon Books, 1973.

Manchester, William. *American Caesar*. Boston: Little, Brown, 1978.

Maraini, Fosco. *Meeting with Japan*. New York: Viking Press, 1960.

Morison, Samuel Eliot. *History of United States Naval Operations in World War II*. Boston: Little, Brown, 1962.

Morris, Ivan. *The Nobility of Failure: Tragic Heroes in the History of Japan*. New York: Holt, Rinehart & Winston, 1978.

Musashi, Miyamoto. *A Book of Five Rings*. Woodstock, N.Y.: Overlook Press, 1974.

Sato, Hiroaki, and Watson, Burton. *From the Country of the Eight Is-*

lands: An Anthology of Japanese Poetry. Garden City, N.Y.: Anchor Press/Doubleday, 1981.

Seward, Jack. *The Japanese.* New York: William Morrow, 1972.

Toland, John. *The Rising Sun.* New York: Random House, 1977.

Turnbull, S. R. *The Samurai: A Military History.* New York: Mac-
millan, 1977.

Winton, John. *The Forgotten Fleet: The British Navy in the Pacific
1944-1945.* New York: Coward McCann, 1970.

Yamamoto, Tsunetomo. *Hagakure: The Book of the Samurai.* Tokyo:
Kodansha International, 1979.

Glossary

aikuchi: short dagger without a guard; preferred weapon for the ceremony of seppuku

ashigaru: ancient foot soldiers

baka; baka mono: a manned aerial bomb, called *"oka"* (cherry blossom) by the Japanese; a fool

Banzai: Live forever

Bi-ni-ju-ku: slang term for B-29 Superfortress bomber

bunraku: the puppet theater

bushi: warrior (Bushido is the Way of the Warrior or code of the samurai)

cha; chashitsu: tea; teahouse

-chan: suffix; term of familiarity and endearment

chanoyo: the tea ceremony

dai: great (Dai Nihon: Great Japan)

daisho: pair of matched swords, the katana and the wakizashi; ancient weapons of the samurai class, often family treasures

-dono: suffix; term of great respect

futon: a bed

gaijin: a foreigner

-gawa: river (Tonegawa: Tone River)

geta: wooden clogs

gimu: partial repayment of an obligation, the full repayment of which is never more than partial

giri: obligation to one's name; a debt that may be paid with mathematical equivalence to the favor received

gumbatsu: military clique

hachimaki: cloth or scarf worn around the head, often decorated for battle with sun disk and patriotic writings

hai: yes

haji: shame

hakama: samurai skirt

-hama: beach (Kujukuri-hama)

hancho: military instructor, a noncommissioned officer

-hanto: peninsula (Boso-hanto)

-jima: island (Iwo-jima)

kaigun: naval; the Navy

kaishaku: sword stroke delivered with the katana by a friend acting as second in the ceremony of seppuku; the perfect cut does not completely sever the head, but leaves it attached to the body by a bit of skin and muscle

kaiten: human-guided torpedo

kami: divine being or force

Kamikaze: Divine Wind, a storm that twice saved Japan from Mongol invaders; name used by suicide pilots

kampai: a toast

kendo: the art of Japanese fencing

ketsu-go: decisive battle (Ketsu-go Number 3: plan for the defense of the Kanto Plain; Ketsu-go Number 6: plan for the defense of Kyushu)

koshaku: marquis

kubimaki: scarf or neckcloth

makoto: sincerity, worthiness

maru: merchant ship

mon; monsho: family crest

mura: compound of a country estate; hamlet

naginata: halberd-style weapon

naze: why

neko: cat

ofuro: bath

ohayo: good morning

on: obligation passively incurred and lifelong; one receives *oya-on* from one's family at birth, *nushi no-on* from one's lord or superior, and *ko-on* from the Emperor

onigawara: demon tiles for roof

renraku-tei: Army liaison boat, used for suicide attacks

ronin: masterless samurai; the tale of the Forty-seven Ronin, a chronicle of loyalty and extraordinary devotion, is a Japanese classic

-sama: term of great respect

-san: term of respect, comparable to Mr.

sensei: learned man, teacher, or master

seppuku: ritual suicide

shinyo: Imperial Navy version of suicide boat

shirei: commander

Shunga: ancient manual on the art of love

sohei: warrior monks

sojusha: pilot

sutobu: stove

Tenno: Emperor

tokko: special attack, by suicide forces

urusai: officious, overbearing, arrogant

Yamato: Land of the Eight Islands; Japan

yobeiki: First Reserve soldier with two years' satisfactory active duty

MILITARY RANKS

taisho: general

chujo: lieutenant general

shosho: major general

taisa: colonel

shosa: major

taii: captain

chui: first lieutenant

shoi: second lieutenant

socho: sergeant major

gunso: sergeant

gocho: corporal

heicho: lance corporal

johotei: superior private

ittohei: first class private

nitohei: second class private

Equivalent ranks in the Imperial Navy are formed by the addition of *Kaigun* (*Kaigun taisa*: Navy captain)

Order of Battle

Y-day, 1 March 1946

GENERAL HEADQUARTERS, U.S. ARMY FORCES
IN THE PACIFIC

Sixth Army

          40th Infantry Division
          11th Airborne Division

  I Corps: 25th and 41st Infantry Divisions
  IX Corps: 77th and 81st Infantry Divisions
  XI Corps: 43rd Infantry and 1st Cavalry Divisions

Eighth Army

          93rd and 96th Infantry Divisions

  X Corps: 24th and 31st Infantry Divisions
  XIV Corps: 6th, 32nd, 37th, 38th Infantry Divisions

Tenth Army

  XXIV Corps: 7th, 27th and 33rd Infantry Divisions
  XXX Armored
      Corps: 100th Mechanized and American Infantry
             Divisions and
      103rd Armored Division

Pacific Strategic Air Forces: Twentieth and Twenty-first
Fifth Air Force   Twelfth Air Force
Seventh Air Force   Thirteenth Air Force
Eighth Air Force

MARINE FORCES UNDER DIRECT COMMAND OF
U.S. ARMY FORCES, PACIFIC HEADQUARTERS

III Amphibious Corps: 1st, 4th, 6th Divisions
V Amphibious Corps: 2nd, 3rd, 5th Divisions

STRATEGIC RESERVE

First Army (redeployed from ETO)

JAPANESE FORCES, CENTRAL KANTO

2nd General Army
51st Army
    44th, 151st, 221st Infantry Divisions
    115th and 116th Independent Mixed Brigades
    7th Tank Brigade
52nd Army
    3rd Imperial Guards Division
    147th and 234th Infantry Divisions
    Matsuo Fortress Division
    3rd Independent Tank Brigrade
53rd Army
    84th, 140th, 316th Infantry Divisions
    117th Independent Mixed Brigade
    2nd Independent Tank Brigade
36th Army (Mobile Reserve)
    1st Imperial Guards Division
    81st, 93rd, 201st, 202nd, 209th, 214th Infantry Divisions
    1st and 4th Armored Divisions
Tokyo Bay Defense Group
    354th Infantry Division
    96th Independent Mixed Brigade
Yokosuka Naval Station Force
    Combined Naval Landing Force
    Special Attack Forces
Tokyo Defense Army
    1st, 2nd, 3rd Garrison Brigades
    Central Kanto District Kempetai
12th Home Army (administrative echelon)
11th Air Fleet